D0184493

Ten Weeks in Africa

Also by J. M. Shaw

The Illumination of Merton Browne

J. M. Shaw

Ten Weeks in Africa

SCEPTRE

SCEPTRE

First published in Great Britain in 2012 by Sceptre
An imprint of Hodder & Stoughton
An Hachette UK company

1

Copyright © J M Shaw 2012

Many writers' work inspired this novel, but the characters and events described are
fictional and the product of the author's imagination.

A CIP catalogue record for this title is available from the British Library.

Hardback ISBN 978 0 340 93405 0
Trade Paperback ISBN 978 1 444 75981 5

Typeset in Sabon MT by Palimpsest Book Production Ltd,
Falkirk, Stirlingshire

Printed and bound by Clays Ltd, St Ives plc

Hodder & Stoughton policy is to use papers that are natural, renewable and
recyclable products and made from wood grown in sustainable forests.
The logging and manufacturing processes are expected to conform
to the environmental regulations of the country of origin.

Hodder & Stoughton Ltd
338 Euston Road
London NW1 3BH

www.hodder.co.uk

For my wife, Caroline – *IMCS*

And in memory of Yusuf Abdi Shirdon,
General Manager of the Somali National Refugee Council,
who remained uncorrupted to the end.

Part One

I

Stephen Odinga stood in the sunlight next to his sister, gazing towards the traffic on the main road in front of their stall. Small children were running in and out between the cars and minicab taxis along Kwamchetsi Wachira Avenue, holding up bags of peanuts, copies of the *Kisuru Telegraph*, bottles of water and orange soda. One little girl in a green skirt marched across the path of a forty-ton lorry, balancing a basket of frangipani flowers on her head.

'How much have you taken?' Stephen asked.

'Four hundred and ten shillings.'

Martha was deep-frying bananas and little satchels of dough in a pan of seething, bright yellow oil. Above her head, the sign on the front of the booth proclaimed: *Aberdare Fried Bananas – Best Value in Kisuru.*

Stephen hitched up his oversized trousers. 'It's not enough.'

'It's early,' Martha replied.

There was a pile of rotting food in the gutter nearby. The smell of it was intensifying with the morning heat, and as he talked, Stephen kept brushing the flies from his face.

'Why don't you help me?' she said. 'I cook, you go to the buses and sell. Like we used to. We make more that way.'

'No. I'm going to Makotsi Avenue. I can get two dollars today, maybe more.'

'Tell Tom to help, then. He's working over there – at Joy and Beauty Valeting.'

Stephen looked towards the traffic-lights where half a dozen small boys were swarming around a white Toyota Land Cruiser. Two had climbed up on the bonnet and were using rags to wipe the windscreen; others stood by with buckets of water, while Tom – clearly visible in his red shorts and blue baseball cap – was standing on the pavement outside the Prosperity Butcher's Shop, holding a plastic bag in each hand.

'He's the toilet boy for that gang,' Martha went on. 'It's a bad job for him. He's not quick enough.'

'Tom's fast. He'll be fine.'

'And when the police catch him, what will you tell Mama?'

'With that fever she has,' he said angrily, 'with fever and no money, what difference does it make what I tell her?'

Martha looked down at the boiling yellow oil, took her tongs and carefully pulled out a deep-fried banana, which she placed on a piece of newspaper. 'Fried bananas,' she called out, raising her voice to compete with the drone of an aeroplane flying low over the market. '*Mandazi*! Best value in Kisuru! Only five shillings.'

A middle-aged man in a jacket and tie stopped by the booth, and stood smiling at Martha, taking his time to examine the strip of printed cotton tied round her hair, and the shape of her breasts, visible through the T-shirt.

'Good morning,' he said, when the plane had passed. 'How are you?'

'Well.'

'So, what have we got here? *Mandazi*?' He grinned at Martha, leaning against the booth. 'Tell me, young lady, what else do you sell?'

'Banana fritters,' she said, keeping her eyes on the boiling oil. 'Good clean food.'

'What if a customer prefers something else? I have a *big* appetite.' And he added gently: 'How old are you, *mchumba*? Seventeen – eighteen?'

'You should try our fritters,' Martha repeated. 'If you want something different, go to another stall.'

'You want to eat?' Stephen asked, approaching the man. 'I recommend it, sir. Take a fried banana. Five shillings.'

4

'No,' the man said, with a scowl. 'I don't think so. I don't like the attitude of this little *mamalishe*.' And he marched off.

'Hot *mandazi*!' Martha cried again. 'Five shillings each, three for twelve, five for twenty – best value in Kisuru. You, ladies, it's a beautiful day. Try our fried bananas . . .'

A group of young women had climbed down from their yellow minibus, marooned in the traffic, and were picking their way across the gutter.

'This way, *visura*,' Stephen called, striding towards them through the crowd of small children. 'Let me help you, ladies – don't let these boys bother you . . . What can we do for you? Banana fritters? Doughnuts? It's such a fine morning, you deserve two each – really. Don't laugh, it's very nutritious food – it will sustain you all day . . .' He yelled to Martha: 'Four bananas and two fresh doughnuts for these beautiful ladies.'

The women stood chatting and laughing together as they ate, and seeing them there, other passengers began abandoning stationary minibus taxis to buy themselves breakfast.

'Thank you, sir.' Stephen pocketed a five-shilling coin. 'You're next, madam. That's right, all our food is cooked to order . . . Here's your double coming up, ma'am – fresh and clean. Ten shillings, please.'

For several minutes the din of the street seemed to rise up around Stephen, and he was too preoccupied to notice the commotion breaking out near the junction where Tom was working. But Martha had raised her head, straining to see what was going on, and other people were looking that way too. One of their customers, a large woman in a saffron headscarf, was pointing towards the traffic-lights. 'That's a real fight.' She chuckled. 'They must have caught a thief. Those street thieves are a holy terror. They can take your mobile while you're still *talking* on it . . . It's true – it happened to my niece. Still, they don't live long. You know what happens to thieves in Makera?' She widened her eyes, slowly running a thumb across her plump throat.

Stephen stepped on to the road to get a better view. A big man in a suit had leaped down from a black Mercedes four-by-four, and was yelling at the two boys on his bonnet. He had already grabbed them by their ankles and was yanking them off into the gutter; then he turned to threaten the rest of the valeting team, who had retreated into the crowd of spectators. 'Keep out of trouble, Tom,' Stephen urged, under his breath. 'You're no match for this *balozi*. Run – go home!'

But the little boy in red shorts had already broken away from the crowd, and was racing in an arc around the angry man, clutching his plastic bags. The man didn't notice Tom: he was looking the other way, standing by the open door of his car. Tom paused to take aim, spinning one of his bags like a sling-shot; then he sprang forward and let it fly into the Mercedes, where it exploded against the cream-coloured dashboard.

The crowd gasped. The big man swivelled round to stare at the inside of his car, and for a few seconds he was motionless with shock. Tom was taking aim with his second bag. Then, jumping into the air, he hurled it at the pale interior, wheeled away and ran for the alleyway.

'Ah, that was the toilet boy!' the woman in orange exclaimed. 'I bet that fellow wishes he'd paid up. His beautiful car will never be the same again. Shit on the leatherwork, shit on the carpet, shit everywhere! And the little scamp who did it?' She snapped her fingers impressively. 'They'll never find him.'

Tom had wriggled through the mass of spectators and was already running down a narrow passage into the Makera slum. The alley was a muddy rut, less than two feet across, half filled with sewage. He sprinted headlong without looking back, dancing from side to side to avoid the sludge, then veered off into another tiny corridor and flew on over greenish pools of waste until he was ten or twelve blocks from the main road.

When he came to a stop at the entrance to a tiny courtyard, he was gasping for breath. He had lost his baseball cap in the crowd. His face and neck were slippery with sweat, his

T-shirt and red shorts saturated. The whole of his body was shaking, and it took him a few moments to be certain he had not been followed. Then he leaned back against the wooden shed. There was no wind: the tin roofs buckled and groaned in the heat, and the air was filled with a rich stench of garbage, diarrhoea, human sweat. The yard was really no more than a gap between buildings, a patch of mud the size of a single shack. Three small girls were playing hopscotch there; an old man sat in the shade of his workshop doorway mending a bicycle tyre next to a painted sign that read 'Christian Fellowship Bicycle Repairs'; overhead, a tangle of electricity cables and aerial masts clung to a capsizing pole. In the shack behind him, Tom could hear a woman's voice, chanting or saying prayers. He pushed the curtain aside to go in.

His younger sister Ruth was sitting on a chair by the door. 'Where've you been?' she hissed. 'Mama was asking for you.'

'I was working.'

'Did you get money?'

'Later I will.'

There were gaps between the wooden boards that formed the wall, and Ruth's face was illuminated with strips of sunlight. 'Go and talk to Mama. She keeps sleeping. Tell her to wake up.'

But Tom didn't move. 'What's Gladwell Oyusi doing?'

'She says we've been cursed,' Ruth said. 'She's going to send away the evil spirit.' And she added, in a whisper, 'I think she's in a trance.'

Tom felt his stomach contract, and he swallowed hard. 'It isn't a bad spirit. The nuns say she's got malaria. Stephen's going to buy medicine.'

Ruth looked towards Gladwell. The old woman was standing over their mother's body, reciting a chant in the Kishala language as she swayed from side to side. She had a stick in her hand, and every few moments she broke off from her prayer to utter a cry, '*Htchoo! Oucha!*' beating the ground as if she had

7

discovered something lurking in the darkness and was sending it on its way.

Tom put his hand on Ruth's shoulder. 'Go and tell Stephen and Martha what's happening,' he said. 'They're at the stall. Tell them Mama won't wake up. Describe the fever. Hurry. Go now.'

And Ruth slipped out into the stinking yard.

2

'The arrogance!' Sarah shut her book angrily. 'Why couldn't we just leave Africa alone?'

She glanced towards her husband, but he hadn't heard. Ed was staring at the architects' plans spread out on the tray-table in front of him. Turning away, she pulled up the plastic blind on the aeroplane window. At once a pillar of copper sunlight slammed into the cabin, illuminating the whole width of the interior and picking out the blond hair of her son, fast asleep on the seat beside her.

'How are you getting on with Makotsi's memoirs?' Ed whispered, looking up.

'Oh, I had to take a break. He's been arrested by the British. For treason, of all things. Can you imagine? Treason in his own bloody country . . . Still, he's got an amazing spirit. He never became bitter. He spent his time in jail writing an account of Makhoto culture, how it was before colonialism.' She leafed through the illustrations in the book. 'Everything was decided by consensus. Nobody was left out. There: that's Kenneth Makotsi's uncle, the hereditary chief. Look at those eyes!'

Ed examined the grainy photograph of a chieftain watching a ritual dance. He was sitting on a pile of animal furs next to a giant fig tree, dressed in the flayed skin of a leopard, while a man in a loincloth held an ornamental parasol over his head. 'I feel sorry for the guy with the umbrella,' he said. 'He hasn't done so well out of the collective decision-making.'

'But there's so much dignity in that face,' Sarah persisted. 'He's so alive, isn't he?'

'Well, that's it,' Ed said. 'It's happened already. My wife's in

9

love with a dead African chieftain. I won't stand a chance once we're out in Batanga.'

She reached across and clutched his hand. 'Come and sit beside me, darling. Go on, change places with Archie.'

Ed got up carefully and lifted his son, who was wrapped in a blanket, then lowered him into his own seat. 'There. Take it easy, mate – don't wake up . . . What a star! Drugged to the eyeballs. He was so manic earlier, I thought he'd never sleep.'

'D'you think he'll be all right?' she said.

'Archie? Of course he will.' He put his arm round her shoulders as he sat down, drawing her towards him.

'I wish he'd had his shots earlier. It was my fault.'

'He's had them, that's all that matters.'

'I keep thinking about spiders and things. Snakes, scorpions . . . God knows. And food poisoning, Ed . . .'

'It won't seem so scary once we've settled into the house. We'll be able to keep things clean. There's a surgery in the compound. Honestly, love, we'll be fine.'

For a moment they sat together under the reading lights, the sound of the engines filling their ears. Then he kissed her briefly on the mouth, sat up again and switched on the little television screen on the seat-back in front of him. 'Let's see where we are . . . There! Juba already. We'll be landing in Kisuru in a couple of hours.'

Sarah opened the blind again and gazed out at the rusty, pockmarked earth. The plane had been flying over desert, its surface broken by fragile islands of vegetation. Now the landscape was turning pale green, and for the first time they could make out the bluish smudge of a mountain range along the southern horizon.

'That's the Ngozi Hills,' Ed said. 'They straddle the border with Sudan. It's no man's land, nowadays. Somewhere down there is the Army of Celestial Peace.'

'It's hard to imagine, isn't it?' Sarah gazed at the ridges of

dark green jungle to the south. 'It looks so primeval and mysterious. My God, it's beautiful.'

The traffic was blocked across the junction. The big man had
refused to move his Mercedes until the valeting team had been
arrested, and a couple of dozen people were standing about,
waiting to see what would happen. When the police arrived,
two officers leaped from their Jeep and dragged the boys out
of the gutter, throwing them down between the road and the
butcher's shop where they started to beat them with truncheons.
Other policemen searched the crowd for their accomplices.

Gradually the spectators began to lose interest, and when the
beating was over, the two boys limped to the big man's car and
started cleaning it up.

'Fried bananas!' Martha cried. '*Mandazi*! Best value in town
. . .' But the customers were moving away, and she caught
Stephen's eye. 'That was Sergeant Mburu, did you see? The one
beating those boys. He's seen us – he's coming this way.'

'Oh, Jesus!'

'Don't blaspheme, Stephen. Go now. Take the money with
you. I'll talk to him. Here. That's seven hundred and eighty
shillings.' Martha handed her younger brother a roll of notes,
which he slipped into his trouser pocket. 'Run, Stephen! Get
downtown!'

But Sergeant Mburu was already close, grinning at them over
the heads of the crowd and swinging his truncheon from side
to side to clear a path for himself. 'Greetings,' he called, as he
reached the stall. He prodded Stephen with his truncheon.

'Good morning, Officer,' Martha said. 'What will you
have?'

'I'll take a doughnut,' he replied, pushing his blue cap to the
back of his head and glancing about the stall. '*Sooo* – where's
your mother today?'

'She's not well.'

'I'm sorry to hear that. Please send her my felicitations.' He rested his stick on the counter. 'I admire Mrs Odinga. Really I do. She's a woman who understands business.'

Martha took a doughnut from the frying pan, and put it on the pile of newspaper.

'I'm late for work,' Stephen said quietly, beginning to move away. 'Good morning, Sergeant Mburu.'

But the policeman shook his head. 'I don't think so,' he said, taking the hot doughnut and biting off a corner. 'There's a little something we need to straighten out.'

'I'm sure our mother will take care of everything when she's well,' Stephen said.

'I'm sure she will,' the policeman replied, his lips glistening as he blew on the hot doughnut. 'But today she's ill, so *you* must take care of it. You are responsible.'

'We can't pay,' Stephen said. 'There's no money.'

'Well, that's a pity.' The policeman took another bite. 'I'd hate to close down your business. After all, I'd miss the doughnuts.'

'Please, Officer Mburu,' Martha said. 'We can't pay until our mother gets better.'

'Oh, I see. You think I should let you have credit, is that it?' She looked down. 'Just a few days.'

'Yes, of course. That's fair. I like to be fair to all my people.' He popped the last piece of doughnut into his mouth and licked his fingertips, watching two men who were pushing a freezer along the dusty pavement in front of DotNet Communications: *We Sell The World For Five Shillings.*

'You see these people?' he said. 'These businesses?' One by one he pointed his truncheon at the temporary kiosks of plywood and corrugated iron that stood along the wide pavement; then he swept it along the concrete shops that lined the side of the street. 'These are all *my* people. I protect them. I look after them. Do you think they have the necessary paperwork to trade on this land? Do you think they have a legal right? Are they politicians? Do they have lawyers who can arrange these things?

Do they have friends in State House?' He widened his eyes. 'No! They are small people – illegal people – people like you! They have no rights. I could shut them down like that!' He thumped the tin counter with his stick. 'But I am a father to them. I overlook their transgressions. I protect them. And they show me gratitude.'

He turned to Stephen, pressing the truncheon against his abdomen again and lowering his voice. 'You listen to me, boy. I don't operate on credit. I operate on cash. And I need to be paid. I have obligations – five children, many cousins, business interests of my own. You think my family should starve because of you?'

Stephen shook his head.

'Do you want my wife and children to die of disease, just to help you? Is *that* it?'

'No,' he whispered.

'Then *pay* me,' he roared, shouting so loudly that people on the avenue turned to look. 'You owe me two thousand shillings.' And he tapped his stick against Stephen's trouser pocket. 'But you think I'm stupid! You treat me like a blind man . . . Let's see what you've got.'

Martha tried to press herself between them. 'Sergeant Mburu, not two thousand,' she said. 'That's too much.'

He shoved her aside, keeping his eyes on Stephen. 'Give it to me.'

And without a word, as though he was hardly aware of what he was doing, Stephen put his hand into his pocket and handed over the money.

'Let's see . . . Five hundred, six hundred, seven hundred and fifty – there's almost eight hundred shillings here. You said you had no money.'

'It's all we've got,' Martha insisted.

'So, that's settled,' Sergeant Mburu declared. 'I accept this as a deposit. I'll be back tomorrow for the rest.' He took his cap from the counter. 'Now, I can't spend all day with you. I have other clients, other business to attend to. Good morning!' And he marched away towards the Family Love Hotel, a half-derelict oxblood shack, calling cheerfully to the three men sitting on beer crates outside.

Ruth had been standing by the stall for several minutes, waiting for Sergeant Mburu to leave. But now, seeing the expression on Martha's face, she was afraid to speak.

'I should have run,' Stephen said in disgust.

'There are police everywhere. He would have killed you.'

'I'll kill him one day,' he declared. 'I swear I will.'

'Ssh!' Martha said. 'Not in front of Ruth.'

Stephen turned on his small sister. 'And what are you doing here?' he shouted. 'You should be at home! Do you know what happens to little girls on the streets? Do you see any little girls here? Do you? No – because it's not safe—' He broke off, his whole body trembling.

'Tom sent me,' Ruth whispered. 'He's with Mama.'

Martha stared down at her. 'Well? How is she?'

'First she was hot,' Ruth said. 'She kept asking for water. Now she's sleeping all the time. She doesn't wake up, whatever we do.' And she added, gazing up at Martha, 'Gladwell Oyusi is with her.'

Everyone was silent for a moment.

'Stephen, are you going to Makotsi Avenue?' Martha asked cautiously. 'There's time. If you got a job right away, you could earn enough for the medicine.'

'Even if I did, we owe Mburu twelve hundred shillings. *Twelve hundred.*'

'I'll pay him from the stall.'

'You can never make that much.'

'If I work hard I can. What choice do we have?'

'I know what I can do,' he replied. 'I'm going to ask Solomon Ouko for work.'

'No, Stephen! What's the matter with you? Ouko's a criminal. Last time you were almost killed by the police.'

'He's not a criminal. Listen to you! He's a businessman – he runs Universal Exports. It's a big company.'

'But you promised Mama you wouldn't work for him. It's too dangerous.'

'I could earn ten dollars quickly – maybe twenty. It would pay for everything.'

'What if they arrest you again? You'll earn nothing in jail.'

'But if I get the medicine?' he replied, stepping towards Martha. 'Mama is dying. I have to make decisions now. I'm head of the family.'

Martha folded her arms, glaring at her brother. 'You listen to me, Stephen. If you work for Mr Ouko again – even if you get paid – do you think Sergeant Mburu will leave us alone?'

'He'll never leave us alone, whatever we do. Don't argue with me. I've made up my mind. I'm going to see him.'

She looked away and let her arms fall to her side.

'Keep Ruth here,' Stephen went on. 'She can help you. Don't worry about me.'

Martha watched her brother walk away from the stall; but before he reached the road, he turned round. 'I'll see you at home,' he said. 'I'll be all right. I promise.' And he disappeared into the crowd.

3

The headquarters of Universal Exports was a four-storey poured-concrete office block on Kwamchetsi Wachira Avenue, about a quarter of a mile downtown from Aberdare Fried Bananas. All day long, on the pavement in front of the building, street vendors cried out to the brightly coloured minibus taxis and cargo lorries that stood rumbling in the heat. And on each side of the building, set back from the road, was a line of shops and bars, their proprietors sitting in the shade of plastic sheets rigged up on poles, guarding their crates of mangoes, old bed-frames, buckets of charcoal, paraffin bottles, bicycles with no wheels.

Stephen paused outside Ebenezer's Super-size Wines and Spirits, directly across the road from Universal Exports. There was a burning sensation of hunger in his stomach and he longed for a drink of water: the whole street had started to reel and rotate around him. But he fixed his eyes on the green door at the other side of the road, brushed the dust from his trousers and marched out into the traffic.

The green door opened directly on to a staircase, and Stephen walked up, emerging into the cool air of the reception area on the first floor. He breathed in the tang of air-freshener, women's scent, his own sour-smelling shirt. Five young women were sitting at desks arranged in a U-shape, speaking into their mobile phones, scribbling in notepads, typing briskly as they stared at their computer screens. Nobody paid him any attention, and Stephen's eyes rested on the face of the receptionist at the end of the room – a beautiful woman not much older than him, with a great number of coloured beads threaded in her hair.

On the wall behind her was a photograph of a benign-looking white-haired man in a field marshal's uniform, above the caption *His Excellency Kwamchetsi Wachira, President and Commander-in-Chief of the Armed Forces of the Republic of Batanga*. Next to it was a picture of a young man in an electric blue suit, smiling broadly at the camera: *Solomon Ouko, President of Universal Exports*.

'What can we do for you, young man?' one of the receptionists asked, peering at Stephen across the top of her screen. 'Are you making a delivery?'

'I'm, er – no. I'm looking for Solomon Ouko.'

The woman raised her eyebrows a fraction of an inch. She was older than the others, about the age of Stephen's mother. 'Is Mr Ouko expecting you?'

'He knows me,' Stephen said, in a voice that came out too loud. 'I've worked for him before.'

'Hundreds of people work for Mr Ouko,' she replied. 'Nobody sees him without an appointment. If it's important, you can explain your business to his appointments secretary, Miss Kimani.' And she pointed towards the beautiful girl with the beads, who was talking on the phone again.

'Ah, Mrs Mwaliko,' the young woman was saying. 'Yes, this is Elizabeth Kimani speaking. I'm so glad you called, madam. Mr Ouko asked me particularly to contact you this morning on his behalf.'

Stephen remained where he was, waiting for her to finish, his eyes coming to rest on the five-gallon water-cooler in the corner by the window.

'There's no need to look so furtive, young man,' the chief receptionist said. 'Go on, help yourself. There's no charge.' And she calmly picked up another of the jangling phones. 'Universal Exports. How can I help you?'

Stephen filled a plastic cup with water and drank it down. His lips and tongue, the back of his throat and his whole oesophagus began to loosen, and he could feel the cold liquid penetrating his stomach. He refilled and drank again. Something was happening in his abdomen: the burning sensation was beginning to subside, and he swallowed another cup of water, closing his eyes in relief.

'Young man,' the head receptionist called out. Stephen started to fill up again. 'Hello, son?'

He turned round, holding his full cup. 'Yes, ma'am?'

'Miss Kimani is ready to see you now. Tell her what you want.'

Looking along the line of desks, Stephen saw the bright, sceptical eyes of Miss Kimani resting on him. 'You want to see Mr Ouko?' she asked, as Stephen gulped down the water.

'Yes, ma'am.'

'But does he want to see you?'

Stephen hesitated.

'Is he *expecting* you?'

'No.'

'Well?' she persisted. 'What do you want to see him about?'

'I want to work for him. I've done jobs for him before. He told me to come back.'

One of her mobiles vibrated on the desk, but she ignored it. 'And?'

'And here I am.'

'Hold on,' she said, with a sigh, glancing at the screen. 'Just a minute.' She answered the phone. 'Hello, Mrs Naliaka. Yes, of course. I'm so sorry – yes, it's very frustrating. He's exceptionally busy at the moment. I'm sure he'll ring as soon as he can . . . Yes, yes, thank you. I'll make sure he has the new number.'

She put down the phone and made a note. 'All right, young man. What's your name?'

'Stephen Odinga.'

'Odinga?'

He nodded, and Miss Kimani's expression softened a little. 'Well, I'll tell you what I'll do. I'll have a word with his recruitment people and see if they're taking anyone on at the moment.'

Stephen gazed back at her, without appearing to understand.

'Well, you might look a little less miserable,' she told him. 'You never know, you may be in luck. Take a seat over there.' She slipped out into the main office.

Stephen sat on the bench by the back window, in the stream of the air-conditioner, leaning his head forward over his knees. He waited a long time for Miss Kimani to come back – half an hour, maybe more. There was a bowl of plastic fruit on the table in front of him, and instead of preparing himself for an interview, or worrying about his mother, he gazed intently at the fake mangoes and bananas. Then his mind began to wander, and he closed his eyes. In his imagination, he had left his cramped, hungry body, and his spirit was flying away. He sailed out of Universal Exports, across the slums and high above the airport until he reached the hills. He could see the farmland of Central Province, the dry savannah, the forests far away to the north. And almost at once he found himself back in his family village, on the farm, in the misty green land he had known as a child. He could see the landscape. He could smell the woodsmoke and the animals. He was home.

Then someone called his name.

'Stephen Odinga! Come and meet Mr Machi.'

He jumped to his feet. An enormous man was standing next to Miss Kimani at the other end of the room, his arms folded across a clean white shirt. 'Come and say hello,' she repeated. 'Mr Machi, Stephen here says he has worked for Mr Ouko before.' She added: 'Mr Machi is in charge of recruitment for special projects.'

Stephen stood in front of him. Mr Machi had a weightlifter's body, his hard, swollen arms and shoulders tapering to a neat waist.

'Look at this boy,' he remarked, with a smile. 'He needs some training. He needs a proper fitness regime . . .' He gave Stephen's shoulder a gentle push with his fist. 'You see?' He laughed.

'There's no *muscle* on him. He's a mop, that's all he is – he's what you call a raggedy boy.'

'Perhaps he's got brains,' Miss Kimani suggested.

But Mr Machi shook his head pessimistically. 'You come with me, child,' he said. 'You got two minutes to tell me why I don't throw you out.' He led Stephen into the next room.

4

The seatbelt signs had come on, and a stewardess was handing out hot flannels in little plastic bags. Ed got up and bundled Archie back into the middle seat.

'There we are,' he said, turning the baby to face the window. 'That's Mount Batanga, Archie – two horns in the distance, you see?'

But the plane was descending in steep steps, dropping suddenly every few minutes before levelling off, and Archie's face creased as though he was about to cry.

'It's okay, mate, don't worry,' Ed said, trying to distract him with a plastic fire-engine, 'we'll soon be there. You should check out the Makera slums,' he added to Sarah. 'You'll never see them so clearly from the ground.'

Sarah was already looking at the neat rectangular gardens of the Kisuru suburbs, each with its aquamarine swimming pool and a clump of tropical trees. 'Is that where our villa is?'

'We're going to be further out,' Ed said, 'a new development. Not as posh as this, but it should be all right – if they ever finish building it . . .'

'And what the hell's that? It looks like Surrey.'

'That's the Aberdare Country Club. Best golf course in East Africa.'

'With Makera, right next door.'

The felted golf course ended abruptly at a big road. All at once, on the other side, the whole landscape turned black and rusty brown, and for a mile or more, as the plane flew in towards the airport, Sarah could see nothing but the tin roofs of the slums, a silver railway running north to south along a dark embankment, and a succession of little hills, which seemed to be crawling with ants.

'Look at those people,' Sarah said. 'What are they doing?'

'Ragpickers. Children, mostly.'

'Jesus! It makes you wonder why they don't just invade the bloody golf club. It would be so easy.' And she turned back to Ed. 'There's just so much to do here. I really want to get working again.'

'There'll be lots of opportunities, love, I promise. With your qualifications, they'll be all over you. Just remember to be extra nice to Milton when you meet him at the airport. He's Pamela Abasi's nephew. If anyone can open a few doors for you, she can.'

'Seriously, Ed? Pamela Abasi? You never told me that. I met her once – well, not exactly. She gave one of the guest lectures I used to go to at SOAS. Wow . . . I wouldn't mind working for *her*.'

The plane dropped another fifty feet, and Archie began to cry.

'I expect his ears are popping,' Sarah said, searching in her bag. 'No, no, it's all right, darling – sssh! Here, have some delicious milk. Go on, take a sip . . .' But Archie knocked the cup away, screaming and arching his back.

Ed gazed down at his son for a few moments. 'Okay, give me the cup,' he said. 'There's nothing for it: we're going to have to violate his human rights. Here – you hold him. I'm going to pour something down his throat. Then he'll have to swallow.'

'Don't, Ed. He might choke.'

'No, no. He's much too sensible to choke.' Leaning across Archie's writhing body, he tipped half a cup of milk into his open mouth.

Archie spluttered and gulped, twisting his head away. Most of the milk shot out of his mouth on to Sarah's cotton jersey, but he swallowed some, and was suddenly quieter, sitting up and gazing about.

'God, I think it's worked,' Sarah said.

'That's it, Archie – good man . . . We're going to try some more.' He gave him another drink, and this time Archie took the cup in his hands. 'Well, that's a relief. I thought we'd have to use the codeine. Come on: let's put you back in your seat before someone arrests you.'

'Did Milton text you back?' Sarah asked, as Ed did up Archie's seatbelt.

'Not before we left. He was probably on the road. It's okay, though. He knows we're coming. I'll call him when we land.'

Stephen was standing with Mr Machi at the back of Solomon Ouko's office, which occupied the penthouse on the fourth floor of the Universal Exports building. To their right, bottles of imported spirits gleamed behind the black and gold mosaics of the bar. In front of him, Solomon was marching up and down by the windows with a phone pressed to his ear. Stephen could see the buildings on the other side of Kwamchetsi Wachira Avenue; when he peered through the back window, he found himself staring out across the rusty roofs of the Makera slums, which stretched away into the distance, with nothing rising above them except the white control tower of Kisuru International Airport to the north and the double peak of Mount Batanga far beyond.

'Of course we'll take them,' Solomon was saying. 'Yes, yes – the whole shipment. Only tell him we won't pay more than ten cents a box for the Durex. Socks are like taxes: nobody wants to pay.' On the wall behind him, hanging between the windows, was a giant poster of Sean Connery and Ursula Andress in *Dr No*, and at the far end of the room, opposite the bar, BBC 24-hour news was playing on a plasma TV. 'The vitamins, that's another matter,' he went on. 'That's a good brand, Nelson. You can pay up to fifty cents per jar . . . Okay, I'll see you then.' Switching off the phone, he swung round to face

Machi and Stephen. 'So, Machi, who's this boy?' he asked, crossing the room.

'Stephen Odinga,' the big man said.

Solomon studied him. 'Where're you from, Stephen?'

'Makera, sir.'

'From the slums? A street boy, huh?' He frowned, and Stephen stared down at the cream carpet. Then Solomon broke into a smile. 'Hey, don't look so sad. You think I am a snob, is that it? I also was raised in the slums. Many of the best people in this country came from the slums. All of us are standing in the gutter, Stephen, but some of us are looking at the stars. You remember that!'

He looked up again. 'Yes, sir.'

'Ah, but not Machi here.' He patted Machi's enormous upper arm. 'No, no. Machi's no slum-boy. He's from the shags. He's a proper farmer – you can tell from his physique.'

'This child says he worked for you before, Mr Ouko,' Machi put in. 'On a special delivery.'

'Yes?' Solomon narrowed his eyes. 'What did you do?'

'I was look-out, sir. I created a diversion when the police came. It was on Parliament Street, near the law courts. I smashed the window of a government car. The police said it was the car of the Interior Minister.'

Solomon laughed. 'That was you?'

He nodded. 'I was smaller then.'

'That was a good job. You did well.'

'I got arrested.'

'Well, I should think you did. You can't go about throwing stones through *wabenzi* car windows.' And he added, 'I expect they gave you a good beating in jail. Still, you've come to work for me again?'

'Yes, sir.'

'He's keen,' Machi said. 'He needs money for his mother's medicine.'

Stephen lowered his eyes, and Solomon shook his head at

Machi. 'What a person needs money for is his own business,' he said calmly. 'You do good work for me, Stephen, you'll be well paid. Machi will decide how to use your talents.'

'I need a boy at the airport tonight,' Machi said at once. 'A new face to carry the cash – load the merchandise. Joe Mwaliko and Alfred Wamba are doing a delivery in Upshala. Geoffrey's in jail.'

'You're willing to take a few risks, Stephen?' Solomon asked. 'In this world, risk and reward always go together – always. If something goes wrong, you can't come squealing to me. You realise that?'

'Yes, sir.'

'Okay.' Solomon nodded. 'All right. Take Stephen with you.' And he added, 'I want to be generous, young man. I want to give you another chance to get arrested – it doesn't seem fair that it only happens once.'

Stephen tried to smile.

'Besides, we Shala should stick together, no? I know what it's like in Makera – everyone's there. Shala, Ngozi, Kishana, they all do their jig together. Even the Makhoto live in the slums, if they're not cousins of Kwamchetsi Wachira . . . There's no tribalism in Makera – not in Univeral Exports, either. I detest tribalism.' He paused. 'But, still, it's good to remember your own people, isn't it? One day you might need them. You take this boy along with you, Machi. Explain the job to him.'

Stephen and Machi turned towards the stairs, but Solomon was still looking at Stephen. 'Have you had any lunch, *kijana*?'

'No, sir.'

'You hear that, Machi?'

'I hear, Mr Ouko.'

'Get this young boy something to eat. Take him to the burger place on Woodstock Road.'

'Thank you, sir.'

'You thank me tonight, when it's all over,' Solomon said, checking the screen of his phone as it started ringing. 'Pay attention to what Machi says, and don't make any mistakes. Go now. I've got to take this call.'

Stephen nodded nervously, and Machi ushered him out along the length of the room.

'Is that you, Constance?' Solomon began as they reached the door, in a gentle voice. 'Listen, I have to see you. I can't stop thinking about you. Is it true that Mr Mwaliko's away? . . . Really? . . . Of course, baby, of *course* I want to. Yes, tonight at the Hilton. I'll fix it . . .'

5

Isaias Murungi, Chief Inspector of Customs at Kisuru Airport, sat in his office beneath a slowly moving fan. He was looking with obvious distaste in the direction of Stephen, who was standing by the open door. Machi had sat down on a wooden chair in front of the desk and was waiting in silence, his eyes resting on the official portrait of the President of Batanga which hung on the wall behind the inspector. 'Under my administration, the Batangan Customs Service will be a corruption-free zone,' the caption read. 'Every member of the public is entitled to polite, honest and efficient service.' – H. E. Kwamchetsi Wachira, President of the Republic of Batanga, Commander-in-Chief of the Armed Forces.

Inspector Murungi cleared his throat, rubbed the puffy sacks of skin beneath his eyes, and peered through the open door towards the soapstone elephant that stood in a glass case in the middle of the reception area.

'Well? What do you want?' He spoke so quietly that Machi had to lean towards him. 'You say you have a proposal? Let me tell you something. Many people come here with proposals and I throw them out of my office – I chuck them out! There are plenty of people who sit here every day, wasting my time.' He paused, examining Machi's dark blue suit. 'All right, get on with it.'

'You have done business with us before, Chief Inspector,' Machi began, after signalling to Stephen to close the door. 'My boss would like to offer you the same opportunities again. He would like to establish what you call a regular business relationship.'

'In that case, he should have come in person.' Murungi glared at Machi. 'Why should I be discussing business with people I don't know – with people of low rank – with you, and this . . .' he sniffed, then cleared his throat again impatiently '. . . this slum-boy? I am the Chief Inspector of Customs.' He picked up a bottle of tablets from the desktop. 'There needs to be trust in business dealings. How can there be business without trust? It's impossible. The risks are too high.'

'My boss was unable to come, Your Excellency,' Machi said. 'He has sent me with his fondest esteem – his highest regards. He asks me to discuss these matters with you, to negotiate on his behalf. We can have what you call an off-the-record discussion. If we cannot agree, there's no harm done.'

'And the boy?'

'He's just a messenger.' Machi swatted an imaginary fly. 'He'll bring us what we need.'

The inspector sniffed once more, leaning back in his chair. Stephen was standing as straight as he could, trying not to sway. For the first time in weeks he had eaten well. His head no longer ached and even the burning pain in his abdomen had gone; instead of anxiety, his brain – his whole bloodstream – was filled with a kind of impatient energy.

'Well?' Murungi said. 'What does he propose? Let me be clear: I am asking just for the sake of politeness. I am giving you a chance to speak – that's all. Besides,' he looked at his watch, 'I have only a few minutes. The London flight is landing at seventeen thirty hours.'

'We would like to drive a truck into the international baggage warehouse,' Machi replied.

'And why would you want to do that?'

He smiled. 'Just one small truck, Excellency.'

The inspector sat up straight, putting the pills down.

'We will take no more than thirty minutes,' Machi went on. 'We will be handling only large suitcases, private cargo shipments – clothes, electronic goods, spirits, perfume . . .'

28

But Inspector Murungi was shaking his head. 'No, no, it's quite impossible. Nobody can enter the warehouse without permission. There is no access for civilians. It's not something that can just happen. It's a complex business – a licence is required. There are many factors, many people to take into account . . .'

'My boss is anxious to do everything properly,' Machi said. 'He understands that there will be expenses. He doesn't want you to be inconvenienced – not in any way.'

Murungi hesitated, casting his eyes across the papers on his desk. 'Let us say, just for the sake of argument, that you were granted a temporary licence, that you had access for a short time, just twenty minutes . . .'

'The whole matter will be over very fast – very efficiently,' Machi said. 'It will be invisible, really, what you call an invisible job. All we ask is access.'

The inspector held his breath for a moment, pressing his hand against his chest. 'No contraband,' he said, in a strained voice. 'If you are dealing in contraband, I will have you arrested – you understand that? The Special Bureau will not permit it.'

'No, sir, no contraband,' Machi assured him. 'We are legiti- mate businessmen, everything above board. Your officers can inspect our work – no drugs, no guns . . .'

'No official property, either.'

'Private goods only. Gifts, for example – gifts and commercial shipments. Clothes, toiletries, electronic gadgets, alcohol . . .'

The inspector took a pill from the bottle and poured himself a glass of water. 'You must realise I absolutely cannot permit this kind of activity. I am responsible for all the passengers at this airport – everyone has a right to pass through unmolested.'

'I understand,' Machi said.

'I take great care to protect this airport from crime. The Minister of Transport himself has congratulated me for bringing an end to the thievery and fraud of the last government. I have posted guards around the whole perimeter.'

Machi said nothing, and the inspector swallowed his pill.

'Of course, it occasionally happens that the guards are absent without leave,' he went on. 'Sometimes they get drunk. They have a great weakness for Scotch. It's a sadness to me. I hate to see the men drunk. But sometimes I believe they cannot help themselves. Then, naturally, when they are drunk or chasing after women, security becomes lax and thieves will take advantage. But it happens less and less: I am bringing the problem under control.'

Machi returned his gaze and leaned closer towards the desk. 'My boss would like to offer you an opportunity to participate,' he said. 'To share his profits as a partner.'

The inspector shook his head. 'How can I be a partner? I am not involved – I cannot be involved in any way. Besides, what if you're stopped by the police?' he demanded. 'That often happens, I must warn you, and if so, I cannot offer any protection. Or what if one of your people is killed by the guards at the perimeter? Those boys are always shooting in the dark, especially if they have drunk too much. I can make no assurances . . .' He cleared his throat a third time and started to get up. 'Well, it's just as I thought. There's no point in pursuing this. I don't want a share of profits. That is the wrong business model. A man in my position requires certainty, insurance – guaranteed compensation. I must know where I stand.'

Machi rose from his chair at the same time. 'In that case,' he said, 'I am authorised to make a transfer in advance of the operation . . . an enabling fee.'

'No, I don't think so,' the inspector said, examining his neat moustache in a little wall-mirror. 'How could such a fee be adequate? The whole business is impossible – I am not some lackey, looking for *kitu kidogo*.'

'Perhaps if I were to write a number on this piece of paper,' Machi suggested. 'Then we could consider the situation in a businesslike spirit, without prejudice.' And he passed the paper to the inspector.

Murungi glanced at the note, and his eyes widened. 'Three hundred shillings!' he said in disgust. 'Three hundred shillings! Are you a joker? Are you a clown?' Stephen turned towards the inspector: beads of sweat were standing out on his forehead, and he seemed to be struggling for breath. 'You – you said you were a serious man, a businessman. I'll have you thrown out. You're wasting my time.' He tossed the paper on to the floor.

'No, Your Excellency, not shillings,' Machi said soothingly. 'I'm talking about American dollars.'

Murungi's face, which had expanded in anger, seemed to deflate as Stephen watched.

'Three hundred dollars?'

'Yes, Excellency.'

But after a brief pause, he shook his head again, and turned back to the mirror to do up the top button of his tunic. 'One thousand,' he said. 'I cannot manage such a thing for less. Take it or leave it. Now I must go. You have occupied too much of my time. The London flight is arriving now. Please leave my office at once.'

Stephen stepped aside, ready to open the door for Machi, but the big man had not moved. 'I quite understand,' he was saying quietly. 'I'm sorry we cannot come to an agreement. My boss will be disappointed. Unfortunately, he has not authorised me to offer more than five hundred.'

The inspector had taken up his peaked cap, and was settling it on his head in front of the mirror.

'Five hundred is not enough,' he said again. 'I have to be realistic. There is a large cost to me, a significant risk, which I am bearing alone. Besides, I have many responsibilities. A great number of people are dependent on me – my family, my business associates, my staff . . . Whatever happens, I cannot help you for less than a thousand dollars.'

'Seven hundred?'

The inspector straightened his tunic and snatched up his swagger stick. 'Seven hundred and fifty,' he said, and he added at once: 'Well? Do I have to repeat myself? For seven hundred and fifty dollars, I might be able to grant you a limited licence.'

Machi paused, as the inspector faced him.

'I make no guarantees about the success of your work,' Murungi went on, fixing Machi in his gaze. 'I only say that a licence can be arranged.' And he swished his stick back and forth for a moment, so that it hummed through the air. 'But why am I saying this to you? You tell me you cannot pay, so it is of no consequence.'

Machi scratched the side of his huge neck. 'Would it be possible to have the licence tonight, sir?'

'Will I have the fee tonight?'

'My boss will be angry,' Machi said. 'I will have to disobey his orders . . .' Then he pursed his lips and gave Stephen a quick nod. 'All right, Excellency,' he said quietly. 'Seven hundred and fifty dollars for an access permit for one truck.' And he turned to Stephen, who at once pulled two bundles of notes from his pocket, and handed them to Machi.

'Here is seven hundred and fifty dollars, Excellency.' He put the money on the desk. 'Please confirm the sum for yourself.'

The inspector took up the banknotes and began to count. Then he folded them, and slipped them into the pocket of his tunic. 'Very well,' he said. 'I will instruct Lieutenant Ngumi. But you must be quick, you understand? I cannot tolerate delays or inefficiency of any kind. I detest tardiness.'

'We will manage everything in twenty minutes, Excellency, thirty at the most.'

And opening the door, Inspector Murungi shouted, 'Ngumi! Lieutenant Ngumi!' Then, in an angry voice: 'You men, bring Lieutenant Ngumi to me. You'll find him in the security office – or at Passport Control.'

'Yes, sir.'

'Hurry up. Tell him it's urgent. Run!' As they hurried off, he called after them: 'If you can't find him there, look in the warehouse.'

6

'You take Archie,' Sarah said. 'I'll make sure we've got everything.'

She peered at the floor in front of the seats, and Ed lifted his son, now waking up, pressing him against his right shoulder. 'Load me up a bit,' he said. 'I can take your coat.'

The aisles were already full of passengers, but nobody was moving.

'Has Milton texted?' Sarah asked, stuffing a tiny sock into her bag.

'Have a look – it's in my top pocket.'

She pulled out his mobile phone. 'Nothing.'

'That's odd.'

'Does he usually get back to you?'

'Yes, he's pretty reliable.'

'Try calling him. I'll take the coat.'

Ed started to carry Archie towards the open door, moving with the queue, and Sarah struggled behind him with baggage. 'He's not answering,' Ed said. 'Perhaps he's in the car.'

It was hard to keep the bags clear of the armrests as everyone moved forward, and Sarah's whole body was sweating long before she reached the door.

'Hi, Milton,' Ed was saying. 'We've just landed. We'll be inside the airport in a few minutes. Let's meet by the stone elephant.'

An atmosphere of reeking humidity had penetrated the aeroplane, and when she reached the top of the steps, Sarah stood in the sunshine inhaling the hot air. 'It's so bright,' she said. 'I thought it would be dusk by now.'

'Come on,' he said gently, glancing towards the Batangan

Army Jeeps parked in the shade of palm trees. 'Let's get Archie inside . . .'

Lieutenant Ngumi was a thin man with anxious, rapidly moving eyes, and a permanent line across his forehead. He listened to Inspector Murungi's orders, the expression on his face impossible to interpret. Then, leading Stephen and Machi out of the arrivals building, he crossed the tarmac to the hangar that served as the cargo store. Two uniformed guards were on duty near the entrance, and Ngumi went up to them with Machi, who shook them by the hand and started chatting. When the Universal Exports truck arrived, he handed each of the guards a twenty-dollar bill, and they retreated to their booth, where they settled down to watch football on a portable TV.

The three men who had been waiting in the lorry jumped out, and started examining the crates and canvas bags arranged in piles all over the building, while Stephen kept watch by the main doors. He could see the London passengers walking towards the terminal building. Behind them, under the fuselage of the plane, a team of porters was unloading luggage from the hold, piling it on to a series of trailers attached to a little tractor.

'Hey, Raggedy! Is the luggage coming?' Machi called, from the darkness inside the hangar.

'No, sir. They're still unloading.'

'So let's get *this* into the truck.' He climbed on to a pile of crates with a crowbar in his hand, prised open the highest one, and held up a six-pack of Stellenbosch beer. 'Come on. Tell Harvey to back up. This is premium lager – two dollars a bottle downtown. We'll take one crate, all right? Hey, Godfrey, what have you found? Show me.' He jumped down and strode off between the lines of boxes.

Sarah put her baggage down on the hot tarmac, and peeled off her cotton jumper, which she stuffed into the mouth of her bag, then hurried to catch up with Ed and Archie. The doors of the arrivals hall were closed, and the passengers nearest the building had formed a queue. Ed was standing next to a group of Indian nuns and a smartly dressed Batangan couple with three young children. Everyone put their bags down. Sarah and Ed squinted towards the windows of the arrivals hall, then back towards the aeroplane and the setting sun. Beyond a high security fence, they could see rows of white Toyota Land Cruisers and black Mercedes gleaming in the car park, a miasma of heat rising from the ground all around them.

'Still nothing from Milton?' Sarah asked.

Ed shook his head. 'We must get Archie into the shade,' he said. 'Does he have a hat?'

'It's in the big blue case.'

'All right, love. I'm going to find out what's going on. You take him for a minute. Put something over his head.' He walked off towards the arrivals hall.

Several young soldiers were standing about in the shade of the palm trees, but the reflection of the low sun made it impossible to see what was going on behind the glass.

'The doors are chained,' someone remarked. 'I suppose they weren't expecting us.'

'Where are the BA people, for God's sake?'

'There's our luggage, anyway,' Ed said, gesturing towards the red tractor with its line of trailers, all piled high with suitcases, which was snaking off towards the cargo hangar. 'At least we won't have to wait about for that.'

'Do you think we could get some water out here?' a woman asked.

'What about some beers? We could be here all night.'

'No, don't worry. Here comes the army.'

There was a sound of scraping metal as someone opened the doors, and Lieutenant Ngumi appeared blinking in the sunlight. 'Ladies and gentlemen, Passport Control is this way. Please have your travel documents ready for inspection.'

35

People in the middle of the queue cheered ironically, and everyone started picking up their things.

'It's okay,' Ed said, getting back to Sarah. 'It won't be long. Hey, look at that. You found Archie a hat . . .'

'Mrs Kimathi has lent us her son's.'

'Mrs Kimathi?'

The woman in front turned with a stern look. 'No, no, not lent,' she insisted, giving the peak of Archie's baseball cap a gentle tug. 'You must keep it. He'll need it.'

'That's incredibly kind,' Sarah told her. 'He was beginning to wilt – hey, Mister,' she added to Archie, 'stop pulling it off.'

'Take it as one mother to another,' she said. 'I know what it's like travelling with small children.'

Sarah beamed at Ed, mouthing, 'So kind!'

'Well, we're moving now,' he said, picking up the bags. 'We'll get Archie into the shade.'

As soon as the baggage train arrived in the hangar, Stephen wolf-whistled, and Machi jogged out of the interior, carrying a box of brand new iPods. Then he chatted to the driver and the baggage handlers, slipping them ten dollars each and opening another case of Stellenbosch, while Stephen and the other men pulled suitcases down from the trolleys.

The truck was already half full, so it was only possible to fit another twelve or fifteen pieces of luggage inside. Stephen started opening the most expensive-looking cases and rummaging through the contents. 'This one's locked,' he called. 'What do we do, sir?'

'If it's everyday kind of luggage, use the screwdriver,' Machi said, pulling open a leather bag and tipping out the contents. 'If you think it's a good suitcase – if it's a luxury model – we'll open it at the warehouse. We can always sell a good case – Louis Vuitton, Longchamp . . .' He called over his shoulder: 'Hey, Harvey, what are you doing? Get back in the lorry, fool. You help Jacob and Hastings load it up.'

36

Stephen had succeeded in forcing open a blue Samsonite case, and he was searching through the shirts and dresses and children's clothes that spilled on to the ground. He held up a pair of little trousers, trying to judge if they would fit his brother Tom. But Machi was standing over him. 'What you doing, Raggedy? Keep focused. We're not looking for baby clothes. What else have you got?'

'Women's stuff. Perfume. Makeup.'

'Labels?'

'I don't know.'

'You've got to learn the trade, Rags. Look at the labels. Study them. We need quality goods – Christian Dior, Ralph Lauren, Giorgio Armani, Dolce & Gabbana . . .'

'Zara,' Stephen read out. 'Topshop . . . and there's medicine, sir.' He held up a bottle of iron supplements. 'Lots of it – all new.'

'Okay, load it up,' Machi said. 'Hurry. Take the whole case.' And he raised his voice: 'We're leaving in five minutes. Take your last items. Concentrate. Look for the labels.'

'Non-Batangan passport holders to the left,' Lieutenant Ngumi called out, as Ed and Sarah finally staggered over the threshold of the arrivals hall. 'To the left, please . . .' There was a row of ten Immigration cubicles, but only three were manned, and the queue stretched for at least a hundred yards outside the building. Behind them, through the glass wall, the sun was now touching the horizon, and the whole hall was filled with light.

'God, it's stifling!' Sarah said. 'It's worse in here than outside.'

'Stand under the fan.'

She stood looking up at the slowly spinning blades, but could feel nothing on her face.

'We've got to find some shade. Archie really needs water.'

Archie had been complaining while they were standing outside, but now he was beginning to bawl, kicking his legs against Ed, who was blowing on his face. 'There must be water

37

somewhere in the building,' he said, looking round the hall. 'There's a little kiosk over there – I'm going to check it out.' He sat Archie down next to Sarah. 'There you are, mate. You stay here with Mummy for a bit.'

But as Ed left the queue, Lieutenant Ngumi strode up to intercept him. 'No one must leave the line, sir. Stand in the queue.'

'I'm just getting water for our baby.' He pointed towards Sarah, who had picked up Archie.

'Do not leave the line.'

'But the shop's just over there.' He gazed at the space behind the lieutenant, where the sunlight was obliterating the grey marble floor. 'It won't take a second.'

'It is closed now,' Ngumi replied. 'There is no one there. Return to your place.'

'I didn't want to tangle with *him*.' Ed put out his arms to take Archie. 'I don't get the impression he's altogether happy in his work. Any movement?'

'Yes, a bit.' Sarah peeled her shirt from her stomach. Her side was sodden with sweat from shoulder to waist. 'Those little nuns got through at once, but it's taking ages for the rest of us. That man in the crumpled trousers has been arguing about his visa all the time we've been standing here.'

'This is where we really need Milton,' Ed said, watching the man's sunburned face, and the nervous movements of the Immigration official as he looked down from his cubicle. 'Milton would steer us through. It's much harder if no one's waiting for you – the guards can take advantage. It happened to me a couple of times last year.'

'What did you do?'

'I sat it out, threatening to call the Ministry of Development, the British High Commission, State House – you name it. Eventually they lost their nerve and let me go. But it took a few hours. I don't want you and Archie going through that.'

'What did they want?'

'Just money.'

'I expect they're not paid very much,' she said, watching the guard thoughtfully. 'Look! They're arresting him.'

A couple of soldiers were escorting the red-faced man away from Passport Control, across the shining floor towards a blue door marked *Customs and Immigration Personnel Only*.

'I'm going to try Milton again,' Ed said, pulling out his phone and pressing the repeat button. 'He must be here by now.'

But as he was leaving another message, four new guards appeared on duty and took up position in their cubicles. The queue immediately broke up, and everyone surged forward. 'Quick, Ed, give me the passports. We're next.' And the guard – a man in his fifties with a neat moustache and white hair at the temples – gestured them to come forward.

7

Stephen was the last to climb on board the truck as Harvey revved the engine and leaned on the horn. He squeezed himself into the cab next to Machi and slammed the door. 'All right, Rags. Everyone on board?'

'Yes, sir.'

'Then we're going home.' He laughed, giving Stephen a gentle shove. 'You still nervous?'

Stephen shook his head.

'All the same, you look out for the airport police,' Machi told him. 'The army, too. Those thugs have a lot of guns.'

Stephen peered about the spaces of the airport as they drove out of the cargo hangar on to a deserted section of runway. In the time it had taken them to load the lorry, the sun had gone down, and all at once it was dark. Harvey drove without headlights, navigating by the glow of a fire half a mile away in the Makera slums, just beyond the perimeter fence.

'That's a nice cargo,' Machi said. 'A good variety of merchandise: spirits, perfume, computers, clothes, toys – all good quality. The boss will be pleased.' He nudged Stephen again. 'You'll get your cash, Rags. You can buy your mother's medicine.'

'Yes, Mr Machi.'

'No, no. You call me Machi.'

Stephen rested his head against the back of the seat, fixing his eyes on the red glow in the slums. For a moment he was unaware of the wailing sound behind them.

'Oh, Jesus,' Harvey said. 'Oh, fuck! Blue lights.'

'I can't see.'

'Here – they're on this side.' He pointed at his wing-mirror.

'Oo-oh, fuck!' he repeated, and raising his voice: 'Jesus – no way! What do we do? They're following us.'

'Keep driving,' Machi told him. 'Don't slow down.'

The sound of sirens intensified as the lorry hurtled towards the white markings on the middle of the runway and Harvey put his foot down, accelerating towards the orange fire, which was throwing up sparks into the darkness.

'How many cars?' Machi asked.

'I can see them now,' Stephen said. 'Four Jeeps. Four blue lights.'

'Jesus Christ! What do we do?' Harvey demanded. 'I can't go any faster – I can't see anything. What's this?' The truck had left the runway and was ploughing through tall grass and giant clumps of thistle, which thumped against the bumper. 'Now we're fucked.'

'If they stop us, we'll have to run,' Machi said. 'Just keep your heads down – you can make it to the fence from here.'

'No way,' Harvey said. 'They'll shoot us – they've got fucking machine-guns.' And he changed into a lower gear, making the engine roar as the truck dipped in the darkness, suddenly reared up again and ground on across the field.

'I think something's happened,' Stephen said, squinting at the blue lights in the mirror. 'Something's going on.'

'Of course something's going on,' Harvey shouted. 'The fucking police are going to kill us.'

'No, look.' He twisted round. 'They're going another way.' The blue lights were no longer directly behind them. Instead, the Jeeps had veered off to the left, keeping to the concrete, and were racing on at a tangent. 'They're not following us. They're on the runway – they're going away.'

Machi leaned forward to see for himself, staring out for a long time before he was sure. Then he sat back and let out a chuckle. 'Hey, Harvey, you can slow down,' he said. 'Why are you going so fast, fool? You trying to kill us?'

'Don't fuck around,' Harvey yelled, keeping his foot on the

accelerator. 'What are they doing? Tell me! I can't see! They'll come back – they'll stop us at the fence.'

'They're not interested in us,' Machi said. 'They're going out by the railway. They could never catch us now.' He laughed. 'Hey, you were frightened, man! They had you scared. Even Rags was getting the fear. Hey, Harvey, slow *down*, I said! Let's get out of this airport.' And the truck rumbled across the last stretch of scrubland, bounced over a narrow ditch, and came to a stop on a muddy track that marked the boundary of the Makera slums.

Sarah and Ed stood at the Immigration officer's cubicle, watching as he studied Archie's medical notes.

'Is there a problem?' Sarah asked. 'We had all the documents checked in the Batangan Embassy in London when we applied for our visas. We were assured it was all correct.'

The officer was now examining the vaccination certificates for a second time, checking each name against the passport, until finally he pushed the paperwork to one side. 'Your son is not well,' he pronounced, resting his hand on the pile of documents. 'It is a serious matter to bring a sick person into the country. It is against the law.'

'But he's only got anaemia,' Sarah said. 'He's not contagious. He just needs iron supplements. It's all in the notes.'

'He cannot enter,' the officer repeated, addressing himself to Ed; and he pointed to the blue door of the Customs and Immigration office. 'Go to that room. Your case will be considered later.'

Ed's head was thumping from the heat, and when he spoke his voice sounded reedy and disembodied. 'Please look on the schedule of controlled diseases,' he said. 'Sideropenic anaemia is not listed. Of course it's not – it's not a dangerous disease. We have a letter from the specialist in London, confirming the diagnosis, letters from the health insurer. The visa department in your embassy checked all the documents.'

'Go to that room,' the officer repeated.

Ed put out his free hand, which was trembling slightly. 'In that case, please give us our passports,' he said.

'All your documents will be returned to you later.'

'I'm not going without them,' Ed told him.

The man shook his head. 'The Customs inspector must see them. Your status is not yet decided.'

'You're not confiscating our papers,' Ed said. 'Absolutely no way. You have no right to do that!'

'Do not tell me my responsibilities,' the man shot back. 'You are bringing a sick child into the country. You are not permitted to do that.'

'At least give us the medical notes,' Sarah put in. 'The letters and certificates. They're private papers.'

'Go to that room,' the officer said again. 'Your case will be dealt with in due course.'

Ed stepped back from the little booth, clutching Archie. The rush of pressure in his chest and skull had reached a climax. He held his breath and tried to calm down. 'Come on,' he said to Sarah, in a barely audible voice. 'Let's go and sort this out.' And he walked across the hall towards the blue door.

There was already a crowd in the Customs and Immigration office. A couple of men in uniform stood behind a high desk at one end of the room, arguing with a group of passengers, while everyone else waited, standing by the air-conditioning vents, or sitting on the wooden chairs along the wall. Sarah collapsed on to a chair with Archie on her lap, while Ed arranged the luggage around her.

'All right,' he said, giving his glasses a wipe on his T-shirt. 'Milton's clearly out of action. Let's just have a look. Who else can help?' Taking out his phone, he scrolled through his contacts.

'What about the British Embassy?' Sarah asked, letting Archie down on to the floor and watching as he wandered away.

'I expect they're closed. It's not a huge operation, these days.'

'The Batangan government?'

'I'm just not sure who to ring, exactly. It seems a bit over the top to call the ministry . . .'

'What about Global Justice?'

'That basically means Milton.'

'Well, there must be *some*body.'

'I don't know,' Ed said. 'I could try Beatrice Kamunda. It's a bit of a long shot.'

'Who's she?'

'She's working on the project for a few months – just an intern on the legal side. So far she's all the staff we've got. The only thing is, I've never actually met her. I interviewed her over the phone.'

'Well, you might as well try. What have we got to lose? We'll be stuck here all night, at this rate.'

'I just don't see what she can do.'

'She may know where Milton is.'

'Yes, it's worth a try.'

More passengers came into the office as Ed got through to Beatrice, and Archie started to explore under the bench so that Sarah didn't hear a word of what Ed was saying. But she watched the anxious expression on his face change. For a while he listened, nodding. Then he spoke again, looking at his watch. Finally he straightened up to say goodbye and his face, which had been shiny and pale, looked almost flushed.

'Well?' Sarah asked.

'*Well*!' He let out a silent whistle. 'Blimey.' He sat down next to Sarah. 'She's quite something. It's like talking to a fifties film star.'

'What did she say, Ed? What did she suggest we do?'

'Well, she's, er – she's coming,' he said. 'She's on her way. And she's going to bring her father. Apparently he's the permanent secretary at the Ministry of Social and Economic Development. That's Pamela Abasi's outfit. I hadn't realised. I suppose that's how she knew about the internship.'

'So when will they get here?'

'She said within the hour.' He glanced at his watch again. 'She told us to sit tight and, whatever happens, not to hand out any bribes. She was very insistent about that. If anyone bothers us, we should tell them we're official guests of the government.' He leaned back on his chair. 'She sounded pretty fired up.'

'What's she going to do when she gets here?'

'God knows. Pull rank, I expect.'

'What if she can't help?'

'Let's give her a chance,' Ed said, getting to his feet again. 'There's nothing else we can do. We're not going to get our passports back on our own.'

Sarah looked to the far end of the room, where the two Immigration officials were besieged behind their counter.

'How's Archie?' Ed said, scooping his son from the floor. 'You found some nice cigarette butts – clever man.'

'He's insanely overtired.' Sarah put her hand across his forehead. 'Overheated, too. He's being amazingly good, considering.'

Ed kissed his son on the top of the head. 'I'm going to look for water,' he said. 'You hold tight.'

Joseph Kamunda was working late at his office in the Ministry of Social and Economic Development when his daughter rang him. He hurried down to the lobby while they were still talking, and by the time he was being driven through the heavy traffic along Parliament Street, he had left a message for the Special Bureau officer in charge of security at the airport, and another for the Commissioner of the National Transport Police, before finally getting through to Isaias Murungi, Chief Inspector of Customs and Immigration. He was still speaking when the car stopped on the driveway of his house in the Aberdare suburbs, and Beatrice got in beside him.

'You only need to understand one thing, Inspector,' Joseph was saying, as he moved his briefcase to make room for his daughter. 'One moment, please, just a second.' He leaned over to kiss her cheek, before telling the driver to take them to the airport as fast as possible. 'Hello? Are you still there?'

'I'm here, Mr Kamunda,' Inspector Murungi replied at once.

'Good. You listen to me. You need only grasp one simple fact. Edward Caine, his wife, Sarah Caine, and their son,' he turned to Beatrice, cupping the phone, 'Archie?'

She nodded. 'He's eighteen months old.'

'That's right, their son Archie, a small child – this family are VIPs, Chief Inspector. They are guests of the Batangan government . . . That's correct. It's a very serious matter. They are in the country at the personal invitation of Her Excellency Pamela Abasi . . .' He held the phone away from his ear while Murungi replied, before resuming in his calm, emphatic voice: 'Well, that's understandable, Inspector, and I wouldn't dream of rushing to blame you personally. After all, I have yet to discover the facts of the situation. But clearly something has gone wrong, and you are the responsible man at the airport . . . Yes, I'm sure it is very hard to find reliable people.' He cast his eyes to heaven for Beatrice's benefit. 'There *is* still a lot of corruption in the service . . . No, no. You can't be expected to root it all out single-handedly . . .' But after another fluent declaration from Murungi, he added in a sharper tone: 'You know, I might well agree with you, Inspector, if we were just having a sociable discussion, I might even sympathise, but I really don't think Mrs Abasi will be interested in how hard your job is, or the moral failings of mankind in general. I expect her view will be that if you're finding your job too difficult, the government should arrange for someone else to take over.' There was another pause. Then Joseph went on slowly and distinctly: 'What I'm trying to say is that if you wish to be Chief Inspector of Customs and Immigration when you wake up tomorrow morning . . .' He waited once more, cupping the phone and whispering to Beatrice, 'This fellow's unbelievable. He never draws breath . . .' Suddenly his face registered pleasure. 'Now that's more like it, Inspector. That's just what I think you should be doing . . . Yes, I think that's an excellent idea: speak to the commanding officer. Of course you have my authority. Now, we'll be with you in twenty minutes, by which time you will have found Mrs Abasi's guests, retrieved their passports and medical documents, made sure they have all their luggage and personal possessions, and made them comfortable in the VIP lounge . . . Yes, well, you'd better go and do that. I'm counting on you, Inspector.'

'The odd thing is, I can't see the blue case,' Ed said.

'What do you mean?'

He was standing by the glass partition near a vending machine, looking out at the luggage carousel in the next section of the airport.

'Well, the luggage is going round and I can see our two black cases but not the blue one.'

Sarah shuffled her feet into her sandals as she got up from the bench to join him. The conveyor-belt was partly hidden by the passengers waiting for their luggage. 'It must be there,' she said. 'You saw the baggage coming off the plane.'

'Perhaps someone's put it aside.'

'It's got all Archie's stuff in it, his clothes and toys – his medicine . . . Shit!' she gasped, standing back from the window. 'Oh, for God's sake! His medicine's in the blue case, three months' supply.'

'We'll find it,' he said. 'It can't have gone far.' And turning away, he saw a man in uniform marching towards them.

'Oh, God, it's that mad-looking man from Passport Control,' Sarah said. 'The one who wouldn't let you get water.'

'Mr Caine?' the man asked.

'Yes?'

'I'm Lieutenant Ngumi, sir. I have come to escort you and your family to the VIP lounge. Please follow me.'

The Universal Exports warehouse was on the edge of the Makera slums, in an unlit yard of workshops and garment factories right next to the railway line. Machi's team had finished unloading the truck and he was walking up and down, supervising the men as they sorted the goods into different piles.

'Yes, hello?' he said, answering his phone. 'Lieutenant Ngumi. A pleasure. What can I do for you, sir? . . . Yes? Yes, I see – I understand. Hold on just a second, Lieutenant.' He gestured to Stephen, turning down the music as he did so, and pressing the phone to his face. 'Okay, sir, I will need a description . . . A blue Samsonite case. And the name? . . . Edward Caine, Global Justice Alliance.' He turned to Stephen. 'The big blue case. Is it unloaded?'

'Yes, Machi. The pills and clothes.'

'Get them right away. Put everything back – neatly. Do it carefully.' And he went on at once: 'Yes, we have it, Lieutenant. It's all right. Unfortunately the lock on the case is broken. I'm afraid one of the boys broke it . . . Where should we deliver it?' He pressed his lips together as he listened. '*Every*thing, sir? The whole cargo? . . . But we have already distributed it. It's what you call pre-sold . . . Yes, of course. I'll speak to the boss. I'll tell him.' As soon as he switched off the phone, he picked up another, calling across the warehouse: 'You're going back to the airport, Rags. Is that case ready?'

'I can't fix the lock.'

'Mo, go and help Stephen with that lock,' Machi roared. 'Tidy it up. Make it look shut. It's going back to the *wazungu*.' He turned away again. 'Hello, boss, it's Machi. I'm sorry to bother you, Mr Ouko. We have a problem at the airport.'

48

8

Joseph and Beatrice found Ed, Sarah and Archie in the VIP lounge with Inspector Murungi and Lieutenant Ngumi.

'We're certainly glad to see *you*,' Ed said, getting to his feet. 'How do you do?' He shook Joseph's hand. 'This is Sarah.'

'Mrs Caine? Please don't get up. This is my daughter, Beatrice.'

'It's very good to see you, Mr Kamunda,' Ed repeated. 'I'm sorry to wreck your evening like this.'

'I'm just sorry you've run into this problem,' Joseph said. He turned towards Inspector Murungi.

'*Shikamoo*,' Murungi said, bowing respectfully. 'I touch your feet.'

'*Marahaba*, Inspector,' Joseph replied, and he went on in English: 'Well? Have you recovered the Caines' documents?'

'Yes, sir. Everything is in order.'

'And why were they held up like this?'

'It was a mistake, sir.'

'I realise that. What you will have to explain is how a mistake of this kind could happen under your command.'

'The official who inspected our passports thought there was something wrong with Archie's medical documents,' Ed put in. 'He didn't think he should be coming into the country with a pre-existing condition. Archie's anaemic, you see. He's on supplements. He's really fine, these days. We just have to keep an eye on him.'

'Anaemia?' Joseph repeated, fixing Murungi in the eye. 'Iron deficiency? Mrs Abasi will want to know how this could have happened, Inspector, how her guests could be held up on such a ludicrous pretext.'

'Yes, Your Excellency.' Murungi withdrew a couple of paces. 'I have already spoken to the man in question.'

'And what about these other people?' Joseph went on, nodding towards the blue door of the Customs and Immigration office. 'Do they all have anaemia?'

'No, sir.'

'Why have they been held up?'

'I'm looking into it, sir.'

Joseph stared straight at him. 'I look forward to your report.'

'Yes, Your Excellency.'

'All right.' He looked round energetically. 'Are we ready to go?'

Inspector Murungi cleared his throat. 'I'm afraid there's another problem,' he said quietly. 'Lieutenant Ngumi has just reported it to me, sir.'

'Well? What is it?'

'Some of the luggage – hmm – is missing from the London flight.'

Joseph paused, keeping his eyes on Murungi.

'We checked three big cases on to the flight,' Ed said. 'We've got these two back all right, but the third seems to have disappeared. A blue Samsonite case – one of those hard plastic ones.'

'I have taken a full description,' Murungi said. 'Lieutenant Ngumi has been making enquiries. We have good hopes of recovering the bag.'

Joseph turned to Ngumi. 'Well, Lieutenant, this is your department. What's been going on?'

'I'm very sorry, sir. I'm afraid some of the men were drinking. I have found this out just a minute ago. They were not guarding the luggage properly. They were not obeying my orders. They were drinking beer – watching football.'

'Let me tell you something, sir,' Murungi interrupted. 'We have a lot of trouble with recruitment. Some of the men are bumpkins – honestly, they are country-boys, Shala, Ngozi, very uneducated, not reliable people.'

'Well, let me tell *you* something, Inspector Murungi,' Joseph replied. 'The government will hold you responsible – you as well, Lieutenant Ngumi – for the return of all the luggage from the London flight. Every last piece. Do you understand?'

'But it's not possible, sir.' Ngumi was barely audible as he leaned towards Joseph. 'The thieves have already got clean away.'

'Then you'd better get after them.'

'But the items have been sold, Your Excellency – I assure you, these villains move so quickly. They are extremely clever – you can hardly believe how fast they work.'

'And how do you know that?' Joseph demanded. He added, in Swahili: 'You can only know so much if you're an accomplice.'

'No, sir.'

'How, then?'

Ngumi stepped back a little. 'I have certain contacts, Your Excellency. I have investigated these thefts in the past. We are making good progress. The airport is becoming a no-theft zone. There are several people who co-operate with me, recovering stolen items, but they cannot perform miracles. We might get one case back after a theft – perhaps two.' He gave Joseph a quick sideways look. 'Sometimes I have to pay out of my own pocket, just to recover lost property.'

Joseph scrutinised Ngumi's well-groomed face, then the plum-coloured pouches under Murungi's eyes. Though the two men avoided his gaze, they seemed to be recovering their confidence. 'I want all of this in the report,' he said, and he added in English: 'In any event, you must get the Caines' blue suitcase back this evening, with all its contents.'

'I'll do my best, sir.'

'If you want to keep your job, Lieutenant, you won't just do your best. You'll deliver that case to the Hilton Hotel before midnight.'

'Yes, sir.'

Joseph pointed at the luggage on the floor by the bench. 'Tell your men to carry this outside. There's a Mercedes van from

51

the ministry on the VIP parking spaces. All right, Mr and Mrs Caine, I'm sure you're looking forward to getting to the hotel.'

Solomon Ouko had driven his open-top Jeep all the way from the Universal Exports warehouse to the airport without speaking a word, while Stephen crouched in the back on top of the Caines' blue Samsonite suitcase, which was hidden under a rug. Parking well out of sight of the airport building, he told Stephen to guard the car and marched off.

Inside the arrivals hall, Solomon spotted Lieutenant Ngumi as he appeared from the Customs area, but Ngumi barely glanced at him, hurrying past towards the exit. He was striding along next to Chief Inspector Murungi, who had his swagger stick tucked neatly under his arm and was leaning to the left, deep in conversation with a perfectly erect, distinguished-looking man in a dark suit. They were followed by a white couple – the man was carrying a small child while his wife chatted to a young Batangan woman – and a soldier pushing a trolley piled with their luggage.

Solomon watched the two foreigners for a few moments, struck by the expression of shock on their faces, as though they were ghosts who had wandered out of the underworld by mistake and were lost in the land of the living. The Batangan girl was different: she was wide awake, talking all the time and laughing in a voice that flew out across the hall – a beautiful, light voice, which took Solomon by surprise.

The little group came to a halt just beyond the automatic doors, and the soldier loaded the luggage into a black Mercedes. Solomon started walking towards Ngumi, who broke away to head him off.

'What are you doing here?' Ngumi demanded. 'You know I can't be seen with you.'

'You think I wanted to come? Well, *do* you?' He added quietly, 'Machi says you've got a problem.'

Ngumi nodded, rolling his eyes towards Joseph. 'This man is

the problem,' he whispered. 'He's a VIP. He works for Pamela Abasi. He's going to have us all arrested. He won't co-operate. I promise you, he's got a heart of iron.'

Solomon looked over Ngumi's shoulder towards the girl. 'That's not true, Dickson. Everyone co-operates. It's just a matter of agreeing a price. You know what VIP stands for?'

Ngumi shook his head gloomily.

'Villains In Power.'

'Not this one, I swear. He wants to ruin us . . . Hey, I'm trying to talk business with you. Stop ogling that girl!'

'I'd rather look at her than you. Who is she?'

'It's his daughter.'

Solomon let out a silent whistle. 'She's a good-looking woman. Check out that dashboard.'

'What are we going to do?'

'You're not going to do anything. Leave it to me. I'll talk to the old man.'

'That's really not a good idea. Don't you have the suitcase?'

Solomon nodded, still studying Beatrice and her father.

'Then bring it in, for God's sake. We've got to give it back. I'm going to lose my job.'

'Hey, use your head, Dickson! I can't bring the case in here. That would be used as evidence against me. I need to offer my help – for a fee, of course. That way he can't prove anything. What did you tell him?'

'I said sometimes you help me investigate baggage theft. I said you had good contacts in the slums.'

Solomon took a deep breath as he looked towards Joseph, who was approaching with Chief Inspector Murungi.

'Is this the young man you mentioned, Lieutenant?' Joseph asked.

'Yes, sir. Solomon Ouko.'

'*Shikamoo*,' Solomon said respectfully, casting his eyes to the ground.

'*Marahaba*,' Joseph replied, scrutinising his face minutely. 'I understand you can help recover the suitcases that were stolen from the London flight.'

'I hope so, *mzee*. I may be able to help; I sometimes assist my friend Lieutenant Ngumi.'

'And may I ask how you come to have such good information?'

'It's simple, Your Excellency. I'm sorry to say that I am slum-boy at heart. I have business interests in Makera – I am involved in the Kisuru garment industry, the export trade. Sometimes I am approached with offers of stolen goods.'

'And what about tonight?' Joseph asked. 'Has anyone approached you?'

'No, not yet, sir.'

'Then you can't help us?'

'Well, I will certainly do everything I can. If you would let me know what you are looking for – a complete description of the cases, their contents – I will speak to some people I know. I don't ask for any fees in advance,' he added. 'I am happy to be paid by results.'

'That's very noble of you,' Joseph replied. 'As it happens, I have been having an interesting discussion with Chief Inspector Murungi here about just this point.'

Solomon watched Beatrice walk towards them. 'I always aim to provide a good service, Your Excellency,' he said. 'How can any enterprise prosper if it doesn't please its customers?' Ngumi glared at him, but Solomon was smiling. 'Yes, Your Excellency. My philosophy is always to include people in business oppor-tunities. When I meet someone with experience, with a wide knowledge of the world, someone like you, Excellency—'

'I don't think His Excellency is interested in your business philosophy,' Lieutenant Ngumi interrupted. He nodded politely towards Joseph and Beatrice. 'Please excuse us. There's no time to lose if Mr Ouko is going to help me track down the missing cases.'

'I'm sorry to interrupt, Father,' Beatrice said. 'Would you like me to go ahead with the Caines or shall we wait for you?'

'Yes, of course. We'll go on together – I'll be along in a moment. This gentleman is going to recover the Caines' luggage for them.'

Solomon offered Beatrice his hand. 'Solomon Ouko.'

'Beatrice Kamunda,' she replied. 'How do you do?'

He held her hand too long, and she looked down.

'Good, good,' Joseph was saying, glancing at the three men. 'I'm glad we've had this little chat. I'm sure Mr Ouko would agree it's important that people understand one another, if they are getting involved in any kind of business together.'

'That's true, *mzee.*'

'So, you'd better understand me, too.' He faced Solomon. 'I am a government official, Mr Ouko. My job is to serve all citizens of Batanga – all, equally – not to enrich myself or favour one person or another. Therefore I am forbidden by law to participate in any business enterprises, and it is against the law for you to offer me any kind of payment or inducement to do so. The maximum sentence for bribing a public official is now forty years in prison. Did you know that?' He tugged gently at his cuffs. 'Now, let me explain something else. The Caines are important visitors to this country, and their luggage has been stolen from the airport. If I asked the Customs Service or the Special Bureau to investigate the matter, I am quite certain they would uncover information about the disappearance of their luggage that is not to your credit. The Special Bureau has wide powers. If he had any reason to suspect your involvement, the investigating officer would have you removed from your posts,' he nodded at Chief Inspector Murungi and Lieutenant Ngumi, 'and your business would not survive such an investigation either, Mr Ouko. If it was discovered that any of you had prior knowledge of this business, you would spend many years in jail.'

Solomon said nothing.

'So let us all be absolutely clear. If the Caines' luggage is not returned to the Hilton Hotel within the next two hours –' he looked at his watch '– that is, by eleven o'clock tonight, I will immediately instigate such an investigation. Do you understand?'

'I'm sure it can be found, Excellency,' Murungi mumbled.

'Excellent,' said Joseph. 'So am I.' He smiled at Solomon. 'Of course, Lieutenant Ngumi, you must give Mr Ouko here all the information you have about the Caines' missing luggage – otherwise, how will he know what he is looking for? Even Mr Ouko, for all his skills, is not a mind-reader. Good night, gentlemen. I look forward to seeing you with the luggage at the Hilton Hotel in the next two hours.' Then he turned to his daughter, putting his arm round her shoulders. 'All right, Beatrice. Let's take our guests to their hotel.' The two of them walked away.

Solomon kept his eyes on Beatrice and Joseph as they strode out of the glass doors. His heart was pounding so hard that he could feel the blood throbbing in his temples. Although he was aware that Lieutenant Ngumi and Chief Inspector Murungi were staring at him, he was too angry to say anything until the car had disappeared from sight.

'Please tell me you've got that case,' Murungi demanded.

'He's got it,' Ngumi answered. 'He just wanted to be *paid* for giving it back. What do you expect? The man's a Shala.'

But Solomon turned on Ngumi: 'And if I'd told him I had it, do you think we'd be standing here now? Do you? Of course not. We'd all be under arrest.'

'Well, you shouldn't have provoked him,' Ngumi retorted. 'Now he's going to investigate everything – everything! The Special Bureau will be all over us . . . Oh, Jesus!' He ran his fingers up the back of his neck and all around his head. 'He knows too much.'

'Listen to me, Ngumi. He knows nothing. He can't prove anything.'

'So what are you waiting for?' Murungi asked. He had taken

his bottle of pills from his pocket, and was unscrewing the safety top. 'If you have the suitcase, take it to the Hilton.'

'It will be there before eleven,' Solomon replied. 'I'll see to it myself.'

'Tell me when it's done, Lieutenant,' Murungi replied, and strode away.

'Why do I do business with you?' Ngumi demanded, after a moment. 'You're a danger to everyone.'

'You worry too much.'

'No. You don't worry enough. What are you going to do now? You're going to fuck that girl, aren't you? You were goggling at her the whole time.'

'And you weren't?'

'I'm a married man,' Ngumi replied. 'I'm a Christian. But you – what do you believe? You have a devil inside you. You want to fuck her out of spite because the old man humiliated you.'

'I'm not going to do anything. I'll take my time. With women you should never be in a hurry.'

'Just don't forget to tell Murungi when the suitcase is delivered. He'll be ringing me every fifteen minutes till it's done.'

'I won't forget,' Solomon said. 'Leave it to me.'

9

Sarah sat in silence, stroking Archie's head and staring out of the window as the Mercedes drove from the airport on to Kenneth Makotsi Road. The traffic jams that paralysed Kisuru all day had begun to disperse, and the driver manoeuvred across the carriageway, avoiding the potholes. Along the side of the road, under advertisements for Tusker beer, mobile phones, Toyotas, mattresses, Sarah could see the half-lit forms of men and women standing by open fires, children playing in the market, young girls in *kikoi* wraps carrying plastic jerry-cans on their heads.

'Look at that creature,' Ed said, as the car turned left into Parliament Street.

Sarah peered out at a giant marabou stork, sitting motionless on a thorn tree a few yards from the road. 'My God, what a face, like some ghastly old man staring at us . . .'

A group of children had rushed up to the car as it turned the corner, holding out their hands, and now as it moved on they ran alongside, yelling and trying to knock on the windows, until the driver entered the grounds of the Hilton and accelerated up the drive.

Ed went to the reception desk with the others, while Sarah sat with Archie on a sofa in the atrium, breathing in the smell of chilled air and furniture polish, and observing the expensive little boutiques that sold carved wooden animals, Ngozi drums, safari hats.

'Beatrice has wangled us an upgrade,' Ed explained as he came back. 'We've got the Imperial Suite on the twelfth floor.' And he added awkwardly: 'It's a bit over the top . . .'

Sarah struggled to her feet, holding Archie and offering her hand to Beatrice. 'You've been so kind – so fantastic. Really, I mean it . . .'

'Don't give it a thought,' Beatrice said. 'I'm just sorry you ran into trouble. My father's furious about it.' She glanced towards Joseph, who was talking to the hotel manager – an Asian in a pinstriped suit and an electric blue turban. 'These things aren't supposed to happen under the Wachira government.' Turning to the two porters who were waiting with the luggage trolley, she said something in Swahili. 'These boys will show you to your room.'

'What are you going to do?' Ed said.

'I'll be with my father – either here in the lobby, or sitting in the Ngozi Bar – waiting for the suitcase.'

'No, no, you mustn't waste any more time on our behalf. I can wait for it.'

But Beatrice shook her head. 'We can't leave until you've got the bag back. We wouldn't get any sleep.'

'Well, in that case we'll come down and join you,' Sarah said. 'Once Archie's settled. We'll have something to eat in the bar.' On an impulse she leaned forward, took Beatrice's hand and gave her a kiss on the cheek.

Forty minutes later, when Ed came back to the lobby, Joseph was walking up and down by the hotel shops talking on his phone, so he went to the Ngozi Bar to look for Beatrice.

She was sitting with a middle-aged white man not far from the stairs. 'Hello, Mr Caine,' she said. 'Is everything all right?'

'Excellent. It's a palace up there. Archie's got his own little room with a cot and everything. He went out like a light.'

'Is Sarah feeling okay?'

'She's having a shower.' The man behind Beatrice was getting to his feet, and Ed turned to him, offering his hand. 'Hello. I'm Ed Caine.'

'I'm so sorry,' Beatrice put in. 'Mr Caine, this is Mike Owens. Mike is an old family friend – a very close friend.'

'Good to meet you,' Mike Owens said, shaking hands.

'You really must call me Ed,' he told Beatrice. 'I'll never get used to Mr Caine. Has Beatrice told you that she's just rescued us from certain disaster?'

'The luggage?' Mike sat down again, scratching the top of his head where his short white hair stood on end. 'That was bad luck.'

'Father's on the phone to the Chief Inspector of Customs,' Beatrice said. 'Keeping up the pressure. He'll be with us in a moment.'

'Well, you're in good hands,' Mike said. 'If Joseph can't sort it out, nobody can. How about a beer?'

'Thanks.' Ed glanced at Mike in the low light, struck by his pale, emphatic eyes and the leathery skin of his face.

'So you've roped in the brilliant Beatrice Kamunda to manage your slum project,' Mike said, his eyes coming to rest on his half-drunk beer. Ed noticed that the backs of his hands, visible in the candlelight, were covered with the red scaly patches of psoriasis. 'The Kisuru law firms are fighting like tigers over this girl, and you've managed to get her for nothing. How did you do it?'

'Don't listen to him, Mr Caine,' Beatrice put in. 'I mean, Edward.'

'Ed.'

'Mike is always over the top.'

Mike finished his beer, and leaned confidentially towards Ed, laying a hand on Beatrice's shoulder. 'Listen, I've known this girl since she was born, and I have to tell you, you've really got something here – I mean it. She's a marvel. She's got her father's brains. Guts, too. You'd better take care of her – this country needs people like her.'

Ed could feel his face flushing, but he lifted his beer. 'Well, here's to Beatrice and her father,' he said.

'And the Makera Slum Project,' Beatrice added, holding up her vodka and lime.

'Yes, of course. The Slum Project,' Mike said, and hesitated, watching Ed with an expression of amused belligerence. 'I've been hearing a good deal about that. Lots of people in the Wachira government seem terribly interested in it.'

'Mike's a journalist,' Beatrice said.

'Yes?' Ed said. 'Who do you write for?'

'Oh, various people.' He wrinkled his nose. 'These days it's usually the wire services that pay the rent. The British media aren't very interested in Africa. Nobody is – unless white people are getting killed.'

'Yes, I've noticed.'

'I've been doing mostly feature pieces for the last few years – magazine articles, book reviews, op-eds. It doesn't pay, but I try to keep my name in print. I don't want the people in London to forget I exist.'

Ed took a long drink of beer, and leaned back against the bench. He was tired, but for the first time since the plane had landed he was beginning to relax, and he looked around the room. The Ngozi Bar occupied most of the hotel basement, with several expensive-looking restaurants leading off it. Young Batangan women in short dresses were sitting on bar stools, or at tables near the dance-floor. Ed peered at two girls sitting opposite one another in an alcove, their heads inclined together as they drank through straws from the same glass of transparent red liquid, which glowed in the candlelight.

'How long have you been in Batanga?' he asked.

'I was born here,' Mike said. 'I'm a Batangan national. My parents came out from Britain in the forties. They bought a coffee farm in the Ngozi Highlands. Everyone expected them to leave after independence, but they went to hear Kenneth Makotsi speak at Upshala Agricultural College, just before the handover of power, and he persuaded them to stay on – them and thirty thousand others.'

'Yes, I read about that,' Ed said. 'A great speech.'

'Makotsi was no fool. He understood the whites and the Asians. He played them like any other tribe.' Beatrice was getting to her feet, and he put his hand towards her. 'Am I driving you away, sweetheart?'

'No, no,' she said. 'Excuse me a second. I'm going to see how Father's getting on.'

Mike gazed after her as she moved towards the stairs.

'So, who's been asking about the project?' Ed asked.

'Oh, you know, "sources" at State House. There's a rumour going about that a certain lady at the Ministry of Development has been making a series of investments in Makera land.' He chuckled. 'She certainly has a reputation to live up to.'

'Pamela Abasi's been very supportive of the project,' Ed said at once. 'She's been involved right from the start – we would never have got this far if it wasn't for her.'

Mike smiled and raised his beer again. 'Well, it's not surprising people are gossiping. There's an awful lot of real estate involved – right next to the Aberdare Country Club. The development potential is colossal.'

'There's no question of anyone having a financial interest in the project,' Ed repeated, smiling to disguise his annoyance. 'After all, the whole thing's on government land.'

Mike nodded, leaning back on the bench. For a moment Ed's attention was caught by the Asian family a few tables away, the women's hair shining with jewels, the men in Nehru jackets, and the children's wide eyes concentrating intently on their banana splits.

'I was involved in a slum project once,' Mike remarked. 'A big operation, rather like yours, in the mid-seventies, out in Manila. You've probably heard of it – the San José Community Project. It became famous, in its way.'

'Yes, of course. It was one of our case studies. I tried to learn the lessons . . .'

'I bet,' Mike said. And he went on with an ironic, easy-going air: 'You know, the sad thing about San José was that the whole project was so cleverly conceived in many ways. It wasn't some back-of-the-envelope scam dreamed up by a charity desperate for new revenue. The World Bank was involved in the planning, and they pulled together half a dozen specialist NGOs – voluntary organisations we called them, in those days. I was doing a stint with Poverty Action International, and they asked me to make an assessment – you know, before and after, a proper analysis of the impact on slum residents.' He stared at Ed. 'At first it went well. A group of American engineers worked night and day to put in the water mains and the sewage system. A Norwegian outfit built two electricity substations to relay power to the whole shitty neighbourhood – there were even plans for getting telephone lines in there. We started late because of various supply cock-ups, and we had to get everything done in three months before the monsoon, which almost killed us – but we did it. So the work was signed off, the funding came to an end, and the Westerners flew off to their next assignments – all except me. I stayed behind, visiting the slums, making notes, interviewing people . . .'

He watched Ed, his lips parting to reveal a row of uneven yellow teeth. 'Well, you know what happened. They say Africa Always Wins, but the Philippines wasn't far behind, as far as I could tell. It turned out that most of the slum land was owned by a friend of the President – a general in the army – and the rest belonged to businesses with factories and warehouses nearby. The fact that six hundred thousand people were living there didn't make any difference at all. They had no rights, nothing to their names. Zero.' Mike took a gulp of his beer. 'As soon as the rains were over, the bulldozers went in, and the general took possession of the entire site, complete with its brand-new sewage system, mains water, electricity – the fucking works. Most of the residents were relocated to a new slum in marshland out of town, far worse than the old one – massive rates of malaria and dysentery – and the landlord set to work building nice big villas for professionals, politicians, expat development workers. The slum was in a great position, you see, just like Makera, about half a mile from the business district. They say the general made more than fifty million dollars from it, and at least seven million of that came from the NGOs.' He put down his empty glass.

'What did you do?' Ed asked.

'What could anyone do? I interviewed people in the new slums, took lots of photographs, wrote my report. Then I sent it off to the World Bank and came home to Batanga.'

'And the bank?'

Mike shrugged. 'Paid me, and buried the report.'

Ed felt giddy with hunger. He swivelled round to look for Sarah, but there was no sign of her. A couple of young Englishmen in polo shirts had sat down nearby and were talking in loud voices. 'I've got to get something to eat,' he said. 'Hold on a second.' He called over a waiter and ordered two club sandwiches. 'Well, I think we've learned a few things from San José,' he went on, after a moment, glancing at Mike.

'I'm sure you have.'

'I've been planning this project for a long time, and we've been working very closely with the Batangan government – the Ministry of Development has advised us all along. It means nobody can muscle in on the property.' He added, leaning forward on the table: 'I haven't run a project before, not out in the field, but I really don't underestimate the obstacles, believe me. I told London I wouldn't do it unless we ring-fenced the assets. We're making certain that the residents get legal title to their homes before we start work on the infrastructure. That's where Beatrice comes in. She's responsible for drawing up the legal documents, meeting the residents' groups, pulling together the land registry data.'

'Yes, I heard about that. It's a good idea,' Mike said. 'It might even work.' He looked up towards the lobby steps, where Beatrice had reappeared. 'Here she comes now,' he said. 'Let's see if they've found your case.'

By the time Sarah came down to the bar, Mike had consumed his fourth beer; he was sitting with one arm round Beatrice, shovelling peanuts into his mouth with his free hand, while he held forth about African politics. Ed sat opposite, picking over the remains of his club sandwich.

'Come and join us,' Beatrice said, breaking away from Mike to greet Sarah. 'This is Mike Owens.'

'Good to see you.' Mike grinned, offering his hand.

'Hi, how are you?' Sarah stared at the sandwich Ed had ordered for her. 'Is that mine, love? I'm bloody starving, I can tell you.' She sat down next to him, putting the baby monitor beside a little bowl of mayonnaise.

'So, how did it happen?' Mike asked, sitting up with renewed energy, but addressing no one in particular.

'How did what happen?'

'Oh, you know, the shenanigans at the airport. I mean, wasn't anyone meeting you?'

Ed let out a discreet sigh. 'Milton was meant to be there.'

'Milton?'

'Milton Abasi,' Beatrice explained. 'He's managing the project for Global Justice.'

'No! Oh, come on . . .' Mike's handful of peanuts stopped where it was, suspended over the table. 'You are joking?' he said slowly. 'Milton Abasi is managing this famous slum project?'

Ed glared across the table, but Sarah swallowed a mouthful of her sandwich and said: 'What's wrong with Milton Abasi? Do you know him?'

'Know him? No, not personally.' Mike turned away from Beatrice, and tipped his peanuts into his mouth. 'What's wrong with Milton Abasi? Well, that's a reasonable question, I suppose.'

'The ministry suggested him,' Ed said. 'It was their call. But I didn't see a problem . . .'

'What would you say, Beatrice?' Mike asked. 'You must know him.'

'Well, he isn't in the office much. But, you know, he has connections. The project needs them . . .'

'You can say that again.'

'So, what is it?' Ed demanded. 'What have you got against him?'

Mike picked up his empty Stellenbosch bottle and signalled to the waiter. Something caught his eye and he pointed towards the far end of the bar, where a white couple in formal evening clothes was emerging from one of the restaurants. 'You see those two over there?' he said. 'That's the British High Commissioner, Martin Sykes, with his wife Angela.' Sarah and Ed watched as the couple stopped to talk to a Batangan family. 'He's been here three years,' Mike said. 'He's a good thing. I like him. Plain-speaking for a diplomat, not too much bullshit. And he's just getting the hang of this country – you know, finding his feet.' He leaned back with a shrug. 'Of course, they're sending him home soon. He's too vocal for the international-development people, keeps talking about corruption. Anyway, three years is the limit out here – nobody stays longer than that.

'There's a kind of natural progression,' he went on, as the waiter put another beer in front of him. 'Everyone goes through it – I've seen it dozens of times. Someone comes out – a diplomat, a development-type like you, World Bank economist, wannabe journalist – and they're full of hope, just fired up, spouting fantastic plans, all the great things they're going to achieve –' He cleared his throat '– and all's fine at first. But after a few weeks the tempo starts to change. They slow down a bit, grow more cautious. They still think they can get things done, but they realise it's going to take longer. It's harder than they imagined to motivate people. There are complex, hidden forces at work – all sorts of disincentives and prejudices and cultural

66

assumptions, which take time to learn and decipher. Still, they keep going, but their lives are getting more complicated. And the more they learn, the less they understand.'

He half smiled to himself, staring into the empty space between Ed and Sarah. 'Little by little a sort of darkness descends on their minds. They work less. They spend more time in places like this, drinking, talking to other expats; or they sit at home smoking dope. They don't want to be in their offices any more. Something's happened. But although it affects them in their secret thoughts, it's not really personal − not fundamentally. It's to do with how they see the world. There's this massive gap − conceptually, morally, in every way − between how things are supposed to be − what they write in their reports to Head Office, what they announce in press releases − and what's actually going on on the ground; and it keeps getting wider.' He took a mouthful of beer. 'They can't explain what's happening − not officially. What would be the point? They know nobody reads reports from the field. And in any case, what's happening can't be described in the official vocabulary. The reports are written in technical language − law, economics, engineering specifica-tions, statistical analysis − but the problems on the ground are never really technical. They're psychological, cultural − *spiritual*. The expat is more and more aware of how little he understands. What matters most to Africans − the things they talk about all the time, like God and the spirits of the ancestors, kinship, tribe − all of that is invisible to him. Not just invisible, it's embar-rassing − childish . . .

'So the months go by, and this gap − this mental disorienta-tion − gets more and more debilitating. The Westerner under-stands less and less. He starts to give in. He becomes fatalistic, cynical. He distrusts everyone, starts to get pissed every night, hangs out with prostitutes.' His pale eyes shot a look at the Batangan girls sitting together around the bar. 'Or he goes the other way. He controls himself, holds it all in, while actually he's overwhelmed by a sense of fear and disgust. He can't admit it to himself so he tries to shut it out. But whatever he does, it ends the same way. Gradually, over the course of a few years, the pressure becomes too much, and he starts to crack up.' He nodded towards the British High Commissioner. 'That's what's happened to Martin Sykes. Everyone's talking about it. They're flying him home in a couple of months.'

Sarah had been glaring furiously at Mike for some time. The more she heard, the more embarrassed she became − not for herself but for Beatrice. When he stopped talking, she tried to catch her eye.

But Beatrice was looking sideways at Mike, with an expression of wary affection. 'Well, that's all very well, but you haven't explained what's wrong with Milton Abasi,' she pointed out. And she went on, in a theatrical aside: 'I think Mr Owens has drunk just a bit too much. Perhaps he's talking about himself − perhaps *he'll* be going mad soon . . .'

Mike put his arm round her shoulders again. 'All right, I'll shut up,' he said, with a contented sigh.

'Hang on,' Sarah insisted. 'What about Milton Abasi?'

'Milton − yes, that's what I've been trying to tell you.' He took one of Sarah's chips with his spare hand, dipped it in mayonnaise and popped it into his mouth. 'Milton's your gap. He's the difference between what you hope and believe − what your NGO expects − and what's actually going on. You realise he's Pamela Abasi's nephew?'

'Yes, of course,' Sarah said briskly.

'Well, doesn't that worry you?' Mike smiled. He added, as he rose to his feet: 'Here comes your pa, sweetheart, bringing the manager with him. Perhaps we'll get free drinks.' And he went to meet Joseph at the foot of the stairs.

'I'm sorry,' Beatrice said, as she got up to follow him. 'I hope you're not offended by Mike. He gets rather carried away. But he's a loyal friend − an old friend. Excuse me, I'll be back in a moment.'

'God, she's much too tolerant,' Sarah said, as Beatrice walked away. 'What a ghastly man. You were so patient with him, love. I wanted to punch him.' She looked towards the stairs, where Mike was now talking to Joseph. 'I really don't know how Beatrice puts up with him. He's so insulting about Africa, and such a lech, slobbering all over her.'

Beatrice returned to the table with the man in the blue turban.

'Mr and Mrs Caine?' he said. 'My name is Parvit Singh. I am the manager of the hotel.'

'How do you do?' Ed got up to shake his hand.

'Good evening, sir. Mr Kamunda has explained the theft of your luggage, and I believe your suitcase has been returned. Would you please come and identify it?'

While Ed and Sarah inspected their suitcase in Parvit Singh's office, Stephen waited outside the door, his eyes moving back and forth across the atrium as he looked at the young girls in their saris and jewellery, the hotel porters, the little shops full of Ngozi carvings. Then, when the Caines came out, he moved aside, glancing nervously towards them.

'Well, I suppose all's well that ends well,' Joseph said. 'Thank you, Parvit.'

Parvit had put his hand on Stephen's shoulder, and was leading him forward. 'This is the boy who delivered the suitcase, sir. Would you like me to let him go?'

Joseph turned to Ed. 'Mr Caine, are you quite sure you have all your things?'

'Certain, thank you. We've been through everything. We've got all Archie's pills.'

Beatrice stepped up to Stephen, surveying his face. 'Where did you find the case?' she asked quietly in Swahili. 'How did you know to bring it here?'

'A man told me to.'

'Who?'

'I don't know.'

'Where was this man?'

'Near the airport, ma'am. In a warehouse. He told me the case belonged to a *mzungu* lady at the Hilton. He said she might pay me if I brought it to her.'

'Did he, indeed?' Joseph interjected in English, fixing him in the eye.

'I have spoken to this boy at some length,' Parvit said. 'This is all he will say. I'm sure he knows more, but what can one do? Do you want me to call the police?'

Joseph shook his head. 'No, I suppose we'd better let him go.' He turned apologetically to Ed and Sarah. 'I'm afraid, quite frankly, we'll never get to the bottom of this business. We just need to be philosophical. At least you got the suitcase back.'

'We're incredibly grateful,' Ed said.

'Still,' Sarah said to Joseph, in a low voice, 'I think this young man ought to get *some*thing for his work, don't you?'

'Well, I'm not sure, Mrs Caine. There's a danger of rewarding theft in a situation like this. You don't want to encourage a boy in a bad course of life. Thieves don't live long in our society.'

'But we don't really know that he was involved, do we?' Sarah persisted. 'I mean, not for certain.'

'That's true.'

'And he looks terribly thin.'

Joseph pressed his lips together, and Sarah turned to Ed. 'Let's give him something,' she whispered. 'What's five pounds in Batangan money?'

'About four thousand shillings.' He took out his wallet and looked at the crisp new banknotes. 'I haven't got anything smaller than five thousand.'

'Go on, then. Let's use that,' she said, taking a note from him. She walked up to Stephen and handed him five thousand shillings. 'Here you are,' she went on, in a slow, emphatic tone. 'This is for you. Thank you for bringing us our case.'

Stephen stared at the note. 'Thank you, ma'am,' he said at last. 'Thank you.' Retreating a few steps, he turned to Beatrice. 'Just a moment. Please wait here, Miss.' He ran out of the lobby and across the driveway towards the car park.

'What's going on now?' Ed said.

'Search me,' Mike replied. 'I'm going to bed.'

'Do you want a lift?' Beatrice asked. 'Come on. We can easily drop you off.'

Mike waved his hand. 'I've got a perfectly good Land Rover outside.'

'Oh, keep us company, won't you?' Beatrice insisted, hooking her arm round his. She turned to the Caines. 'Good night, Sarah. Good night, Ed. I'll see you in the morning.'

As Ed and Sarah walked away, Stephen ran back into the lobby, carrying an enormous bunch of pale yellow roses wrapped in cellophane. 'This is for you, ma'am,' he told Beatrice, holding them out. 'There is also a letter. Here.' He pulled an envelope from his trouser pocket.

'Who gave you these?' Joseph asked Stephen, as he retreated towards the door. 'Who? Come here, young man.' But Stephen's thin form had already slipped out through the automatic doors, and was dissolving in the darkness outside.

Beatrice tore open the envelope.

'Blimey! Pretty good flowers,' Mike remarked. 'Who're they from?'

'Solomon Ouko,' she said, smiling in bemusement as she cast her eye over the letter.

'Who?'

'The young man at the airport,' Joseph explained. 'I don't suppose he admits his involvement in trying to steal the luggage, does he?'

'No, Father. I'm afraid not.' She stuffed the letter into her bag. 'Just a lot of nonsense in Sheng. Come on. Let's go home.' Cradling the flowers in her arms, she walked out of the hotel with the two men.

Martha and Ruth shut up Aberdare Fried Bananas a little after eleven that night, carrying the kerosene stove and cooking oil, with the remaining bananas and dough, to Mrs Buwumbo at the Eclipse Beauty Salon, where they stored their things each night. All along Kwamchetsi Wachira Avenue people were shopping for groceries, drinking at the bars, chatting under the electric light-bulbs that were strung out

72

zigzag across the market. The two sisters hurried through the crowds with a green plastic jerry-can, which they filled from a pump outside the Prosperity Butcher's Shop. Then, manoeuvring the canister on to her head, Martha gripped Ruth with her free hand and they started off together into the corridors of Makera.

Gladwell Oyusi was sitting in front of the Odingas' shack with Tom, who looked up at Martha but said nothing.

'What's the matter?' She put the can down on the mud. 'What's happened?'

'There was a spirit here,' he said flatly.

'What are you talking about?'

'Gladwell Oyusi sent it away.'

'Is Mama all right?' Martha asked. 'Is she alive?'

'She's sleeping,' Gladwell said. 'Tomorrow, she'll be well. I lifted the curse.'

'There were some rags,' Tom explained. 'Gladwell Oyusi found them buried under the floor. She dug them out with a stick.'

'They had been there a long time,' Gladwell put in. 'Someone has cursed your family. Perhaps some woman is jealous of your mother – jealous of her four children.'

'She carried the rags outside,' Tom went on. 'I watched her burn them.'

'Well, that's fine,' Martha replied. 'That's good. Now it's cleaner inside. What's the matter with you? You should be pleased.'

'There was something alive,' Tom insisted. 'The rags were panting like an animal. I could hear them.' Martha squatted beside him, resting her hand on his head. 'What if there are other bad spirits in the house? Our mother thinks there are – she said so. What if a witch has cursed us?'

'Nobody's cursed us. Our mother's ill, that's all. When you're ill, you have bad thoughts. Stephen is going to buy more medicine.' She got up to carry the water inside. 'Come on. It's time to sleep. Say your prayers with Ruth. Pray to Jesus and Mary to look after you. Ruth, come here. Say sorry to Jesus for your sins. Ask Him to help us. Ask Him to send the right doctor. I'll make the bed.'

There was a stench of diarrhoea in the shack; something was scuttling back and forth across the tin roof; mosquitoes droned all around. Gradually, as her eyes adjusted, Martha discerned the shape of the chair near the door, the picture of the Sacred Heart on the roof beam, the slender form of her mother on the floor at the back of the room.

'Who's that?' Ann asked weakly.

'It's me, Mother.'

'Martha? You shouldn't be here. Why aren't you working? You must work.'

'It's night, Mama. It's late.' She knelt down beside her.

'Where are the children?'

'Outside. I'm going to make the bed.'

'Stephen?'

'He's working.'

Ann nodded in the darkness.

'I brought water.' Martha leaned over, putting out her hand to feel her mother's forehead.

'I keep dreaming we're back home,' Ann whispered, 'on the farm, and your father's with me – standing right here. Then I wake up and I'm lying in this place . . .' She grasped Martha's T-shirt, raising her head with difficulty from the blanket. 'We must leave, Martha. There are spirits here. I can feel them inside me, pushing me down – planting me in the ground like a tree. They're trying to bury me . . .'

'It's the disease,' Martha said. 'Here. Try to drink.' Supporting her mother's head with one hand, she put the cup to her lips.

Ann swallowed, but she jerked her head away, coughing. 'Everything tastes like poison,' she said, in Kishala.

There was silence, apart from the whining of mosquitoes. Martha called Ruth and Tom to come and lie down, and taking the wooden chair from the doorway, she set it down beside her

74

mother. 'Go to sleep,' she told them. 'Don't worry about anything. Just pray and go to sleep. I'm going to pray, too.'

The children fell asleep some time after midnight, but Martha stayed awake, propped up in the chair and clutching the image of the Sacred Heart to herself, while her mother wheezed and groaned. After a few hours, Ann was quiet for a while, breathing more evenly, so Martha wrapped a blanket around herself and finally dozed off in her chair. She woke with a cry some time before dawn. Ann had drawn her knees up, and was rolling on to her side, trembling all over and crying out. 'I'm cold,' she complained, in a small, distant voice. 'Oh, my dear Lord Jesus, I'm cold. I'm nothing but ice.' She pulled up her thin cotton wrap. 'What's happening? My heart's turning to ice . . .'

Martha took her blanket and laid it over her mother. Then she lay down and tried to hold her, but Ann had started to thrash about. Martha climbed on top of her, using the whole weight of her body to press her down on the floor. 'Don't die, Mama,' she said. 'You're not going to die . . .' She closed her eyes, listening to her mother's teeth as they rattled in the darkness, and the groan that came from her throat.

Stephen woke up on a pile of blankets in the Universal Exports warehouse. He sat up at once, checked the money in his back pocket as he rolled off his bed, and hurried to the washrooms. Then, when he had held his head under a cold tap, and pulled on a T-shirt, he went outside into the dawn.

The garment district was already crowded. All along the railway lines – on the embankment and rubbish tips on the far side, where the sun was rising, and in the yard outside the warehouse – men and women were rising from the ground, folding the rags they had been sleeping on. Dozens of small children were at work, scavenging on the rubbish tips beyond the tracks with the goats and giant marabou storks, while small girls with plastic jerry-cans queued for water at a pump by the warehouse.

Stephen turned away from the train tracks, moving as fast as he could around the side of the building, his shadow stretching out along the corridor ahead of him. The smell of the slums had retreated in the night, but it was rising again with the heat, and when Stephen reached his own little courtyard and stood outside the shack, the stink of excrement was so strong that he pressed his hand against the wall and bent over while his stomach contracted. Then, wiping his mouth, he went inside.

Martha was sitting on the chair next to Ann, and she turned to Stephen without a word.

'What's happened?' he said, standing beside her. 'Is she alive?' Ann moaned in her sleep, and he crouched down. 'I have the money.'

'Where have you been?' Martha demanded.

'Working.'

'I was frightened to death.'

'Go to the nuns and fetch a doctor,' he said. 'They can tell you what drugs to buy. Here, take it.'

'What about Tom and Ruth?'

'They'll stay here and look after Mother.'

'You stay with them, Stephen.'

'No, I have to work.'

'Please. They need you.'

'They need *money*. Look at Mama – she's half dead.'

'Ssh! Don't say that,' Martha replied, and went on in a different tone: 'I stayed with her all night. I had to lie on top of her. She was shaking badly – beating the ground. I used all my weight to calm her.' She turned her eyes towards him. 'She kept saying she was cold – but it was so hot. I thought she was going to die.'

He glanced at the slight figure under the blankets.

'Then I thought about Jesus in the Garden of Gethsemane,' Martha said. 'I asked him to help.'

'And did he? Did he come and help?'

'You've come,' she replied.

'I'm not Jesus.' He let go of her hands. 'I can't cure her.'

'We have money now. We can get a doctor.'

'Go on, then.'

But she remained where she was, keeping her face turned towards him. 'Can I tell you something? I want to explain it, only you mustn't be angry. You promise?'

'What is it?'

'In the night, when I was lying here, something happened. I was frightened. I couldn't even pray – my head was full of terrible thoughts . . . But I was holding the Sacred Heart in my hands, saying his name – Jesus, Jesus – and he *did* come, I'm sure he did. He sat down beside me right here. I could feel him. He heard me. And after that everything changed. I was peaceful – the house was calm.'

'Nothing changed,' he said. 'If he came, why didn't he cure Mama?'

'He will. It was real. He was here. Compared to that, nothing is important.' And she nodded her head. 'It was a grace.'

Stephen got to his feet. 'Go to the doctor,' he repeated. 'Hide the money. I'll come with you to the avenue.' He turned to the children, who had been sitting on the cotton cloth they slept under. 'Put away your bed,' he said. 'Stay here with mama. We're going to get help. We'll be back soon.' He led Martha out into the sunlight and set off with her towards Kwamchetsi Wachira Avenue.

Part Two

II

Global Justice Alliance had set up a temporary office on the two-acre site near the edge of the Makera slums where the clinic and school were going to be built. The site was about half a mile from the Hilton, and to start with Ed made a point of walking to work. On the first morning, he got as far as the marketplace on Kwamchetsi Wachira Avenue before attracting the attention of the street-children, who ran up with newspapers and bags of nuts, then followed him the rest of the way, whistling, jeering and shouting in English. The same thing happened the next day, but on the third morning Ed found himself surrounded almost as soon as he turned off Parliament Street, so that for at least ten minutes he was unable to move at all. After that he decided to go to work by taxi.

However early Ed arrived, Beatrice's scooter was always parked outside the box-like office when he approached the compound, and he found her working in the inner room, where Milton Abasi had installed a couple of desks and a metal filing cabinet for which they couldn't find the key. For the first two weeks after Ed arrived in Batanga, Milton never came to work, so he and Beatrice sat together with the windows open, drinking bottle after bottle of water as they sorted through the chaos of cheque stubs, handwritten notes, invoices and receipts they had found in the drawers of Milton's desk, trying to match the sums he had spent with the figures that had been reported to Ed in London before he had come out.

The office was unbearably hot. Air-conditioning units had been fixed under the windows, but they had not been connected to the power supply, and once the sun was up, Ed and Beatrice sweated continuously, even if they sat perfectly still. Outside the windows, a brown savannah of warped tin roofs and makeshift aerials stretched out before them in the sunshine; and all day long, the sharp, bitter stench of the slums invaded their little room – burning tyres and rotting vegetables, chicken droppings, human excrement, and something heavy and pungent, like putrefying flesh, which seemed to permeate everything else.

By the end of the first week there was still no sign of the bank statements, despite Ed's repeated visits to the branch manager, and it was clear that Milton had lied about the money he had spent. Beatrice found a locksmith on the Avenue who came to open the filing cabinet, and after that, for another few days, they sorted through the paperwork in the files: letters to Milton from a property company called Matiba Development; some receipts from building contractors; a pile of expensive-looking brochures from an architect's firm called Alfred Kimathi Associates; and scraps of paper covered with Milton's handwriting, notes of phone numbers, various sums of money, dozens of names. When they had arranged everything in order, they sat together at the desk and tried to calculate the discrepancy in the figures: the difference between the modest expenditure recorded in Milton's reports to London, and the very large sums named on the paperwork in the office. Then, when she had added up the columns several times, Beatrice underlined a figure of $2,300,000, and passed it to Ed.

'That can't be right,' he said at once. 'There must be an explanation. Where the hell are the bank statements?'

'Where's *Milton*?' She looked down the list of payments, tapping her finger on one of the names. 'This company is getting most of the money. Mount Batanga Construction. Their name keeps coming up.'

'Any idea who they are?'

She shook her head.

'Well, we're meeting Milton's aunt on Wednesday,' Ed said. 'Let's just hope we get to the bottom of it then.' And he threw the paper back on to the desk. 'Come on, Beatrice, let's get out for a few hours and clear our heads. I've been here almost three weeks, and I've hardly been into the slums at all. We won't achieve anything if we don't get to know the neighbourhood.'

Ed had set up a meeting with Pamela Abasi at the Ministry of Social and Economic Development many weeks earlier, but now, as the day approached and it became increasingly clear that Milton had been misusing project funds, he worried about what exactly he should tell the minister and her officials. He spent hours going over the financial information with Beatrice, trying to separate what they knew for certain from what was still open to question, and preparing a report that would set out the difficulties without seeming to blame Milton too directly. After Beatrice had gone home in the evenings, he rehearsed his presentation in the office, before going back to the hotel where he tried it out on Sarah.

On the morning of the meeting, Beatrice came into the office before dawn to check the presentation for the last time, then print up and collate copies of the report for the minister and her team. She sat alone as the sun rose over the slums to the east, concentrating intensely, unaware of the noise of traffic on Kwamchetsi Wachira Avenue, or the dense crowds in the slum corridors around the compound. Ed had ordered a car to pick her up at ten thirty and bring her to the Hilton, before taking them on to the ministry building together. She was already nervous. It seemed to her that every time she reread the report she found some new mistake. And then, a little after nine, as she was about to print a corrected page, the power supply failed.

'Oh, for goodness' sake!' She gazed about at the papers neatly laid on the table. Then she slapped the side of the printer, and prodded the start button angrily. There was a noise in the compound. A car door slammed and, after a moment, there were footsteps and voices in the next room. 'Who's there?' she called. 'Is that you, Ed?'

'*Hodi*!' Solomon Ouko's voice sang out. 'Miss Kamunda? I hope I'm not disturbing you.'

He sauntered into the room, ducking his head to clear the top of the door and carrying an enormous bunch of red roses. Outside in the sunlight, surrounded with building materials, Beatrice recognised the anxious-looking boy who had brought the Caines' suitcase to the Hilton.

'A small gift,' Solomon announced, closing the office door. He approached her slowly, holding out the flowers. 'A token of the joy you provoke within me.'

She looked at him blankly.

'I have also brought an invitation,' he continued, coming to a stop a couple of feet from her.

'A – what? What are you talking about?'

'An invitation,' he repeated. 'I'm throwing a *heppi* in my penthouse.' He stayed where he was. 'I thought perhaps you would not be pleased to see me. Naturally I hoped for a generous reception but, frankly, I was afraid. I have been out of town, Miss Kamunda. I have been on the road. All the way to Upshala and back, I was thinking about you – nothing else.'

Beatrice folded her arms, her eyes defiantly hostile despite a sensation of excitement in her stomach.

Solomon stepped a little closer. 'I promise you, I could think of nothing else. Your face was fixed in my mind. Fixed. Now I am back in Kisuru so, naturally, I had to see you again. I really had no choice. What else could I do?'

'You could stay away,' she said. 'I'm extremely busy this morning.'

'Yes, of course. I will be quick – I promise.' He took an envelope from his jacket pocket and handed it to her. 'Here. Please.' She took it from him. 'Thank you, Miss Kamunda. I can't explain how much I wanted to see you again – even for just a few minutes.'

She kept her lips pressed together, refusing either to smile or to look at Solomon's eyes. 'Well, you've seen me,' she said, tossing the invitation on to the desk. 'Now you can go.'

'Aren't you going to open it?'

'Perhaps. If I have time.'

'Aren't you at all curious?'

'I have more important matters on my mind.'

Solomon hesitated, still holding the flowers. 'These are for you also,' he went on, laying them on the desk beside her, but keeping his distance.

'Listen, Mr Ouko,' Beatrice said. 'You can save us both a lot of trouble. I'm working. I'm under a lot of pressure. My boss is arriving any minute. Go away and try your patter on someone else.'

Solomon watched her with his head on one side. 'You are a beautiful woman, Miss Kamunda. You have the power to tear a man up – you can destroy his strength. That is a great power, greater than statesmen and oligarchs, greater than the power of an army . . . '

Beatrice shook her head as she examined the roses on the desk. 'Do you own a florist's, Mr Ouko?' she asked. 'Maybe you are a florist – perhaps that's your profession.' And she half smiled. 'I mean, where do these flowers come from?'

'Would you despise me if I was a florist?' Solomon asked. He looked about the room. 'Who put up this box? You don't even have electricity. My builders would never do a flimsy job like this. They can construct a whole row of houses in a single night, good family houses. We always satisfy our clients.'

'By stealing their luggage?'

'I didn't steal anything. Through my contacts, I got the luggage back.'

She watched him for a moment, and her voice softened. 'I never despise a man who knows how to work.'

But Solomon had stepped away and was moving round the office. 'And what about you?' he asked. 'What are you doing

85

here? How are you making a living out of the slums, Miss Kamunda? You know how poor people are in Makera.'

'We're going to build a school,' she said. 'A school and a clinic. And I'm not making money. I'm a volunteer.'

'Really? A volunteer?' He picked up a framed photograph from Milton's filing cabinet and examined it. 'And is your boss a volunteer?' The picture showed Milton with his aunt Pamela, smiling at the camera from a rooftop terrace in Manhattan, the Chrysler Building visible in the sunlight behind them. 'Well?'

Beatrice said nothing.

'I'll tell you something. You are working for *wabenzi*.' He held up the picture. 'With people like this, there is always a profit. Always. If there wasn't money to be made, he wouldn't be involved. There's no business like the aid business, Miss Kamunda. Every villain in Batanga wants to work in development.'

'You can think what you want.'

'You don't believe me?' He shrugged his shoulders. 'It doesn't matter. You'll see I'm right.'

'Please go,' Beatrice repeated. 'I've got work to do. My boss will be here soon. We're going to a meeting downtown.'

'Good! Will you introduce us? I'd like to meet him.'

'Not that boss. The director of Global Justice. He's from England.'

'That little *mzungu*?' Solomon laughed. 'He's your director? I saw him at the airport. He looks like a ghost.' But seeing the haughty, deadpan look on her face, he retreated to the door. 'Hey, Stephen, let's get back to work.' And he added, with a broad smile: 'It was a great pleasure to see you, Miss Kamunda. I'm sure we'll meet again very soon. If you can't come to my party, perhaps we can have dinner together.'

He walked away without waiting for an answer, calling as he approached Stephen, 'Hey, *kijana*, what's going on here? Who's this pretty girl hanging on to your shirt? Why's she crying? What have you done?'

'Nothing,' Stephen said, attempting to push away Martha, who was standing in front of him clutching his shirt. 'She's just my sister, Mr Ouko. She's going now.'

'No, Stephen!' Martha remonstrated. 'You must come with me. We have to find a doctor.'

'Go to the hospital,' he told her. 'The emergency department.'

'You know they won't help. I'll wait all day, and our mother will die.' And she raised her voice: 'You must come!'

'What's the matter?' Solomon asked.

'It's nothing, sir.'

'This is your sister?'

Stephen shuffled in embarrassment. 'It's all right, Mr Ouko. It's not important.'

'Stephen!' Martha protested.

'Go away!' he insisted. 'You see I'm busy.'

'Then she's going to die,' Martha yelled, finally letting go of his shirt. 'She'll die because of you!'

Beatrice appeared at the door.

'Tell me what's going on,' Solomon said again, stepping down on to the dusty ground.

'Our mother's sick, sir,' Martha said, coming up to him. 'We bought her medicine, but she's getting worse. There are no doctors at the convent. Everyone's busy. They can't help us. Please tell Stephen to come with me.'

'What's wrong with your mother?' Beatrice asked.

'She has malaria,' Martha replied. 'She's not conscious.'

Beatrice took out her mobile phone, stepping back into the shade to read the screen.

'You have an idea, Miss Kamunda?' Solomon asked.

'Perhaps,' she replied. 'Don't you? You must know a doctor.'

'We have money,' Stephen put in. 'We can buy more drugs.'

'Hello?' Beatrice said. 'Can I speak to the doctor on duty, please? . . . Yes, it's an emergency.' Keeping the phone pressed to her ear, she turned to the others. 'The project has a partnership with a medical charity. They're advising us about the clinic.

They do visits in Makera – one of them was telling me about it . . . Hello, is that Dr Mutua? Robert Mutua? . . . Yes, it's Beatrice Kamunda here . . . That's right. I'm at the project now . . . Yes, thank you. Fine, fine . . . Listen, Robert, we've got an emergency with one of the people connected with the programme – a medical emergency. Yes, of course . . .' Turning away, she disappeared inside the building.

When she came out again, Beatrice was wearing a pair of ankle-length rubber boots and carrying a shoulder bag with a Red Cross emblem. 'All right. Dr Mutua is coming here directly – it should take him about half an hour. He will need someone to show him the way to your mother's house. Stephen, can you do that?' Stephen looked towards Solomon. 'Is that all right, Mr Ouko?' Beatrice asked. 'You can spare Stephen for an hour or two?'

'Yes, of course. You do as Miss Kamunda says, Stephen. Wait here for Dr Mutua.'

'Yes, sir.'

'What about you?' Solomon asked. 'Where are you going in those green boots of yours?'

'To see the patient,' she said, a little self-consciously. 'I've got a thermometer, water, rehydration salts, antiseptic wipes – I'll see what I can do. I can ring the doctor and bring him up to date. Martha, will you show me the way?'

Solomon looked at her quizzically. 'Where's your appointment, Miss Kamunda?'

'I may be late,' she replied. 'It can't be helped. I'll ring my boss on the way.'

'But where is the meeting taking place?' he asked again. She merely glared at him. 'Oh, don't be stubborn.'

'It's at the Ministry of Development. A car's coming at ten thirty.'

'Then you won't make it.'

She looked at her watch, biting her lip.

'I'll tell you what,' he went on. 'I'll send a motorbike for you.'

She laughed. 'Are you serious?'

'Of course. Motorbikes are the only way to get about in this city. My driver will have you at the ministry in less than ten minutes. He'll be waiting for you here.'

Beatrice hesitated. 'Why, Mr Ouko?' she asked quietly.

'You're helping me,' he said. 'You're helping one of my people. Why can't I help you? Are you going to refuse? I don't believe you're such a fool.'

'No. Under the circumstances, I accept. Thank you,' she added thoughtfully, 'I'll be back as soon as I can.'

Solomon watched her hurry across the compound. 'I'll tell the driver to bring a spare helmet,' he called after her.

'You don't know my size.'

'That's not hard, Miss Kamunda. I'll tell him you have a very big head!'

Gladwell Oyusi was sitting on the wooden chair by the door. She had been drifting in and out of sleep, her head resting against the wall and her feet stretched out in front of her, almost touching the edge of Ann's blanket. But she was awake now, and her eyes snapped open the moment Beatrice came in.

'This is our neighbour, Mrs Oyusi,' Martha explained. 'She's been helping us since our mother got ill.'

Gladwell drew in her feet, watching Beatrice hesitate at the door, overcome by the stench of diarrhoea. 'You *people*,' she spat, struggling to stand up. 'Can't you see the woman is ill?'

'It's all right, Mrs Oyusi,' Martha said. 'Miss Kamunda is not from the development company.'

'No?' She dropped back on to the chair.

'She's come to help. She has telephoned a doctor.'

Gladwell kept her eyes on Beatrice's neat, well-dressed figure.

'She's a friend, Mrs Oyusi. We can trust her.'

Beatrice took a breath of foul air, stepped past Gladwell and went to squat beside Ann. 'Mrs Odinga,' she said, 'I want to take your temperature.' Ann was breathing heavily, and she gave no sign of having understood. 'I'm going to put this device on your forehead, Mrs Odinga.' She took the thermometer from her bag. 'It won't hurt. Please lie still.'

'You must tell her I drove away the evil spirit,' Gladwell remarked, apparently addressing Martha, although she had closed her eyes. 'I sent the children for water.'

'The Odingas are fortunate to have a neighbour like you, Mrs Oyusi,' Beatrice said, making a note of Ann's temperature. 'At times like this, friendship matters so much.'

Gladwell opened her eyes in the dark, and sat upright on her chair. 'I have known Ann Odinga since we were children in the Highlands,' she declared. 'We are both Shala. The Shala understand friendship.'

Beatrice had put the thermometer back in the bag, and was now peering at her watch. 'I'm going to take your pulse, Mrs Odinga.' After half a minute or so, she spoke again: 'The Upshala Highlands are my favourite place in Batanga. There's nowhere like them. I used to visit them when I was little. My mother's family came from there.'

'Then you are a Shala, too,' Gladwell said, with satisfaction.

'I was born in Kisuru,' Beatrice replied. 'Really, I consider myself a Batangan. I'm afraid I don't much speak Kishala these days.'

But Gladwell shook her head. 'You are a Shala. It's written in your soul. Nothing can change that.'

Beatrice wrote down Ann's pulse, then wetted a clean piece of lint and laid it across her forehead.

'She has been troubled by an evil spirit,' Gladwell explained. 'It was worrying her a great deal. She was so frightened – that's how she became delirious. But I sent the spirit away. She will be well soon.'

'What was she worrying about?' Beatrice said. 'I mean, was there something in particular?'

'Money,' Gladwell said. 'She has four children: she is always worried . . .'

'There's never enough,' Martha put in. 'I should be working now – we have to pay the school fees for the children, the rent for this house, for our stall, for storage. The cooking oil must be paid for, the bananas, the flour, and the police always demand more money. All of us are worried. My mind is never at peace. Our mother is frightened that our family will break up. She's worried about Stephen – that he'll lose his faith, lose his way in life and become a thug.'

Beatrice nodded in the darkness.

'Last night she kept crying out,' Martha went on. 'She was talking about the house – the development company. She had a dream that we were homeless again.'

'Who are these developers?' Beatrice asked.

'Matiba Development. They come all the time handing out leaflets. They want to buy our home. Can you imagine? Why would anyone want to buy this house?'

'They're buying the whole neighbourhood,' Gladwell said. 'They paid one man four hundred dollars for his workshop and flat. Four hundred! Just like that! And he's still living there – they haven't even asked him to leave.'

'Last week they threatened my mother,' Martha said. 'A man with one eye came here and menaced her.'

'Why?'

'Because she refused to sell. This is a slum, but it's near the city. When people move away, they end up miles from nowhere, beyond the airport, in the hills. Then they spend all day getting to work.'

'Tell me about this man,' Beatrice said.

'He has two eyes,' Gladwell explained, 'but one of them is false.'

'He left a card for my mother,' Martha said. 'I'll show you.' She had gone over to a small chest on the floor beside the children's blankets and was looking inside. Then she came back to Beatrice and handed her a white business card, with a red and yellow flyer.

'Luther Magari,' Beatrice read, and getting to her feet, she went over to the door. 'Can I keep the leaflet?'

'Yes, of course. Those things are all over Makera.'

Beatrice wrote down Luther Magari's name and phone number in her notebook. Then, glancing at her watch, she handed the card back to Martha and went outside to telephone Dr Mutua.

'I'm going to leave this water here,' she said, when she came back in. 'Dr Mutua is on his way with Stephen. They should be here soon. He's bringing drugs and an intravenous drip. He will try to treat your mother at home, Martha, but it may be better to move her to the clinic. He can't decide until he's seen her. Try not to worry. Many people recover from malaria, with the right treatment.' Martha watched Beatrice as she put the bottles of water next to Ann. 'I must get back to the office now.'

'Let me come with you,' Martha said. 'I'll show you the way. You mustn't go on your own. It's dangerous, even for people who live here.'

'Are you sure?'

'Yes. Please follow me.' Martha led Beatrice out, past the large, immobile form of Gladwell Oyusi, into the glare of the sun.

12

A sergeant in jungle fatigues stood leaning against a green armoured car outside the Ministry of Social and Economic Development. He was smoking a cigarette, laughing and shouting to the man on top of the vehicle, who had trained his machine-gun in the general direction of the Makotsi Memorial Park across the road. The other soldiers, lined up along the front of the ministry, stared at the street through dark glasses, listening to the continuous thunder of traffic and building work all around. A few yards away, a team of shoeshine boys called for customers, and a blind man with no legs sat propped against the wall of the ministry building. But one noise in particular had caught the sergeant's attention. Slowly he stopped laughing and held up his hand for silence. Somewhere in the distance a wail of police sirens had begun to isolate itself, and as the sound intensified the sergeant threw his cigarette to the ground, turned to face his men and called the detachment to attention.

Inside the building, too, the sirens had caused a change in atmosphere. The porters straightened their caps and lined up along the wall to the left of the door, while the smartly dressed receptionist by the lifts produced a little mirror from her bag and applied lipstick. Even the sniffer dog, which had been lying in the shade by the marble fountain, lifted its head and looked towards the door.

The head porter called, 'Hold the lift. The minister's arriving.' With extraordinary suddenness, a formation of police motor-bikes sped down the driveway outside, immediately followed by three Mercedes with darkened windows, more motorbikes and a couple of police Land Rovers. The first group of riders came to a stop across the exit to the street, while the Land Rovers blocked the entrance. Then, as the sergeant gave the order to present arms, six or seven men in suits jumped out of the first and last Mercedes, and surrounded the one in the middle. The soldiers stamped their boots on the stone; the sergeant saluted; one of the detectives opened the passenger door of the second car.

At first nothing could be seen of the person sitting behind the dark windows. Then a plump hand emerged into the sunlight, grabbing hold of the leather handle over the door, while at the same time a black-patent leather loafer touched the marble pavement below, the sunlight catching the buckle. The sergeant watched as another foot was planted on the ground, and the large torso of a middle-aged woman rose stiffly from the car. The minister batted away the hands that were held out to help her; for a second or two she stood adjusting her business suit and straightening the diamond ring on her left hand. Then she looked about the driveway with an expression of intense fastidiousness on her face, as if she was disappointed with everything she saw, until she caught the sergeant's eye, gave him a rapid nod and was escorted inside the atrium.

'Her Excellency is going straight to the twenty-fifth floor,' one of the officials told the head porter as he entered the building. 'Bring the post and telephone messages to me there.'

'Right away, sir.'

'Are there any petitioners?'

'Yes, Mr Wanjui. Fifteen people are waiting upstairs. I have a list here.'

He glanced at the paper. 'You can send them away. The minister won't receive anyone until this evening. I'll keep this.'

'Very well, sir.'

'Send up the head of Hospitality. Also, get a message to Her Excellency's nephew, Milton Abasi. He needs to be here by eleven for the meeting with the British.'

'Do you know where he is, sir?'

'How should I? You find him.'

'I don't believe he's in the building, sir,' the head porter ventured. 'I haven't seen him for several days.'

Charles Wanjui hesitated. 'Well, speak to Luther Magari. He'll know where to look. And Joseph Kamunda – bring him to us.'

'There's no need, sir. Mr Kamunda is already in his office.'

'Good. Go and find Milton, then.'

The head porter withdrew as Pamela Abasi stepped into the lift, quickly followed by Charles Wanjui.

'What time are the *wazungu* coming?' Pamela asked, when the doors had closed.

'Eleven, Your Excellency. Actually, we're only expecting one Englishman – Edward Caine, the director of the Global Justice project. He's bringing Beatrice Kamunda with him.'

'Beatrice?' She sniffed. 'How is little Beatrice Kamunda mixed up in this Global Justice business?'

'She's doing an internship with them, ma'am, just a few months.'

Pamela swallowed to clear her ears as the lift shot up towards the twenty-fifth floor. 'Charles, have you spoken to Milton?'

'We haven't been able to find him this morning, Minister. I've told the head porter to contact him. He's going to co-ordinate his efforts with Luther Magari.'

'Well, tell Luther I want to speak to him.'

'Yes, of course.'

The lift doors opened, and Pamela Abasi stepped into the reception area of her office, waiting in silence while one of her assistants hurried forward to take her handbag and jacket. Her lips were pressed together gravely, and her eyes darted about with a kind of defiant watchfulness. 'Have you got me the Matiba Development files?' she asked, as the double doors to the next room were opened.

'Yes, ma'am. They're on your desk.'

'And the diary?'

'Here, Excellency.' The assistant held up a big red book.

95

'Well, bring it to me, girl. I can't read it from here . . .' She sank into the soft chair behind the desk and settled a pair of half-moon spectacles on her nose. 'What's this at two o'clock?'

'The World Bank, ma'am. The new East Africa director, Mr Anders.'

'Tell him to come tomorrow – no, next week. Say something's come up. Apologise for me.'

'I believe he's in Norway next week, ma'am. He was hoping to see you before going on leave.'

'Too bad. The week after, then.'

'I'll speak to his assistant, Excellency.'

Pamela opened the Matiba Development folder, leaned back on her chair, and began to rifle through it. 'So the first payments have gone through,' she remarked. 'Has Deepak Zaidi processed them?'

'Yes, ma'am,' Charles replied.

'I want to talk to him this afternoon. Tell him to come here, Lucy. We need to keep an eye on that Asian snake . . .' She was searching through the papers. 'So, do we own the land or not? I want to see the registration documents. Where are they, Lucy?'

'This is the file that Milton left for you, Excellency.'

'Well, it's not complete.' She slapped the folder shut. After a pause, she went on: 'The Global Justice team will be here at eleven. Make sure they're comfortable in the conference room.'

'Of course, ma'am. It's already prepared.'

'See to it yourself. Make sure of everything – coffee, tea, plenty to eat. Make them feel appreciated, Lucy.'

'Yes, ma'am.'

'Now, let's have some space in here. You girls give me half an hour with Mr Wanjui. When Luther Magari arrives, show him in right away. Go on – stop gawping, for goodness' sake. Shoo-shoo!' The two assistants hurried from the office, closing the double doors behind them.

Ed set off from the Hilton on his own, and almost immediately his car was stuck in traffic along Parliament Street as it headed for the ministry. He had spent the morning in the suite, practising his presentation, and was now more anxious than ever about the meeting with Pamela Abasi. As the car crawled along, he kept his briefcase shut and leaned his head back in the blast of the air-conditioning, trying to keep his mind clear until he felt a little calmer. Then he stared out at the hectic movement of the crowds. A few blocks from the ministry, a small boy came up and pressed a copy of the *Kisuru Monitor* against his window: *Ngozi Girls Are Best In Bed*, ran the headline. *Read Our Groundbreaking Survey*. On the pavement behind him, a child in a soldier's cap stood by the shop-front, a cardboard sign around his neck, holding up the amputated stumps of his arms. Ed pulled out his wallet and opened the window; as the car moved on, he threw a screwed-up two-hundred shilling note towards the little soldier. But it landed a yard short of him, and immediately a man in the crowd snatched it from the ground and shuffled away.

'Well?' Pamela Abasi demanded. 'Have you found him?'

Luther Magari stood a few feet from the minister's desk, his good eye looking down politely while the glass one swivelled out towards the skyscrapers and building sites framed by the window. 'Yes, ma'am,' he said quietly. 'He was at the nightclub. He's having a shower now.'

'Is he all right?'

'He just needs some coffee, Your Excellency, and a cigarette.'

'Don't let him drink anything – or take those pills of his.'

'No, ma'am.'

Pamela hesitated slightly. 'Is he *compos mentis?*'

'Madam?'

'Can he cope with this meeting?'

'I think so, ma'am.'

'All right, then. We'd better say he's had the flu.' And she turned to Charles Wanjui. 'His eyes look terrible – very red. It *looks* like flu.'

'Just as you say, ma'am,' Charles replied. 'There's a lot of flu going about.'

Pamela let out a benevolent sigh. 'All right. Thank you, Luther. A good job.'

Luther bowed his head. 'I'll bring him here myself,' he said. 'I'll see to it right away.'

'You do that. The *mzungu* will be here soon.' And she added: 'Make sure the boy puts on a suit and tie. I don't want him letting me down.'

Ed was met by Joseph as he arrived in the conference room, and Pamela's assistant Lucy came up to offer him a cup of tea.

'The ubiquitous Thermos of tea,' Joseph said, smiling at Ed. 'You find one in every government office in Kisuru. Rather a *good* custom left us by the British.'

'Well, I could settle for a post-colonial glass of mineral water,' Ed said, with a laugh, 'if that would be more diplomatic . . .'

'No, let's both have tea. Lucy, perhaps you could bring us a fresh pot.'

'Yes, Mr Kamunda.'

'And cold milk for our guest.'

'Of course, sir.'

Joseph put his arm out to Ed. 'Come and look at the view, Mr Caine. On a day like this you can see pretty much the whole city from up here.' As they walked across the room he went on, in a quieter voice, 'Are you alone? I thought Beatrice was coming with you.'

'I'm afraid she had an emergency. She was called away to a sick woman in the slums. She should be here soon.'

Joseph knitted his brows as they approached the window, but his voice was perfectly calm: 'Here we are, Mr Caine.'

'Please call me Ed.'

'Yes, of course. You must forgive us Batangans if we seem a little hidebound. There's a lot of formality here in the government service – especially among people of my generation – not always matched by efficiency, I'm sorry to say.'

'The formality is probably a legacy of the British, too.'

'I don't know about that,' Joseph replied affably. 'One of the West's misconceptions about traditional culture in Africa is that it was all terribly easy-going and egalitarian. Actually, the opposite is true. A linguist I knew, who spent a few years here in the sixties, used to compare the modes of address in Bakhoto to the nuances of courtly Japanese. It's hard for modern British and Americans to understand that. Your cultures really belong on the other end of the spectrum in that respect.'

Ed squinted out towards the Kisuru business district with his arms folded. The sun was still rising behind the glass tower of the World Bank, and the top section of the building was almost obliterated by silver light. To the south, away from the glare, the new Batangan Treasury building stood on its own in the midst of half-constructed concrete towers and yellow cranes, with the cylindrical tower of the Hilton behind it.

'Most of this has happened very recently,' Joseph said, following Ed's gaze. 'Really since President Wachira's election. To be honest, I'm a little mystified by it, but it's notoriously hard to interpret economic data in a country like Batanga. Officially, we're in the middle of a boom. In reality—' Lucy arrived with the tea, and he guided Ed to a table along the adjacent wall. 'Well, you can see for yourself – personally, I prefer this view.' And he nodded at the old Parliament buildings and law courts – single-storey structures of whitewashed porticoes and pillared terraces, surrounded with parkland. 'Those gardens cover twelve acres,' he said. 'On a hot day like this I'd rather be down there than up here. There's always plenty of space and fresh air in the old government quarter.'

Ed looked out towards the north. Half a dozen yellow and red kites were swerving and pitching in the sky above Parliament Gardens, their strings controlled by tiny figures on the grass below; higher up, rising and falling on the wind, a couple of marabou storks glided in circles. He gazed for a moment at the department stores and office blocks immediately beyond, then let out a low whistle, and leaned forward, pressing his forehead against the glass.

'Yes,' Joseph replied. 'There's Makera. These days it almost reaches the city centre. You can see why the government is so keen to improve the area.'

Quite suddenly, beyond the last line of shops, like brown floodwaters held back by a dam, the ramshackle roofs of the slum surged in from the north, swamping every patch of open ground as far as the warehouses along the airport road.

'Two economies,' Joseph remarked. 'Two ways of life, really – juxtaposed, but totally unintegrated. There's a boom in the official economy, the one inhabited by the business élite, Western expatriates, UN personnel, NGO people like you. But what's happening in the *real* Batanga? Nobody knows. In the boom economy Toyota sells Land Cruisers for eighty or ninety thousand dollars a shot and the country's full of them. But the average income in Batanga is about four hundred dollars a year. Four *hundred*. Even civil servants and company directors earn just a few thousand. Of course, you can feed a family on very little. It's not quite as bad as it sounds. But the fact is, there's almost no point of contact between the two systems. They hardly ever meet.'

'But they do down there,' Ed pointed out.

'In your school and clinic? Well, yes, let's hope so.'

Lucy, who had been standing nearby, cleared her throat. 'Excuse me, Mr Kamunda. The minister has asked me to let you know that she is a little delayed. She is in a meeting with her nephew, Milton Abasi. They will be joining you at about eleven fifteen.'

'Thank you,' Joseph said, checking his watch. To Ed he added: 'Let's hope Beatrice can make it by then. I don't want her turning up late for your first official meeting.'

Beatrice arrived at the Global Justice office just before eleven, and was immediately confronted by a huge man in a leather jacket. 'Miss Kamunda?'

'Yes.'

'I am your driver, ma'am. My name is Machi. Please try this on.' He offered her a black helmet. 'I can store your bags in these boxes,' he added, indicating the black containers on the sides of the bike. 'They are very secure.' And when she hesitated, he insisted gently, 'It would be better, ma'am. You will need to hold on tight.'

'Do you know where I'm going?'

'Mr Ouko has told me. The Ministry of Development, as fast as possible.'

'Just a minute.' She ran over to the door of the office, let herself in, kicked off her boots and put on her working shoes.

'Try your helmet, ma'am. The traffic is very bad today. I will need to execute what you call advanced manoeuvres. If you are frightened, just close your eyes.'

'That's very reassuring.'

'Get on behind me, please.' He mounted the bike and switched on the engine. 'Put your arms round my waist.'

Beatrice hitched up her skirt to climb on behind Machi.

'There's nothing to worry about, ma'am. I have excellent driving techniques. I am an instructor. You can trust me.' Briefly taking Beatrice's hands in his own, he placed them together across his stomach. 'Hold tight, Miss Kamunda. Like that.' Then he drive off down the service road towards Kwamchetsi Wachira Avenue.

'Just look at you!' Pamela Abasi exploded, banging the desk with the flat of her hand. 'You're a disgrace! What's the matter with you?'

Milton had dropped into the armchair opposite her desk, holding his head between the fingertips of his two hands. He winced as she slapped the desktop. 'I'm sorry, Aunty. I overslept. I had a lot of business to attend to at the club last night—'

'Business! I know what kind of business you get up to in that club. Your business is to manage this project in the slums. That's your job. Do you know how much this programme is worth?'

'Yes, Aunty.'

'You've got no sense of priorities – no discipline . . .' She glared at him. 'Drink your aspirins, for God's sake. What were you doing last night? Attempting suicide?' She checked her watch. 'We're meeting them in twenty minutes.'

Milton looked up towards Agatha, who was waiting by the door. 'Get me a glass of whisky,' he said hoarsely. 'A mini bottle. There are some in the bar.' And turning to face his aunt he added, 'I need it, Aunt Pamela. It's medicinal.'

She sighed, nodding to Agatha. 'Get it for him.'

'Yes, ma'am.'

'Well, I'll tell you what we're going to do. We're going to tell Mr Caine that you've been ill. A bad case of the flu. But you must apologise. You were meant to meet him at the airport, remember?'

'Yes, Aunty.'

'Say you've been ill and your phone was stolen. Say you're *terribly* sorry – say it like an Englishman.'

'Yes, yes. *Terr*ibly sorry.'

'They were nearly robbed at the airport because of you. And Mr Caine hasn't seen you at the office. What will he think?'

Milton tipped back his glass of aspirin, closing his eyes as he swallowed.

'You have to restore confidence. If they think you're unreliable, they'll change the programme.'

'It's too late,' he said. 'I've already paid Batanga Construction. There's nothing he can do.' And, turning to Agatha, he took the gleaming tumbler of Scotch she was holding for him, squinted at it through one half-closed eye and tossed it back. Then he sat still, waiting for the sensation of fire to travel down his oesophagus and spread out across his stomach. 'Oh, Jesus,' he said, his eyes snapping open. 'That's better than aspirin.'

'Don't blaspheme,' his aunt said. 'And don't be *complacent.*

The British Minister for International Development is coming to Kisuru in a few months. We don't want Mr Caine complaining about a lack of co-operation. Keep him happy. Let him have everything he needs. Reassure him, Milton. Batanga Construction have got the money? Well, fine. Introduce them to him, give him a schedule of works, tell him it's all happening according to plan, that everything's above board. You've got to see it from his point of view. He needs to believe you. He has to write reports . . .'

'You know what these foreigners are like.' Milton shrugged, his voice a little more assertive. 'They have to spend their money – they want to give it away. They need us more than we need them.' He rubbed his bloodshot eyes with the heels of his hands. 'They never dare ask what's happening to the cash. Edward Caine is no different. I've met him. He's not a big man.'

She pursed her lips, surveying him disapprovingly. 'Just don't wreck this Global Justice programme, Milton. It always pays to be tactful, and it costs nothing. You've got to learn a bit of diplomacy.'

'Yes, Aunty.'

'In this life, one has to make people believe they're doing the right thing,' she went on, as she sat back on her wide chair, which creaked a little under her weight. 'That's the key to the aid business. Of course everyone knows things go wrong and that these programmes usually don't work out, but you mustn't rub their noses in it.' She turned to her assistant. 'Is everything ready upstairs?'

'Yes, ma'am.'

'Joseph Kamunda?'

'He's there, ma'am.'

'Good. Bring me a mirror, Agatha. And you, Milton, go and put a tie on. Please tell me you've *got* a tie.'

Milton pulled a gold one from his jacket pocket and held it up in his fist.

'Go on, then. And wash your mouth with something. I don't want you smelling of whisky.'

He got slowly to his feet and walked to the wall-mirror.

'Charles Wanjui's going to be with us,' she went on. 'Let him do the talking. Don't say a word. You've been ill, remember. Don't start trying to remember the numbers – you've got no head for it.' She added lightly: 'If Caine wants some extra reassurance, Charles thought we could offer him Joseph Kamunda.'

'What do you mean?'

'As a liaison officer between the two governments. He's perfect. The *wazungu* love him. Caine will trust Joseph Kamunda – everyone knows he's incorruptible – and Joseph will keep an eye on things for us.'

'If you say so, Aunty,' Milton replied, straightening his tie.

'I do,' she shot back. 'You just be polite and keep quiet. All right, let's go up.'

'Hold on tight, Miss Kamunda,' Machi shouted. 'I'm taking a short-cut.'

Beatrice was already clasping her hands around his rigid stomach. Now, as Machi revved the engine and started to steer towards the pavement, she hugged him harder and turned her head sideways, pressing her helmet against his back. Immediately the motorbike dipped down into the gutter, then jumped out with a roar between the brightly coloured market stalls.

'No, for heaven's sake!' Beatrice screamed. 'What are you *doing*?'

'There's an alleyway here,' Machi shouted through his helmet. 'Trust me, ma'am.'

The bike rumbled and bumped across the pavement, swerving to avoid a goat tethered outside a butcher's shop, then ploughing through a puddle of black slime. The engine pitch rose again, and Machi accelerated towards the mouth of an alleyway that lay between two tall office buildings. Beatrice watched in silence as the contents of the alleyway shot past – dustbins on wheels, metal fire-escapes, cardboard boxes. Then the walls of the alley started to narrow, and the bike bounced violently up and down, juddering and whining as it climbed a great mound of rubbish.

'Oh, mercy!' Beatrice cried out, closing her eyes. But Machi was laughing, and almost at once she felt a change in the angle of the bike, which lurched downhill and ran along a relatively smooth surface before making a sharp left turn.

'Parliament Street, ma'am,' Machi called out calmly. 'The ministry is over there.'

Beatrice opened her eyes again. They were travelling at a terrifying speed, overtaking a lorry, but she could see the World Bank tower and the vast building site to the south. 'I'll drop you at a side entrance, Miss Kamunda,' Machi said. He accelerated through a red light, drove diagonally across the junction, mounted the pavement on the far side and stopped at a small door.

13

Ed watched two elderly waiters moving around the conference table, stopping beside each chair to straighten the pencils and writing pads or to pick up a tumbler, holding it up to the light and rubbing it with their white gloves before setting it down next to a bottle of mineral water.

'Ah, here she is!' Joseph said, hearing the lift arrive in the hall outside.

He stepped towards the door to greet Beatrice, but Lucy hurried in with a sheaf of files. 'Her Excellency is coming up now,' she announced as she finished setting out the papers. 'She has Charles Wanjui with her, and her nephew, Milton. Are we expecting anyone else?'

'Yes,' Joseph said flatly. 'My daughter Beatrice.'

Lucy nodded, counting the places. 'Well, that's fine. She can sit next to Mr Caine. This will be Her Excellency now,' she added, as the lift doors opened again. But there was no sound from the hall; and after a moment the heavy door opened a few inches and Beatrice peered in.

'Thank goodness you're here,' Joseph said, swinging round to face her. 'The minister's arriving at any minute.'

Beatrice's face was glowing and her short hair was pressed out of shape by the motorbike helmet. 'Hello, Father. Sorry I'm late.'

'Where on earth have you been?'

'I had to visit someone in Makera.' She turned to Lucy. 'Is there somewhere I can wash?'

'There's a cloakroom over here, Miss Kamunda,' Lucy said. 'I'll show you. Let me take your bags.' She led her away.

'For goodness' sake, be quick,' Joseph called after them. He shook his head at Ed. 'I could do without these dramas. Nobody turns up late for a ministerial meeting. It just isn't done.'

'I very much wanted to greet you in person,' Pamela Abasi began in her deep voice, planting her elbows on the armrests of her big chair and looking directly at Ed. 'I'm sure I don't need to tell you, Mr Caine, the Ministry of Social and Economic Development is involved in at least two hundred development projects at any time. But, as far as I'm concerned, this work you're doing in Makera is the most important. It's very close to my heart. I want you to be in no doubt about that.'

'Thank you, Minister,' Ed said, glancing involuntarily towards Milton, as he breathed in Pamela's sweet, rather stifling scent. 'It's enormously reassuring to have your support.'

'I know a country like Batanga can be a challenging environment for foreign development workers,' the minister went on, smiling at Ed, and pausing for a moment as she surveyed the expression of perfect composure on Beatrice's face beside him '. . . but you have a lot of support here, Mr Caine. The purpose of this meeting is to assure you of that, by setting up a clear chain of accountability and advice. Since the project involves a three-way partnership – an alliance between my department, Oona Simon at the Department for International Development in London, and Global Justice – I want you to feel able to ask this office for anything at all, any time. You can use my name, Mr Caine. You can talk to my people here, or come straight to me personally.'

'I really don't know what to say,' Ed replied. 'I appreciate it enormously. It makes all the difference. I'm sure we can succeed with such emphatic official support.' He straightened his papers in front of him. 'I would like to talk you through my report, if that's all right. I've come across one or two problems that need to be sorted out quickly, if we're going to get the school open for the autumn term. I would very much value your advice and guidance.'

'Yes, of course,' Pamela said genially. 'By all means. And let me tell you something, too, Mr Caine. As far as I'm concerned, we *must* succeed with this project. The development of Makera will affect the whole of Kisuru. I'm just sorry my nephew has been so unwell over the last few weeks. It has been very unfortunate timing. I understand you had a bad experience at the airport.'

'Well, it was all resolved very quickly,' Ed replied. 'Beatrice and Joseph fixed everything – I mean, Mr Kamunda.'

'There, you see. Your project already has friends in high places,' Pamela said. 'And I must say, in defence of my nephew, it's not like him to be defeated by a little flu.' She looked at Milton, inhaling briskly through her nose. 'In any case, he assures me that he's on the mend.'

Milton's shoulders had dropped down towards the table as if he was barely able to support the weight of his head. 'Yes, I've had the flu,' he said, clearing his throat as he spoke and sitting up a little. 'I've been out of action for a few weeks. It was unfortunate that I couldn't meet you at the airport.'

'It's all right,' Ed said. 'I knew it must have been something like that. Please don't mention it.'

'So, you have the backing of the ministry,' Pamela repeated. 'And not just that. President Wachira is personally concerned about this project – he asks me about it often. Any problems at all, any delays or difficulties, just shout.' She indicated Joseph Kamunda and Charles Wanjui, who were sitting together at the far end of the table. 'Let me introduce Charles Wanjui, Mr Caine. Charles is our chief permanent secretary – head of the civil service. I asked him along this morning so that you'd know who to turn to if you come across an interdepartmental problem of any kind – if the Treasury is sitting on a payment, or the Interior Ministry takes too long granting you building permits, or you can't get clearance for your engineering works. Whatever it is, Charles can sort it out.'

'I look forward to working with you, Mr Caine,' Charles Wanjui said, leaning across the table to pass him his card. 'I have already briefed the other permanent secretaries and their senior officials about your programme in some detail, so you will have top-level support in all departments from day one.'

'Thank you,' Ed said.

'Of course you know Joseph Kamunda,' Pamela Abasi went on. 'Joseph is our permanent secretary here at MSED. He's also chairing the President's anti-corruption unit, down at State House. President Wachira has staked his reputation on achieving a cultural change.'

'His approach is hugely admired in London,' Ed said, looking up at the portrait of Kenneth Makotsi, the Father of the Nation, which hung on the wall. Makotsi was wearing a Western-style field marshal's uniform, but he was decked out in the trappings of the Makhoto kings, a fly whisk in his right hand, a leopard skin over his shoulder, a long spear planted in the ground beside him. 'It's one of the main reasons the UK government was so keen to get on board with the Makera project.'

'Well, everyone's talking about governance issues,' Pamela said. 'Joseph's job is to see that the President actually succeeds – isn't that right, Joseph?'

'Yes, Minister, so far as it lies within my power . . .'

'There, you see, that's typical,' she said, with a chuckle. 'With Joseph there's always an escape clause. You ought to know, Mr Caine,' she went on, 'that in the old days, the Kamundas were prime ministers to the Makhoto kings. The position ran in the family. Joseph's great-grandfather negotiated with the British from the first days of white settlement around Mount Batanga; and sixty years later, his father was at the forefront of Kenneth Makotsi's independence movement. They lived together in exile for many years – in a bedsit in Camden Town. That's right,' she added, with another baritone laugh: 'Joseph was born in

London. That's probably what makes him such a shameless Anglophile.'

'Well, of course I've read Robert Kamunda's autobiography,' Ed put in enthusiastically, 'but I didn't realise how close the connection was.'

'Father and son,' Pamela said, looking down the table at Joseph, who was sitting with his head perfectly erect and his hands folded on the table in front of him, as he waited for the discussion to move on. 'In any case,' she concluded, 'the President and I are going to burden Joseph Kamunda with another responsibility.'

Joseph's face barely moved, but the muscles tightened around his mouth. 'Yes, Minister?'

'We want you to act as liaison officer, Joseph, as the link between our people here at MSED, and the British Department for International Development.'

'Very well, Excellency.'

'The key point is that not only does Mr Caine have the full support of the Batangan government, but also the UK officials understand what's going on at this end.'

'Yes, of course,' Joseph said, and focused on Ed. 'I've been in close contact with Clive Bird at DfID – do you know Clive, Mr Caine?'

'We've spoken on the phone,' Ed said. 'I don't know him very well.'

'Well, the two of us are quite used to co-ordinating the efforts of our respective offices.'

Ed was aware that he had been nodding rather idiotically for some time. Glancing towards Beatrice, he was impressed by her attentive, inscrutable expression. 'This is a really tremendous start for the Makera Project,' he said, looking towards Joseph and Charles, and back again at Pamela. 'I know how often programmes like this go wrong, and nine times out of ten the problem is in the dialogue between the NGO and the local administration, some crossed wire. It's terrific to have so much support.' Placing his hand on his report again, he went on in the same slightly anxious tone: 'If it's all right with you, Minister, I'd be very grateful if we could run through some of the points I've raised here. I mean, there are things I don't understand – especially in the financials – but it's probably because Milton's been out of action so I haven't had the whole picture.' He glanced at Milton, who had taken a navy blue handkerchief from his jacket pocket and was pressing it to his nose. 'Now that we're all together for the first time, I'm sure we can get to grips with it very quickly.'

'I'm sure you can,' Pamela said, and turned her head impatiently towards the door. 'Well? What is it, Agatha?'

Agatha had approached the minister with a tan folder. 'Excuse me, Your Excellency,' she muttered. 'This is urgent.' Leaning down, she handed her a note.

Pamela read in silence, while Ed looked down the column of figures on the paper in front of him.

'That's fine,' Pamela said in a low voice. 'Tell Mr Zaidi someone in the UK office will be in touch later today to finalise the arrangements.'

'Yes, Mrs Abasi.'

'You must forgive me.' Pamela addressed the whole table as Agatha walked out of the heavy doors. 'I have another meeting right away. Please carry on with your discussions. Lucy is having some lunch brought up. Are there any questions you particularly need to ask me before I go?'

Ed hesitated, his index finger resting on one of the bar graphs. 'Yes, as I say, I do have some questions, Minister, but I certainly don't want to take up any more of your time.'

'And how about you, Beatrice?' Pamela asked, as she heaved her weight forward and started getting to her feet. 'Do you have any questions of your own?'

Beatrice had been staring at her notepaper, on which she had written 'Matiba Development?', but she stood up along with everyone else and smiled at the minister. 'No, ma'am. With the official involvement of the ministry, I'm sure everything will become clear before long.'

'Of course it will,' Pamela replied. She turned to Ed. 'I expect you've already discovered that Batanga is a very small world,' she said, as they shook hands. 'The Kamundas are old family friends of ours. Joseph's father was my late husband's mentor in many ways. And as for this young lady,' she waved a benevolent hand over Beatrice, 'Beatrice Kamunda and my daughter Joyce are practically twins. They used to play together the whole time when they were little.' She went on in a stage whisper: 'Joyce is no dunce, I can tell you, but this girl, ha! You'll have to watch out for her, Mr Caine.' She clung to Ed's hand, though her eyes were no longer focused on him. 'Yes, Beatrice always had such a serious expression, even when she was a tiny child – just like her father . . . Whenever he saw her playing in the garden, my husband used to say, "There goes the next President of Batanga."'

'How is Joyce, ma'am?' Beatrice asked. 'It's been a long time. I hear she's at university in London.'

'Yes, King's College,' Pamela said. 'She's studying law.' And she added by way of explanation: 'I sent her away to boarding school in England after her father died, Mr Caine. Do you know Roedean?'

'Roedean?' Ed said. 'Er, no, not really. I've heard of it, of course.'

'Joyce was head girl,' Pamela said, finally letting go of his hand, and for a moment she fell silent. Then she glanced at the clock. 'Lucy? I'm running late. Good luck with the project, Mr Caine. Please keep in touch.'

'Yes, I will, Minister. Thank you for your support.'

Pamela began to turn away, but she hesitated. 'Mr Caine, are your family with you here in Kisuru?'

'Yes. My wife Sarah and our little boy, Archie.' On an impulse he added: 'Sarah's a great admirer of yours, Minister. She heard you give a lecture at SOAS last year.'

Pamela raised her eyebrows. 'Is Sarah in the development business, too?'

'Yes,' he said, 'Her speciality is women's health, reproductive issues . . .'

'Really?' Pamela smiled. 'Well, I must meet her, of course. It isn't every day I get a chance to talk to someone who shares my passions.' She called, 'Lucy!'

'Yes, ma'am?'

'Please invite Mrs Caine to join me for lunch one day, as soon as it can be arranged. Lunch or dinner, whichever is sooner.' Nodding to the two civil servants she swivelled round, put her hand out to take a file from Lucy, and glided off towards the lifts.

While Pamela was saying goodbye, Milton loitered near the open door, half hidden by his aunt's substantial figure. Then, when Pamela marched out of the conference room, he followed her. Ed assumed at first that Milton was seeing her to the lift, but after ten minutes, when he had still not come back, he realised that his project manager had taken the chance to disappear without a word.

'Where's Milton?' he asked, laying his hand over the papers on the table in front of him. 'We really need to get started on these figures.'

Joseph kept his eyes on Beatrice, who was sitting opposite him, and slowly – almost imperceptibly – shook his head in warning. Charles Wanjui looked about with feigned surprise. 'He didn't seem at all well,' he said drily. 'I expect he's gone back to bed.'

'He can't have!' Ed let out a sigh. 'I mean, I wish he'd told me. I only needed a minute or two of his time. We just have to get hold of the project files. There are very few documents on site and it's impossible to make out what's been happening.'

'I'll talk to his office,' Charles said. 'I'm sure we can get a message to him in the next few days.'

'But he was right here just minutes ago.' There was a kind of exultant pressure at the top of Ed's head, and he had to make a conscious effort to stop himself saying more.

'Perhaps we can manage without him,' Beatrice suggested. 'We've had difficulty getting duplicate statements, but I'm sure the bank manager will be more helpful if he has a visit from someone at the ministry. And we need to talk to Mount Batanga Construction. They must have costings and invoices.'

'Yes, of course,' Ed said. 'It would just have been so much easier and quicker if Milton had let us see the project records . . .' He closed the file and waited for the sensation of dizziness in his head to subside.

'If you let me have a schedule of the internal documents you need, Mr Caine, I'll task someone in my office to speak to Mr Abasi's people about them,' Charles put in. 'I'm sure they'll be able to track them down, even if Mr Abasi himself remains *hors de combat* for a week or two.' Looking at the door, he went on at once: 'Ah, here comes lunch! We'd better clear away these papers so the boys can lay the table. Come and admire the view, Mr Caine,' he added, as he got up. 'We can see the whole of Makera from here.'

'And the scavengers,' Beatrice remarked.

'Scavengers?'

'Our famous Kisuru scroungers.' She pointed through the north-facing window at the pairs of marabou storks circling the slums at different altitudes. 'They're dying out from all the rubbish they eat, but that doesn't stop them. They gobble everything up. I should think they could devour a whole school project, if they wanted.' She spun round to face the business district. 'Up there, you see. They're nesting on the half-built skyscrapers downtown – the higher the better. They frighten the hell out of the workmen, but nobody likes to disturb them. It's considered bad luck.'

'Well, you've set yourself quite a challenge, Mr Caine,' Charles Wanjui said, after a pause.

He smiled weakly. 'The marabou storks?'

'The slums. You've got your work cut out.' And when Ed nodded, he went on quietly, 'I'm sure we all wish you the best of luck. Really. I mean it,' before adding, in a commanding voice: 'Well, what do you think, Joseph? Why don't we drink to the Makera project? Come on, let's have an aperitif. We'll open a bottle of the ministry's Chablis.' And he called for the waiters.

14

Sarah was standing at the bathroom basin when Ed got back to the hotel, washing her underwear and a pile of Archie's T-shirts and shorts, while Archie lay on the sofa in front of the plasma TV, staring up at a cartoon.

'Hey, love, how did it go?' she called, as Ed came in, and immediately Archie started shouting, jumping up and down on the sofa.

'Hi, darling.' Ed gave her a wave as he threw his bag and jacket on to an armchair, and went to turn down the volume of the TV.

'Well? I'm dying to hear what happened.' Sarah took her soapy hands from the water and peered out towards him. 'Was Pamela friendly?'

'Oh, yes.' He kissed Archie on the head, and came to stand at the bathroom door. 'Everyone was ex*treme*ly friendly.'

'Daddy! Monster, *D*addy!'

'You sound a bit fed up,' Sarah said, and raised her voice: 'Quiet, Archie. Mummy and Daddy are talking.'

'Well, the whole thing is pretty frustrating. Pamela ran out of time and left before I got a chance to make my report to her.'

'You're joking! After all that . . . Couldn't you have insisted?'

'Daddy – dragon!'

'Yes, Archie,' Ed said, glancing round. He folded his arms, leaning against the doorframe. 'It just wasn't that easy. Pamela rather dominated things.'

'Daddy!'

'Archie, do be quiet for a minute. Watch your monsters. And don't jump on the sofa, darling.' Sarah wiped her forehead with the dry part of her arm, then turned back to the dirty water. 'Did Milton turn up?'

'Yes, just about. He hardly said a word. And he ran out at the end before I could talk to him.'

'Honestly, Ed, he sounds a complete nutcase.'

'He's definitely a problem. He says he's been ill, but it's more than that.'

'What are you going to do?'

'I'll just have to bypass him and manage the project myself. I've already discussed it with Beatrice. There are lots of things we can get on with – working on the database of Makera residents, canvassing opinion . . .'

'And what about the money?'

'We'll get to the bottom of that,' he said, with a sigh. 'Either we force Mount Batanga to do the work or we claw back the cash—' He broke off suddenly, hurrying over to Archie, who was about to jump off the sofa on to a glass table. 'President Wachira's on board,' he explained, as he sat Archie down again. 'That's the good news. Pamela's given us high-level access within the civil service. We've even got an office at the ministry so we don't have to work on site all the time – Beatrice's father set that up. We couldn't have asked for more support.'

'Did you tell them about the money that's missing?'

'I explained everything to Joseph and Charles Wanjui over lunch. I left them a copy of my report.'

'What did they say?'

'They agreed with me. Charles Wanjui said it was perfectly straightforward: either the builders do the work or they pay us back. So then I said I thought Milton should be able to help us sort it out – that we must have copies of the work schedules and everything – but Wanjui didn't like that at all. He changed the subject. I thought I'd broken a taboo or something. Even Beatrice was embarrassed.'

Sarah wrung out a little T-shirt. 'You don't *know* that Milton's acted dishonestly – not for sure.'

'I didn't say he *had*. I just said he should be able to help us sort it out . . .'

She put the T-shirt with the other clean things on the grey marble surface and pulled out the plug. 'I suppose if the officials have their doubts about Milton they won't want to say too much, out of loyalty to Pamela.'

'I expect so. Anyway, I'm sure she's a bit worried. Why else wouldn't she let me explain the position? I mean, she was so friendly and encouraging, it's hard to believe she's covering anything up, but she seemed a bit evasive. I couldn't get a word in edgeways.'

'I imagine she's looking into it right now, don't you? After all, she doesn't want to be in a position where she knows less about this than you do.' Sarah started hanging up the washing on a line she had rigged up over the bath. 'Look at it from her point of view. If Pamela suspects Milton of incompetence, she'll want to deal with it in her own way – keep it inside the family. If she talked about it with you in an official meeting like that, she and Milton would both lose a lot of face. It would make it hard for him to work with you. And it would be embarrassing for the civil servants.'

'Well, I certainly hope it *is* incompetence,' Ed said.

'Oh, come on, Ed. You said it yourself – she's helping you. She wouldn't deliberately do anything to harm the project.'

'Okay. But in that case what's Milton up to?' He hurried across the sitting room again to catch Archie, who had lost interest in the cartoon and was running into the bedroom. 'I mean, it's just an impression,' he went on, as he picked him up, 'but I had the sense that Milton wasn't really frightened of her. If he'd spent all that money without her knowledge he'd be nervous, wouldn't he? I wouldn't want to cross a woman like Pamela Abasi. And when you look at Milton, he's such a wreck – it's hard to see him acting against her wishes.'

'There's just so much we don't know, darling,' Sarah said, coming out of the bathroom. 'We can't be sure if Milton has cocked up. Perhaps this building company is going to do the work after all.'

Ed rolled his eyes, putting Archie down on the sitting-room carpet.

'Well, it's possible, isn't it?' she persisted.

'Yes, I suppose so.' As Sarah walked towards him, he added: 'She wants to meet you, by the way.'

'Who does? Pamela?'

'Yes. I told her about your work. Her assistant's going to fix up a meeting.'

'Wow, Ed.' She stopped in front of him. 'Thank you.'

'That was the easiest part of all,' he said, and he put his arms round her waist, pulling her towards him. 'It just came up in conversation. I told her you're a rising world authority on women's rights, development economics, multi-agency co-ordination, mutual societies, co-operatives, you name it.'

'No, seriously, Ed, did you say I want to work in the field?'

'Absolutely.' He looked at her anxious, bright green eyes. 'She was excited. She wanted to meet you. It's good news, love. If anyone can get you a job, she can.'

'Yes. Except I really can't take one until we've found some-where to live.'

'I know. So much for our beautiful new villa . . .'

'Well, it isn't just us, if that's any consolation. The housing agent was telling me that the whole development won't be ready for at least a year. The contractors have taken the money and done a runner.'

For a moment Ed was silent. Then he said: 'How did it go today? Did you see anywhere nice?'

'Not really. I spent this morning looking at houses in St Jude's. Everyone keeps saying how nice that place is but, honestly, it's pretty basic. There were cockroaches in the first place.' She glanced towards Archie. 'Two minutes, darling. Then it's time for your bath.'

'No, no, no, no, no, no!' Archie protested.

'Yes, my love. Don't argue. If you're good, Daddy will read you a story.'

'We need to make a decision soon,' Ed said, looking down at Sarah's bare feet, and her bright cotton wrap. 'We're running through the entire housing budget.'

'Don't tell me about it. I'll go mental if we have to live here another month. We really need a garden for Archie – somewhere he won't keep running into the lunch buffet or the wheelie-bins – but I haven't yet seen anything we could really live in.'

'You looking again tomorrow?'

She nodded. 'Something in Aberdare – not that we can afford it.'

'I'll take some time off next week,' Ed said. 'We can look together. Try not to worry.' He kissed her on the mouth. 'Let's have supper up here tonight. Just us. We can get something sent up from the bar. We might as well enjoy this place while we're here.'

Over the next two or three weeks, Ed and Beatrice worked together in their air-conditioned office at the ministry throughout the heat of the day. One of their main concerns was to make contact with Mount Batanga Construction, but Ed received no reply when he wrote to the directors, and it didn't take him long to discover that the company was not actually a functioning business. When he and Beatrice drove out to Mount Batanga's registered office one morning, they discovered an empty building site on the airport road, guarded by a man with an Alsatian. After that, Ed asked his boss in London for permission to engage a firm of Kisuru solicitors to collect the money that had been paid to Mount Batanga, and begin legal action if necessary.

Ed also made a point of ringing Milton several times in the course of a fortnight, leaving messages for him in which he explained the actions he was taking. At the same time, he and Beatrice started to investigate the Matiba Development Company, whose representatives had been threatening Ann Odinga and her neighbours in Makera, but which, as far as they could discover, had no official status.

Ed and Beatrice were almost never in the office for an entire day. In the early mornings and the evenings, when the sun was low, the two of them went out into the slums. Ed had mapped out the area to the east of the project site, dividing it into grids of ten or twelve blocks each, and he and Beatrice started working outwards from there, block by block, interviewing the residents and building up a systematic database. Each time they arrived at a house for the first time, Ed greeted the residents politely in Swahili or Kishala. Then Beatrice went inside with her notebook and tape-recorder and asked the women questions about their work, their families, their contact with Matiba Development, while Ed stood at a distance outside, assessing the condition of the house and making notes about sewage, the power supply and access to water.

One evening Beatrice took Ed to meet Ann Odinga. 'I'd like to photograph this rubbish tip for the Global Justice website,' she said, as they passed the hill that overlooked the Odingas' courtyard. 'That's forty feet of solid refuse – rotting food, dead animals, human excrement. Everyone in the neighbourhood throws their waste up there, but most of it lands on the roofs – there, you see.' She pointed at a cluster of plastic bags baking on a sheet of corrugated tin. 'Flying toilets. There's literally nowhere for the sewage to go.'

'Come on,' he said, 'let's keep moving before something lands on us.'

Beatrice led him to the Odingas muddy yard, which was only a few yards away. 'This is their place,' she said. 'I'll see if Ann is well enough to talk. Hey, Ruth, *hujambo*? How's your mother? Can I come in?' She stepped inside. 'Mrs Odinga? It's Beatrice Kamunda.'

There was a movement in the darkness. 'Beatrice?'

'*Shikamoo*,' she said.

'*Marahaba*,' Ann replied. 'Wait a minute, let me get up. I have to wash . . .'

'Please don't disturb yourself.' She moved forward in the half-light and knelt down. 'Save your strength.'

'I heard a man's voice,' Ann replied, struggling to sit up.

'He's a friend.'

'Tell Ruth to come back in,' she said at once. 'It's not safe.' Beatrice got up to fetch her.

'You stay here, child,' Ann told Ruth, when she came inside. 'Stand where I can see you. Fetch a cup of water for our guest.' She let her head drop down on the blanket. 'I'm sorry we have no tea, Miss Kamunda. It's because I've been unwell. We're in no state to receive visitors.'

'Actually, I would prefer water,' Beatrice said. 'It's such a hot day.'

'The girls have to be so careful.' Ann sighed, her hand darting from side to side as she brushed away the flies. 'I worry about Ruth and Martha – when I had the fever, I was worried all the time. Worry is a terrible thing, like having another person in your head.'

'I'm so pleased you're recovering,' Beatrice said.

She laughed faintly. 'For a long time I thought I was dead and had been sent to hell.'

'And now?' Beatrice asked. 'Has the fever gone?'

'Now I feel like a rag,' she said simply. 'No muscles, no bones. No strength in me.'

Beatrice reached forward and placed her hand across Ann's forehead. Then, lifting her head off the blanket, she put a cup of water to her lips. 'I have a friend waiting outside, Mrs Odinga,' she said. 'He's an Englishman. He has come to Kisuru to improve the Makera neighbourhood. I would like him to meet you, if you are willing.'

'He must come when I'm well,' she said. 'I can't meet strangers today. What can I offer him?'

'There's no need to offer him anything,' Beatrice assured her.

'He's coming to hear about these men who ask you to sign contracts. He wants to help. It would be good if you could speak, just for a moment. He will stand at the door. He doesn't need to come inside.'

Ann closed her eyes, nodding, and Beatrice called to Ed in a low voice.

'I'm sorry to disturb you, Mrs Odinga,' Ed said in Swahili, as he came in, then went on in English: 'I know you haven't been well. Beatrice and I have been hearing a lot about Matiba Development . . .'

'You must talk to Gladwell Oyusi,' Ann said. 'Gladwell has spoken to those men.'

'Mrs Oyusi has already talked to us,' Ed said. 'She told us you had been threatened. Is that right?'

Ann stared towards the tin roof and tried to sit up again. 'That man came back two days ago – the one with the glass eye. When he came before, he offered us money for this house.'

'How much?'

'He said he would give us four hundred dollars if we went to live in the hills, more if we persuaded our neighbours to go with us.'

'And what did he say this time?'

'He said we had missed our chance to take his money. I told him that was fine and we had nothing to discuss. But he didn't go. He took hold of Ruth – he picked her up and held her in his arms. He kept saying what a nice girl she is, and how dangerous the slums are. He said there are a lot of fires in Makera, a lot of landslides. It's true,' she added. 'Last month a hill collapsed near the railway and many houses were buried.'

'What did you tell him?' Ed asked.

'I said it's dangerous everywhere for poor people. I told him I brought my family to Kisuru from the north, that we escaped Patrick Ochola's army, and we're not fleeing again. He was angry when I said that.'

'Were your family targeted by the Army of Celestial Peace?' Ed asked.

Ann nodded. 'Patrick Ochola took my husband. His soldiers were looting our region. Paul was in the fields with my son Stephen, just five miles from our village. As soon as they saw soldiers coming out of the jungle, they started to run. But Paul fell down and they caught him. Stephen saw everything – he saw what happened. The ACP always take children, young girls and boys, but if they find a man like Paul, a strong man . . .' She closed her eyes and pulled the blanket up to her chin. 'He was a good man. No one can replace him.'

'So you came south?'

'I knew they would come back to seize my children. They take the pretty girls as prostitutes, the others they turn into killers, like the boys. They give them guns and force them to shoot their mothers, their baby sisters. Once a child has done a thing like that, he is a killer. He has no peace of mind – his soul has been destroyed. There is nothing worse that can happen to a person. Nothing. I have tried to teach my children that if you lose your soul you have lost everything.' She looked up towards Beatrice. 'We live here, Miss Kamunda, but we don't belong in this place. You see us living like this and you think we are slum-people. But my people were farmers. Stephen, our first-born, is a good farmer. He used to help his father. Only now, because he has lived in Makera a long time, he looks like a troublemaker. People mistake him for a thug, even though he is not one.' She turned towards the image of the Sacred Heart on the wall. 'In the future, with God's grace, I hope we will return to the Highlands. Stephen and Tom will be farmers. Yes, I would like them to be farmers, like their father. That's what I ask God for every day.'

'Mrs Odinga,' Ed said, 'we would like to stop these men from Matiba Development. Would you be willing to work with us?'

Ann looked at Beatrice for a moment. She whispered in Swahili, 'Look at me. What can I do?'

'He's an honest man,' Beatrice replied. 'You can trust him.'
She went on in English: 'If you agree, Mrs Odinga, I would like
to work with you when you're feeling better. We need to talk
to your neighbours so we know everything these developers are
doing. Then we can go to the courts with our evidence and get
an injunction to stop them.'

'An injunction?'

'Yes. An order from the court. They will have to obey it. They
will have to leave you alone after that.'

'You think you can stop these men with a piece of paper?'

'The government will support us. But we need evidence.'

'You can meet my neighbours,' Ann said. 'I'll explain to
everyone.'

'It would be good if they could come to our office. Stephen
and Martha know where it is. We can talk to them more easily
there, and write everything down.'

Ann nodded, but she had closed her eyes and held out her
hand to Ruth, who was already squatting beside her and now
helped her to lie down again.

'I'll come back tomorrow,' Beatrice said gently, getting to her
feet. 'Try to rest.' She pressed her hand to Ruth's head, then
followed Ed outside into the burning sunshine.

'Good Lord, he's tracked me down to this place now.' Beatrice
laughed, but she was silent for a while, admiring the great pile
of roses Solomon had left for her at the ministry building. She
added, more quietly: 'I suppose we'll have to find another office.'
She pulled an envelope from the paper wrapping. 'To the
aromatic, incorruptible, delicious Miss Kamunda,' she read,
shaking her head. 'What does Solomon do when he writes these
notes? Eat a thesaurus?' She ripped open the envelope. 'Oh, for
goodness' sake, there's a whole poem in here. He's copied out
a poem.' She surveyed the round, childish handwriting that
covered both sides of the paper. 'He's really a lunatic. It's impossible to read all this – it'll take hours.' She turned away, smiling

and shaking her head as she folded the letter carefully. 'I'll have to look at it later.'

'We should buy some vases for the office,' Ed remarked. 'Flowers die so quickly over in Makera. It seems a waste.' And he added with a grin: 'Perhaps your friend Solomon could give you a more practical present next time – like fixing the air-conditioning out there.'

'He probably could,' she replied, putting the letter in her bag. 'But if he did that, I'd really have to go out to dinner with him. I mean, I'm already in his debt – he got me to that meeting with Pamela Abasi.'

Ed was struck by the ambiguous look of pleasure and embarrassment on her face; he turned away to look through the post on his desk.

'Hey, Beatrice, look at this. We've finally got something from the bank.' He opened the first envelope. 'They've sent us the duplicate statements. What a miracle!' For a moment his eyes narrowed in concentration as he examined the first two pages of figures, leaning forward over the desktop, but his expression began to change. 'Wait a minute . . . This isn't right. No, no, no. It doesn't add up.' As Beatrice drew up a chair beside him he took a knife from the desk and started slitting open the rest of the letters.

Beatrice laid the statements out on the desk, arranging them in chronological order, and the two stood side by side to study them.

'I mean, what are these, here?' Ed pointed at three big payments. 'That can't be right. I thought we had two point three million dollars unaccounted for . . .'

'Yes, just under.'

'But look at these figures! It's much more than two point three, more than twice that amount.'

Beatrice added up the figures in silence. 'I make it four point nine million.'

Ed experienced a fierce sensation of panic and nausea in his stomach. 'That's the whole fucking building budget,' he said, taking hold of the chair and sinking down on to it. 'How the hell could this happen? It's a disaster – Milton's blown the entire project!'

'We don't know that the money's gone,' Beatrice said.

'Well, he made all these payments – just look at them. Nobody authorised him to do that.' Ed took off his glasses.

'We need to find out who all these payees are,' Beatrice said. 'There are some new names here.'

'We won't learn anything,' Ed declared. 'It'll be Mount Batanga all over again. We've been trying to discover who they are for weeks, and what have we learned? Nothing at all. They're shells – I'd put money on it. It's a series of dummies.'

Beatrice leaned over the papers and scanned them again, one by one.

'Even if these people are going to perform,' Ed went on, 'Milton had no authority to pay in advance. What was the point? It's crazy – but it's my fault. I should never have left him in charge.' Wiping his face, he added angrily: 'God, I'm thirsty – it's so bloody hot today.' He stared at his hands, which had started to tremble.

After a moment, Beatrice cleared her throat. 'There are still things we can do,' she said. 'There must be people who know these companies. I mean, they must have a reputation, a track record. I bet Mike Owens would know something – or he could tell us who does. You should talk to him.'

Ed had taken a long breath, and he let it out all at once. 'You're joking, right? That drunk guy at the Hilton?'

'Mike's never as drunk as he seems.'

He shrugged. 'Okay, I'll talk to him. It's not as though I've got any better ideas.'

'Ask him about Alfred Kimathi Associates.'

'Kimathi?' He wrote it down. 'What are they – accountants?'

'Architects,' she said. 'Alfred Kimathi is Milton's cousin. He has a stack of their brochures in his filing cabinet at Makera, remember? They're a well-known firm – they do a lot of government contracts.' And she added: 'I ought to go home. I promised Father I'd be there for dinner.'

'Yes, of course,' he said, without looking up.

'Are you all right, Ed? I can stay if you want – I can ring Father.'

'No, no, I'm fine.' He looked up at her. 'Don't worry. We'll get the money back. I'm going to speak to the lawyers now. There must be a way . . . There has to be, doesn't there? I'll see you in the morning.'

15

Beatrice slowed down on her scooter, sounding the horn as she approached the house. Immediately a couple of shaggy dogs shot out from under the wide veranda, bolted across the driveway and leaped up against the wire security fence, barking continuously. Then, after a few moments, a middle-aged man in blue overalls hurried out from a side door into the sunlight. 'Good evening, miss,' he called, as he reached the gate.

'Hello, John,' she said. 'Everything well?'

'Yes, miss. Your father's at home. Just a moment, Miss Beatrice.' He growled, 'Stop it, Sherlock,' taking the bigger dog by the collar and securing him with a rope. 'Behave yourself! Sit down, *pumbavu*! Sit down!' Then he grabbed hold of the other dog, which was leaping against the mesh. 'Mycroft, you *mhuni*! Come with me – come on, that's right. Mrs Mgiro's got a nice piece of chicken for you . . . Yes, biscuits and chicken . . .' He led them back to the house, reappearing a few moments later to unlock the gate for Beatrice.

Beatrice sprang up the three front steps, but rather than going inside, she walked along the wide veranda that ran the whole way round the house, looking out across the tumbling, half-wild lawn towards the rose bushes and the little plantation of banana trees in the distance. At the back of the house, the veranda was broad enough to form a kind of outdoor living room, with wickerwork chairs and low tables where Joseph sat reading in the evenings. There was a disused swimming pool, half hidden behind a screen of orange bougainvillaea about fifteen yards away, and Beatrice stood peering at it, listening to the cicadas in the trees, and the police sirens on the main road half a mile away, before turning to go inside.

'Father?' she called, moving along the dark corridor that led to Joseph's study.

'Hello, Bea,' he replied, from the interior. 'I'm here, just wrapping up.' As she appeared in the doorway, he glanced up at her over his half-moon spectacles.

'Look at you, Father,' she said, 'all huddled up in the dark. Why don't you come outside? You can work in the fresh air. The garden's full of sun. I'll tell Hope to bring you a whisky.'

'Yes,' he said. 'I'll be out soon.'

The study windows looked out on to the veranda, but they were protected from sunlight by the wide roof, which was overhung with jasmine, so that the room was always dark. Beatrice sank down on the sofa and picked up one of the photographs from the table. Her mother, Rachel, was standing with Joseph on the steps of the Roman Catholic Cathedral of Kisuru on the day of their wedding: the photographer had caught her in a moment of extraordinary happiness, her eyes laughing and her head tipped back, as if she was about to sing. For a moment Beatrice studied her face. Then she leaned back and watched the shadow of the jasmine trembling on the carpet.

Despite her many suggestions over the years, Joseph had never done anything to the interior of the house, and this room in particular seemed to be stuck in another era. The previous owners – a British colonial intelligence officer and his wife – had sold him the house complete with all their furniture and books, so Beatrice had grown up with a collection of tropical butterflies in glass cases, the mounted heads of wildebeest, kudu and cheetah in the hallway, and a library that overflowed from Joseph's study into the shelves along the corridors. Most of the books were academic works of anthropology, psychology, history, archaeology, dating from before the Second World War, but there were also dozens of nineteenth-century novels, volumes of poetry, and – laid out on the shelves behind Joseph's desk – the complete works of Conan Doyle, John Buchan and P. G. Wodehouse, some of which he had reread so many times he knew whole passages by heart.

'Well, that's done,' he said, turning off the desk lamp and taking one of the hardbacks from the shelf by the door. 'Let's go outside.'

Beatrice hesitated, sunk on the sofa. 'Father?'

'Yes?' He rested his hand on the Bakelite switch.

'I want to talk to you about the slum project. I need your advice.'

'Well, of course. We'll talk outside.' He disappeared into the passage.

Joseph clasped a glass of Scotch close to his chest, gazing out into the garden as Beatrice began to tell him about the duplicate bank statements, the unauthorised payments to Mount Batanga Construction, Milton's absenteeism. For ten minutes or more he made no comment, apart from raising an eyebrow or nodding absentmindedly. And by the time Beatrice was explaining the behaviour of Matiba Development and the threats to Ann Odinga, the sun had gone down. Mrs Mgiro had come out to light the mosquito coils, and Joseph was looking up at the beams of the veranda roof, where countless insects were thrashing about and colliding with the light-bulbs.

'Well, Father?' He took a sip of whisky, and Beatrice was suddenly aware of the din of bullfrogs and cicadas in the pitch-black garden. 'What should I do?'

'It's hard to say. What does Ed think?'

'He's going to explain everything to his boss in London. I suppose they'll shut down the project.'

'I'd be surprised. It's really not in their interest.'

'But the whole budget's gone, Father. Almost five million dollars. They can't carry on. We've got to open the school in September.'

'Perhaps the builders will do the work. Perhaps they're just behind schedule, these Mount Batanga people.'

'Oh, Father!'

'Well, you can't be sure until you've spoken to Milton. He must have some kind of explanation.'

'And if he hasn't?'

Joseph finished his Scotch with a sudden movement, and put the glass down on the wickerwork table.

'Even if we do manage to talk to him,' she went on, 'what if we find out that he's basically stolen the money? I mean, that *is* what it looks like, you have to admit. What do I do then?'

'Well, Bea, in that case, which has not happened yet, you finish your internship, and you go to work for Mutoko Shackleton Gethi in the new year. Unlike Global Justice, they'll actually be paying you, remember?'

'Is that all? I can't just walk away from a fraud like that.'

'That's exactly what you should do. Believe me, any other course of action would be extremely foolish.'

'You know something, don't you?' she said, in a lower voice. 'Tell me what's going on.'

But he shook his head. 'I don't know what's happening. All I know is that you have your whole future ahead of you, Bea.'

'And what about you?'

'Me?' He laughed. 'I've already got a career, thank you very much.'

'But you'll have to explain everything to the British. You're the link between the two governments. Besides, you're in charge of the President's anti-corruption task force.'

'Oh, that? They're not interested. You know what these committees are like. We meet once a month for a good lunch. There's lots of gossip from State House and the diplomatic circuit, we look serious for a few minutes and talk about the World Bank's governance agenda, the attitude of the donor nations, the problem of capital flight, the fungibility of aid, and then we go back to our various offices. Everyone on the committee is fully occupied with other work. There's Charles Wanjui, a couple of the President's policy advisers, someone from the Special Bureau and yours truly. It's not a working group.'

'Why don't you resign, then, if it's such a farce?'

'I've thought about it. I do think about it. On balance I feel I should stay. Unofficially I hear things because of the committee: people come to me from time to time with tales of corruption and the abuse of power, and I file the stories away. Usually the whistleblowers are lowly government employees, underpaid clerks with a grudge against a boss who has his snout in the trough. I feel sorry for them – they're taking a big risk in contacting me. I have to bury their testimony – I've put it all in code. But there's nothing more I can do. I've got no power of investigation. Really, I'm blocked in.'

'Can't you lobby for more authority?'

'Nobody's interested, Bea. The thing's a PR exercise. The President wants the Anti-corruption Unit to exist because it pleases the donors – they can tick the box that says *improving standards of governance* – but he doesn't want us to do anything.' He laughed. 'That would frighten the hell out of everyone.'

Beatrice stared at him defiantly. 'Doesn't it bother you? *Please* tell me it does.'

'Of course,' he said. 'The reality of it bothers me, that this country is eaten up with corruption. The politics of it bother me, too – but perhaps that's just my vanity. The President wants me around to reassure foreigners that things are improving when, quite obviously, they're not but actually getting worse in many ways. So, I'm being used. My reputation is being used to mislead the *wazungu*. Just about everyone knows it.' He paused. 'Then again, if I resigned, what would that achieve? I'd know even less about what's going on, I'd have less influence, I'd be frozen out.' He turned towards her, and his dark eyes scrutinised her face. 'Kwamchetsi Wachira and Pamela Abasi know that. We have a

133

tacit understanding. I won't investigate what's going on – I haven't got the mandate, in any case – but if they want me to keep quiet, they mustn't rub my nose in their affairs.' He pressed his lips together and glanced at her. 'Is that a good compromise? Not at all. But it's the only one available.' And he added, after a moment: 'As for this slum project of yours, I just want you to be careful. If Milton's behaving badly, you must remember he's got very heavyweight backing. Too much for *you* to take on.'

'Don't we have a duty to speak out, Father? Isn't that what you always say?'

'We have a duty to avoid corrupt practices ourselves. Believe me, in this country that's pretty much a full-time occupation and it makes you extremely unpopular. Speaking out about other people's corruption – well, that's a whole different thing. I sometimes think that blowing the whistle is a bit like going to war: if you're going to do it, you have a duty to make sure you succeed. Otherwise, even if you manage to survive, you're going to leave an awful lot of casualties behind you.'

'Informants?'

'Informants, witnesses, small people. They've already suffered for being honest. If you go public with their information, and you don't do it exactly right, then it's all over for them.' He added: 'Remember, my darling, in this context we're the little people. We don't have the government machine behind us.'

'Because you never played the game.'

'We've survived by being discreet, Bea. That's the price we pay for a clear conscience.'

'What about going to an external authority?' she suggested. 'I mean, if the slum project is all eaten up by Milton, you'll have to tell the British something.'

'Well, I'm certainly not going to worry about that,' he said. 'Let's see how things pan out. Ed seems very capable. He'll probably get some kind of programme off the ground, whatever Milton's up to. The British are used to aid projects going off the rails. It happens all the time.'

'Even so,' she said, 'they'll want to know what's happened to their money.'

But her father shrugged. 'It's not so much a matter of knowing exactly what happened to the money. Very often, in cases like this, the donor would rather not know. The real point is deciding how to present everything in the public accounts, and there's usually a way of doing that.'

'Even if it means telling a lie?'

'Not a *lie*, if possible. That's never a good idea,' he said, picking up his empty glass and peering into it. 'It's just that there's never much appetite on anyone's part for seeing the whole truth put down in black and white.'

Beatrice looked at her father, his head silhouetted by the light from the hurricane lamp behind him, and let out a long, deliberate sigh. 'Well, it's hopeless,' she said at last. 'Even you, Father . . . It's such a compromise.'

'Yes of course it is, but it's not hopeless. One has to be patient.'

'You could die of frustration, living like this, keeping quiet all the time, putting up with all the endless threats, lies, evasions . . .' She glared at him. 'How can anyone keep their sanity?'

'You know what Ken Saro-Wiwa said?' Joseph asked, closing his eyes in concentration. 'There was his beloved Nigeria, his magnificent country, so full of injustice and corruption, murder, robbery, maladministration, hunger, knavery, treachery and God knows what – plain stupidity. But it still remained a blessed country to him.'

'Yes, Father,' Beatrice said. 'It was all very blessed, until he was hanged by General Abacha.'

'What I'm trying to say, Bea – the point is that we have to accept the basic limitations of the situation. It's not the way we want it, but it's complex, large-scale, systemic. You can't pit your will against a whole system: that's just quixotic. Plough your own furrow as straight as you can. You don't have the time or strength to plough everyone else's. We have to fight our own daily temptations, our own demons.' He tapped the cover of his book. 'Look at me. This is the time of night when I have to decide whether to sit up late reading P. G. Wodehouse and drinking Scotch, or go to bed. I can feel my mood deteriorating. Once the sun's down, memories ambush me. Don't ask me to take on the reform of public life in Batanga, Bea. I'm not the President.'

Beatrice had got up and was looking down at him from the back of the veranda. 'I'd better tell Mrs Mgiro to bring the supper,' she said. 'I didn't realise how late it is.'

16

The next evening as they were walking back through the slums, approaching the gates of the Global Justice site, Beatrice stopped abruptly, laying her hand on Ed's arm. 'That's Milton's car,' she said, pointing through the fence at a brand-new metallic-grey Range Rover parked outside the office.

'Close the gate behind us,' Ed replied, 'then follow me in.' He made his way to the little building and crept inside. 'Hello, Milton,' he called, as he entered the office. 'How good to see you. I was hoping you'd drop by.'

Milton spun round from the open filing cabinet. 'What are you doing here?'

'Well, this is my office,' Ed pointed out, with a forced smile. 'I work here. So do you – remember?'

'That woman has been screwing around with my things,' he declared, as Beatrice came in. He marched up to her, brandishing a sheaf of papers. 'What is this? What have you been doing with my things? You stole these documents – I found them in your desk.'

He thrust them into her face, too close to read, but she replied quite calmly, 'Oh, yes, the bank statements. They're not your papers. They belong to GJA. All your personal things are over there in the filing cabinet. We've been keeping them out of sight – there are so many break-ins around Makera.'

Milton continued to wave the bank statements. 'These are mine. My name is here – look.'

'Those are duplicates,' Ed put in. 'Since you haven't been around, I asked the bank for a full set of statements.'

Milton folded his arms across his purple polo shirt. He seemed about to say something, but instead went back to the filing cabinet and started to collect his things in silence.

'I've been trying to contact Mount Batanga Construction,' Ed went on, moving sideways to stand next to Beatrice in front of the door. 'We need a schedule of work, the contract, basic information. I haven't yet been able to speak to anyone.'

Milton shrugged, without looking round, and crouched to sort through the lower drawer.

'I'll have to tell my boss what's happened to the money,' Ed said. 'At the moment, all I can say is that the building budget has been paid to a company I know nothing about, and we have no idea when the work will be done, whether it'll be done, to what standard, or anything at all. I haven't even met the quantity surveyor. What do you think I should tell the trustees, Milton?'

Milton stood up with his parcels and letters. 'It's not my problem. I shouldn't even be here. I'm going up-country to stay with my aunt.' Crossing the room, he stood in front of Ed, who was now leaning against the closed door. 'Get out of my way,' he said quietly.

'Tell me where the paperwork is,' Ed said. 'You don't have to do anything else. It won't take a second. Where are the contracts with Mount Batanga? Where are the work schedules?'

'I don't have them. You think I carry these things about with me?'

'Where are they?'

'They're still being agreed.'

'But they've got our money!' Ed said, his voice rising in pitch. 'You can't have paid them before you signed a contract.'

'You don't trust me?'

'I trusted you completely. I left you in charge out here.'

'Oh, that's big of you. You put me in charge!' He gazed at Ed with an expression of derision. 'So I'm not your servant. Get out of my way!'

Ed kept his back to the door. 'You really don't give a damn,' he said. 'What do you think will happen to this project? Give me your opinion. Is Mount Batanga going to do the work? Will they build the school and the clinic?'

'Why not?' he said mockingly. 'That's the plan, isn't it?'

'Can I tell the trustees that you've made the arrangements?'

'You can tell them what you want.'

'But is it true?'

'You trust me, don't you?'

'And the paperwork?'

Milton narrowed his eyes and stepped up closer, so that he was six inches from Ed's face. 'You sort out the paperwork,' he said. 'It's your job. You think I'm a clerk?'

'No, you're not a clerk,' Ed replied. 'You're the manager of this project, and you paid a construction firm to do the work – remember? You did it months ago, before I was here. You made that decision. All I'm saying is, it's your responsibility to see that the contract is drawn up. That's pretty elementary stuff.'

'Are you telling me I don't understand business?'

'On the contrary, I think you understand much more than you admit,' Ed replied. 'That's what worries me.'

'Oh, right! Because you really understand what's going on, don't you, Mr Caine? You're a real expert! Let me tell you something. I'm an Abasi. An *Abasi*,' he repeated. 'Do you know what that means?' He drew a deep, unhurried breath through his open mouth as he hovered over Ed, his shoulders hunched. 'Understand one thing, Mr Caine. You know nothing about Batanga. You understand nothing about doing business here. This is a dangerous country. If I were you, I would go back to England.'

Beatrice had snatched up a piece of paper from her desk and was now advancing with it towards Milton. 'And what about Matiba Development?' she cried. 'Do you know nothing about that, either, Milton? That they're threatening the people in Makera, trying to drive them out?'

Her voice fell away, and there was silence. Then Milton looked about in mock-surprise. 'Did you say something?' he asked. 'I could have sworn I heard your voice.' He stood directly in front of Beatrice. 'But, of course, it can't have been you. You're only an intern. You can't be talking to me like that.' He grabbed the document from her and screwed it into a ball.

'What do you know?' she said again. 'You have to tell us.'

'I don't have to tell you anything.' He dropped the paper on the floor. 'I am not answerable to you!'

'And if people are forced to leave Makera? If families are driven away?'

'You think that matters?' he demanded. 'They only arrived a few years ago. They can move again – why not? There are better places. This is good land – they're in the middle of Kisuru. That's it. I'm wasting my time.'

'So Matiba is part of your scheme,' she persisted. 'They clear the land, get rid of the Shala riff-raff. Then you tell Mount Batanga to put up the school and the clinic, install the water system. Of course! It's a perfect development opportunity.'

Milton stood at the door, still gripping the packages under his arm. Though the back and armpits of his purple T-shirt were dark with sweat, his face seemed calm. 'If I were you, Miss Kamunda,' he said, fixing his eyes on Ed, 'I'd get yourself a proper job. Believe me, you don't want to work for people like this. In NGOs it's always the *wazungu* who are in charge. Always. It doesn't matter how many Africans there are with better qualifications, more experience. And you know what happens after a few months, when the funds are spent? They fly off to the next project – you never see them again.'

They listened to the muffled roar of Milton's Range Rover as it drove out of the compound, and for a long time neither of them said a word. Ed sank into his chair and sat staring at the floor. He was conscious of the blood throbbing in his temples, and for a while his brain and his whole body were paralysed with shock.

Eventually, he raised his eyes to Beatrice. 'What the hell do we do now?' he said. 'I mean, I had my suspicions – I knew he was tricky, but this blatant fraud . . .'

'It wasn't your fault,' she said. 'How could you know?'

'I'm responsible for the project. The buck stops with me.' And he sat up. 'He won't pay it back, will he? Not a penny.'

Beatrice shook her head. She was walking slowly towards the desk and had taken out her mobile phone.

'What are you doing?' he asked.

'I'm going to speak to Solomon.'

'What's the point? What can he do?'

'He runs a firm of builders. He was boasting about it. They put up shacks in the slums. If I get him over here and show him the plans for the school, will you talk to him?'

'Beatrice, we don't need a slum builder, we need to get the government back on board. If we don't do that, if Milton is acting for the administration, the project's totally screwed.'

'Solomon might be able to put up the school. That would be something.'

'But we've got nothing to pay him with.'

'We could use the equipment funds – the money for the playground, the whiteboards, computers. It won't be a proper building with air-conditioning and everything, but at least we can have classrooms for the new term.'

Ed was still staring at the floor.

'Ed? Are you all right?'

'No,' he said. 'Definitely not.'

'What about Solomon?' she urged. 'Shall I talk to him?'

'I suppose there's no harm in asking,' he said wearily. 'If he can give us some kind of estimate, I could take it to London.'

'Would they authorise a new builder?'

'No. I'd say they'll close us down, wouldn't you? It must be obvious that I've blown the project.'

'But if we can put up a school, we'd still achieve something worthwhile.'

'A slum school? Built out of metal sheets? What if it falls down with the children inside?'

'I'll tell him that,' she said. 'I'll make sure he understands what's at stake.'

'I just can't believe it,' he went on. 'It's a fucking mess.' He rotated his head to relieve the tension in his neck. 'And I can't even stay and think it through. I've got to go back to the hotel. Sarah's having dinner with Pamela Abasi tonight – of all people . . . Jesus!' His arms and legs felt heavy, and it it was an effort to stand up and pull on his jacket. 'So much for my planning skills. So much for learning from experience. This project was over before it started. What a disaster.' He turned towards her as he reached the door. 'I'm sorry, Beatrice.'

'Don't say that. There's nothing to apologise for.'

'You know you don't have to go on. You can call it a day – you understand that?'

'I'm going to ring Solomon,' she said.

'All right,' he replied. 'Thanks, Beatrice. Thanks for not giving up. Most people would.' With that, he let himself out into the compound.

17

Sarah sat opposite the glass doors in the lobby of the Hilton, waiting for Pamela Abasi, who was more than an hour late. She had been telephoned so many times in the last few days by Pamela's assistant, changing the time of their meeting, that she was half expecting Lucy to ring again to tell her that the minister wouldn't be coming. And after the miserable argument she had just had with Ed, she would have been almost glad.

All the time she waited downstairs, Sarah had been going over the quarrel in her mind, and for a long time she was too upset to make any sense of it. Ed had come home furious about Milton – angrier than Sarah had ever seen him – and tried to persuade her to call off the meeting with Pamela. No doubt she should have sympathised with him, but the pressure he put on her was maddening. Ed made no effort to see things from her point of view: he was trying to stop her accepting Pamela's help simply because of his own frustration with the Abasis.

'I can't believe you're treating me like this,' she told him. 'I'm seeing Pamela tonight. It's been planned for weeks. What do you expect me to do? Cancel? Do you have any idea what I've been doing all week? Walking about St Jude's, in and out of shitty little houses, trying to find somewhere halfway decent for us to live. Can you please try to imagine what it's like house-hunting in Kisuru, with half the budget we need and Archie running off the whole time, playing in piles of rubbish? And now, the first chance I get to meet someone who might actually help us, who can help me do something for myself, you want to stop me. Jesus! What's that about?'

Archie had started crying, but neither of them moved.

'I thought you left him here,' Ed said.

'What are you talking about?'

'Archie. I thought you left him in the hotel when you went out.'

'Leave him how? On his own? How *can* I?'

'You said there was a girl.'

'Oh, she's been ill . . . Shit, now I'm going to be late.' She went to pick up Archie. 'Ssh, it's all right. Quiet, darling.'

'Aren't you going to change?'

'There isn't time.'

'Of course there is. Pamela's bound to be late. Here, give me Archie. Go and have a shower. You'll feel better.'

'It's all right. It doesn't matter. I'll go as I am.' And she had hurried out.

Sarah sipped her glass of wine and stared towards the automatic doors. A black Mercedes drew up outside the hotel, but it was not Pamela's, and she closed her eyes, leaning her head against the back of the chair. She was still angry with Ed, but she was tired, too, and somehow less sure of herself. Picking up a copy of the *Kisuru Telegraph*, she surveyed the front page, tossed it aside and got to her feet. There was a full-length mirror a few feet away, outside one of the shops, and she walked over to examine herself. All around her in the lobby, chatting under the tubular chandeliers, were groups of women with flawless skin, wrapped in brilliant saris or in close-fitting evening gowns, with jewels around their necks the size of men's knuckles. As Sarah surveyed her own crumpled linen dress, her blotchy face, with a swollen mosquito bite on the jaw, a feeling of childlike embarrassment and vulnerability took hold of her. For a moment she wondered whether to go upstairs and change, but she was sure Pamela would arrive the instant she went away. She retreated to a chair at the edge of the hall and sat down, listening to the beautiful, confident young women as they chatted away in a mixture of Hindi, Swahili and English.

'Excuse me – Mrs Caine?'

Sarah looked up despondently at the two men approaching from the doorway. 'I'm Mrs Caine.'

'The minister will be with you shortly, ma'am. We are just making a preliminary security sweep.' Sarah watched half a dozen uniformed policemen make their way along the row of little shops in the foyer, peering through the carved animals and bolts of brightly coloured fabric. 'Her Excellency asks that you wait for her in the Ngozi Bar, ma'am. This way, please. I will show you the table.'

A solidly built mahogany chair had been set out for Pamela Abasi in an alcove, near the entrance to the famous Mawana Coast Restaurant. By the time Sarah reached the table, a waiter had already brought out an ice bucket containing a bottle of champagne and set two tall glasses on the table. 'Here, ma'am,' the bodyguard said, indicating the banquette. 'Her Excellency will be arriving soon.'

Sarah perched on the edge but she was too nervous to sit still, and after a moment she got to her feet again, looking up towards the lobby, which was now pulsing with blue lights from the driveway outside. The women in evening gowns had moved off, and the hallway was almost clear, but Sarah recognised the figure of Parvit Singh in a saffron turban and dark blue suit, waiting by the shops. Then Parvit bowed his head, and another six or seven large men hurried into the lobby, followed immediately by the round, bustling form of Pamela Abasi, who was escorted down the stairs.

'Mrs Caine,' she boomed as she reached the alcove. 'Pamela Abasi.' She put out her hand.

'How do you do, Minister? I'm delighted to meet you.'

Pamela pressed her lips together gravely as she accepted Sarah's hand. The minister's round body was wrapped in a gown of purple and gold, and she wore a tall, cylindrical hat of a type Sarah recognised from old photographs of the Bakhoto queens. 'I hope you've had something to drink,' she went on, in the same declamatory tone, glancing at the table. 'I told Lucy to warn you I was running late.'

'Oh, yes, absolutely. I've been very well looked after.'

'I was in a meeting with Mr Anders,' Pamela went on, raising her head with a dignified, slightly defensive air. 'He's the new director of the World Bank office here. Do you know him? No? He's a Norwegian. A specialist in *transparent administrative systems*. He's written a book about it.' She chuckled, and Sarah was conscious of her rich, rather claustrophobic scent. 'I'm sure he means well, but in my opinion there are far too many outsiders theorising about Africa, too many foreign officials laying down the law.' She indicated the banquette. 'Shall we sit down? Please.' Lowering herself into the armchair, she said something in Swahili to the wine waiter, who stepped forward to open the champagne.

'I think the World Bank is much too prescriptive,' Sarah said, speaking a little loudly to mask her nervousness. 'They seem to want full control of the recipient country.'

'It puts us in a very difficult position.' Pamela raised her eyebrows slightly as she looked at Sarah. 'We have to choose between basic education and healthcare for our people, and paying the interest on historic debts. I wish Mr Anders and his team could spend a few months in Makera – or in the north, among the refugees. That would change his perspective.' She put out her hand towards her glass of champagne, but paused to adjust her ring. 'Well, let's not waste time discussing Mr Anders,' she went on. 'Your husband tells me you have done research into women's health.'

'Reproductive health was an important element in my thesis,' Sarah said. 'I was looking at the cultural determinants of women's progress – traditional approaches to health and child-rearing, gender roles, the impact of education . . .'

'I'm a staunch supporter of girls' education.'

'Oh, absolutely. I've studied your work on girls' primary education and fertility rates.'

Pamela nodded, with cautious approval, her heavy eyelids half lowered. 'Where were you studying?'

'King's College, London.'

'Yes? My daughter Joyce is at King's.'

'I enjoyed my year there,' Sarah said enthusiastically. 'I spent a lot of time at SOAS, too. I heard you talk when you came last year.'

'Really? . . . The dean at SOAS is an old friend. Actually, I get asked to talk at a lot of seminars – I can't possibly attend them all but I do what I can. It's important to reach out to the next generation of officials, aid workers, activists . . . I want them to understand the reality of African life.'

'It was a brilliant lecture,' Sarah said. 'I promised myself then that I'd take up your challenge, that I'd work with Africans – within African civil society, not through external agencies and intermediaries.'

The head waiter of the Mawana Coast Restaurant had been waiting anxiously a few yards away, but now, seeing that the minister had stopped talking, he stepped up to let her know that her table was ready.

'All right, let's go in,' Pamela said. Getting to her feet, she led Sarah through the double doors of the restaurant into a spacious dining room. 'Have you eaten here before?' the minister asked, as they sat down on opposite sides of a broad white tablecloth.

'I'm afraid we've been living off room service.'

'This restaurant has the best seafood in town. You should try the crab curry – it's the speciality of the house.' She handed the menu back to the head waiter. 'We'll both have crab curry, with some okra or spinach, whichever is freshest today, and a bottle of white Burgundy – you can decide which.'

'Certainly, Your Excellency.'

'So, tell me,' Pamela went on, as the waiter withdrew, 'what exactly was your dissertation about?'

Sarah took her napkin and pulled it open. 'Well, it does seem rather theoretical, thinking about it now. I mean, I agree with you so much about the need for practical development work . . . Basically, I was trying to investigate how cultural attitudes can help women or hold them back. For instance, assumptions about girls' education, or the sort of work they can do when they finish school.'

'Well, I don't call that theoretical. What could be more practical than getting girls into school? Were you focusing on East Africa?'

'Not at first. I was trying to find a general relationship between certain basic cultural factors and economic opportunity – measurable outcomes, like female employment and income, higher education . . . I mean, there's always this conflict in people's minds between the traditional culture of a society on the one hand and economic development on the other – as though only people who are deprived economically can still live their traditional culture. But does development really require everyone to adopt a Western-style, post-enlightenment mind-set? Is that what modernity means?'

'Well? What did you conclude?'

'In the end, I couldn't prove any clear causal relationships. It's hard to pin down the cultural factors. But I'm sure it must be possible to have the best of both worlds, to get material progress – women's rights, improved healthcare, more education – while maintaining traditional values.'

'A lot of people are talking about this now,' Pamela remarked. 'African values – an African renaissance . . .'

'One of my lecturers at King's was an expert on pre-colonial Africa,' Sarah went on. 'The consensual basis of decision-making in tribal societies – the sort of political traditions Kenneth Makotsi describes in his memoirs. I found that very interesting. It's so different from the individualism and the – I don't know – the dog-eat-dog competition in the West.'

Pamela sat back. 'If you want to see how tribal society works, you need to go up-country. There are still places where the elders gather under the fig tree and the boys are circumcised in the river. But here in the city – in places like Makera – those tribal customs have gone. People feel an identity with their parents' tribe, especially when times are hard, and they rely on the tribe for support, but if you ask the girls in the workshops and offices here, they don't know much about their traditional cultures. In the old days, people in Kisuru thought of themselves as visitors – migrant workers. If you said, "Where are you from?" they would say at once, "From the Ngozi Highlands", "From Bakhotoland", or "From the coast." There was a sense of belonging to the land of your people. When someone died in Kisuru, the family used to pay for the body to be brought back to the homeland for a traditional burial. Nowadays, if you ask a young person where they come from, they say, "Well, I come from Kisuru", or "I'm a Batangan". That's what Joyce would say, or Beatrice Kamunda. They're not interested in Bakhoto traditions. So what culture *do* they belong to now?'

The waiter served the crab curry.

'But someone like you,' Sarah said. 'I mean, to me you still have a very impressive Bakhoto identity, and at the same time you're an inspiration to African women who are trying to achieve their independence.'

'There's nothing traditional about that.' Pamela raised her glass of wine to take a sip. 'I inherited this position among the Bakhoto when my husband died. It's as simple as that.' And she went on, a little louder: 'Let me tell you a few things, Sarah, things you may not have learned at university, about the day-to-day reality of these questions. First of all, tribes still exist in this country – I meet a lot of Western academics who insist that they don't matter any more, but they do, believe me. Only, as I say, they're not cultural groups any longer. No. Nowadays the tribes exist as political networks, the providers of social security. And, more than anything, it's multi-party elections that keep them alive. For instance, I have a responsibility to the Bakhoto people, who looked to my late husband, Philip. His family had been prominent in the Mount Batanga region since before the British came and our people still expect us to provide for them – to see to their needs. Therefore they tolerate me, they vote for me, but that doesn't mean they want their own daughters to be independent women – God forbid!' She picked up her fork to spear a piece of crabmeat.

'Every child has to contribute to the household income,' she went on when she had swallowed the mouthful. 'It's essential. Survival depends on it. A child who strikes out on his own – let alone *her* own – is letting everyone down. If someone does that, he becomes an outcast – a non-person – and in this city, let me tell you, girls who lose their family's protection end up as prostitutes, if they live long enough.' She drank some more wine. 'Most women in Africa have no idea of a life outside the family. The family and religion are the centre of life for most people. They are operating within the limits of necessity all the time – there is no room for manoeuvre. But you Westerners, you never understand this, never. You cannot imagine a world-view so different from your own. Either you're incurable romantics, who look at tribal society and say, "Oh, how beautiful! How authentic! We Westerners should never have come here and destroyed this wonderful way of life!" Or you're liberals – progressives – who see the power of unelected old men in the tribe, the low status of unmarried people, the sexual taboos, and you don't like it. You start asking, "Who are these self-important *wazee* – these elders? Why can't the young people be free? Why are the girls locked up in the family compound until they marry? What about their human rights?"' She fixed Sarah with her fierce, protruding eyes. 'You see? We Africans can't win! We're damned either way. And, these days, we have to listen to lectures from post-modernists, too – ridiculous people determined to maintain both positions at the same time: tribal society and personal freedom, feminism and a warrior society. Don't ask me how they do that. God only knows!'

Sarah could feel herself flushing, and her mouth was set in a defensive half-smile.

'I want you to understand,' Pamela went on, arching her eyebrows, 'even the poorest people here have to support their relations. Even a beggar – a ragpicker – has to provide for his cousins, his wife's grandparents, his brother's children, the family elders. Poor people sometimes emigrate from city to city – they leave the country – just to avoid their relations and enjoy the little money they earn. As for me!' She expanded her eyes as she reloaded a fork with rice and curry. 'Every day I receive letters from kinsmen of my husband, asking for help – a scholarship for a son, a job for a nephew, a loan, a visa to the UK. I employ Agatha full time just to deal with these requests, and she's always behind. I'm not exaggerating – there's really no end to it.'

'But that's so amazing, in a way,' Sarah said. 'I mean, people in Britain are so individualistic – there's so much selfishness.'

Pamela watched her with an expression of slightly arch incomprehension in her eyes, while the waiters cleared away the plates. 'I'll tell you what,' she said. 'If you're serious about this, I'll introduce you to some people who do good work in the field of women's welfare, not just the NGO and UN people who are always coming and going, but Batangans – social entrepreneurs, proper activists. You should go and see the programmes set up by Batangan women operating in civil society – co-operatives, shelters for battered wives, AIDS orphanages. There's a lot of excellent work going on out there. It doesn't all come from Western agencies.'

'That would be fantastic,' Sarah said at once. 'I'd like that very much.'

'Talk to Lucy in the morning. I'll tell her to set up some appointments for you.'

'I'll ring her first thing. Thank you.' And she added, after a moment's hesitation: 'It would be so good to get stuck in to proper work as soon as I'm free. At the moment I'm spending half my time house-hunting.'

'Really? Haven't Global Justice fixed something up for you?'

'They were meant to. We'd hired a new villa outside Aberdare but it's not finished yet – not nearly. I've been going out every week with the agents, but we're not really getting anywhere.'

'I didn't know this,' Pamela said. 'Why didn't you mention it?'

'I'm sure we'll sort something out, but it's just taking up a lot of my time until we do. And things are surprisingly expensive. I mean – I hadn't realised how high the rents are.'

'That's *your* fault,' Pamela shot back, with a chuckle. 'There are so many of you development people in Kisuru, these days. Nobody else can afford to live here any more – certainly not the Batangans—' She broke off. 'Now, let me see, I may be able to help. Listen, here's an idea. I own a place in Aberdare which is vacant at the moment – a good house, colonial era, very comfortable.'

Sarah looked down. 'I'm afraid Aberdare is a bit out of our league. I've been looking more at St Jude's and the McPeak district.'

'McPeak? No, no, that's not suitable. Edward would be sitting in traffic all day, just to get to Makera. You do something for me, Sarah. Go and have a look at the house – take Edward along. Don't worry about the price for now. If you like it, we can discuss the rent. It was going to be let to an American journalist and his wife – nice people. They were taking it for a year, probably longer, but CNN sent him to Jerusalem instead so the house is vacant. I'd be glad to have a reliable tenant.'

'It's incredibly kind,' Sarah said. 'Of course, I'd have to discuss it with Ed . . .'

'Of course, of course . . . We have a saying in Bakhoto, "The men must talk, but the women decide."'

Sarah smiled, still avoiding Pamela's eyes. 'Well – I'll talk it over with him right away. It's terribly kind of you. And I'm sure Ed would love to see it.'

'Good – that's agreed, then.'

'Thank you so much,' Sarah said, putting down her glass as Pamela pushed her chair back from the table. 'That's wonderful – really.'

'I'm glad to help,' she replied, getting to her feet with the help of two detectives, who had stepped forward to assist her. 'Now, unfortunately, I must go. I'm travelling up-country tonight. There's a meeting of the Party in Makhotoland tomorrow morning, and they've asked me to make the opening speech.'

'It's been a great pleasure,' Sarah said, also standing up.

'No, the pleasure was mine. I'm glad we were able to meet.' Pamela nodded as they shook hands, but her expression had changed and her eyes were no longer focused on Sarah. She adjusted her headdress rapidly and set off at a dignified pace across the floor of the restaurant, followed closely by her body-guards. There was a lull in the conversation as she glided over the carpet, staring directly ahead, and the manager hurried to open the door for her. Then Pamela Abasi strode out without a word and disappeared from view.

18

Solomon was with Machi in the penthouse when Beatrice texted him. 'Oh, so she's decided to contact me, after all. I suppose she must want something. Why else would she text? She *never* does.' He passed Machi the phone. 'Take a look at that.'

Machi studied the screen.

'When I call her – when I send her gifts – she doesn't even answer. But, of course, this is different. I must ring her right away because she wants something. She expects me to come running to the slums just like that –' he snapped his fingers '– like a puppy! What does she think?' He went on angrily: 'And I had started to forget about her, too – do you know that? Yes. I was really forgetting all about her. But now . . .' He looked directly at his friend, an expression of pain in his eyes '. . . what should I do, Machi? I wish I'd never seen this woman.'

'Ignore her, boss. Don't answer.' Machi handed back the phone. 'Women like that – proud, *wabenzi* women – they're always trouble. She'll be a curse to you.' Getting up, he padded across the room to fetch another bottle of Johnnie Walker from the bar.

'She thinks she's a Bakhoto queen,' Solomon mused. 'No, that's not true. She believes she's an empress.'

'There was a man in my village who was tormented by a woman like Beatrice Kamunda.' Machi passed the bottle to Solomon as he sat down and stretched out his feet on the thick carpet. 'She wanted to marry him, so she cast a spell over him – a powerful spell. But his parents forbade it. He had to marry a girl from his own clan who owned land in the next village. The poor man stopped eating. He could never sleep. He was visited by his ancestors every night. And if he did sleep, he always dreamed about this woman. Soon he had a fever—'

'Maybe he loved this girl,' Solomon said, picking up the phone again. 'This witch.'

'That's what he believed. He swore he loved her. But he was sick. Little by little, he stopped being a man. He didn't want to go outside. He just wanted to hide. He lay down in his hut and the spirit went out of him.'

'He died?'

'Yes. After three months, he died.'

For a moment Solomon watched Machi. Then he shook his head and smiled. 'Machi, let me tell you something.'

'What is it, boss?'

'That is a ridiculous story. Totally ridiculous.'

'It's true. Everyone in my village knew about it. It happened when my parents were young.'

'And they all blamed this poor girl?'

Machi nodded. 'They drove her out of the village one night. What else could they do? You should do the same, boss. You must get this woman out of your life.'

Solomon's eyes rested on Machi's face; then he glanced down at the stack of *Playboy* magazines under the brown-glass table. 'If I could banish her,' he said quietly, 'I would do it right away.'

'You should see a doctor,' Machi said. 'I know a man who can help you – a proper Shala wizard. Let me ring him.'

But Solomon had picked up his phone again and was rereading the message. 'You know, I hate this girl,' he said thoughtfully. 'Even when I first saw her, I had a bad feeling.'

'Then why don't you avoid her?' Machi asked. 'There are women everywhere. You don't need this little *balozi* . . .'

'At first I wanted to teach her father a lesson – you remember? Besides, she's very beautiful. Proud and beautiful.' He put the phone down, waiting while Machi refilled his glass. 'She pretends to hate me. She's quite abusive.'

'She's wasting your time.'

'No, but if I can just talk to her, perhaps she would start to trust me – do you understand?' He looked down at Machi's grey socks. 'If I could be with her for just one night . . .'

Machi leaned forward and put his tumbler on the glass table. 'You're the boss,' he said. 'Tell me what you want.'

'I can't see her now. She'll know I've been drinking. You have to do this for me. Go down to that stupid office of hers in Makera and find out what she wants. Don't make any promises. Just see what the job is.'

Machi started to put on his shoes.

'Tell her I'm busy this evening – say I'm in meetings – and I'll contact her in the morning.' As Machi got up and pulled on his jacket, he added: 'Get back here right away. I want to know what she says.'

Machi returned an hour later with a bundle of architect's plans, and a letter from Beatrice.

Dear Mr Ouko,

You said your builders can construct houses overnight in Makera. If you can build this school for us, the whole community will honour you as their benefactor – and so will I. If you are able to do this, let's discuss the cost tomorrow. The project has only small funds. In hope of many great things,

Beatrice Kamunda.

There was a surge of adrenalin in Solomon's stomach as he read the letter. Then, sitting on the carpeted step by the bar, he spread the drawings around him; and as he discussed the job with Machi, the sensation of heaviness and frustration he had been carrying for so long seemed to disperse.

'It can be done,' Machi conceded. 'I could speak to our foremen in the morning. We will need twenty, maybe twenty-five men, no more. It's a simple structure. I'll check the warehouse for materials. We can use iron for the roof. The cost is less.'

'No, we should use wood,' Solomon said. 'We don't want to cook the children. We'll need a generator on site. I'll speak to Wellington in the morning – see if his brother can find us something. That office Beatrice uses, it stinks of the slums. Really, like burning shit. There's no air-conditioning, not even a fridge.' He cast his eyes over the plans again. 'All right, Machi, we're going to help this arrogant girl. Yes?'

'If you say so, boss.'

'Make an estimate of the price for the work tomorrow – a proper price, Machi. We'll go through it together.' He folded the letter. 'Start contacting the men. I want everyone on site early on Saturday. They can dig the foundations while we bring in the timber and bricks. And these channels, here, they can cut them, too, for the drainage pipes.'

'Yes, sir.'

'I'll talk to Wellington first thing tomorrow – he can meet us on site. I'll see you there before nine.'

'Yes, Mr Ouko.'

'If the men work all weekend, we'll have the job finished by Monday.'

'That will be hard, sir.'

'Hard? It's not hard. You tell the men I'll give them a bonus if it's ready by Tuesday morning. Make sure they're good men, each one a proper *fundi*.'

'Yes, sir, skilled men. I'll choose them myself.'

'All right. Go home, Machi. Get some sleep.'

'Good night, boss.'

Beatrice spent most of the next few days in the slums, gathering survey information for the Global Justice database. She was accompanied some of the time by Ann Odinga, who was strong enough now to walk about her own neighbourhood. Ed had been with them at first, but on Sunday he went back to the office in the ministry to start entering the hundreds of names they had collected, and the descriptions of shacks and workshops, on to a spreadsheet, carefully mapping out the shape and position of each plot of land.

As a result, neither Ed nor Beatrice had seen the crowd that had gathered around the perimeter of the Global Justice compound during the weekend, shouting encouragement to Solomon's workmen as they began to lay the foundations of the school. The numbers had continued to grow throughout Sunday morning, and by lunchtime, when the timber framework of the building was standing in the compound, women from the market had set up braziers to fry doughnuts for the spectators, and children moved about selling Tusker beer and hot *mandazi*.

Late on Sunday afternoon Beatrice returned to the site, but long before she reached the compound she found the corridors blocked by crowds. She could hear chanting ahead, and the percussion of countless tins and Fanta bottles, held up and beaten with sticks. As she struggled out on to the open land around the building site, people all around were swaying as they sang and stamping on the ground. At first, as Beatrice pushed on through the mass of bodies, she was unable to see what was happening inside the compound. But ten yards from the gates, she stopped. The brick walls of the school had been built up against the timber frames, and a solid-looking L-shaped shell now stood inside the fence, with empty holes for the windows and doors. 'He's done it,' she muttered. 'He's actually done it already.' And she struggled on through the crowd.

Solomon was arguing with the foreman on the other side of the compound, not far from the project office. 'What's the matter, Mr Ouko?' Machi asked, as he approached.

'This fucking generator is the matter.' Solomon kicked the diesel engine. 'We can't make the office air-conditioning work with it. It's not powerful enough.' He turned to the foreman. 'Is that what you're saying?'

'It's all right for the lights and the power points, Mr Ouko, but not the ventilation.'

'You hear that, Machi?'

'Yes, I understand. I'll see to it. I'll speak to Wellington again.'

'You tell him I'm angry.'

'Yes, boss.'

'I don't expect this kind of problem when I deal with friends.'

'No, sir. I'll talk to him.'

Solomon looked down at the reddish earth. His white shirt was stained with dust, and his face was red, too, except for two streaks where the sweat ran down from his baseball cap. 'I want the internal structures finished by tomorrow midday,' he said to the foreman, pointing at the plans, which he was holding out for him. 'The ventilation shafts, the plumbing – everything. Even the cupboards, and the shutters on the windows.'

'I've got the carpenters working all night, Mr Ouko.'

'All right. If you have any problems, you call me – understand?'

'Yes, sir.'

'Don't stand about. Go and check that roof. I don't want a roof that leaks.'

'It won't leak, boss.'

'Never say that,' Solomon replied. 'Every roof leaks in a flood. You make sure they're doing a proper job. Go on.'

Solomon wiped his forehead with his shirtsleeve and put his hat back on, pulling the peak down to shield his eyes from the sun. A group of workmen was passing in front of the compound gate, each man carrying a heavy roll of roofing material on one bare shoulder as he walked to the school building. Beyond them, outside the fence, Solomon saw a deep, constantly shifting field of headdresses and *kanga* wraps: the women in the crowd were swaying from side to side as they sang. Then he saw Machi open the gate, and Beatrice's face appeared at the entrance. Solomon narrowed his eyes, watching her intently as she looked at the L-shaped school building and the deep trenches that ran the length of the site. An almost painful sensation of excitement and apprehension seized hold of him, and as he tried to read her expression, he felt like a frightened child. Then he saw her smile at Machi, who was approaching her across the building site, and she looked towards the dirty yellow generator and the trestle table where Solomon was standing.

'This way, Miss Kamunda,' Machi said, leading her forward. 'The boss is waiting.' Beatrice followed him across the broken ground.

'Well, Miss Kamunda,' Solomon said, tossing his cap on to the trestle table. 'Here is your school.'

She stood in front of him, examining his dusty face. She was struck by how tall he was – her eyes were level with a smear of engine oil on his shirt collar.

'You don't look too pleased,' he remarked. 'Shall I tell the boys to pull everything down again?'

She smiled. 'I bet you would, too – you're capable of it.'

'I don't know.' He lowered his voice. 'Perhaps I'd do it for you.'

'Then, please don't,' she said. 'I like it the way it is . . . Thank you for doing this.'

'Well, to tell you the truth, I didn't want to get involved,' he replied. 'In fact, I told Machi to manage everything himself. I only came down to see how it was going.'

Beatrice examined his shirt, red with dust, his strong arms and neck. Then she looked up at his eyes, which were staring directly at her. 'But you stayed,' she said, returning his gaze.

'I wanted to make sure of everything. There's a lot to do – we have to work fast.' Taking his eyes off her face, he pointed towards the school. 'We still have to complete the fitting out – services, classrooms. We're fixing your air-conditioning, also, in the office. I told the boys everything has to be ready by tomorrow night. Then we'll have a party.' He put out his hand towards her, about to touch her face, and Beatrice held her breath. 'I hope you can come this time,' he said gently. 'If you're not too busy in that little office of yours.'

She smiled. 'I expect I can take a night off.'

'Is that a promise?' he asked, suddenly serious, and as she nodded, he grabbed her hands and held them up in front of her, as if he was about to kiss them. 'In that case, I'll organise a proper band. Yes, a real Shala band. Then we can dance, Miss Kamunda. We can go out for dinner, too, if you want. I'll take you somewhere we can talk – somewhere elegant.' He smiled, watching her minutely. 'What do you say?'

'Yes,' she said quietly. 'I'd like that.'

19

By the time Ed reached the gates of the compound late on Sunday evening, it had been dark for several hours. He made his way towards the L-shaped school and stood in the playground, bemused, listening to the smooth chug-chug-chug of the diesel generator and watching the carpenters at work through the open windows. Then he walked slowly to the office.

Beatrice was sitting at her desk, going over the survey information. 'Good evening,' she called. 'What do you think of our school?'

'I honestly don't know what to think. We pay millions to a firm of builders everyone recommends and nothing happens for months. Then you make a couple of phone calls, I go off for a few days – and just look at it. I think I should keep away from this project altogether. I seem to be bad luck.'

'Don't say that. It's all your work – they're following the plans. The only thing you didn't decide was the timing.'

'Or the price. We've already spent the budget. How are we going to pay this time?'

'They don't need much. I told Solomon it had to be slum-building rates.'

'Even so, we'd better sit down with him tomorrow and get to grips with the figures before we find we've spent another small fortune.' He looked out of the window towards the school. 'You think the building will last?'

'Solomon says it will. They put down a concrete foundation and they've dug the drainage channels.'

'I saw that. It certainly looks good. I wonder what Milton's going to make of it.'

'He probably knows already,' she said. 'We had a visit this afternoon from some official gentlemen. Machi spoke to them. He thought they were Special Bureau.'

'Why did he think that?'

'He says he can tell by their shiny black shoes. According to Machi, they want us to stop work. They asked to see our building licence, the title deeds, planning agreement, employers' insurance – all the paperwork.' She gestured at the files. 'He told them to come back tomorrow.'

'We'd better ask your father down here to give us a hand,' Ed said.

'Yes. I'll tell him what's happening. He might be able to come in early, before he goes to the ministry.' But she hesitated, looking at the papers on her desk. 'I was out with Ann Odinga today. We were talking to the people in her neighbourhood. We've seen most of them now – about three hundred altogether.'

'That's great,' Ed said. 'Of course, in percentage terms it's a drop in the ocean – but at least we've made a start. It's a representative sample.'

'There've been more threats,' she went on. 'Some people are getting frightened. They want us to take their names off the database. Those two thugs have been preying on Ann especially. They follow her everywhere. She says she's not afraid, but I'm sure they're going to beat her up.'

'Well, the sooner we involve your father, the better. We need to mobilise some high-level support, what with Milton and the Special Bureau people.'

'Did you talk to Mike Owens?'

'I just spent three hours with him.' He nodded with a kind of wary respect. 'Bloody hell, what a pessimist! But he knows his stuff.'

'Was he drinking?' she asked.

'Not a drop. He told me to tell you that. He said you gave him an earful for getting drunk at the Hilton.'

'Yes, I did.'

'I don't really know what to make of him. I mean, he's so bloody rude. He told me I'd end up working for the UN – as though that would be the ultimate sell-out. Then, in the next breath, he virtually offered me a job with the UNHCR in Upshala. He said he'd put in a good word for me.' He paused, facing Beatrice, watching her reaction. 'We talked about recovering the money. Mike's sure Milton wouldn't have done anything like that on his own. And he says the money's probably in Switzerland by now. Jesus! You spend a bit of time with a man like Mike Owens and pretty soon you're convinced you can't trust anyone.'

'Is he going to help?'

'He's promised to look into it. He says if the money's being laundered, there's a handful of people who are bound to hear about it. He's going to call in some favours.' Ed shrugged, holding out his hands. 'What can I say? He seems to know what he's talking about. He's worried about you. He doesn't want to see you getting caught up in the middle of a big scandal. I'm sure he'd like me out in Upshala, with this project wound up nice and quickly. He says I can move on to other work, but you need to be careful.'

'He's just being protective,' she said, taking her bag and moving to the door. 'He thinks I'm still a child.'

'Well, he wants to talk to you about it. I think you should hear him out.'

'Yes,' she said. 'I'll talk to him. See you tomorrow, Ed.'

'Okay. Thanks, Beatrice.' And he added, as she was walking out: 'I almost forgot. Mike said you're right about those architects – Kimathi Associates. If someone's working on a commercial redevelopment of Makera, it'll be them. They're the Abasis' people.'

By the time Beatrice arrived on site on Monday morning with Joseph, crowds of families were already pressing against the perimeter fence. Climbing out of the ministry car inside the compound, Joseph did up the middle button of his jacket, glanced at the school without comment, and followed Beatrice into the office. 'Is there any tea in this place?' he asked.

'There's a *mamalishe* on the avenue. I can send someone out.'

'Don't bother,' he said, glancing at his watch.

'Are you sure, Father? Her tea's not bad. I've been living on it.'

'No, we'd better get on. Where's Ed?'

'He'll be here in a few minutes. He stopped at the ministry to pick up some papers.'

'Hmm. Is that the builder?'

Beatrice peered out towards the school building, and smiled. 'Yes, that's him.'

'I recognise him from the airport.' Joseph watched Solomon walk towards the office, followed by Machi, gesturing rapidly as he talked. 'He's got energy, I give him that.'

'He's saved the project,' she said.

'So it seems. I wonder why he did that.'

'Because he's a good man, Father. He was a slum-boy himself.'

Joseph pursed his lips.

'Here he is now. *Try* to be nice, Father.'

Joseph tugged at the cuffs of his shirt as Solomon came into the Portakabin.

'Father, this is Solomon Ouko. Solomon, my father, Joseph Kamunda.'

'*Shikamoo*,' Solomon said, bowing his head.

'*Marahaba*,' Joseph replied, nodding at him without offering his hand. 'I see you've been busy.'

Solomon smiled, glancing at Beatrice. 'I was glad to help.'

'And if you don't mind my asking, what motivated your decision?'

'*Father!*'

'Well, Mr Ouko here is a businessman, Bea. He and I have already had a discussion about his approach to commercial matters – at the airport. I'm sure you remember, Mr Ouko?'

'Yes, sir, I remember. But this . . .' Solomon's eyes briefly crossed Joseph's face, before he looked sideways at Beatrice '. . . this was a special job. It was not simply a business decision.'

'You agreed to do the work for charity?' Joseph asked.

'For friendship, let us say. After all, there are more important things in life than profit.'

'I'm sure you agree with that, Father.'

Joseph turned away, towards the building site. 'No doubt we could have an interesting discussion about what matters most in life, Mr Ouko. Friendship, as you say. Or loyalty.'

'Yes, sir. Loyalty and love.'

Joseph turned back to him, examining the expression on his confident, handsome face. 'Well, you have done the people here a service,' he observed cautiously. 'Don't let me keep you – I'm sure you've still got a great deal to do.'

Solomon bowed his head, smiled rapidly at Beatrice and walked away.

'I do hope Ed will be here soon,' Joseph said, checking his watch. 'I have to be at the ministry by ten.'

'He's on his way, Father – he texted me a few minutes ago.'

'Well? And what's going on with you, Bea?'

'Nothing. Nothing's going on.'

'No? I hope you're not getting too mixed up in all of this. It's only an internship, remember?'

She could feel herself blushing, and Joseph sat down in an office chair, looking out towards the gates, where Ed's taxi had just arrived.

'Here he is,' Beatrice announced, going to the door. 'I'll let him know you're here.'

Joseph watched her cross the compound. The sight of Ed's sunburned, smiling face, as he got out of the car, caused him to sigh. '"Behold,"' he recited under his breath, '"I am sending you out as sheep among wolves . . ."'

'Beatrice has outlined the situation to me,' Joseph began, when Ed had sat down. 'Have there been any developments overnight?'

'Nothing definite. A couple of Solomon's men saw a boy with kerosene outside the fence, and chased him away. That was early this morning.'

'Kerosene?'

'Machi thought so. Apparently the boy had a jerry-can.'

Joseph looked down at the table. 'And the Makera residents?'

'Their mood is calmer,' Beatrice said. 'They are encouraged by this building work. They say if the *wabenzi* allow a new school to be built here, they won't force them to move. They regard it as a kind of guarantee.'

'Who has been threatening them?'

'An outfit called Matiba Development,' Ed said. 'We're not sure who they are. The company seems to have some kind of official backing, but we don't know. We need to talk to someone in authority at the Special Bureau – the City Police, the Ministry of the Interior.'

'You're seeing the minister this morning, aren't you, Father?' Beatrice said.

Joseph nodded. 'I'll make sure she's up-to-date.'

'I'm very grateful,' Ed said. 'Really, without your help, we'd be terribly exposed. I mean, we've obviously rattled someone's cage. There were these men here yesterday asking to see our paperwork, too – our building permit, employers' insurance, planning approval, all the rest of it. I suppose that's standard practice. I don't know what you think . . .'

'Well, I don't want to speculate,' Joseph said with a brief smile. 'There's no reason why the city council shouldn't send an inspector. Stranger things have happened. As for the threats to the slum residents, there really isn't a great deal of evidence to go on, is there? A few hearsay reports of visits from various unidentified men, no photographs or recordings. Presumably these men are agents of some party seeking to buy land once the improved infrastructure is put in place. That's hardly surprising.' He pulled at his cuffs again, distracted by the repeated sound of a car horn, coming from a black SUV waiting outside the compound gates. 'Has anyone actually been harmed by these people?'

'Not that we know of,' Ed said, looking towards the source of the noise. 'Of course, we're only in touch with the residents in this immediate area – basically the Shala neighbourhood a little to the east of here,' he pointed on the map, 'about a quarter of a square mile around Ann Odinga's house. I'm sorry, Mr Kamunda, but I'd better go and see what the fuss is about.'

Two of the workmen had opened the gates for the SUV, and the driver, who had been pounding on the horn, drove rapidly into the compound.

'What's up, Machi?' Ed asked.

'Some big *balozi* from the Ministry of the Interior, Mr Caine. I had to let him in. He says he's come to check our permits.'

'That's all right. I'll talk to him.'

He strode towards the car as the passenger door started to open. A man climbed out, wearing a pair of sunglasses with black frames.

'Ed Caine.' Ed offered his hand. 'I'm the East Africa director of Global Justice Alliance. I understand you want to see our files.'

The man dismissed his extended hand with a scowl and walked ahead.

'All the paperwork is in the office,' Ed said. 'I'm sure you'll find it's in order.'

'I will decide that,' he declared. 'I already see many infractions on this plot of land, many illegal activities.' Before Ed could reply, he moved away again. 'This, for instance.' He pointed at the L-shaped building. 'What is this?'

'That's the school,' Ed said, his voice firmer and a little louder than before. 'It's the first stage of our building programme.'

'It is an illegal structure,' he replied. 'No permission has been given for this building. You must demolish it. It's a criminal offence to build without a permit. As a director, you are person-ally liable.'

168

Ed shook his head. 'Let's go inside,' he said. 'I'll show you the permit, the building specifications, all the planning documents. The school building is an essential part of the programme, specifically required by the Batangan government – they made it a precondition of their involvement, Mr . . . ?'

The man continued to look away as he surveyed the site with exaggerated attention. 'My name is Luther Magari.'

'Please come inside, Mr Magari. The project adviser from the ministry is here this morning – you might want to discuss the situation with him.'

Luther stood at the door of the little office without removing his sunglasses. He stared at Joseph and Beatrice. 'Good morning, Luther,' Joseph said cheerfully. 'Won't you join us? Have you met my daughter, Beatrice?'

Luther nodded to her. 'Miss Kamunda.'

'Here,' Joseph went on. 'Take a chair.'

'Mr Magari is concerned about the planning permission for the school building,' Ed put in, sitting down beside Luther. 'He wants to see the paperwork.'

Beatrice had already taken out the file, and now put the papers in front of Luther. 'These are all copies,' she explained. 'The originals are at the ministry building. This site is not very secure.'

Luther took off his dark glasses to examine the first document, which he held up to the light for a few moments, as if he was reading the small print, then dropped it back on to the desk and took up the next.

'Everything's in order,' Joseph said calmly. 'I have checked the papers myself. As it happens, the staff at the ministry were responsible for all the paperwork. Mrs Abasi's office supervised the whole application.'

'Copies are not valid,' Luther declared, putting down the last page and fixing Joseph with his good eye. 'I must see the original certificates.'

'They're in the safe at the ministry,' Beatrice repeated. 'Just let me know when you would like to inspect them.'

'And that building,' Luther went on, pointing towards the school. 'That is not right. It is not scheduled.'

'But the school is essential,' Ed said again. 'It was agreed right at the outset. And the term starts later this week.'

'Actually, the school building is several months overdue,' Joseph put in, catching Ed's eye. 'I think that is what Mr Magari means. It should have been finished in May. Of course there will have to be an inquiry into the delay. I am seeing the minister this morning so I will discuss the matter with her. I know she is most anxious that every aspect of the project is kept on schedule – especially as the UK Minister for Overseas Development will be visiting the site when she comes in October. I'm sure the British will be glad the school has opened on time.'

Luther took his sunglasses from the top pocket of his jacket and stood up. 'I also will see Her Excellency today,' he announced, watching Beatrice with the ferocious dark iris of his left eye. 'I will make sure she is aware of the situation.'

'It's reassuring to know that the Special Bureau is taking such a close interest,' Joseph said.

'The Special Bureau is concerned with everything that affects the position of the government. It is our job to be vigilant always.' And, shaking his head disapprovingly at Beatrice, he walked out into the burning dust.

'That's him, isn't it, Father?' Beatrice said, as soon as he had left. 'That's the man who's been bullying Ann Odinga and the others.' She glared at Joseph. 'You know him. You knew his name.'

'Yes.'

'Then why didn't you tell me? Why didn't you say the Special Bureau is behind Matiba Development?'

'We still don't know that,' he said. 'Luther's not above acting on his own account, throwing his weight around.'

'Slow down a second,' Ed said, a look of ferocious attention in his eyes. 'Just hold on. This guy Luther Magari – the man who's been threatening to clear people out of the slum – belongs to the Special Bureau. Is that right?'

Joseph nodded reluctantly. 'He's a colonel in the SB.'

'But you're saying he's not actually working for the government.'

'I'm just saying we don't know. When officials abuse their positions to extort bribes, they're often acting on their own.'

'But, Father, this isn't some *kitu kidogo* – some backhander. This is a business operation. Matiba are clearing out the biggest slum in Kisuru. They're going to make tens of millions. Even a colonel in the SB wouldn't get involved in a scam like that without backing.'

Joseph held out his hands as the others glared at him across the table. Ed's face had turned bright red. He was staring directly at the older man, while a physical pressure in his chest made it hard to breathe. 'So, what are you saying?' he asked, after a silence. 'What does this mean? No, wait. I'll tell you what I think. This man Magari proves that the ministry is involved – that's clear, isn't it? It shows that Pamela Abasi's definitely involved. It's not just Milton getting greedy. No. This is a co-ordinated effort: clearing the land to develop it. It's a scam – a gigantic scam.'

'Father?' Beatrice urged.

'Well, it certainly looks that way,' he said quietly. 'It's possible. No,' he corrected himself. 'Let's be honest. On the basis of what we know, it's probable. Luther works closely with Pamela Abasi. He does a lot of her unofficial work.'

'Oh, well, that's wonderful,' Ed said, bringing his fists down on the table. 'That beats everything. The nephew steals the building funds while the hired muscle clears the land. Then the big men – the big women – sell Makera off to the highest bidder.'

'So, what do we do?' Beatrice asked.

'I'll talk to London,' Ed said. 'And meanwhile, I suppose, we carry on here. At least the school can open.'

'Well, whatever you suspect,' Joseph said, 'keep it to yourselves, won't you? I'll see what I can find out at the ministry. But keep your heads down – especially you, Bea.'

'Yes, Father.'

'I mean it. If this scam is what it seems, you'd better watch yourself.' He got to his feet. 'All right, I must go. I've got a meeting with the minister in half an hour.'

'What are you going to tell her?' Ed asked.

'I'm not sure. It requires some thought.'

Ed took out his phone and read a text. 'Oh, great. I forgot about that. I'm meeting Sarah in Aberdare. We're going to look at a house belonging to Pamela Abasi. I suppose I have to go.'

'Well, perhaps I can give you a lift as far as the roundabout,' Joseph said, holding the door for him. 'You should be able to get a taxi from there.' And he added to Beatrice: 'I'll see you later, my darling. Look after yourself.'

20

Ed reached Pamela Abasi's property on Villiers Street, in the Aberdare suburb, about ten minutes after Sarah and Archie. He found Sarah standing with Pamela's assistant Agatha on the driveway at the side of the house, looking down across a wide, well-watered lawn.

'Would you like to see the garden first?' Agatha suggested, when Sarah had introduced Ed. 'Your son could run around for a while.'

'That would be great,' Sarah said. 'Isn't it a lovely garden, Ed?'

He nodded, picking up Archie and giving him a hug. 'How far does it go?'

'The property extends to the river, Mrs Caine,' Agatha said. 'About three acres. But there's excellent security.'

'Come on, Archie,' Ed said. 'Let's look for monkeys. This way . . .' As soon as he put him down, the little boy toddled off across the driveway and on to the wide lawn.

'I'd better keep an eye on him,' Sarah said. 'He's a bit stir-crazy.'

'We can ask Ory to play with him, if you like.'

'Ory?'

'Oh, I'm sorry. Let me introduce the staff.' Agatha put out her hand towards the elderly guard, who was standing a few yards away with two young women. 'This is William, your *askari*, and these are his daughters, Mary and Ory.'

'Hello,' Sarah said. 'I'm Sarah Caine. This is my husband, Edward.' Ed smiled rigidly. 'That's Archie, over there.'

The women cast their eyes down diffidently, while Agatha and William exchanged a few words in Makhoto. Then William said something, and Ory set off in pursuit of Archie, who was halfway down the lawn by this time, tottering towards a group of flat-topped acacias.

'We can keep an eye on him from the veranda,' Agatha said. 'William's wife will be with us in a moment. She's fetching some lemonade. I'm afraid they weren't sure when to expect us.'

'Please don't apologise,' Sarah said, and she looked round for Ed, who was standing on his own at the edge of the drive, gazing out into the smoggy valley that separated Aberdare from the city centre. 'Are you coming, darling?' she called. 'Ed?' And to Agatha she added: 'I'm sorry. We'll be up in a minute.'

'Please take your time, Mrs Caine. There's no hurry. I'll be on the veranda.'

'What's the matter, love?' Sarah said, as she walked over to him. 'You hardly seem to be here.'

'No. I, er—' He glanced at Agatha. 'Are we alone? We really need to talk.'

Sarah took his hand. 'What's going on, love? You look so hassled.'

'Well, I've just been catching up with reality.'

'The project?'

He nodded. 'The whole thing's being eaten up by the *wabenzi* – it was never intended to help anyone in the slum. All the money's going straight to the politicians.'

'Oh, Ed, there are rumours like that with every development project.'

'Well, this time they're true.' He folded his arms, staring down into the valley that separated Aberdare from the rest of Kisuru. 'Joseph's come clean. You know how much I don't want to believe it, but there it is.'

'And you think Pamela's involved?'

'She's right at the centre of it. Like a fat bloody spider.' He glanced towards the villa. 'We need to be very careful, love. She isn't offering us this place out of the goodness of her heart. It's a bribe. She's keeping us on board.'

'Oh, come on, Ed! You can read too much into these things. How does it help her if we're living in one of her houses? God knows, she doesn't need the money.'

'That's not the point. It would put us in her debt. There's a clear conflict.'

'But how can you be sure? I mean, she's always been supportive – you said so yourself. She's stuck her neck out for the project. Hasn't she?'

'Of course she supported it. It's going to make her a fortune.'

'Joseph said that?'

'Joseph works for her. How much can he say? Solomon said it – but everyone thinks the same.'

'Solomon? The builder guy? So, really, we don't know – I mean, not for certain.'

'Everything points to her being involved, love. Everything.'

Sarah turned round distractedly to acknowledge Agatha, who was standing on the balcony next to a stout woman carrying a tray of glasses. 'That must be the housekeeper,' Sarah said. 'We should go and say hello. We don't want to be rude.'

But Ed took hold of her arm. 'All right. We'll look round the house, but we can't accept.'

'Darling,' she said, standing directly in front of him. 'Please look at this from my point of view. Where are we supposed to live? This is the first house I've seen that we can actually afford and which isn't a complete bloody dump. Absolutely the first.'

'We don't need all this – it's huge, far too big for us.'

'I know. But the other places were miserable, Ed. Please don't be impossible. We're not in the Home Counties. We can't weigh everything up so legalistically. Loads of expats rent from the Abasis. The new World Bank man is living in one of their houses. Agatha told me.'

'Just because everyone's doing it, that doesn't make it right.'

'God, darling, you can be so rigid sometimes. We've got to adjust a bit to the local culture.' But she had narrowed her eyes and now stood back a little. 'Oh, hold on. I know where all this

175

is coming from. You've been talking to Mike Owens, haven't you?'

'Yes. Among others.'

'I knew it. I knew that man would poison you against Pamela. He obviously can't bear her. He's obsessed with the Abasis. If you ask me, he hates seeing clever, well-educated black people in charge of this country. He can't reconcile himself with modern Africa. I thought so as soon as I saw him. He's a racist – I'm sure of it. There. I've said it. Don't tell me you haven't had the same thought.'

'I don't think so,' Ed said. 'I really don't get that impression. There are lots of people who share Mike's point of view – most of the Batangans I've met. I come across them every day in Makera. Mike's no different from other people in what he thinks about Batangan politics. He doesn't trust the tyrants.'

'Well, I don't trust him,' Sarah said. 'So we're square. Come on. We really must let Agatha show us round.'

'Yes, all right.'

'Look at Archie,' Sarah said. 'He's having a riot.'

'It's certainly a great garden.' Ed looked out towards the valley, the highway running through it, the city in the haze beyond. 'They say the whole of Kisuru used to be like this. Someone was telling me this valley was open savannah until the seventies. It was protected by planning laws. Imagine that. They called Kisuru "the Safari City". You could sit up here watching herds of giraffe and elephant kicking up the dust. God! Look at it now – warehouses and slums.'

'Come on, love,' Sarah said, and, taking Ed by the hand, she led him across the drive to the steps of the veranda.

'I'm hearing bad things about Makera.' Pamela Abasi sat behind her desk at the ministry, looking up at Joseph, who was standing directly in front of her in the middle of the room. 'Luther tells me you are using an unlicensed builder.'

'That's true, Minister – technically. Very few firms have the proper documentation, as you know. But I've seen his work and he seems capable enough.'

'That's not acceptable.'

'It certainly isn't ideal.'

'I assigned you to this project to make sure things were done properly. You must get rid of this firm.'

'They'll be gone by this evening, Minister.'

'Oh?'

'The building is almost complete.'

'And what about Mount Batanga Construction? You know they were scheduled to do the work. The whole thing had been agreed. Now these other people – these slum builders – have taken their place.'

'I'm afraid Mr Caine lost faith in Mount Batanga some time ago, Minister. He found it impossible to contact anyone there. And since the school building was already three months late, he felt he couldn't rely on them. The school has to open this week – he was quite determined about that. I really wasn't able to persuade him to wait any longer. The term is starting on Wednesday.'

'Don't talk to me about school terms,' she said, in a controlled monotone.

'I only mention it because I know Oona Simon is particularly interested in the educational aspect of the project. She will be reassured to see the school open and full of children.'

'You worry too much about the *wazungu*,' Pamela said, taking her eyes from Joseph and surveying the clean surface of her desk, on which were arranged half a dozen gold brooches in the form of miniature assegais. 'I've met Oona Simon. Actually she's an unimpressive, stupid little person. She comes out with a lot of embarrassing clichés about the responsibility she feels for the world's poor. You could take her to any school in Makera – she wouldn't know the difference. Anyway, they say she's in trouble. She won't be minister for long . . . And Edward Caine won't be

177

here much longer, either – you should remember that. You know what these NGO projects are like – they're mosquitoes. They come and go in a season.'

He smiled cautiously. 'That's quite true, Minister.'

'Of course it's true,' she shot back. 'The important thing is to manage them while they're here. That's what the government is paying you to do.'

'Of course, the bulk of the building work is still to be done,' Joseph pointed out calmly. 'The clinic is a high-specification unit and Global Justice are still relying on Mount Batanga to build that. It cannot be done by slum workmen. I'm sure even now that Edward Caine would be delighted to work with Mount Batanga, if they will only communicate with him. After all, they have already received their payment.'

'He needs to understand that business is managed differently in this country. He has to make a cultural adjustment. Everyone has to be patient in Africa.'

'I will tell him that, ma'am,' Joseph said. 'I believe he is a patient man. And a thorough one. Unfortunately, he's upset about the payments to Mount Batanga – the Global Justice money that has been paid out, with nothing to show for it. It makes him mistrustful.'

'You mean he is critical of my nephew's decision-making?'

'Not exactly, Minister. I'd say that more than anything he cannot decide what to think. I'm certain he would gladly work with Milton in order to straighten everything out.'

'Then you'll have to reassure him.'

'I will do my best, of course,' Joseph said, 'but it would be easier if I knew what Mount Batanga and the other contractors are intending to do.'

'Who can say? I'm as much in the dark as you.'

'Matiba Development have been particularly active in that neighbourhood,' he ventured. 'Some people are saying that Luther Magari is working for them. He has been identified several times, talking to residents.' He paused, watching Pamela's

178

hands as she took one of the ornamental spears from the desktop and pressed it end to end between her thumbs.

'And what have you said?'

'As little as possible, Minister. If Mr Caine believed there was a connection between Matiba Development and State House, or with this ministry, he would be forced to raise the matter with his trustees in London.'

'So, what does he think?'

'I'm not sure, ma'am. I've avoided asking him. I don't want him to form a definite view. It's much better that he remains in a state of uncertainty, looking for an honourable way forward, hoping for the best. As you say, Minister, he won't be here for long. He may come to accept that he'll never get to the bottom of things. In many ways that's the best outcome we can hope for.'

'We?'

'The government, Excellency.'

'The government. That's right.' She settled back in her chair and peered up at him. 'Your family has always served the rightful rulers of this country, Joseph. Long before the British came, and after they went away.' She held out the little spear towards him. 'Your father was one of the first men to be granted this honour, wasn't he? Warrior of the Burning Assegai, first class. Kenneth Makotsi himself presented the award.'

'Yes, Excellency.'

'It's time your services to the country were recognised, Joseph. Many people feel the same. It's hard to see why men like Charles Wanjui should be honoured and not you. It isn't right.' And when Joseph remained silent, she added, 'The President agrees. I have discussed it with him more than once.'

'It would be a great honour,' Joseph said.

'Well, loyalty must have its reward.' Pamela put the little assegai back into its dark blue box and snapped the lid shut. 'It's up to you, of course. There are many people in this country – *wazungu*, too – who would pay a good deal for your expertise.

As a matter of fact, I hear Matiba Development are looking for a non-executive director.' She chuckled. 'There's so much money being made in Kisuru property these days . . . Those boys really need someone like you – someone who won't let it go to his head, who'll take the long view.'

'Perhaps when I've retired, ma'am.'

'Well, these chances don't come up every day,' she said impatiently. 'I hope you don't wake up one morning and find your opportunities have all passed, that people are questioning your motives, and all of a sudden there's nobody to protect you. Don't spurn your own people, Joseph.' And she went on in Bakhoto: 'Even the greatest warrior cannot defeat the whole tribe. You should remember that. Beatrice must remember it, too. She has her whole future ahead of her.'

'Beatrice is leaving the project soon enough,' Joseph replied at once, his voice rising slightly for the first time. 'It's just work experience.'

'I hope she understands that,' Pamela replied. She nodded towards the door. 'I'm expecting Deepak Zaidi at five o'clock. Tell Lucy to show him in.'

'Yes, ma'am.'

'And, Joseph . . .'

'Minister?'

'Think it over, won't you? Don't get left out in the cold.'

Joseph raised his head as though he was about to say something, but he kept his lips pressed together, nodded to Pamela and walked out of the office.

21

At around seven on Monday evening, Machi climbed up on to the roof of the newly built school and waited in full view of the crowds, holding out his arms for silence. Hundreds of people were standing in the dark beyond the perimeter fence and along the road that led to Kwamchetsi Wachira Avenue. Here and there he could see their faces illuminated by the fires of the street traders, while inside the compound, the whole school was lit by the builders' floodlights. Gradually, as he waited there, in full view of the crowd, the singing and chanting around the site began to subside and he stepped towards the edge of the roof.

'Can I have silence?' he shouted. '*Karibuni*! Good evening – thank you. Just a moment – I have something important to tell you.' There was an outbreak of cheering somewhere near the main road, and a group of women started chanting, but then the sound died down again. 'Tonight the building work is finished,' Machi yelled. 'On Wednesday the Makera Project School will open for the new term. You can bring your children.' There was a long roar of approval, but Machi immediately raised his voice again: 'Tonight – tonight we are celebrating,' he shouted. 'Welcome to the party! Everyone is welcome.'

There was a kind of murmur in the dark, as the word spread out towards the edge of the crowd. Then, after a minute or so, when Machi had climbed down from the roof, the singing that had been going on and off all day was suddenly taken up by everyone at once, and the compound was filled with the sound.

Beatrice was in the office and broke off from her work to listen, first to Machi and the singing, then to the crowd closing in on the site from all around, as people surged through the gates. Turning off the desk lamp, she got up to look out of the window, but almost at once the door was thrown open behind her. She spun round with a gasp.

'Hey, Beatrice!' Solomon called, standing at the door. 'What are you doing in here? Everyone's asking for you.'

'No way,' she said. 'None of these people have heard of me.'

'Yes! They all know you ordered this work – everyone knows.' He went on more quietly as he walked towards her: 'Half of Makera is here tonight. Machi says the whole Shala neighbourhood is deserted – not a light on anywhere.'

'You're the one they've come to see,' she replied. 'You should make a speech.'

'Oh, no speeches. I keep my head down.'

'That doesn't seem like you.' She breathed in the strong, gingery smell of his aftershave. 'In any case, they all want to thank Solomon Ouko. You mustn't disappoint them.'

Outside, through the window, they could see the crowds moving across the compound, their faces caught for a moment in the builders' lights.

'The band is coming now,' Solomon said. 'Machi is fixing it. Then we can dance.' Calmly, keeping his eyes on hers, he touched her cheek with the back of his hand. 'Or we can go somewhere quiet – just us. We can be alone. It's up to you.'

Beatrice remained as she was, examining his neck and jawline in the half-light, listening to the chanting in the compound outside. 'Don't you think we should go outside?' she said quietly.

'If you like.' Putting his arm round her waist, he pulled her close. 'We can do whatever you want.'

'Perhaps I don't know what I want.'

'I think you do,' he said.

But she shook her head. 'How can I? I hardly know you.'

'You think I'm not serious? You think I could change my mind?'

'People change their minds all the time. Besides, is it really me that you want?' She bit her upper lip, resting a hand on his chest and very gently pushing him away. 'You see me, and you start to imagine things. You think if we were together we'd understand each other. I imagine that, too, as though we're connected – secretly linked together.' She raised her head, looking up at him. 'But that won't happen. We're not free like that. There are so many things to keep us apart – so many obstacles. We'll never know each other, not really.'

'I'll tell you something,' he said, after a moment.

'Yes?'

'In your heart, I know you're afraid.'

'So, now you're reading my mind?'

'Of course it makes you angry, but I'm right. I'm afraid, too. That's how I know.' He went on, as she turned away and the crowd started singing again. 'When I was a child, a good man – a priest – told me something I always remember. I was scared when I was small, always terrified. And I used to do bad things, violent actions, to show how brave I was. But this priest said to me: "You do bad things to conquer your fear, but the opposite of fear is not violence, not pride or hatred. No, those are the consequences of being afraid. The opposite of fear is gentleness . . . patience. Love."'

Beatrice had stepped back and was studying his face with minute attention. 'And when you heard that,' she asked, 'did you stop being afraid?'

He smiled. 'No. Not for a long time. But I remembered what he said.' Taking her hand, he raised it to his lips and kissed her fingers. 'Well, the band's starting. I think we should dance, don't you?' And he led her outside.

The crowds were still spread throughout the surrounding corridors and access road, as far as the marketplace on Kwamchetsi Wachira Avenue. All around the compound, male voices were chanting in Kishala, overlaid by a descant from the women and children, while the diesel generator chugged along in the background. Coloured spotlights had been rigged up in the school playground, illuminating the musicians on their raised platform as they set up their equipment, but beyond the compound, when Beatrice peered out into the slums, everything was pitch black. Even the stars in the sky were blocked by the smog.

Solomon and Beatrice walked through the crowd towards the band. Someone struck a chord on an electric guitar, and one of the singers roared a greeting to the audience. Immediately the chanting in the streets disintegrated into thunderclaps of shouts and whistling. Then the three singers lined up at the front of the little stage, the man with the guitar nodded at the others, and the music started.

Beatrice was pressed against Solomon by the crowds. At first she concentrated on the rapid, intricate singing as she danced, looking about to avoid staring at Solomon, surveying the faces in the crowd instead: the three singers sharing the microphone, the drummer with a sweatband round his head. Stephen and Martha were standing by the office, and Beatrice caught sight of Ed, who was standing on a pile of building timber, taking a swig from a bottle of Tusker.

It was still unbearably muggy, but she could feel a breeze from the north and put her head back to let it cool her face, smiling to herself.

'What's so funny, Miss Kamunda?' Solomon called, above the music.

'I don't know.' She watched his face in the coloured light, and an intense feeling of exultation seized her heart. 'I feel so strange, like a boat – a little boat floating down a big, wide river . . .'

He came up close again, raising his hands to frame her face. 'Do you want to stop dancing?'

'No,' she said. 'I want to go on all night.'

'Then I'm glad!' he exclaimed. 'I'm so glad!'

The tempo of the music was increasing, the singers rapping out their words faster and faster, but Beatrice and Solomon had started to dance more slowly, and for half an hour or more, despite the deafening noise and the pressure of the crowd, it seemed to Beatrice that she was alone with him – that they had retreated far away and were together in private, dancing and turning around one another. Then Solomon took her hands, pulling her towards him. For the first time she put her arms around him, closing her eyes.

She didn't look up until Solomon stopped dancing. The band had finished a song, but instead of another starting, the music died away completely. Then Beatrice heard someone cry out at the far side of the compound. When she looked up she saw Ed, still standing on the pile of timber, gazing towards the slums to the east.

'What is it?' she asked. 'Something's happened.'

'Look at the horizon,' Solomon said, pointing to the other side of the compound. 'The sky's turning red.'

'*Moto! Moto!*' a man shouted. And at once other people began to yell, '*Moto!* Fire!'

The people around them were trying to get away, running out from the area around the school and crossing the compound to reach the gates. Beatrice could feel herself being pushed away from Solomon.

'What shall we do?' she cried, raising her voice over the screaming.

Solomon continued to look out across the heads of the crowd towards the red glow to the east. 'Get to the band,' he said at last. 'Tell them we need to use the microphone.'

Beatrice pushed against the flow of the crowd, trying to reach the stage.

'It's moving fast,' someone yelled. 'The fire's getting bigger – the wind's taking it!'

'Out of my way!' a woman shrieked. 'My children are there – all my children! I have to get back!'

Stephen was one of the first to get out of the compound gates. He raced into the labyrinth of corridors to the east, sprinting the length of a dozen alleyways before he came to a stop about twenty yards from the flames. Although the fire had started less than an hour before, it was already consuming whole sections of the streets between his own house and the Global Justice site. Seeing at once that it was impossible to get through that way, he turned north, hurrying along the alleyways a couple of blocks from the edge of the blaze.

Even at that distance from the fire, he could feel the heat pricking his eyes and tightening the skin across his face. He raced on against the flow of refugees who filled the corridors, and pushed his way through families with young children who were standing bewildered at the intersection of the corridors. Then, as he turned east, he noticed something glistening and seething in the gutter ahead of him; and leaping into an open doorway, he watched as an exodus of rats stampeded past, screeching in terror.

Stephen hurried on into the undamaged area to the north of the fire, where teams of young boys armed with sticks were roaming from house to house along the edge of the blaze, searching for loot. He ran past them, without slowing down, and along a series of narrow corridors until he turned right on to one of the principal alleyways that led south from the airport road into his own neighbourhood, near the centre of Makera.

Then, quite suddenly he came to a stop, peering about through his stinging eyes. He could see at once where he was. The neighbourhood rubbish tip was clearly visible in the firelight to his left – parts of the lower slopes were still smouldering – and he knew for certain that his own street lay directly in front of him. But when he tried to identify the familiar landmarks, he could make out nothing at all. Every shack had collapsed. The contours of the alleyways and the line of the sewers had been obliterated by a landslide of corrugated iron. There was no courtyard with the bicycle-repair shop, no washing lines, no overloaded telegraph post – no noise, even, except the roar of the fire being driven south by the wind. The only object he recognised was a tin sign, painted with the words 'Christian Fellowship Bicycle

Repairs', and he moved towards it, stepping on to a sizzling metal sheet. But he jumped back with a shout when it slid sideways underfoot. Then, as he retreated, there was a muffled explosion directly in front of him, and the flattened wall of a house, which had been steaming and hissing all this time, suddenly burst into flames.

Stephen stared at the debris. His body was shaking, his heart pounding violently. An almost photographic image asserted itself in his mind: of his mother, Tom and Ruth buried under the wreckage. And at once a new feeling filled his heart, a perfectly simple, unsentimental consciousness of hatred, which seemed to give him strength and blocked out every other emotion. As he watched the remaining sections of corrugated tin buckle and subside with a groan, he declared out loud, in Kishala: 'I will kill the men who did this. I myself will find them and kill them.' Then, forcing himself to turn round, he walked away.

Joseph arrived in a car, but it was impossible to get through from Kwanchetsi Wachira Avenue, so he set out on foot to the Global Justice site. All around him in the dark streets family groups were sitting on the mud or standing between the tin buildings, and everywhere he could hear children crying.

Beatrice saw him as he reached the gates. She ran to him through the crowd and threw her arms around him.

'Are you all right, Bea? Are you hurt?'

'I'm fine.'

'Thank God.'

Her eyes moved around the compound. 'A lot of people are missing, Father. We don't have time to write down the names so we're telling everyone to form in groups according to their neighbourhoods – it's all we can do.' She nodded towards Martha, who was crouching by the gatepost, rocking back and forth in the half-light. 'Her little brother and sister were in the fire,' she said quietly, 'and her mother – Ann Odinga, the woman

I've been working with. The poor girl sent the children home just before the fire broke out.'

Joseph stared down at Martha's head. Then he crouched beside her, laying his hand on her shoulder. Beatrice turned away to survey the horizon. The sky was still orange, but the fire was no longer moving southwards, and when she looked back to her father, she caught sight of Machi, hurrying into the compound with a group of workmen, followed immediately by Solomon and Ed.

'Petrol,' Ed said at once, wiping his eyes as he came towards them.

'Petrol?'

'The fire was started with petrol. We found the canisters – five-gallon drums. I saw them myself.'

'Are you sure?'

'We both saw them, didn't we, Solomon?'

'Machi, too,' Solomon said. 'One of his boys found them.'

'Whereabouts?' Beatrice asked. 'Where did the fire start?'

'Near Ann Odinga's place – next to that rubbish tip. Literally in her backyard. We found four drums there.'

'They used rats to spread the fire,' Solomon put in. 'Some children saw the whole thing. They had rats in big sacks, soaked them in petrol and threw them on to the fire. The rats ran out in every direction, burning everything.'

'It was deliberate,' Ed broke in. 'No question. Even the timing – while everyone was here at the party. Otherwise it wouldn't have spread so far.'

'Those boys,' Joseph said, 'the ones who saw it all, where are they now?'

'They wouldn't leave their homes – there are looters everywhere.'

'You got their names?'

Solomon nodded. 'Stephen is with them. He's in a bad state.'

'Father?' Beatrice said. 'What are we going to do?'

'Let's collect the evidence,' he said, 'put together a case. I'll have a word with Wycliffe Gatere tomorrow.'

'He won't help,' Beatrice declared. 'Everyone knows he's a government stooge.'

'He's still Chief Superintendent of the Kisuru Police,' Joseph replied firmly. 'I'll make sure he takes witness statements, treats the area as a crime scene.' He glanced at his daughter, but her attention had been caught by something on the ground near the compound gates. Martha had got to her feet, and was now making her way towards the mass of bodies outside. They watched as she pushed through the crowd, shoving people aside, until she reached a group of small figures in the half-darkness.

'She's found somebody,' Joseph said. 'There – that boy and girl. Is that them, Beatrice?'

'I don't know. I must go and see.'

Beatrice found Martha crouching by the gate, hugging two small children, one in each arm. 'Where have you been?' she was sobbing. 'Where *were* you? You were supposed to be at home, Tom – at home. I thought you were with Mama. Oh, God – oh, my dear Lord! I thought you were in the fire . . .'

22

Ed sat on the veranda at the Kamundas' house, on the opposite side of the table from Beatrice, clasping a big cup of coffee and squinting into the morning sunshine.

'As I see it, we have three options,' Joseph was saying. 'The first is the easiest. We ignore the fire – simply put it out of our minds. You would have to say in public that you believe it was an accident, and carry on with the project – try to build the clinic, run the school, go on with the water supply . . .'

Ed shook his head. 'We can't do that. It's impossible.'

'It's the safest thing,' Joseph said. 'Safest for us, and safest for the people in Makera. Also, if it worked, it would mean not all the money had been wasted.'

'But we can't say it was an accident,' Ed insisted. 'People know it was arson. Nobody would trust us.'

'That's true,' Joseph said. 'You'd have to manage the reaction in the slums.'

'What's the second option?' Beatrice said.

'I know you think the first is bad,' Joseph went on, 'but the second is a great deal worse. Option two is that we make our suspicions public – that we speak out right away, without solid evidence. We rattle a lot of cages, get ourselves into a fight with Matiba, the Special Bureau – these people, whoever they are – and we're not prepared. Then we're in great danger ourselves – even you, Mr Caine, you and your family. The Makera residents will be in peril, too. So the project will be destroyed. No school. No clinic. Nothing to show for the money that's been spent. Failure all round.'

'London would intervene before that happened,' Ed said. 'They're not going to turn a blind eye.'

'London would need evidence, too,' Joseph replied. 'Batanga is a regional ally. The British are not going to jeopardise friendly relations without a rock-solid reason. And, besides, the Wachira government will say, "You think we're corrupt, you don't like us. All right. But what happens if you undermine us? Who's going to take over? Do you really want to see Batanga ruled by Patrick Ochola, bankrolled by the Chinese?" No, no, believe me, the British will be cautious.'

'So, we're stuck,' Beatrice said. 'That's it, isn't it? That's how we do things, economic and social development Batanga-style.'

'There is another possibility,' Joseph said.

'Don't tell me, the worst of all?'

'No. On balance, I think it's the least bad option. First you say that the fire is under investigation. I will speak to Wycliffe Gatere this morning and get him to commit the resources. Then we build our case. We establish proof before we make any public accusations.'

'What if he refuses?' Beatrice said.

'Well, I won't succeed,' Joseph replied. 'There is a chance of that. Wycliffe may be implicated in some way. I can still ask him to act correctly. Or would you rather I said nothing?'

'No, Father.'

'All right. I'll talk to him. He is family, after all. Wycliffe was a cousin of my late wife, Rachel,' he went on, addressing Ed. 'They were childhood friends, very close. He's always been a loyal friend. I will talk to the British High Commissioner, too – off the record. I'm seeing him tomorrow night in any case. We need to gather our allies, but we must do it discreetly. I'll have a word with my colleague Charles Wanjui as well – you've met him, Ed: the head of the civil service.'

'Yes, of course.'

'If anyone knows what's going on, Charles will.'

'What about us?' Ed asked. 'What should I do?'

'Talk to your people in London. Let them know what's going on. Find out who your friends are – who'll fight for the project if the politics turn against it. You'll need to go there, talk to them face to face.'

'I was thinking the same.'

'But, Father, what about the evidence? You say we need proof.'

'That's true. But we need to build our case carefully. You mustn't do anything that will alert Matiba. You can't go about asking for witness statements or voicing your opinions. If the Special Bureau is involved, everyone who knows about it is in danger. You can't ask people to risk their lives if you won't be able to protect them.'

'What can I do?'

'You keep your head down, Bea. Don't let them know what you think.'

'Do nothing?'

'I didn't say that. Bide your time, that's all. Don't make yourself conspicuous. After all, we may get the evidence we need from Gatere's investigation – or from Charles Wanjui. All right,' he went on, getting to his feet. 'We've got a long day ahead of us. I'll call you this evening, Ed.'

Solomon and Machi were at the compound when Ed and Beatrice arrived. 'We have a problem with the fire area,' Machi said at once. 'The residents want their land back. They want to start rebuilding. People are angry at the delay.'

'But how can they rebuild?' Ed asked. 'The ground's still hot.'

'It's not too hot for them,' Machi said. 'Slum people are always ready to build – and they know how. They'll find the materials somehow. If we let them move back on the land, the new houses will be up by tomorrow morning.'

'Well, we can't have that. We'll lose the crime scene – the evidence.'

'I'll go and talk to them,' Solomon said. 'I'll explain things . . .' And he called to Stephen, who was standing in the shade of the office building a few yards away, 'Hey, *kijana*, we've got a job to do. I need your help.'

Stephen stared towards Solomon with bloodshot eyes, without seeming to hear him.

'Machi, you come, too,' Solomon said. 'We'll sort this out.'

He walked out of the compound in silence, followed by Stephen and Machi. Then as they approached the fire site, he addressed Stephen, in a low voice: 'I'm very sorry to hear about your mother, young man. That is a great sorrow.'

'Yes, Mr Ouko.' Stephen kept his eyes on the ground, controlling his voice.

'I know what it's like to lose people you love. It's the worst pain you can feel.' And he added, as Stephen looked away: 'Where are your brother and sisters now?'

'The little ones are with Martha, sir. She's gone to see about the stall. Our things were looted in the fire – the stove and the frying pan. Everything's gone.'

Solomon nodded. 'If you and your sister need a business loan, talk to Machi. He'll introduce you to a man who can help.'

'Thank you, Mr Ouko.'

'You don't want to deal with the moneylenders along the avenue.' Stephen looked sideways at him. 'Where are you all going to sleep tonight?'

'I don't know, sir. Maybe in the school building. Lots of people are staying there.'

'Is there any space at the warehouse, Machi?'

'Yes, sir, plenty.'

'Well, we need a caretaker there,' Solomon said, as they approached the site of the fire. 'A proper *askari* to keep the place secure. I want you to move in there, Stephen, you and your family. You stay as long as you need, till you've rebuilt your house. Can you do that for me?'

'Yes, Mr Ouko. Thank you.'

'Don't thank me. It's a job. You keep an eye on the warehouse – there are lots of thieves in the garment district, especially now. We can't leave the place without a guard.'

Wycliffe Gatere was sitting in his office in the old colonial police headquarters at the edge of the government quarter. An ancient fan rotated above his desk and, through a half-raised venetian blind, he looked out over the high wall of State House gardens across several acres of well-watered lawn. He was pouring himself some tea when Joseph rang, and it took him a moment to put aside the cup and switch on the machine that recorded his telephone conversations. 'Joseph, how good to hear you,' he said, in an easy-going bass voice, as he sat back in his chair. 'How are you? How's that marvellous girl of yours?'

'We're fine,' he said. 'Very well. And you? Alice and the boys?'

'Yes, all well. They're on holiday at the coast.'

'Well, please give them my regards,' Joseph said. 'It's been too long . . . Listen, Wycliffe, I've just come from Makera. Pamela Abasi has put me in charge of government liaison with a British NGO working on a project there. There was a fire last night.'

'There's a fire every night in Makera. The place is a liability.'

'This one was started deliberately. A lot of people have died.'

'It's too bad,' he said, rotating his cup so that he could pick it up by the handle. 'I wish we could clear the whole damn area. It's impossible to police a slum like that. My men can't even make foot patrols there.'

'Even so, I think you should deploy them now.'

'What on earth for?'

'There are political implications. The British are getting concerned: there have been a lot of delays and irregularities – and now this fire. We need to reassure them that the authorities are behind the project. If not, they'll start to pull out.'

'You've discussed the situation with the minister?'

'We talked yesterday. I'm on my way to see her again now.'

'What do you want me to do?'

'Seal off the area to the north of the fire. Treat it as a crime scene. Get the fire department down there. They refused to come out last night.'

'What can they do? You can't get the vehicles into Makera. There's no water. We can't ask the men to piss on the fire.'

'They must send their forensics division. We need to treat the deaths as murder.'

'I can't do that,' he protested. 'Do you have any idea how many murders there are in Makera every week? How many rapes, robberies? We don't have the manpower to log them. There's Shala on Shala violence, drug gangs, communal violence – it's the law of the jungle down there.' He gulped a mouthful of tea. 'The fact is, we've started finding weapons and explosives in Makera. We're dealing with an Army of Celestial Peace fifth column – we could find ourselves fighting the war in those corridors. Seriously. And you want me to start allocating resources to one crime?'

'At least twenty-five people have died. To say nothing of the destruction of property.'

'But what evidence is there, Joseph? We can't work on the basis of rumours.'

'There's physical evidence – empty petrol cans.'

'Well, if you know something definite, you must let us have it.'

'I'm just saying we need to show we're serious, Wycliffe. This project is worth a lot of money. If the British pull out because of this . . .'

'The donors never pull out.'

'There's always a first time. Just start an investigation. I'm not asking this as family, I'm asking it as a servant of the government.'

There was silence while Wycliffe finished his tea. 'I'll tell you what. I'll send one of my captains up there with a couple of Jeeps. He can make an assessment and we'll take it from there.'

'Thank you.'

'Don't worry about it. You're right. We don't want the *wazungu* jumping to conclusions. Please greet Beatrice for me.'

'I will. My regards to the boys and Alice. Let me know how your captain gets on.'

'I'll keep in touch.'

Wycliffe sat in silence after he had hung up, gazing across the room at the portrait of Kwamchetsi Wachira that hung between the tall windows. The friendly expression on his face slowly faded. For a moment he winced and closed his eyes. But he roused himself, put aside his Thermos, and called to his secretary in the next room. 'Esther, get me Luther Magari's office. Tell him we need to speak on the red line.'

Late in the afternoon, when the ground had cooled, Ed and Solomon set off across the burned-out districts of the slum with Machi, Stephen and a dozen others spread out in a line to search for bodies. Looters had picked over the whole area during the night. The petrol cans had disappeared, along with every knife and spoon, cooking pot and metal cup from the shacks that were still standing. Even the smouldering debris had been looted for sheets of corrugated tin, aerials, doorknobs, nails. Under the surface, the rats had returned.

By about six o'clock, they reached the area below the hill of rubbish that marked the boundary of Stephen's own neighbourhood. Stephen slowed, then stopped, pushing his stick carefully into the gaps between the collapsed houses.

'Hey, Rags, you all right?' Machi called.

Stephen wiped sweat from his neck as he peered into the blackened debris.

'Is this your neighbourhood?' Machi asked, walking up to him across the crunchy metal sheets, while Solomon approached from the other direction.

Stephen had stopped searching, and was standing with his face turned up towards the sun and his stick over his shoulder. 'There's a body here,' he said.

Machi signalled to a team of stretcher-bearers.

'I know it's her,' Stephen said, watching the men as they started uncovering the body. 'I should get her out. It's my job – I'm her first-born son.' He looked at Solomon. 'I should have protected her. It was my responsibility.'

'Nobody could have known,' Solomon said.

'But I know now,' Stephen replied. 'Everyone knows the fire was started by the Bakhoto. I will wait, Mr Ouko – I can wait a long time. Then, one day, I will find the men who did this.'

'Is that what you think? You're going to have your revenge?'

'You would do the same. You are Shala, too.'

'When you're angry, *kijana* – when you've suffered – there seems no other way. But in the end, violence and anger will crush us all. There's no end to injustice in this world, Stephen. If we all took our revenge, who would be left alive?'

The men had uncovered the body – a shrunken, charred figure, curled in the foetal position – and laid it on the stretcher. Then, putting a blanket over it, they started to carry it away, humming a Shala lament.

'Go with her to the compound,' Solomon said. 'Pay your respects, you and your sister. Machi and I will come. We'll see you later.'

Sarah had been waiting up for Ed, sitting behind the mosquito mesh on the veranda, reading her way through the annual reports and press releases of the various women's co-ops and self-help organisations she had visited over the last couple of weeks. When she heard Ed's taxi, she turned off the light and went to the front of the house, watching while he climbed out of the car and slouched towards the house.

'Oh, darling, you look terrible.' He dropped his bag at the top of the steps and for a moment they held each other. 'Let me get you something to eat. I bet you haven't had anything all day . . . Grace made a lamb stew.' She pressed his face between her hands as she examined it. 'Why don't you have a shower while I heat it up? Go on, love. You'll feel more human.' And when he didn't move she asked: 'What happened today?'

'We found some of the bodies,' he said. 'Thirty-six so far. And we're nowhere near completing the search – we've covered about a quarter of the area. In some houses a whole family was killed together. You can see them all lying there – parents, grandparents, babies, children Archie's age, pregnant women. Just charcoal shapes. They had no time to get out, the fire spread so fast.'

'Oh, my love . . .'

'I keep going over things in my head. We've got to make some decisions.'

She put a hand out anxiously towards him, but he stepped away. 'I'd better have a shower.'

'Yes, of course. Go on. We'll talk while you're eating.'

'I think the fire was deliberate,' he said, as he went upstairs. 'It was started on purpose.'

'But why? Who would do that?'

'The people who control the land.'

'God, it's unbelievable.'

'Well, nobody seems all that surprised. Beatrice, her father, Solomon – none of the people who really know the country. It's almost as though they expected it.'

'I've got to go to London,' Ed told her, as he started to eat. 'Why don't we all go? Archie can see his grandparents. I might even make some progress sorting the project out – things may start to look a bit clearer.'

Sarah had poured herself a glass of Sauvignon Blanc. 'I can't just disappear to London, love. I'm still getting fixed up here – I'm meeting people every day, thanks to Pamela. I'm expecting a job offer.'

'It wouldn't be for long.'

'How can you be sure? It could take ages. In any case, I don't see how anything's going to get sorted out in England. What can they do?'

'They control the funding.'

'But, my darling, we've only been here two months – we've barely moved into this place and Archie's just beginning to acclimatise. The warmth is really good for him. He loves it – he loves Ory, too. Do you really want to uproot him again?

198

Besides, you haven't explained what's going on – it's all so mysterious.'

'Okay,' he said, pushing aside his empty plate. 'I'll tell you what I think. Where do I start? First, the project has been adopted by the Batangan government so that various very rich people can make a lot of money out of it. They're waiting for us to put in the basic infrastructure, then they'll get the police to move the people off the land, bulldoze the slums and turn Makera into a suburb of expensive flats and shopping malls.'

'Who are these people? You're talking about Pamela.'

He nodded. 'She certainly did it very well. I never suspected.'

Sarah picked up her glass. 'What about Beatrice? Or Joseph? You're not seriously saying they're out to steal from the project?'

'No. Joseph and Beatrice are caught in the middle, Solomon, too. I'm pretty certain about that. It's one of the things that worries me. If I blow the whistle, what happens to them? Pamela appointed Joseph to look after her interests. If he fails, his career's over.'

'I can't understand Pamela's involvement . . . She's been so good to us, and she's got a fantastic reputation. Why would she do this?'

'She has different reputations in different places, love. Somehow or other, she's accumulated a gigantic amount of money.'

'Well, of course. She inherited it from her husband. Besides, she's a clever businesswoman.'

'I know you like her. I quite like her, too. But she's taken a great interest in this project, and her nephew – whom she appointed – has grabbed the entire building budget.'

'Can you actually prove all this? I mean, is there any definite evidence?'

'We know Milton's got the money, and we know Special Bureau people are trying to clear the site. Now they've committed murder. But you're right. There's no legal proof that Pamela's behind it all. We need evidence. That's what Joseph keeps saying.'

'So, until then, we've got to give her the benefit of the doubt, haven't we? That's just ordinary fairness.'

Ed looked at her blankly. 'The thing that worries me is that Joseph and Beatrice are so exposed. Even if we had our proof, how can I blow the whistle on the Batangan government without endangering them? In the time it takes to explain everything to London – by the time Sue and the trustees have decided what to do – it'll probably be too late. You know Milton threatened me,' he added, after a while.

'Milton? That's just macho stuff.'

'He threatened you and Archie, too.'

'How?'

'He said this is a dangerous country.' Ed fixed Sarah in the eye. 'It was before the fire – before all those people were killed. He said, "You and your family ought to go home." He was quite serious.'

Sarah thought for a moment. 'Well, one thing's clear. We can't be bossed about by *him*. I'm sure he'd love to pack us back to London – it'd be perfect for him. He'd have the whole project to himself. Why do what he wants?'

'I'd just be so much happier if we were together,' Ed said. 'I don't want to leave you here alone. It doesn't feel right.'

She reached out across the table and took his hands. 'You're tired, love. Let's talk it over tomorrow. We both need some sleep.'

'You'll think about it?'

She nodded, leading him towards the door.

'There's no point lying down,' Ed protested. 'I won't sleep – my brain's racing.'

'I'll get you a tranquilliser,' she said, turning off the lights and putting an arm round his waist. 'Come on, love, come to bed.'

Part Three

23

The architects Alfred Kimathi Associates had their head office in one of the brand new tower blocks to the south of the Ministry of Development, at the edge of a six-acre building site, its glass and steel façade washed all day long by a storm of red dust.

'I have important documents for AKA,' Beatrice told the woman behind the desk, brushing the sleeve of her grey suit.

'Eighth floor,' she said. 'Take the middle lift – the others aren't working. You're supposed to sign in.'

'It's all right,' Beatrice called, as she crossed the hall, 'I won't be a moment.'

In the reception area, two women in suits were sitting behind a counter of green glass, overlooking a balsawood model of a big urban development. Beatrice paused to examine the miniature city. There was a circle of office blocks around a piazza with fountains, palm trees and open-air restaurants. Little Jeeps and Land Cruisers had been placed on the ramp approaching the car park of the mall and on the wide roads, while tiny plastic figures sat on the benches or stood on glass-covered escalators.

'Can I help?' one of the receptionists asked.

'Yes, of course.' Beatrice approached with a diffident smile. 'I wonder if I could make an appointment to see your human-resources director.'

'You want to make an appointment?' The woman had an elongated face with high cheekbones. 'You need to have an appointment before you come here.'

'I've tried to contact him many times and he's always busy. I just thought if I came in person, he might be able to see me.'

'I don't think so, young lady.'

'Oh, please!' she said. 'It means so much to me. This is the firm I want to work for – I don't care what kind of job. And I don't mind waiting – it doesn't bother me at all. I'll just sit over there. I won't be in anyone's way.' She indicated the sofa by the entrance to the office. 'If he can't see me today, I'll leave my CV and come back tomorrow.'

The two receptionists looked at each other; the one with the long face cast her eyes to heaven. 'All right. I'll tell his secretary you're waiting. Go and sit down.'

At first Beatrice sat up straight on the sofa, but gradually she let herself slip down, until her head was out of sight of the reception desk, hidden behind the model city. Then, for an hour or more, she remained where she was, watching the firm's employees come and go. Sometimes the office door was held open as people stopped to talk, and Beatrice could see architects working inside at special drawing tables, poster-sized technical plans displayed on large boards and, at the far end of the office, right next to the lavatories, a door marked 'Archives'. Finally, around one o'clock, the long-faced receptionist went out to the lifts, and a few moments later a group of middle-aged men arrived and stood around the model, discussing it in loud voices, until the other receptionist led them to the board room.

Beatrice jumped up, straightened her skirt and let herself into the main office, gripping her briefcase and marching straight towards the archives. A couple of young men looked up to watch her pass, and she smiled in acknowledgement without slowing. At the door, she hesitated, glanced behind her and went inside.

A series of tall metal cases ran the length of the room, each holding hundreds of files. Beatrice could hear someone moving about and coughing, and there was a whispered conversation going on to her right, but she immediately walked along the ends of the cabinets, turned quickly into the stack marked 'L to M' and, leaning down, started to search for the file on Matiba Development. At first she found nothing except plans for beach houses and suburban villas – there was no file where Matiba's should have been – and she crouched on the floor in frustration, pressing her head against the metal cabinet. Then, not knowing what else to do, she opened the drawer to the right and examined the first set of papers. It took her a second or two to understand what she had found. The folders in this drawer were not named after individual clients: each one referred instead to a particular project. As she checked the information on the front page of one file after another, she found that in every case the project had been commissioned by Matiba Development. She knelt on the floor, ran her finger along the tabs and stopped suddenly. She let out a silent gasp, then pulled out a big set of papers, much thicker than the rest, labelled 'Makera Development Project'.

There was a reading table at the far end of the stack, and she carried the file over to it and sat down. She had the impression that the man and woman who had been whispering to each other had left the archives, but she could still hear someone coughing out of sight behind one of the cabinets so she opened the papers as quietly as she could. The file contained a great deal of correspondence, most of it between an executive at Matiba Development and one of the senior architects, and a series of plans. Beatrice started to unfold them, looking for the most recent draft, and found herself staring at a map of the Makera slums, from Kwamchetsi Wachira Avenue in the west to the railway tracks in the east. But instead of Makera's rabbit warren of corridors and tiny yards, with its tens of thousands of shacks and hundreds of rubbish heaps, the land was neatly dissected by a network of suburban streets, with large houses standing in their own gardens, blocks of flats and a shopping centre. She started to refold them, intending to put them into her bag – when a man's voice addressed her from the next bay. 'How are you getting on?' he said.

Beatrice, lowered the plan. 'Fine, thank you.'

'I don't think we've met.' He approached her, clutching a sheaf of papers under his arm. 'Moody Maore.'

'How do you do?' She got up to shake his hand. 'I'm Alison Kantai,' she said. 'I'm doing a short internship here.'

'Not *too* short, I hope.' He held on to her hand and stepped a little closer. 'If there's anything you need, you let me know.'

'Yes, I will.' Beatrice moved sideways, so that she was standing between him and the open files. 'Perhaps we could have tea together,' she suggested. 'There's so much to learn – I'm still getting my head around it all. I could do with some help . . .'

'It would be a pleasure,' he said.

'This evening, perhaps?'

He released her hand, smiling. 'You come and find me.'

'Oh, I will.'

As he backed away, she cleared her throat. 'Mr Maore . . . ?'

'Moody, please.'

'Moody. Where can I photocopy a sheet like this?' She held up the plan, blank side towards him.

'Right there,' he said, pointing to the next alcove. 'Do you want me to show you?'

'No, thank you. I mustn't detain you. I'll be fine.'

'I'm sure you will,' he said. 'I'll see you later, Alison.'

Beatrice marched back through the office, heading for the reception area, with her bag under her arm and a serious, preoccupied expression on her face. The two receptionists were back behind the desk, and when she came out the woman with the long face raised her head. 'And where have you been, young lady? No one gave you permission to go into the studio.'

'I had to go to the *choo*,' she said. 'I didn't think anyone would mind.'

'That is the toilet for visitors,' the receptionist replied, pointing at the sign beside her desk.

'I'm sorry. I didn't see.'

'Well, you should be more observant.' She went on: 'I have made an appointment for you. The personnel manager is willing to see you at one thirty.'

'Oh, thank you. Thank you so much.' Beatrice looked at her watch, backing towards the door. 'That's so kind of you.'

'And where are you going now? You should stay here. He wants to see you in fifteen minutes.'

'I'm just a bit nervous,' Beatrice said. 'I'm going to get some fresh air. I'll be back right away . . .' She opened the door to the main hallway and the lifts, but as she did so, Moody Maore appeared from the office.

'Ah, Alison, did you get that photocopy? All well?'

'Yes, thank you,' she said quietly.

The receptionist rose abruptly from her desk, staring at Beatrice.

'I'll see you later,' Moody said. 'Six o'clock in my office?'

'Yes,' she replied, backing out through the door. 'I look forward to it.'

'Mr Maore,' the receptionist asked, hurrying towards the hallway, 'do you know that young woman?'

'Alison? I was just chatting to her in Archives.'

'Did you say she was photocopying something?'

'Yes. Some plans, I think.'

'She had no business being there.'

'But she's an intern – she told me so.'

'Miss Sitanik,' the woman said, 'call Security right away.'

Joseph had found it exceptionally difficult to contact his old confidant Charles Wanjui. First thing on Monday morning, Charles's secretary at State House had promised to pass on Joseph's message, but Joseph had called another three times before he rang back.

'I was sorry to hear about the fire,' Charles said smoothly. 'It's bad luck.'

'Is it?' Joseph replied.

There was a pause, while Charles turned his back on the people he was with in the Cabinet Office. 'Listen, Joseph, I think we should talk.'

'Good. So do I.'

'I'll come to your house. Let me see . . . seven this evening?'

'Wouldn't you rather we met at the club?'

'No. Let's keep it private. We can have a drink together in peace – go over things.' Charles hesitated. 'Will Beatrice be there?'

'I don't know. Shall I ask her?'

'She's been involved in the Makera project.'

'Very much so.'

'Well . . .' Charles rubbed his forehead with his thumbnail '. . . probably better if you speak to her yourself – father to daughter.'

'Seven o'clock, then,' Joseph said.

'You know how much everyone admires you,' Charles said, when he had swallowed a mouthful of whisky. 'Your integrity, Joseph.'

'Do you think so?' He raised his eyebrows in amusement. 'I never thought integrity was a particularly popular character trait.'

'Well, of course you worry people. They think you're going to catch them out.'

'Not me. I made up my mind long ago not to be a whistle-blower – not even a spoilsport.'

'That was wise.'

'Prudent, anyway,' he replied. 'Who knows what sort of trouble wisdom might get you into?'

The two men sat in silence for a while, looking out from the terrace towards the bougainvillaea and the path to the empty swimming pool, where John was sweeping up jasmine petals.

'I hope you're not planning to abandon the habit of a lifetime,' Charles said.

'Is that what people are saying?'

'Well, some of your friends think you're getting too involved in this Makera project.'

'I don't think so,' Joseph said. 'The minister asked me to keep an eye on it, which I've done, but you know my opinion of projects like this. The thing had a bad look from the start.

Beatrice is upset – she's not as cynical as the rest of us, and she knew one of the women who was killed. They were quite friendly.'

'I'm sorry.'

'She was here earlier. She said she'd be back by eight. You'll probably see her.'

'I'm very fond of Beatrice. She reminds me of Rachel.'

Joseph nodded.

'She's got a lot of *you* in her, too – but that profile . . . She's a beautiful girl.'

'Except that now, all of a sudden, she's a beautiful woman.' Joseph contemplated his friend. 'The fire was started deliberately – you do realise that?'

'What kind of evidence have you got?'

'Pretty overwhelming. Witness statements, petrol canisters, evidence from the remains. It's all there if one takes the trouble to look. The fire started near Beatrice's friend's home. The people in the slums are saying the Special Bureau were hanging about: that they've been making themselves conspicuous over the last few weeks. That rumour has taken hold. You know how it is – once a thing like that is generally believed, nobody's going to listen to me, a Bakhoto in a suit, telling them otherwise.'

'There are other rumours, too,' Charles said. 'Not just rumours, either, reliable intelligence reports – ACP cells in the slums recruiting young boys to bring the war to Kisuru, arms caches, explosives, bomb-making materials. One of Patrick Ochola's lieutenants was arrested in Makera on Friday.'

'Yes, I heard.'

'He's being held at St Jude's.' Charles took another gulp of whisky, peering across the table at Joseph in the half-light. 'Under the circumstances, I'd be surprised if the Special Bureau wasn't keeping an eye on things in Makera, wouldn't you? I'd say they wouldn't be doing their job. After all, it's the biggest concentration of Shala in the city. The fact is, the military position in the north isn't as good as our people are being told. Wilson Abako has lost a lot of ground. Our men are deserting – going home for the harvest. Morale is very poor.' He added confidentially: 'You were right about that appointment. Abako's a politician, not a military leader. He's got no business wearing a general's uniform. But there's no point in going over that now. The last thing we need is an ACP bombing campaign in Kisuru. We must prevent that at all costs. We can't afford to be choosy about the Special Bureau's methods.'

'You think they started the fire?'

'I don't know,' he said. 'That's not a question I want to ask. And nor should you. You know the proverb – "No matter how faded and shabby she is, she's still my mother."'

Joseph looked away into the dark valley of the garden. 'I always wondered about that,' he remarked. 'Who is our mother, exactly?'

'You know what I mean,' Charles purred. 'Whatever happens, we can't allow the country to fall into the hands of the uncircumcised. We must maintain our discipline.'

Joseph shut his eyes in the darkness. There was a quite physical sensation of heat in his stomach, but when he spoke he sounded calm, almost indifferent, as if he was discussing an academic question. 'Unfortunately, it doesn't make much difference what I tell Ed Caine,' he said. 'The minister wants me to guide his responses, enable him to see things in a positive way. But the fire has frightened him – he's in a state of shock. It will take him time to come to terms with it.'

'Can't you persuade him to take a break?'

'He's going to London this week.'

'That's good.'

'I hope he'll get a sense of perspective.' Joseph raised his glass without putting it to his lips. 'Even before the fire, he was worried about the misuse of project funds. And I have to be careful what I say about that. He'll lose all confidence in me if I try to block his investigations. He's already beginning to think that some parts of the government are working against him.'

'You'll just have to manage him as best you can,' Charles said. 'He won't be here for long.'

'Well, it would be easier if I knew what was actually going on,' Joseph replied. He sipped his whisky. 'If I had the full facts, I could guide him in the right direction. As it is, he might come to all sorts of conclusions.'

'What does he know, exactly?'

'It's more a question of what he suspects. He realises that Milton is connected with Mount Batanga Construction.'

'Can he prove it?'

'I don't think so. Naturally he assumes that Matiba Development is controlled by the Abasis, although he can't be certain. And meanwhile everyone's telling him that the Special Bureau were responsible for the fire.' He shrugged, his eyes resting on Charles's placid face. 'Put yourself in his position. His worst nightmare is that members of the government have taken the project money to develop the land commercially, using the security service as their bailiffs. If he doesn't get to grips with the situation, if he goes along with it, he's complicit.'

'He's not complicit if he doesn't know.'

'He knows *something*'s going on,' Joseph said, and tipped back his tumbler. 'He couldn't prove it in court – but what difference does that make? A thing like this would never come to court, would it?' And he added, in a more urgent but quieter voice: 'Listen, Charles, you need to trust me with the facts. I can't stop him drawing his own conclusions, but if you tell me what he mustn't know – what I should lead him away from – we'd have a chance of neutralising him.'

Charles uncrossed his long legs and sat forward, propping his elbow on the table as he observed Joseph. 'A thing like this involves a lot of different players,' he began. 'A great number of interests are at stake – a lot of agents and only one or two principals. The agents are disposable. They know the risks. The important thing as far as Mr Caine's concerned – the only thing that really matters – is that he doesn't disturb the principals . . . the principal, I should say. That's all I care about.'

'And how does the principal benefit?' Joseph asked. 'Is it simply a commercial proposal?'

Charles shook his head. 'Not at all. There's a commercial aspect to it, of course. Given the right conditions, Makera's worth a lot of money. But there's the demographics to consider, too. Makera ought to be a Bakhoto stronghold.'

'Do the Abasis have shares in Matiba?'

Charles smiled and shrugged his shoulders. 'I don't think that's a matter of public record.'

'What about the five million dollars that's already been paid to Mount Batanga?'

'That's gone,' Charles said at once.

'Gone?'

'Out of the country.' He made a gesture with his right hand like a conjuror. 'Deepak Zaidi has spirited it away. There's no way of tracing it – the money's been laundered a dozen times. It never existed.'

'And the principal has it?'

He nodded. 'It's in the UK, less Mr Zaidi's handling charges. Five million, which is about one per cent of the funds held abroad by a certain prominent family . . .'

'You believe that?' Joseph said. 'You think the Abasis have amassed half a billion?'

'It must be in that region. Don't look so shocked.'

'I'm not shocked,' Joseph said, 'just a little surprised. I mean this Mount Batanga business, it seems very quick work. It must have been prepared well in advance.'

'Why do you think the minister was so interested in this project?'

Joseph took the whisky bottle, pulled out the stopper and refilled both tumblers. 'So, we have to keep Mr Caine away from Zaidi and the capital flight,' he said.

'Correct.'

'And when it comes to the slums?'

'It doesn't matter very much what he learns about that. Anything that happens in the slums can be repudiated. If some of the boys from the Special Bureau are throwing their weight around, they can be disciplined. Developers? Well, of course they're interested in a slice of Makera – who wouldn't be? And if the contractors are proving unreliable, that's hardly news, is it?'

'What about the UK authorities?'

Charles waved a hand dismissively. 'The *wazungu* just want to know that the funds were spent. They're under a lot of departmental pressure to raise the budget every year and the last thing they want is to follow up on a project like this. Edward Caine will be gone in a few months, and his successor will have some new programme. You know what these people are like. I'm sure you'll handle your man. Still, have a word with Beatrice, won't you? We don't want her getting caught up on the wrong side of something like this. I hear she's been spending a lot of time with the Shala residents.'

'That's just geography,' Joseph replied. 'They're mostly Shala in that part of Makera.'

'Well, tell her to be careful. There's always a danger of some little upstart in the Special Bureau accusing her of disloyalty, and it's really not worth the risk – she's only an intern, for goodness' sake.'

'Why do you say that?' Joseph asked. 'Have you heard something?'

'No, no, nothing definite. It's just that those security boys don't use very subtle methods. If they decide to arrest people in Makera – if they make a trawl for Ochola supporters, hidden weapons – I'd hate to see Beatrice caught in the net.'

'All right,' Joseph said. 'I'll talk to her.'

Charles got to his feet. 'I'll see you tomorrow. Don't move, I'll see myself out. Thanks for the Scotch.'

He walked back through the house towards the front door,

but almost at once the lights came on in the hall and Beatrice appeared from the corridor that led to Joseph's study. 'Good evening, Mr Wanjui.'

'Well, what a pleasure,' he said, taking her hand and pressing it between his own. 'Where have you sprung from?'

'I just got back from work,' she said. 'I heard voices so I was on my way to investigate.'

'I wish you'd come earlier. I've just said goodbye to your father. I have to get home myself, unfortunately.'

'I'll walk you out,' she said. As she opened the front door, she called: 'John! John?' The outline of a man's figure appeared from the garage near the gates, and hurried across the drive. 'John, Mr Wanjui's leaving now. Please open the gates for him.'

'I'll see you soon,' Charles said, taking her hand. 'You keep out of trouble.'

'Oh, yes. I'll be careful,' she replied, as he walked down to his car and was driven away.

24

'He's gone,' Beatrice said as she reached the veranda.

'I wish you'd been here,' Joseph replied. He hadn't moved from his chair, and hardly looked at Beatrice as she leaned down to kiss him. 'Charles talked a lot. He said things I never expected to hear from a man like him – from a friend . . . Stupid things. He was trying to warn me.'

'It was aimed at me, too,' she said, sitting down beside him and taking his hand.

'You heard?'

'I came back a while ago. I didn't want to disturb you so I sat in the study – right there, on the sofa by the window. I could hear everything.'

Joseph shook his head. 'I honestly can't believe the attitude he took. I mean, I knew he was compromised – he was very close to Kenneth Makotsi and he's made an awful lot of money in government service – but even so, to be so crude, to rub my nose in it like that . . .'

'He sounded like a thug,' she said. 'That stuff about the uncircumcised.' She added thoughtfully: 'I should write some notes now, while I remember.'

'Absolutely not, Bea. What would you do with them? They could be used as evidence of your disloyalty.'

'I'm meeting Mike Owens later,' she said. 'I'll give them to him, along with the other things I've found out.'

'What things?'

'I don't want you to know, Father.'

'Oh, so now *you*'re protecting *me*.' He kept his eyes on her accusingly. 'And with this information – this evidence – you'll do what, exactly?'

'I don't know. I was thinking Ed could take it to London. Once it's out of the country, what can they do?'

'What can they do? Is that a serious question?' Joseph leaned forward and took her hands. 'You listen to me, Bea. You've got to be sensible. You're getting mixed up in things you can't begin to control. If one word of this gets out – if anyone even thinks you've been collecting evidence about this business – you're dead. Do you hear what I'm saying? Not arrested and left in St Jude's, or barred from the legal profession, or ostracised, or sent into exile – they can do any of those things to you for much less. No, if this comes out, they'll kill you, Beatrice.'

'But Father, how can they possibly know? I haven't spoken to anyone. Not a soul.'

He gazed at her insistently.

'What?' she said.

'Are you saying you haven't confided in that young man – the builder?'

'Solomon? Oh, Father . . .'

'Well, he's obviously keen on you. He can see for himself what's going on.'

'He's not going to talk.'

'So you *have* talked to him?'

'Not exactly. I trust him, though. I do trust him.'

He sighed, pressing her hands together. 'That's not good. You need to be extremely careful with a man like that. He's not someone you can let into your confidence.'

'Why? Because he's a slum-boy?'

'Because he's an operator, my darling. He lives a dangerous life. Apart from anything else, he ought to keep clear of the slum project for his own sake. He certainly doesn't want the Special Bureau investigating his affairs. Keep away from him, Bea. Steer clear. You promise?'

She bit her lip.

'I've always respected your freedom,' he went on. 'You know I don't interfere in your friendships, but now, Bea, with this man Solomon . . . Well, you understand.'

'Yes, Father.'

'All right,' he said, after a pause, and sat back on his chair. 'What are you going to do with your evidence?'

'Mike will know how to hide it.'

'I certainly hope so. All I know is, it cannot be here. Absolutely cannot. If they discover you've been investigating this business, we're both finished.'

'They wouldn't do that – they wouldn't investigate us.'

'Don't you believe it. When are you meeting Mike?'

'Soon,' she said. 'Nine o'clock.'

'Good. Come straight back afterwards. I don't want you running around town any more, in and out of Makera. I don't like it. You should stay here till this fire business blows over – the ACP arrests . . .'

'I'll be careful, Father.' She got to her feet and kissed him again. 'Please don't worry about me.'

Mike's house was entirely dark and, as she drove her moped into the yard, Beatrice was afraid he had gone away. She parked under a Christ's-thorn tree, out of sight of the road, and made her way with her shoulder bag along the path that ran down the side of the house to the garden and the swimming pool. Then, seeing a light, she tapped on the window of Mike's study.

'I'm sorry,' she said, as he opened the kitchen door. 'You weren't asleep?'

'No, no, I've been working. Let's go into the study. What's up, Bea? Are you all right?'

'I'm fine.' She put her bag on the armchair where he had been reading. 'I've got a favour to ask.'

'Sit down,' he said. 'Move those books off the sofa – go on. Give them a shove.'

'No, I can't stay.'

'What's this? Something for me?' He opened the bag and took out the papers. 'Kimathi?'

'Kimathi are developing Makera. The plans are all there.'

'So I see. What else?'

'All the financial information we've been able to find. The witness statements about Matiba Development and the fire. And here,' she handed him her phone, 'I've got a recording of Charles Wanjui talking to my father. He admits the Abasis' involvement.'

Mike whistled. 'You're sure nobody knows about this?'

'Certain. I took notes, too, in case the sound quality isn't clear.'

'You want me to make a transcript?' he asked, taking the jotting pad from her.

'Yes.'

'Then what?'

'Look at the whole thing for me, Mike. Tell me what else we need to prove our case.'

Mike created a space on his desktop for the papers and the phone. 'Okay,' he said. 'I'll look at it all. Come on, Bea, do sit down a second.' He came over to clear away some of the books from the sofa, piling them up on the floor. 'Let's just talk this through. Who knows you've got this stuff?'

'Ed's seen most of it,' she said, perching on the edge of the sofa. 'Not the recording, though. That only happened tonight.'

'And your father knows about that?'

'I didn't tell him I'd recorded it.'

'What *does* he know?'

'Only what he learned for himself. I haven't shown him the documents.'

'And Milton?'

'It's hard to say. He hasn't been on site for weeks.'

'Were you followed here tonight?'

She looked surprised. 'I don't think so.'

'All right.' Mike went to the desk, where he poured himself a whisky.

'What are you going to do?' she said.

'I'll read it through.'

'Will you show the British?'

'Perhaps.' He took a mouthful of his drink, sitting down on the armchair.

'And the newspapers?'

'Definitely not.'

'But if we have proof, Mike – if we can show that Pamela has stolen the project funds – then we have a duty to blow the whistle, haven't we?'

'First and foremost, we have a duty not to put people in danger, Bea.'

'You don't have to worry about me,' she said. 'I'll be all right.'

'Well, even if that were true, what about your father?'

She avoided his eyes. 'That's why I want you to go to the British,' she said. 'If *they* blow the whistle, nobody can blame Father.'

'They can if his daughter provided the evidence.'

'But they won't know. How can they?'

He looked at her reproachfully. 'Listen, Bea, you want the British to change their approach without provoking the Special Bureau to arrest your father. Right? What you do *not* want is for the British to do nothing while your father gets beaten to death in a cell in St Jude's. Well? Am I right?'

'Yes,' she said, folding her arms. 'Of course.'

'Okay. Leave it to me. And don't talk about this to anyone. Beatrice? What's the matter now?'

She had leaned back on the sofa, turning her face away from him. 'I don't know,' she said with a kind of baffled fury. 'It's impossible, isn't it? Nobody can ever do the right thing in this country. Everybody has a perfect excuse for saying nothing. We just go on lying the whole time. Keeping silent. Even Father. It's enough to give you an ulcer!' As she got up, he saw that her eyes were full of tears. 'Mike, can I ask you something – I mean, something personal?'

'Hey, come on, Bea, of course you can.'

'I just – I mean, there's nobody I can tell. No one at all. And I don't know what to do.'

'What is it?' he said, moving forward on his armchair.

'It's Solomon,' she said. 'Solomon Ouko.'

'Your builder?'

She nodded. 'He's not just a builder. He has a lot of businesses – I don't know everything he does . . .'

He watched her wipe her face with the back of her hand. 'And you like him?' he said gently.

'Yes.' She turned to face him. 'I love him, Mike. I keep thinking about him – I keep seeing his face in my mind, like he's inside me, all around me.' She sat down on the floor. 'Oh, I want to tell people – I want to talk about it all the time – but I don't dare . . . When I first met him, I thought he was just a good-for-nothing – I mean, good-looking but a real vagabond. I tried to ignore him – I didn't want to get involved with someone like that . . . But in his heart he's a good man – that's the trouble. He's gentle. And I lied to Father. I said I wouldn't see him any more.'

Mike watched her in silence for a moment. 'But you are seeing him?' he prompted.

'We're meeting for supper tomorrow. It'll be the first time we've been alone. Up to now, we've always been on site, but we can never talk properly. There's always something going on.'

Mike tried to smile. 'There's not much I can do, Bea,' he said. 'I hope he deserves you. I hope he loves you.'

'But what about Father? Do you think I should tell him?'

'Tell him when you're ready. *Intend* to tell him. Trust him. He'll understand.'

'Yes, you're right. He's bound to understand, isn't he? I just have to find the right moment . . . But it frightens me. I feel like I'm doing something wicked – like I'm being disloyal.' She went on, with a grave expression in her eyes: 'Only I can't pretend. When I wake up in the morning, I'm already thinking about

Solomon. He's fixed in my head and I'm so happy. I can't believe he's real – that he's alive and I'm going to see him. Then I get terrified of all the things that could happen.' She scrambled to her feet. 'I've got to go. Father will be worried. Thanks, Mike. I'm sorry to unload on you.'

'It's okay. Really.' He went up to her and gave her a hug. 'You be careful, that's all. Make sure this man loves you before you commit yourself. Whatever you do, just make sure of that.'

25

Ed arrived by taxi near the main entrance of the Holy Souls Cemetery, a couple of miles north of Aberdare. He had arranged to meet Beatrice there in time to join Ann Odinga's funeral procession, but when he reached the gates he found himself surrounded by an enormous crowd. Burials of those killed in the Makera fire had been taking place all morning, and hundreds of people were now standing along the highway and at the gates. Young men had climbed on to the high walls of the necropolis, and half a mile to the south, Ed could see the next procession emerging from a great dust cloud as it made its way along the road towards him. Instinctively he withdrew from the area around the gates and went to stand a hundred yards away, in the shade of a little shop that sold crucifixes and plastic Madonnas.

Some of the people in the crowd were holding up posters of Patrick Ochola, a red bandanna round his head, Kalashnikov in his right hand. Others were chanting in Kishala, breaking off from time to time to jeer at the riot police, who had lined up on the other side of the road, next to Heavenly Archangels Funeral Services. But most people were singing hymns, or crying out in a high-pitched wail.

Ed was wearing a dark suit, and it was becoming unbearably hot, but nobody else had taken off their jacket and he was determined not to do anything disrespectful. He was the only white person in the crowd – one out of a thousand or more – and as the singing and wailing grew louder, and the coffin came into sight, he felt increasingly out of place. By now he could see the priest: a short man in a black chasuble, walking in front of the coffin, preceded by three boys in white tunics, the tallest of whom was swinging a metal vessel from side to side, from which little clouds of incense smoke rose into the air, while another carried a crucifix on a long staff. The mood of the crowd seemed to change as Ann's body approached. By the time the pallbearers came to a stop outside the cemetery gates, the young men on the walls were no longer taunting the police, and everyone turned to the coffin. For a few moments there was silence everywhere, except for the crying of babies and the rise and fall of sirens on the airport road to the south. The priest said something to one of the mourners, and a choir of young children started to sing. The coffin bearers moved on towards the open gates, and Ed saw Stephen, Martha, Tom and Ruth, walking directly behind the coffin.

Nobody had been paying any attention to Ed, and he was starting to feel less self-conscious. Keeping his eyes on the coffin, he stepped out of the shadows and moved forward with the rest of the crowd, heading towards the cemetery. He knew the tune of the hymn the children were singing, and some of the people around him were starting to join in, but he couldn't make out the Swahili words. All around, as he approached the entrance of the cemetery, he could feel the pressure and movement of the crowd closing in, the sun burning his face, the reverberation of the voices in his chest. Even if he couldn't join in the prayers, it seemed to him that he was still a mourner, like everyone else, and for a few minutes, as he made his way with the crowd into the burial ground, he forgot how alien he looked.

The crowd came to a stop, unable to move any further, and Ed found himself beside a stone angel on a slightly raised piece of ground from which he was able to see the little chapel. Ann's coffin was resting on trestles in the sunlight, draped in a white sheet, and the four children stood to one side. Then, as the priest raised his voice to address the congregation, the people around Ed stopped singing, and the entire cemetery, which had been so full of movement and noise, was overtaken with a sort of electric silence.

Beatrice had managed to reach a place near the front of the crowd. After the burial she spotted Ed and telephoned him.

The great body of mourners had started to file out of the cemetery past the police lines, heading back to Makera. But there was no jeering, no Shala war-chants, and the Patrick Ochola posters had disappeared.

'I saw you standing by the chapel,' Ed said, as Beatrice came up, 'but I couldn't get to you. I really wanted to say something to those children. How are they?'

'A bit shocked. They weren't expecting this.' Beatrice watched the retreating crowd. 'The whole of Makera has turned up for these funerals. I thought there was going to be a fight with the police – there would have been, if the priest hadn't spoken so well.'

'I couldn't follow what he said, but it seemed to calm everyone down.'

'Yes. He talked about the Resurrection. He said that if you could see Ann's whole life from the point of view of eternity – from God's point of view – however unjust and corrupt things are in the world, you'd understand everything and have no thought of vengeance.'

Ed pointed towards the gate. 'We'd better get going. My plane's taking off at two thirty.'

'In a situation like this, Christianity can overcome tribalism,' Beatrice continued, as they hurried on. 'It's something universal – something we all understand.'

'*I* don't understand it,' Ed said.

'No. It's different with Westerners. But in Africa people acknowledge God – it's common ground; it can reconcile enemies. That's why Father Augustine made a point of speaking in Swahili. Some of the men were chanting in Kishala – he's a Shala like them, and they wanted him to speak in the tribal language, but he refused. He told them that Ann had lots of Bakhoto friends, *wazungu* friends, Ngozi, Bontai, Kishana, that the Church recognises no boundaries. Then he told the boys on the walls to put away their posters of Patrick Ochola.' She shook her head. 'He's brave, he has a good reputation. I don't think

224

Stephen was pleased.' Then she said, in a different tone: 'Oh, no. Here comes Gladwell Oyusi.'

Gladwell had been waiting by the gates, dressed in a raincoat and clutching something in her fist. Now that she had seen Ed and Beatrice, she left her place and ran towards them. 'Tell him to go,' she yelled in Swahili, white circles around her irises as she glared at Ed. 'Tell this man to leave us. Tell him to go away!'

'Ssh, Mrs Oyusi,' Beatrice said. 'He's a friend, you know he is. He was a friend to Ann.'

'And you – you Bakhoto.' Gladwell turned to Beatrice, thrusting a fist towards her forehead. 'You lied to me. You said you were a Shala – you gained my trust – but you are not one of us. There are men here who will kill every Bakhoto in Makera. Yes, when the time comes, you will be wiped out.'

'And if they do?' Beatrice shot back. 'If these people murder their neighbours, who are just as poor as them, who will benefit? If there's war in the slums, how will the tyranny ever end? How? You tell me that.'

'*He* is one of them, too,' she spat back, extending her fist towards Ed. 'He is their servant. Ann's blood is on his hands.' Raising her hand over Ed's head with a short cry, she released what she had been holding, and half a dozen white feathers fluttered on to his suit, then to the ground.

Twenty or thirty people had stopped to listen to Gladwell's outburst, and many remained where they were as she marched away, including a group of men in suits and shiny shoes, who stood talking together in low voices. 'Come on,' Beatrice said, taking Ed's arm. 'We'd better get to the airport.'

Ed was still gazing after Gladwell's retreating figure, his feet planted on the ground as if he were paralysed. 'What was all that? What does she think I did? Does she seriously imagine I wanted Ann to die?'

'Don't say anything. Keep your voice down.'

'But it's not rational,' he persisted. 'It makes no sense – she must see that.'

'Come on! Let's get to the car.'

The crowd around them was closing in, and some of the young men were standing across the entrance, blocking their path.

'It's all right,' Beatrice said. 'Gladwell's not thinking straight. She's upset – the fire has changed her.'

'The fire's changed everything,' Ed replied, stepping over the feathers. 'It's polarised opinion. That's what they wanted, isn't it? That was the intention.' Guided by Beatrice, he walked reluctantly towards the men in suits who were lined up across the gateway, paused as two of them stepped aside, just a little, and shuffled out between them on to the road.

Beatrice drove Ed to the airport in her father's big car. She checked her rear-view mirror every few moments, half convinced, long before they reached the terminal building, that they were being followed by a Mercedes four-by-four. 'I'll get a porter,' she said, glancing in the mirror again as she drew in.

'I can manage. I've only got a small case.'

'You'd better start going through Security,' she said. 'It can take ages, these days.'

'Don't I know it. Especially if you don't want to pay up.' But he hesitated, looking at her. 'Listen, Beatrice, do you think I should give up? You understand what's happening. Tell me honestly. Have I got in too deep?' Struck by the uncertainty in her eyes, he added quickly: 'I'm not too proud, Beatrice, or stubborn – whatever you might think.'

'I don't think that.'

'I mean, I'm not convinced I have to be right. If we're not doing good, if this project is making things worse, we should pull out. To me that's obvious. I'd be happy to tell the people in London. We could shut off the funding, put the whole thing down to experience. What's the point of pouring money into Milton Abasi's bank account?'

'Is that what you're going to say?'

'I'd like to. I want to get the whole thing off my chest. It's not up to me what they do, but they'd have to listen.' He checked his watch. 'I'd better go.'

Beatrice and Ed hurried across the marble floor of the terminal building towards the queue at the check-in desks.

'You've got your passport and tickets?' she asked.

He held them up and stepped forward to pat her shoulder. 'Don't wait here. It's a waste of your time.'

'Okay. I'll see you in a few days.'

She gripped the car keys in her hand as she marched towards the entrance, her eyes fixed on the brilliant light beyond the open doors. Then she stood humming to herself, as she waited for a Batangan family to push their trolleys into the building.

'Miss Kamunda?' a man's voice asked.

Beatrice looked round at a chubby man with a small moustache, dressed in the olive green uniform of the Customs Service. 'Yes?'

'Miss Beatrice Kamunda?'

She nodded. 'I'm Beatrice Kamunda.'

'Isaias Murungi,' the man said. 'Chief Inspector of Customs.'

'Oh, yes, Inspector, I remember.'

He cleared his throat, watching her for a moment, then grasped the end of his swagger stick and whooshed it through the air. 'These gentlemen would like a word with you.' He pointed his cane at the men in suits standing on either side of Beatrice. 'They are from the Special Bureau.'

'What do you want?' she said, immediately recognising the driver of the Mercedes.

'Come this way,' Murungi replied.

'Why?' she said. 'I'm going back to my car.'

'My colleagues will take care of the car,' one of the men said, taking hold of her wrist.

'But it's not mine,' she protested. 'It belongs to my father. Let go of my arm.'

'Give me the keys, Miss Kamunda.' He tightened his grip.

'Inspector, tell him to release me.'

'I can't do that,' he replied quietly. 'They are not my men.'

'This isn't lawful,' she declared. 'I refuse to co-operate.'

Murungi smiled almost apologetically. 'If you will take my advice, Miss Kamunda, that's really not a wise attitude. You should assist these officers. They can make life very unpleasant for you.'

'Come with us,' the second man insisted, staring at Beatrice through his sunglasses.

'Wait a minute,' she said. 'What's this about? Tell me what you're doing. Let go of my arm! Will you *let go*!'

'Give me the keys. Do as I say, Miss Kamunda, or I'll handcuff you.'

'What do you mean? Are you arresting me? What's the charge? You must tell me the charge.'

'Just come with us,' he repeated. 'It won't take long.'

Beatrice stood where she was, clutching the keys, as the men stood over her. Then she dropped them into the officer's open palm, shoved him away and followed Chief Inspector Murungi towards a door marked 'Security'.

There was no window in the interrogation room, and its pale grey walls were undecorated, apart from a large portrait of Kwamchetsi Wachira, which hung next to the ventilation grille. Beatrice was told to sit on a wooden chair, in front of a table that had nothing on it except a blue file. For a long time the two men ignored her. Taking her bag, they tipped the contents on to the table and started going through them. The larger man removed his dark glasses and spent a good deal of time examining her mobile phone, writing the names and numbers from her contacts into his notebook, while the other went through her purse, and made a rapid examination of her house keys, a packet of painkillers, her lipstick and an ancient photograph of her mother. 'Give me your watch,' he said. 'Your ring, also, the necklace. All your jewellery.'

Beatrice unfastened her things and handed them over.

'Now take off your jacket.'

'Why? What's going on?'

The man came up to her and peered into her face. 'I won't repeat myself,' he said. 'If you don't co-operate, Sylvester will take care of you.' He indicated his friend, who looked up from the notebook and smiled at Beatrice. 'Sylvester is very skilled with a knife, Miss Kamunda,' he said. 'It would be his pleasure to undress you.'

Beatrice stood up and started to unbutton her jacket.

'Take off your shirt also,' he said.

'You've got no right to do this,' Beatrice said. 'I want to see your warrant. This is not legal.'

'Miss Kamunda,' the man said, 'we are officers of the Special Bureau. I want you to understand something: if I tell you to take off your clothes so that I can search you, you must do it. I have the power to do anything that is necessary.'

'But it's *not* necessary.'

'I will decide that,' he said. 'Do you understand?'

Beatrice nodded, but the man seemed to be getting angrier. He put his hand under her chin and lifted it so that she was looking directly into his face.

'If I want you to stand naked in front of me,' he said, 'that is lawful. If I put my hand up your *kuma*, Miss Kamunda, that is my business. Nobody can stop me. I do not need a warrant to enter you. So take off your shirt, take off your skirt, take off your shoes.' He shouted: 'Do it now!'

Beatrice started, but almost at once she began to undo her shirt.

'And the skirt,' the officer repeated, seeing her hesitate. 'Everything will be searched.'

Beatrice took off her shoes, unzipped her skirt, and let it fall to the floor.

'Now sit down,' the officer said.

The two men bundled up her clothes and jewellery and put

229

them with the contents of her bag and the blue file on a plastic tray. Without another word, they left the room. Beatrice heard the lock turn in the door, and for a long time she remained on the wooden chair, naked except for her bra and pants. At first her heart thumped furiously, and she stared at the wall. But when she had been alone for ten minutes or more, with nothing to listen to except the rattling of the air-conditioner, the effects of adrenalin began to wear off and a cold, almost physical sensation of terror spread out from the pit of her stomach. She leaned forward, crossing her arms, determined not to show her fear or let her limbs shake as she sat there. But eventually, when her legs began to lose circulation, she got up and walked up and down, then leaned against the wall, below the portrait of the president, and slid down to the floor.

After about an hour, a woman officer came in, carrying the plastic tray. 'Put your clothes on,' she said, dropping it on the table.

'Can I go?' Beatrice asked. 'Am I being released?'

'Get dressed,' the woman repeated.

She struggled to her feet, steadying herself on the back of the wooden chair, and put on her skirt. 'Where are my shoes?' she said, looking at the things in the tray. 'What's happened to my watch – my cross?'

'Your valuables will be returned when you're released,' the big woman said.

Beatrice was doing up her shirt, her hands fumbling with the buttons. 'I need to use the *choo*,' she said.

'Later.' The woman folded her arms, taking up a position with her back to the door.

'Please,' Beatrice said, pulling on her jacket. 'I have to go. What am I supposed to do? You must help me.'

The officer tilted her head disapprovingly. 'Come with me,' she said. She unlocked the door and led Beatrice into the corridor, across a pool of water, which was collecting beneath an air-conditioning duct, past a number of closed doors to a

230

row of pit latrines enclosed in cubicles. 'Two minutes,' the guard said.

Luther Magari was waiting in the interrogation room when the officer led Beatrice in.

'Miss Kamunda,' he said, surveying her with his good eye, 'I hope you have been treated well? No?' He sat down on the other side of the table.

'Why am I here?' she demanded. 'What do you want?'

He had opened the blue file and was gazing at some photographs that Beatrice could not see. 'I understand you've been busy with our Shala cousins. You have been getting very involved with their affairs.'

'That's nonsense. I'm working on the Global Justice Alliance project in Makera. That's no secret. We're dealing with all kinds of people – loyal people, Batangans.'

'Really? Batangans? Do you think Ann Odinga was a loyal Batangan? Or her friend Gladwell Oyusi?' He held up a picture of Beatrice and Ann talking to Gladwell at the project site. 'And what about Ann's son, Stephen? Do you think he's a patriot, Miss Kamunda?'

'Why not?'

'Because he is a member of the ACP!' He raised his voice. 'He is a rebel.'

The sensation of panic intensified in Beatrice's stomach, and her eyes, which had been trained on Luther's face, dropped to the tabletop.

'We know things about your friends,' Luther went on, starting to spread the pictures out in front of him. 'You should have realised, too – any good Bakhoto would suspect a boy like that. He has an unhealthy attitude.' And he looked at her. 'But you are not a loyal Bakhoto, are you?'

'I'm a Batangan,' she replied hoarsely.

Luther leaned back on his chair, watching her. 'Miss Kamunda, your country is at war with Patrick Ochola. If a person is not

231

supporting that fight, they are part of the rebellion – they are the enemy. If a person says that the people in Makera should fight against the government, that person is a traitor.'

'I didn't say that.'

He looked down at the file. 'You said, "If there's war in the slums between the poor, how will the tyranny ever end?" The tyranny, Miss Kamunda? What tyranny is that? Do you mean the tyranny of Patrick Ochola – the Army of Celestial Peace? Or do you mean President Wachira's government? The lawful government, the government of your own people.'

Beatrice's face seemed to be growing colder.

'Miss Kamunda?'

'I want to speak to a lawyer,' she said.

'You are a lawyer. You are free to consult yourself. I am investigating treason. That is the most serious crime a person can commit.'

'I'm not a traitor.'

'In that case, why are you giving confidential information to this man?' He held up a picture of Beatrice parking her bike in the yard at Mike Owen's house. 'This was taken yesterday evening. What was in that package? Oh, but you don't have to tell me now,' he went on soothingly. 'You can explain it all when the boys have spent more time getting to know you. There's no hurry. Interrogations are like making love, Miss Kamunda. One should always take one's time . . . Ah, now that is an interesting picture also. Your father is very friendly with the British High Commissioner.'

'That's his job, you idiot,' Beatrice almost shouted. 'Of course he's friendly. Do you want him to be *un*friendly?'

But Luther put the picture away and slapped the file shut. 'You are an arrogant woman. I don't think someone in your position should be accusing anyone of being an idiot. You are the one under suspicion of treason.'

'I'm not a traitor. You know that. You haven't any evidence. You can't have – there isn't any. You have to let me go.'

Luther got up with a sigh, and went to the door. 'Go and get Sylvester,' he told the large woman officer, who was standing outside. 'Njenga, too. Fetch them both. They have work to do.'

'Yes, Colonel.'

Njenga appeared with Sylvester, who was carrying a black plastic holdall, and stood grinning at Beatrice while the woman officer shut the door behind them. Then, walking up to the table, he put the bag down in front of Luther and went to stand a few feet from Njenga near the wall.

'Well, let's see . . . What have we got in the bag today?' Luther peered inside, then took out a riding crop with a leather handle. 'This is good. I like old-fashioned equipment. Of course, I could have you taken to St Jude's, Miss Kamunda. At St Jude's we have a lot of very modern kit – it's all very up-to-date. But when it comes to a young woman like you, I prefer to start with traditional methods.' Getting to his feet, he flexed the whip between his hands, raised it in the air and smacked it down on the tabletop. 'It's a pity I can't stay,' he said, turning back to observe the trauma in Beatrice's eyes. 'I have so many things to attend to. But I am leaving you in good hands. I know you'll want to make a statement soon, and I'm sure the boys will let you do it – just as soon as they've finished.' He turned to them. 'Give Miss Kamunda everything she needs. Make sure she's not neglected in any way.' And he added, as he walked over to the door: 'I want your report by tomorrow morning, Lieutenant.'

'Yes, Colonel,' Njenga said.

Then, nodding at Beatrice, he knocked at the door, which immediately opened to let him out.

26

Joseph had gone straight from the ministry to a dinner at the Aberdare Country Club. When it was over, at about eleven, and everyone else had gone to the bar, he slipped away without saying goodbye and started to walk home. As soon as he had left the club grounds and entered the residential area, it struck him that the neighbourhood was unnaturally silent, even for that time of night; and when he approached his own house he paused, looking in through the wire mesh as he searched for his key in his jacket pocket. The whole place was dark: there was no hurricane lantern on the veranda, no lights in Beatrice's room or in the Mgiros' quarters to the side, no sign of the dogs.

He let himself in and stood on the driveway, halfway between the front steps and the Mgiros' cottage. 'John?' he called. 'Mrs Mgiro?' Then he walked in darkness towards the veranda. The front door was open, and as he came up the stairs he could see that it had been jammed in that position by the end of the hall dresser, which was lying on its side in the doorway. 'Beatrice?' he said more loudly, stepping over the corner of the dresser. 'Bea?' He tried the light switch by the door, but the hall remained pitch black. Walking on, he felt something brittle under his shoes, and stooped to pick up a shard of ceramic from the bowl that used to stand on the hall table. Then, hearing a subdued shout somewhere inside the house, he moved towards it.

None of the lights was working, and it was too dark in the corridor to see anything, except the overhang of the veranda roof through the open back door. As he passed the passage leading to his study, he found himself walking over a great number of books and papers – the contents of the shelves that lined the walls – and he could hear someone crying. He reached the wide veranda, but it took him a while to understand where the sound was coming from. The wickerwork chairs and table had been thrown over the banisters on to the lawn, and many of the floorboards had been torn up, but he found the oil lamp that hung from the central beam, and managed to light it. Then, holding it up as he walked over the broken boards, he saw John's face staring up at him from the far corner, Mrs Mgiro and Hope lying beside him. They were wriggling, trying to sit up.

'What's happened?' He ripped the duct tape from John's mouth. 'Where's Beatrice?'

'She's not here, sir. She didn't come home.'

'What do you mean? Hasn't she rung?'

'No, sir. She never said anything.'

Joseph crouched in silence opposite John. His heart seemed to be shaking within him and his hands and feet were unnaturally cold. 'Turn round,' he said weakly. 'Let me untie your hands.'

'She didn't come back this evening,' John repeated automatically, shuffling round. 'We were waiting up for her, Mrs Mgiro and me. Mrs Mgiro had Beatrice's supper but she didn't come. I kept looking out for her – we were sitting in the yard. Then Sherlock and Mycroft started barking at the gate, and I went to see.'

'Who was it?'

'I don't know, sir. They didn't say. They wouldn't tell me. They were big men, Mr Kamunda. Strong men. And they had guns, too. I'm so sorry, sir, I let them in. They said they'd kill me if I didn't. They said they'd shoot Hope and Eliza – they knew their names . . .' And he added quietly, as if he didn't want the others to hear: 'They killed the dogs, sir. They shot our two boys in the garage.'

Joseph had untied the cord, and pulled it away from John's hands. 'Help Mrs Mgiro and Hope,' he said. The blood had drained from his head, and he had to steady himself as he got to his feet.

'Oh, Mr Kamunda!' Mrs Mgiro burst out, as John untaped her mouth. 'Oh, dear Lord Jesus, we've been so scared – I can't tell you, sir. We've been lying here like this – we thought we were going to die – and we couldn't stop them. We couldn't do anything. They said if we moved, they'd kill us. They were so violent, sir – they smashed everything . . . everything . . .' She gave a low-pitched wail. 'All your best books, sir, they tore up all your books.'

'How many men?' Joseph said.

'Six. All big men – real vagabonds, sir. They came in a van.'

'Did they hit you?'

'They hit my John. They beat him!' Mrs Mgiro was crying now. 'Oh, Lord – oh, sweet Jesus . . .'

'Ssh, Eliza,' John said. 'I'm not hurt. It's not serious.' He put his hand to his forehead, which was bleeding, and turned back to Joseph. 'I told them they mustn't go in your study, sir. I said that was your private work in there – important work. That's when they hit me. And they tied us up, like you saw, and started breaking everything.' Hope was helping her mother to her feet, and John started to look about the veranda. 'I'll fetch your chair. They threw the furniture into the garden. I'll get it now.'

'Yes, fetch the chairs. We need one for Mrs Mgiro, too. Don't worry about anything else. Come, Mrs Mgiro. It's all right, they've gone.'

'Oh, Mr Kamunda – what's happened to Beatrice? Have those men got her, sir? What do they want?'

'Ssh, Mother, stop it!' Hope put her arms round her.

'I'm sorry, sir,' John said. 'I let them in – I let those devils into your house.'

'You did the right thing. They would have killed you.'

'Oh, dear Jesus,' Mrs Mgiro repeated. 'Dear Lord Jesus . . .'

Joseph stood at the railings, looking away from the veranda and taking a series of deep breaths to counteract the sensation of nausea in his stomach. Then he made himself turn back to where Mrs Mgiro and Hope were standing at the open door.

'Mrs Mgiro, you need to sit down,' he said. 'You've had a terrible shock.'

Mrs Mgiro had stopped wailing, but she was still sobbing. She nodded now and put out her hands towards the chair John had set in front of her.

'Why's it so dark?' Joseph asked. 'What's happened to the power?'

'When the men left us, all the lights went out,' John said. 'I'll check the fuse-box, sir, I'll take a look . . .' He set another chair on an undamaged section of floor. 'Here, sir. I'll bring the sofa up, too.'

'Where are you going, Hope?' Joseph asked.

'To make your bed, Mr Kamunda,' she said, peering nervously into the dark house. 'They were in your bedroom – I could hear them there.'

'No,' he replied. 'Leave everything till the morning. Don't worry about the bed – I won't sleep tonight.'

Hope was about to protest but caught her father's eye and said nothing.

'We all need a drink,' Joseph said. 'See if you can find something, Hope. See if they left the whisky. Then come and sit down.'

'Come on, Hope,' John put in. 'Come with me, child . . .' He led her into the house, holding up the oil lamp ahead of him.

By two in the morning, the airport was deserted, except for the security men around the perimeter fence and the little army of Ngozi women, who went about the terminal building with wide brooms, sweeping the marble floor. Sylvester and Njenga had spent more than six hours with Beatrice in the interrogation room. Early in the evening, the air-conditioning vent had stopped rattling and the temperature had started to rise. Now the air was stifling, and the walls of the room were slippery with moisture. Beatrice was unconscious, face down on the table, her swollen face turned to one side, her naked legs and back purple with bruises.

'What do we do now?' Sylvester said, wiping his forehead and nodding at the half-naked body on the table. 'You want me to keep beating her?'

'No. Colonel Magari said no real damage, just bruises.'

'What, then?'

'You heard her yourself,' Njenga said. 'She made a confession, didn't she? She agreed to sign.'

Sylvester shrugged. 'If you say so, Lieutenant.'

'You say so, too. We both heard it.'

'Yes, sir.'

'All right.' Leafing through the papers, Njenga took his pen and signed Beatrice's initials at the bottom of each page. 'It's done,' he said. 'She's confessed. Help me with her.' He closed the file and started to untie Beatrice's wrists. Sylvester wiped his mouth with the back of his hand, turned Beatrice's body over to check her breathing and put the whips in the black bag. Then the two men laid a blanket over her, carried her out along the corridor past the duty officer's desk, and into the car park, where they pushed her on to the back seat of a Land Cruiser.

'You drive,' Njenga said. 'I've got to finish the report.'

'Where are we taking her?'

'Makera, the railway tracks. I'll show you.'

The first thing Beatrice saw when she regained consciousness was an enormous grey rat standing on its hind legs as it gnawed its way into a bag of rubbish a couple of feet from where she was lying. She raised her head and tried to sit up, but as soon as she moved, every muscle in her back and thighs, her arms and neck burned, aching so much that she gave up in shock and lay as she was, in a puddle of green slime. The sun was already high but she couldn't tell if it was morning or afternoon. Almost at once, the stench of human excrement and rotting food made her choke.

After a few moments, keeping her eyes on the rat, she rolled over, pressed one hand on to the ground and managed to get into a kneeling position. Despite the throbbing all over her body, she got to her feet. Then, finding it impossible to straighten up, she wrapped herself in the muddy blanket that had been lying next to her, and started to limp along the valley between two mountains of rubbish where she had been dumped, heading towards the railway tracks.

As she emerged from the shadow of the rubbish tip, she could see the control tower of the airport, the dark green hills beyond it, and she shuffled on along a narrow path that led to the railway, her back bent at forty degrees, until she reached a yard of wrecked cars. From there she could see the main road, about a hundred yards away on the other side of the building, and she followed the metal fence of the scrapyard, moving along the line of an open sewer.

At some point between the slums and the highway she stood still, not wanting to wade on through the shining green mud with her bare feet; but she made herself do it, emerging among the crowds on the pavement. Then she picked her way between the goats and chickens, past street stalls and tiny hotels, through groups of children playing ballgames, limping on in the direction of Aberdare.

By the time she reached the palm trees and jasmine bushes of the suburbs, her whole body was shaking with shock and she felt as though she had a fever. For a few minutes she sat hunched against a wall with her eyes closed, thinking she was about to vomit. Then she struggled on along the empty streets, until she reached the side entrance of her house where she stood, pressing her head against the bell, until John ran up to the gate.

'Miss Beatrice! Oh, thank God, thank God! Come in, miss – give me your hand.'

'Oh, John – where's Father?' She fell through the door, clutching his arm.

'He's here, miss. He's all right. He's been waiting for you. We've all been waiting. Oh, what's happened to you, Miss Beatrice? Who did this to you . . . ?'

'I'm all right. Tell me about Father. They didn't arrest him?'

'No, miss.' He shook his head, a look of profound shock in his eyes. 'What a night, miss. How can these things happen? Everything's changed. Look at you – just look at your face . . .'

'Tell me what happened here,' she said, leaning on John's arm and walking forward.

'Some men came when Mr Kamunda was out. They destroyed his papers, his books, too – all his favourite books. They broke everything.' John stopped again, halfway across the drive, lowering his voice. 'They killed the dogs, miss. They shot them in front of me – there, by the garage.'

'Oh, John.'

'What kind of men would do that?'

She tightened her grip on his arm and they shuffled on. 'What about Hope and Mrs Mgiro? Are they hurt?'

'They're safe. Here, miss. Shall I carry you up the stairs?'

'No, I'm all right.'

'I'll ring the doctor,' he said, as he watched her struggle up the three stairs, pulling hard on the banister.

'Yes, call Dr Kiraitu. Tell him I've had an accident.'

Joseph had heard their voices. 'John? Who is it?'

'It's me, Father,' Beatrice called, as she reached the corner.

'Bea?' He hurried towards her, stepping over the broken floor-boards, and she tried to stand up straight. 'Oh, thank God! What happened, my darling? What have they done to you?' He stared at her swollen, purplish face, the hair covered with mud. 'What happened? Tell me.'

'Ssh, Father. It's all right.'

'But your face – who did this to you?'

She looked away from him into the garden.

'Come on, my darling,' he said gently. 'You need to wash

– we must get you upstairs. Don't try to talk now.' And as he took her hand, he called, 'Hope? Hope, are you there? Come and help us.'

After her bath Beatrice slept for a few hours, and woke when Dr Kiraitu arrived to examine her. She had a pounding headache and her body was so raw that it was painful to move, but she was intensely hungry. Before he left, the doctor brought her downstairs to sit with Joseph on the veranda, and told Hope to fetch her a bowl of *ugali*.

Joseph sat in the chair next to Beatrice so that they were both looking out towards the jasmine that screened the empty swimming pool. 'What are we going to do?' she said quietly.

'I don't know. Last night I couldn't even think about it. But now that you're here . . .' He took her hand. 'All the time you were missing, I kept asking myself how we had got to this point. I was going over it in my mind, over and over, trying to find the turning point, the critical moment.'

'It's my fault,' she said.

'No, my darling. You must understand how wrong that is. Whatever happens, you can't believe that. I was thinking a lot about Charles Wanjui, Wycliffe Gatere – all my childhood friends from the Sacred Heart Academy. Even Philip Abasi. You see a man like Charles, and you think, He knows what he's doing – he's made some definite decisions. But what I was thinking was, he probably never made a conscious choice, never really committed himself to the system, to eating at the trough. That's not the way it works. It's a gradual process, a kind of envelopment, like the dusk – like the light going out. Suddenly you look around and you realise it's night, pitch black, and it's impossible to change – there's no going back. From a certain point on, everyone's guilty, everyone's complicit, but nobody ever said to themselves, "This is what I'm going to do."'

'You're not complicit,' she said. 'You never took a penny.'

'I'm still guilty. I kept my mouth shut. I knew how things

were going – I could see the Bakhoto Mafia taking over. It started before independence, in the last phase of British rule. You could see exactly who was going to benefit from the end of the colonial regime. And when they started helping themselves to the country's productive assets – the newspapers and farms, haulage firms, fishing fleet – putting themselves in charge of every state-run utility . . . I mean, when Philip and Pamela took over a twenty-mile stretch of the Mawana Coast Nature Reserve – an act of pure undisguised theft – even then, I said nothing.'

'What could you do?'

'I should have spoken out. I should have made my voice heard. But I censored myself – we all did, my generation. Nobody had the guts to break ranks. And now, after fifty years of self-censorship, what kind of country have we got?'

'And if you had spoken out, what then?'

'I don't know. Perhaps back in the sixties and seventies I might have made a difference.'

'You don't know that.'

'Well, I know one thing. Nobody can change this country now. Corruption is a way of life. It's in the national DNA. It's like watching an old friend dying of cancer: there's nothing you can do. Until it's over, you can't even start mourning.'

She was silent, watching his face in profile. Then she squeezed his hand. 'What are we going to do?' she repeated.

'We can't stay here,' he said. 'They'll kill us both.'

'They'll kill us if we leave.'

'Yes. If they catch us.'

Beatrice looked down at the broken floorboards. 'But all our things, Father . . . What about the house? What about John and Mrs Mgiro?'

'John has a brother in the south, not far from the border. They should go down there for a while. We can send them money if they need it.'

'What money? If we leave, we won't have any.'

He smiled for the first time. 'If only I'd played the game,' he said, 'we could fly to London, disappear for a few years, live on my corrupt earnings . . .'

Hope had come up with a tray and was standing a couple of yards away, looking at Beatrice. 'Here, Miss Beatrice,' she said hesitantly. 'I've brought you some *ugali*.'

'Eat it,' Joseph urged. 'Sit forward a bit. Hope, bring a cushion to put behind her back.'

Beatrice sat up and took the spoon, but her hand was shaking. 'I can't do it,' she said.

'I'll help you.' Joseph held the spoon for her, raising it to her mouth. 'I thought we could ask Mike for help. He'll know what to do.'

She swallowed, but immediately shook her head. 'They were asking about him. They think he's a British spy. We mustn't put him at risk.'

'He doesn't have to come here. I'll get a message to him.'

'They took my phone, too.' Beatrice closed her eyes as she swallowed. 'They know all the calls I've made – my contacts.'

He moved the spoon towards her mouth again.

'What's wrong with me, Father?'

'It's just the shock. Leave things to me now. Matthew Kiraitu is coming back later. He's going to bring you some pills.'

'Don't leave – you're not going, are you, Father?'

'I'm staying right here,' he said. 'When we leave, we'll leave together.'

27

That afternoon Solomon and Machi drove out to the Universal Exports warehouse. They had been arguing in the car, and now Machi walked away in silence, letting himself into the storerooms ahead of his boss, while Solomon waited outside. There was a big white van parked in the loading bay with the words 'Universal Exports' painted on the side, and Solomon walked around it. 'These tyres are worn out,' he announced, when Machi reappeared from inside, accompanied by Stephen. 'We need new ones.' Climbing up into the lorry, he looked about the empty hold. 'This is fine. There's plenty of room. How soon can we be ready?'

'It'll take a few hours, boss. New tyres, engine oil, loading the cargo . . .'

'Stephen can help you,' he said, jumping down again, 'but nobody else. I don't want anyone to know.'

'If you're going, boss, if you've made up your mind,' Machi said, 'I'm coming with you.'

'No, I need you here. Who's going to run the business?' And he added quietly: 'You've got to make the arrangements with the Wahindi, too. Whatever happens, we're going to need cash.'

'Not if you're dead.'

'Hey, come on, we've been over that.'

'This is stupid, boss. It's plain stubborn. Nobody's going to the north any more. We haven't sent a delivery to Upshala this whole month.'

'Then it's time we did.'

'No, sir. The war's getting worse. Nobody's safe on the road.'

'I'll be all right.'

Machi stared at Solomon. 'You could lose everything, boss. You could get ambushed, and – bang! – the ACP takes your cargo. All your cargo. If they don't kill you, too.'

'If I don't go,' Solomon answered, 'if she's arrested again . . .' He put his hand out towards Machi. 'Hey, let's not argue. We never argue.'

'Never before, Mr Ouko.'

Solomon glanced at Stephen, who was standing on the loading platform. 'Start with the big boxes,' he said. 'We'll come soon to help you.' He turned back to Machi. 'Listen, you've got to understand. I was awake all night. I waited for Beatrice at the restaurant, and right away I knew something was wrong. Long before I got the news, I was certain she was in trouble. I could feel it.' He tightened his grip on Machi's arm. 'Now I have a chance of helping her. If I don't do it, if she's arrested again, if they kill her, how would I live? How? I love this girl, Machi.'

'Well, you should take someone with you, boss.'

'It's too dangerous.'

'Not in the Central Province. Take Stephen with you as far as the National Park. He can come back before you get to Ngoziland.'

'Okay, I'll ask him,' Solomon said. And he pushed Machi gently with his fist. 'Hey, don't look so worried, man. Come on, let's give the boy a hand.'

Beatrice woke up and lay still on her back for a long time, breathing in the smell of diesel exhaust as she tried to work out where she was. She was in a confined, almost lightless space, and all she could see at first were two walls of cardboard boxes on either side of her. But she was aware of the noise of an engine grinding along in low gear and realised, with a spasm of fear, that she was being driven somewhere. Every few moments the whole confined space lurched to one side as the vehicle hit a pothole, causing the boxes around her to strain against the cords

245

that tied them to the sides, and each time this happened, the bruises on her back and legs seemed to take the full shock of the impact. She shut her eyes, waiting for the pain to subside. Then, cautiously, she put her hand to her head, which was throbbing violently.

'You're awake.' She heard Joseph's voice in the darkness behind her. 'I hoped you'd sleep till we stopped.'

'Father?'

'Yes.' He took her hand. 'How are you feeling, my darling?'

'I don't know . . . Thirsty. My back hurts. And my head.'

'Matthew Kiraitu gave you some powerful tranquillisers. You've had a good long sleep.'

She blinked, trying to concentrate. 'Where are we?'

'About fifty miles north of Kisuru. We're crossing Central Province.'

'How . . .' she began. 'I mean, what is this place?'

'It's the back of Solomon Ouko's lorry.'

'Solomon? Is he here?' She tried to sit up at once, despite the pain. 'Where is he?'

'Lie still, darling. You must rest as much as you can.'

'But, Father, I don't understand. I was at home – we were at home together . . .'

'We had to leave, darling. We had to get out of Kisuru.'

'But why this – how did Solomon . . . ?'

'He offered to help. It was Mike's idea.'

'Isn't it dangerous for him?'

'Yes, it's dangerous.' He watched her anxious expression in the half-light. 'Solomon's on his way north to sell whisky and cigars to the army.' He raised his eyebrows with a kind of reluctant admiration. 'Apparently he does it every month – him or one of his men.'

'He's not worried about the war?'

'He says he's never had any trouble. Apparently he supplies *both* sides. I wanted to drive down to the coast but Mike said the Special Bureau would be watching the ports. Flying was out of the question. This seemed the only option. Solomon's going to get us to the Sudanese border, if he can.'

'What happens when we get to Sudan?' she asked. 'What will we do? Do we have any documents?'

He shook his head. 'The Special Bureau took everything. All we've got is the cash that was left in the house. It isn't much. That and six spare tyres, two drums of water and food for a week. He's a resourceful man, your Mr Ouko. He's even packed coffee around us to confuse the police dogs.'

Beatrice began to sit up again, moving more carefully this time and drawing a long breath as she did so. 'You see, Father? I told you. I knew he was a good man.'

'Well, let's see how things turn out . . .' He checked himself. 'He's certainly taking a big risk for us. For you, I should say.'

Beatrice smiled in the dark, and for a while she said nothing. Then she started to sit up. 'Is that a window?' she said, confused for a moment by the spots of sunlight coming in through the roof. 'Can we get any air in here?'

'Solomon's going to let us out every few hours,' Joseph said, 'whenever he gets a chance. If something's wrong, he bangs on the partition three times and we have to keep still. But there's a spyhole,' he went on. 'You can look out. Only be careful. We've been stopped three times already.' He sat back and carefully removed one of the boxes – a half-case of Johnnie Walker – from its place in the stack beside him. Immediately a flat beam of sunlight landed on Beatrice's stomach.

Beatrice leaned across her father and put her eye to the slit. At first she could see nothing at all in the glare. But gradually she made out the landscape they were travelling through. The highway had been running in a straight line across the savannah, but the lorry was climbing now, and she could see the unmistakable mountain range of the Bakhoto heartland all across the horizon. For a long time she gazed up into an amphitheatre of irregular fields stacked up against the valleys. Every patch of level ground was dark green with coffee bushes and banana fronds, while all around an impassable wilderness of eucalyptus was crisscrossed with deep crevices and mountain streams.

'It's like Paradise,' she said.

'They say you don't need to cultivate the land here. You just look at it and the crops grow.'

'How long have we been driving?'

'About four hours. It took us a long time just to get past the airport.'

She sat back on her blankets, letting herself down carefully. 'Don't you want to look out?'

'I don't think so,' he said, putting the box back in its place. 'I was looking earlier. Somehow it didn't seem the right way to say goodbye to Batanga.'

'Oh, Father, we'll come back.'

'If we get out of the country alive, that's enough to be thankful for. What happens after that, God knows.' As he said this, there were three loud thumps on the metal partition between the driver's cab and the hold. 'Police. Keep still.'

'What do you mean they've left Kisuru?' Pamela Abasi glared at Luther, whose good eye was fixed on a section of carpet in front of her desk. 'How could they? You mean they just walked out of their house like a couple of tourists?'

'No, ma'am. The house was under surveillance.'

'Oh, I'm pleased to hear that. I'm *very* reassured. Evidently the Special Bureau is so efficient that nobody could possibly give them the slip.' She picked up the large piece of polished black stone that she used as a paperweight and clasped it in both hands, as if she was trying to crush it.

'We had four men watching the house, Minister,' Luther went on.

'Well? How do you explain it, then?'

'I'm still investigating. They had some visitors – a doctor, Matthew Kiraitu, and Michael Owens.'

'That spy? How could you let him in?'

248

'His car was searched on the way out, ma'am.'

'Well, he must have hidden them in his pocket.'

'No, Your Excellency. They were still in the house after he left. We could see Mr Kamunda on the veranda – we had a man in the garden.'

'Well, they're not there now,' she shouted, bringing the stone down on to the desktop with a crash. 'You listen to me, Magari. Find them and bring them back. I want them in custody in forty-eight hours. If you can't do that, you can find another job. Do you understand?'

'Yes, ma'am.'

'Where are you going to start?'

'We know they cannot leave by air or sea,' Luther replied. 'With your permission, Minister, I will contact the army in Ngozi Province. They should set up roadblocks along the northern highway.'

'They won't go that way! You're not thinking. Why would they head straight into the war zone?'

'Because they have no choice,' Luther said, his voice barely rising, despite the throbbing in his head and neck. 'They have no passports – no time to get false documents. There's chaos in the north, no border controls. If I was them, I would go that way.'

'If they're travelling north, someone must be helping them.'

'Yes, ma'am. I'm certain of it.'

'Find them,' she repeated, turning away from Luther as if he disgusted her.

'You can rely on me, Excellency.'

As he left, Pamela called through the open door, 'Lucy! Come here. I need to see Deepak Zaidi. Get him here – this minute, do you hear?'

'Good evening, officer,' Solomon said with a broad smile, climbing down from the cab. 'What a beautiful night.'

'Your licence.'

'Yes, of course.' Solomon handed over his driving licence, watching the thin, anxious face of the young policeman as he inspected it.

'What are you doing here?' the other officer asked, observing Solomon warily and crossing his arms over his pot belly.

'My partner and I are travelling to Upshala, Sergeant.'

'What is this? Universal Exports?' He squinted at the side of the lorry. 'What are you carrying?'

'I supply the army,' Solomon said. 'These are important supplies for the high command in Upshala, private goods for General Wilson Abako, luxuries . . .'

'Show me.'

'By all means. Stephen, please show the sergeant our cargo.'

Stephen led the fat sergeant to the back of the van and released the padlock. 'Here, sir,' he said nervously, pushing up the rolling door.

The officer's eyes widened. 'Whisky!'

'Yes, sir. The general's favourite brand,' Solomon said. 'He relies on me to keep him supplied.'

The sergeant whistled, and his eyes, which had been fixed on the boxes, shifted sideways as he examined Solomon again. 'This kind of trade requires a permit,' he said.

'I answer to the general,' Solomon replied. 'I am an authorised supplier for the army. If any of the cargo is missing, His Excellency will want to know why.'

The policeman pushed his lips out. 'Show me,' he said, pointing at random. 'Open this box.'

Solomon nodded to Stephen, who pulled the case out, lowered it on to the roadside and pulled open the lid.

'Twelve bottles of Johnnie Walker,' Solomon said.

The policeman gazed admiringly at the neat bottle-tops. 'You must know,' he remarked, 'the police force is not well paid.'

'There is a lot of injustice in this world,' Solomon replied sympathetically. 'We traders, too, are often forced to sell at a loss. We have no security.' And he went on, watching the reaction on the fat man's face. 'I believe that men of all kinds must work together. That is my philosophy. We must help one another whenever we can.'

The sergeant sniffed. 'Constable Karua tells me there is a problem with one of your brake lights,' he said, folding his arms again across his tight tunic.

'Yes? I will have it mended as soon as I reach Upshala.'

'You should not be driving a vehicle in this condition. It's a long way to Upshala.'

Solomon nodded gravely. 'I understand your concern, Officer. And to be honest with you, normally I would not want to lose any of the general's goods – not a single bottle. The general is very scrupulous, you see. If he orders one hundred bottles, he expects one hundred to be delivered – not ninety-nine. But if you gentlemen are able to assist us, if you can enable us to drive on in peace, I'm sure His Excellency will understand.'

The sergeant looked at him through cautious dark eyes, and for a moment his head didn't move. Then he nodded briskly, and Solomon bowed his head towards him. 'Officer Karua has my driving documents,' he reminded him.

The fat man said something in Bakhoto, and the younger man handed Solomon his licence.

'Stephen, close the back of the van,' Solomon said. Stephen bent down to pick up the case of whisky, but Solomon shook his head. 'No, no. Just close up.'

'Yes, sir.'

'It seems that we have mislaid one case of Johnnie Walker,' Solomon said. 'I will have to explain to the general that the police in the Central Province gave us a great deal of assistance.'

The fat officer muttered to his junior, who picked up the case and carried it to their Jeep.

'Perhaps on our return journey we can do some more busi-ness,' Solomon suggested, as Stephen got back into the cab. 'If you need anything at all from the north,' he took out a notebook and scribbled a mobile number, 'do not hesitate to call me.'

Tearing out the sheet of paper, he thrust it into the soft, fleshy hand of the sergeant, then climbed up beside Stephen, started the engine and saluted the two policemen through the open window as he drove away.

Part Four

28

The UK headquarters of Global Justice Alliance occupied the fourth floor of an office block on a busy road near Waterloo, with windows overlooking the Thames and the London Eye on one side, the railway tracks on the other. Ed arrived at ten, in time for a meeting with Sue Davies, the chief executive. He was told she had been held up, and spent more than an hour sitting in Reception, rereading his own forty-page report into the failure of the Makera project, and listening to Sue's distinctive nasal voice through the doors of the conference room.

At eleven she came hurrying out, offering her cheek for him to kiss. 'Come in, Ed. It's good to see you – how was your flight?' She pushed a strand of frizzy hair back from her face. 'Listen, I want you to meet Derek Powers. Derek's an expert on the assessment process. He was with the World Bank for twelve years.'

Ed followed her inside, where a weather-beaten man in a blue moleskin jacket offered his hand. 'I've read about your work,' Ed said. 'Weren't you involved in the Millennium Development Goals?'

'In a small way.' He gripped Ed's hand a little too tightly. 'A great deal's happened since the millennium. I was working on partnership development at the bank, engagement with civil society in the recipient countries. That's still a cause close to my heart. When Sue invited me to advise Global Justice, the project I was most excited about was your work in Makera. It ticked a lot of boxes for me.'

'Well, I certainly thought we'd considered most of the angles.'

'And you *had*.' He went to stand on the other side of the

table. 'Really, it was a great piece of work, Ed. Tremendous. And now it's time to move on.'

'Move on?'

'Well, let's all sit down, shall we?' Sue put in rapidly. 'Would you like a coffee, Ed?'

'Er, no – no, thanks.'

'I just mean we have to move on to the assessment phase,' Derek said, as they sat down. 'Measurement of the outcome.'

'Well, that won't be hard,' Ed said. 'You've seen my report?'

'Yes, of course.' Derek and Sue caught one another's eye.

'I'd say the outcome is pretty obvious,' Ed said. 'We've achieved precisely none of the objectives we set ourselves, not one.'

'Well, that's something we clearly need to discuss with the trustees,' Sue said, straightening out the copy of Ed's report that was lying in front of her, the Global Justice logo on the cover, with its strap-line in red: *Poverty isn't a misfortune – it's an injustice.* 'I've asked Derek to help us with the evaluation,' she continued. 'He'll be reporting with you to the chair and the board, and managing the post-project transition with our development partners. Obviously we need to keep DfID and our recipient partners on board—'

'Recipient partners?'

'Your civil-society stakeholders in Batanga,' Derek said.

'Yes, well, that's something else we need to talk about,' Ed said. 'It's the main reason I came back. I couldn't discuss this by email. We have to face the fact that we made the wrong decision about our partners. If we're going to salvage anything from this project, we need to change the team.'

Sue's eyes rested on the front page of Ed's report. 'Look, Ed, I've been discussing this with Derek,' she said. 'We both feel that you place a bit too much emphasis in your report on the original timetable – the building schedule.'

'How do you mean?'

'Well, of course it's good – I mean, it's very important – to go out into the field with clear operational objectives, such as clinics and schools to be built, measurable targets, but at the same time we've got to be flexible about how we reach them. You know that better than anyone. We must be willing to work *with* the local culture and conditions, not just with*in* them.'

'And what happens when our entire objective – not just our timetable or budget, but every principle we stand for – is jeopardised by one of our partners?' Ed said. 'You read the report. It's not a question of running overtime with the building work – God knows, I can live with that. It's the theft of our funds by the Abasis – by Milton Abasi – the murder and forced eviction of the slum residents. If we go ahead now, the only people who'll benefit from the project will be Batangan oligarchs. Not a single poor family will be better off – not one – even supposing they survive.'

Derek nodded thoughtfully, but he avoided Ed's eyes and focused on the piece of paper in front of him, on which he had written a series of bullet-points. 'I know how you feel, Ed, and I sympathise – I've been in your position quite a few times. But we do need to move carefully. We've got to carry DfID with us.'

'Fine. Show them the report,' Ed said. 'I've no objection. They can judge for themselves.'

'I do want to share the final report with them,' Derek said at once, 'only we must give them more to go on. I absolutely endorse your views – the approach you've taken here – but we're dealing with the UK government. They work closely with Wachira's people and we'd have to give them solid evidence if they're going to adjust their approach.'

'They can have all the evidence they want,' Ed said. 'Everything's on record. I've got a shedload of paperwork.'

'Here in London?'

'No. I couldn't risk being searched on my way out of Batanga.'

'Where is it, then?' Derek said.

'It's safe. I'll get it to you. In fact, I'd like to show the trustees. I want them to see the whole picture.'

'The trustees?' Sue nodded. 'Interesting idea.'

257

'But it doesn't make any difference,' Ed continued. 'We're not taking Milton Abasi to court, are we? From the GJA point of view, all we need to know is that he's corrupt, that he's stolen our funds and obstructed our objectives. There's no doubt about that. Even on the basis of my reports from Kisuru, you must have known what was wrong.'

There was silence for a few moments. Sue pressed her hands palm down on to the table. 'I was concerned, of course,' she said. 'We're relying a good deal on Milton – on the Abasi network . . .'

'*Were* relying,' Ed corrected her. 'He's got to go. I can't work with him now. Nobody could.'

'There's certainly a case for repositioning him,' Derek said.

'Repositioning him where?'

'I think we need to restructure the project – I'm sorry, Sue. Is this an appropriate moment?'

She hesitated, glancing at Ed. 'Yes, I think so.'

'Okay. What we've been thinking, Ed, is that we need to reconsider the project assessment criteria before we release the final report. That's something I recommend in most cases.'

'You mean, moving the goal posts?'

He smiled, shaking his head calmly. 'Not at all, not at all. You set the objectives, and nobody's challenging that – Makera was your project from the start. I simply mean that we have to absorb the lessons you've learned – absorb them – and feed them into the assessment process in a positive way, not use them as proof of failure. It's simply a matter of handling the feedback. That way we can carry DfID with us and start rolling out Makera-style programmes in other cities.'

'That's what I want you to do, Ed,' Sue put in. 'I want you to take on a global planning role, building our partnerships with recipient governments, putting together the programmes.'

Ed paused, narrowing his eyes. 'What about Makera? What about the people there?'

'I want you to move on,' she said. 'I'm offering you a strategic

258

role.' And she added, a little defensively: 'It's a promotion, Ed. You'd be running project development worldwide.'

'But we've just learned that the Makera model doesn't work,' he said, sitting back on his chair, his eyes wide as he looked from Derek to Sue and back again. 'Haven't we? I mean, at the very least, we know there are more pitfalls than we imagined. Despite all our due diligence – all my preparations over the last eighteen months – a major project can still be hijacked, even in a country like Batanga where we thought we knew the ruling élite pretty well.' He paused, his eyes resting on Sue, who was blushing. 'We can't pretend none of this happened. If Milton Abasi remains associated with Global Justice – if he continues to have some kind of role . . . Well, it's a joke. We can't work like that. Nobody in Batanga would take us seriously. He has to go.'

Derek shook his head. 'I know how you feel, but Milton's not in play.'

'Not in play?'

'Technically he's not our appointment,' Sue said. 'We can't sack him because we don't employ him.'

'But we can refuse to work with him. We can close down the project and start again with new partners.'

'You know we can't do that,' Sue said. 'I realise it's frustrating, but you've got to see how much is riding on this. DfID are very fired up about it. They want Makera to be the first of a whole series of projects in the world's slums.'

'I've been discussing it with them,' Derek said. 'It's an extremely exciting opportunity for GJA. The government wants to focus twenty per cent of its MDG funding on the mega-slums of Africa and Asia – that's where the action is now. The urban poor are the fastest growing demographic on the planet.'

'But we're not going to help the urban poor if we let local élites muscle in on the funding.'

'Nothing works perfectly,' Derek said. 'The Wachira government isn't so bad by African standards.'

'How bad would it have to be?' Ed asked. 'We seem to apply different standards to Africa and the Middle East than we do anywhere else in the world. What's that about? We're talking about rich people stealing from the poor.'

Derek frowned. 'DfID's view is that Wachira's achieved quite a lot. Of course there's still leakage, but the overall trajectory is positive. He's grown Batangan GDP – six per cent per annum over the last four years. If you look at it in a long time-horizon, it's an encouraging record.'

'So you're basically saying we shouldn't learn anything from Makera,' Ed said. 'We just keep handing money to our clients so that they can make a fortune pushing poor people out of the slums. Oh, and we make sure there's no evaluation – no follow-up that might upset the funders. Terrific. *That*'s ethical.'

'That's not fair, Ed! You know our motives.'

'Our motives? You're talking about motives? What about consequences? What about the impact our work has on the people we're supposed to be helping?'

'That's where you come in,' Derek said. 'Obviously we keep refining our approach, keep learning from past mistakes . . .'

'Well, good. Let's start learning. First off, we've got to close down the Makera project.'

'We can't do that,' Sue said.

'Why not? It's easy. We just send DfID the report and say that, for totally obvious reasons, we're pulling out before we do more harm than good.'

But Derek was shaking his head. 'We can't afford to get hung up on one sub-optimal project, Ed. I've been spending a lot of time at DfID recently – I've been briefing Clive Bird and Oona Simon and they fully understand the problems we've run into in Kisuru, but they're keen to roll the model out, learn the lessons, raise our game, move on. They want to meet you.'

'It's a huge opportunity,' Sue said. 'They're talking about a whole series of Makeras, Ed, twenty to thirty million dollars per project.'

'Clive's working on a financing formula with the EU. They're looking at a joint aid strategy, sharing the costs between a consortium of donor countries, the World Bank, the EU, a couple of the UN bodies, with the recipient governments providing expertise in the field.'

'If we don't run with it, DfID will partner with Housing for Health,' Sue went on. 'They've been trying to move into third-world slums for years.'

'Yes, I know,' Ed said flatly. 'They tried to headhunt me last year.'

'Well, there you are,' she replied. 'Look, you've got to see the big picture. Our turnover will be more than fifty million next year if we agree to Makera Two. There's a lot riding on it – influence, the chance to make a difference on a big scale . . . We mustn't let our feelings get in the way. We have to think strategically.'

Ed picked up his report, weighing it in his hand as he waited for the sound of police sirens on Westminster Bridge to fade away. 'Do you remember what we talked about when I first joined Global Justice?' he said at last.

Sue tapped a pen on the table. 'What was that?'

'About the pressure on NGOs to come up with impressive-sounding goals to attract funding, then ignore bad outcomes so that the donors maintain the income stream.'

Derek folded his arms, keeping his eyes on Ed's sunburned face.

'There are basically two ways of assessing a project,' Ed went on. His voice was beginning to break, and he cleared his throat. 'Two ways. We can either look at what actually happened in the field – in Makera, say: the misappropriation of funds, the failure to achieve our objectives, the worsening conditions on the ground – or we can ignore it and simply look at the amount of money we disburse, the growth in our turn-over, staff numbers, the advertising budget . . .' He gave his report a shake. 'That's easier, of course. You don't need to visit the project to count the money – you don't even need to *have* a project. You just transfer cash from one government to another.' He got to his feet. 'I told you I didn't want to work like that,' he said, 'and you agreed with me. At least, you said you did.'

'A lot's changed in the last few years,' Sue said. 'This organisation's growing very fast. We need to be realistic.'

'You're right.' He took his jacket and pulled it on. 'I'm resigning, Sue. I'll send you an email.'

'I'm sorry,' she said, clearly surprised. 'That wasn't what I wanted – not at all.'

'No?' He picked up his report.

'You know it wasn't. I was offering you a promotion.'

Ed shrugged his shoulders, but he was blushing now and twitching the report against his jacket. 'I should go,' he said. 'I don't want to say anything else.'

Derek stood up and offered Ed his hand. 'Let's keep things friendly,' he urged. 'There's no need for bad feeling. It's a small world out there.'

Ed looked at the hand for some time, before taking it. 'I'm going,' he repeated, turning away. 'I'll email.' He walked out into the reception area, past a Global Justice poster of a child in Makera with flies on his face, and out to the lifts.

Mike's phone went off when he was stuck in traffic on Freedom Avenue.

'Hey, Ed, what's happening? You back yet?' He gripped the steering wheel with his knees as he set up the phone.

'No, I'm still in London,' Ed's voice replied. 'Look, Mike, I've, er – something's happened . . .'

'I'm listening.'

'Well, it's GJA. I've resigned.'

'Shit, that was quick.'

'Yes, well, there it is. I didn't exactly plan it.'

A man with a dirty bandage over one eye had started banging

on Mike's window with the stump of his right hand. 'Hold on a minute,' he told Ed. 'Don't go away.' Winding down the window a few inches, he put a hundred-shilling note into the man's left hand.

'You know that job you mentioned in Upshala?' Ed went on. 'The refugee co-ordinator?'

'Yeah, yeah – the UNHCR.'

'Do you think they're still looking?'

'I can find out. You want me to recommend you?'

'That would be good,' Ed said. 'Really, I'd be very grateful. I'm definitely in the market.'

'All right. You hold on. I'll ring you from the office.'

29

Sarah was working at her laptop on the veranda, her documents spread out across the table and on the floor beside her. She had almost finished writing the speech she was going to make the next day to supporters of the Mbari Women's Co-operative. In the sitting room behind her the lights were on, and she had set up a powerful reading lamp, which shone down over her shoulder. Beyond the mosquito mesh, the garden was dark, stirred by a northerly breeze that smelt of jasmine and hot earth.

Sarah snatched up her phone as it started to ring and, saving her document, got up from the chair. At first it was hard to hear what Ed was saying over the din of cicadas.

'Why, love?' she asked, after a moment. 'What's happened?' She took her empty wine glass from the table. 'You're not serious . . . Oh, it's unbelievable – Sue Davies did this? Look, we should talk when you get back. We can't decide over the phone. Give me a chance to take it in. I'm right in the middle of things.'

'That's what I'm trying to explain,' Ed said. 'I have to go to Upshala tomorrow . . . I'm sorry. It's the only way I could get the job – they've lost their director and they need someone right away.'

Sarah could feel her heart expanding in anger, but she let out a long, controlled breath as she went to the fridge and took out a half-drunk bottle of white wine.

'Actually, it's a good job,' Ed was saying. 'I just wish we'd had time to discuss it. I had to make a decision. It's only a three-month contract. We can decide what we want to do next, whether to renew—'

'I don't understand,' she interrupted, refilling her glass. 'What did Sue Davies actually say? She couldn't just ignore you after everything you've learned out here.'

'She wants to whitewash the whole thing. She's worried about the donors. They think I've gone bush. It's like I was talking a different language.'

'I never trusted Sue Davies,' Sarah said. 'There's something so calculating about her, like she's managing a supermarket.'

'That's true. I was banging on about justice and helping people in Makera, and Sue was talking about increasing the turnover. I felt so stupid.'

'Oh, darling.'

'How's it going with you? How's Archie?'

'He's fine.' She took a mouthful of wine. 'Never better.'

'And the Mbari Women?'

'Fantastic. I've been flat out. They're incredible people – so much attitude. I'm meeting the sponsors tomorrow.'

'You see? I told you you'd find a job.' And he added, in a different tone: 'Listen, I've been thinking about our situation – now that I'm not with Global any more, and we don't know how long this UN contract will last, I really think we ought to move out of the villa.'

'Please don't tell me that, love. The villa's great. It's the only secure thing in our situation at the moment. And we're still settling in. Archie's just getting used to everything.'

'We don't know if we can afford that house any more – even with the discount.'

'What about my salary? I'm earning enough to cover the rent.'

'I just want to make a clean break. I mustn't say too much on the phone but it's important that we stand on our own feet.'

'You want me to give notice?'

'Yes.'

'Well, at least let's get something lined up first. We can't become homeless again. We've got three months, anyway.'

'Yes, I suppose so.'

'God, darling, the time I wasted house-hunting. I can't do that again – I'm literally flat out.'

'I'll help you this time,' he said. 'I'll come down to Kisuru every weekend, and we'll look together.'

'Okay. I'll talk to Pamela if I get a chance, but I don't want to offend her. I don't care what Mike says, she's been very good to us.'

Ed hesitated. 'You know Beatrice and Joseph have disappeared?'

'What do you mean?'

'They've left town. Nobody knows where they are.'

'You think they're in danger?'

'Mike does.' He added quietly: 'The project's been a curse.'

'But it doesn't make sense. Do you want me to ask around?'

'No, don't say anything. Let the dust settle. They may come back.' His tone changed: 'What's Archie been up to?'

'Oh, he's just loving the whole thing – the villa, the garden. He's really running now – he's started kicking a ball, too, and he's pretty good. He spends hours outdoors with Ory. He's not at all interested in me. I'm getting quite jealous.'

'He loves *you*,' Ed said. 'I'm going to miss you both.'

'How long will you be?'

'I don't know. I'll need a couple of weeks to find my feet. The Dutch woman who was running the programme got flown out to Dubai with a fever. It'll take a while to pick up all the threads. Apparently the staff are fighting.'

Sarah stared into the dark garden. 'I'm so sorry about Makera,' she said.

'So am I.'

She surveyed the mass of papers on the table and floor. 'I should finish this speech.'

'I'll ring tomorrow,' he said. 'Get some sleep. Give Archie a kiss from me.'

Pamela Abasi was being driven at high speed through the streets of St Jude's to the Methodist church that housed the Mbari

Women's Co-operative. She had been held up at a crisis meeting with President Wachira, discussing the military situation in the north, and was now on the phone to her brother-in-law, General Wilson Abako, in his headquarters in Upshala.

'No, Wilson. No, no, *no!*' she was saying. 'You shut up before I tell the President to sack you! I'm not interested in your excuses. If Patrick Ochola is supplied by the Sudanese, then cut him off – encircle him. What's the matter with you? Is Ochola a wizard? Can he fly through the air?'

She hung up and handed the phone to Lucy, who was sitting next to the driver in the front. Then, taking a small mirror from her bag, she checked her makeup. There was a standpipe on a street corner, a couple of blocks from the church, where a queue of young girls carrying brightly coloured jerry-cans had formed early in the morning. By this time, as Pamela's car drove into the neighbourhood, dozens of women in *kanga* wraps were lining the streets to cheer her, while a group of policemen walked up and down the line, swinging their truncheons. Pamela sat up straight, waving through the window. As her driver slowed down a choir of children, standing outside the church in Mbari Women's Co-operative T-shirts, started to sing a traditional Makhoto greeting.

Lucy jumped out of the Mercedes and hurried towards Sarah, who was standing a few yards away with Dido Buwembo, the director of the co-operative. 'Her Excellency can stay for only ten minutes,' she explained.

'Will she be able to address the girls?' Dido asked. 'They have been so excited about this visit. They know this centre wouldn't exist without Pamela Abasi.'

Pamela was walking slowly towards them now, surrounded by her guards, raising her right hand in acknowledgement of the singing children and the cheers from the rest of the crowd.

'How do you do, Minister?' Dido said, extending her hand towards her. 'Welcome to the Mbari Women's Co-operative. We're deeply honoured by your visit.'

'It's good to be here,' Pamela said.

'I believe you have met Sarah Caine, Minister,' she went on. 'She has been assisting us with our latest fundraising campaign, reaching out to international donors.'

'Yes, I know Sarah,' Pamela said, gripping her hand. 'How are you?'

'Well, thank you, Minister. I'm delighted to see you again. The women are so excited about your visit – they've been talking about it for weeks.'

'We should go inside,' Pamela said, her eyes scanning the crowd. 'The SB are worried about this area.' She kept hold of Sarah's hand as she strode on towards the church. 'I was pleased to hear you'd got this job.'

'Thanks to your kind introduction,' Sarah said. 'It's a superb organisation. And Dido is exceptional. I've never worked for anyone so inspiring.'

'She's a good manager,' Pamela replied, nodding towards Dido, who was marshalling the crowd in the hall to move back and make space for their visitor.

'They all owe you so much,' Sarah said. 'Without your support, there would be no centre, and their lives would be far, far harder. Everyone is conscious of that.'

'I do what I can,' Pamela replied, her smile fading as they entered the church. She stopped at the threshold. 'I have to tell you, Sarah, I've been very worried about Joseph and Beatrice over the last few days. Last night I was kept awake, thinking about them.'

'Why? What's happened?'

'Well, we don't know. Nobody has heard from them for two days now.'

'You think they're in danger?'

'Who knows?' She sniffed, glancing towards the women waiting to meet her. 'I hear rumours, and it frightens me . . . If I knew where they were, I could help, but as it is . . .' She turned aside, and Sarah noticed the watery surface of her eyes. 'We know there are rogue elements in the security forces – Shala agents – men in the pay of Patrick Ochola. They would dearly love to kidnap a senior official like Joseph. They are targeting civil servants, professional people . . .' And she moved closer to Sarah. 'You know them, don't you, Edward and you? Have you heard anything?'

'No,' Sarah said at once, putting her hand towards Pamela's arm in sympathy, then standing back respectfully. 'We don't know what's happened. Ed's in London. Actually, I wanted to talk to you about our situation, about the villa, but this obviously isn't the time.'

'No, no. You tell me what's happening.'

'Well, Ed rang last night. He – well, he's decided to move on from Global Justice.'

'Move on?'

'He's resigned.'

Pamela stood still, watching Sarah minutely.

'Yes, it's extraordinary, after all the work he's done, but it seems they've come to a parting of the ways – I don't know why, exactly. I didn't want to interrogate him over the phone. Ed's such an idealist – he was very upset by the problems with the Makera project.'

'It must have been frustrating,' Pamela said. 'It's a shame for Global Justice to lose such a good man, but I'm sure he'll find another job.'

'He's taken a short contract with the UN,' Sarah said, 'but he's worried about money. He wants us to give notice on the villa. He's not sure we can afford it after the new year.'

'No, no. That I won't hear of.' Pamela glanced over Sarah's shoulder. 'You must stay. You have enough worries without moving house again – am I right?'

'Well, Ed was very insistent.'

'Yes, of course, and so am I,' she said. 'We can't let the men decide everything. We girls must look after ourselves. You stay. If you need a rent holiday in the new year, we'll talk about it. Well, Lucy? What is it?'

'It's time,' Lucy said quietly. She had come up behind Pamela, clutching a leather file, from which she now took out a sheet of A4. 'Here's your speech, ma'am.'

Pamela offered Sarah her hand. 'If you have any thoughts about Joseph and Beatrice, you'll let me know, won't you?'

'Yes, of course,' Sarah said, and went on cautiously: 'Actually, there is someone you could ask – a young man who's been quite involved, Solomon something. He helped Ed with the building work.'

'Really? You don't know the surname?' Pamela asked. 'It might help.'

'No, I'm sorry. He's a businessman, with his own building firm.'

Lucy made a note.

'Well, we'll just have to keep praying,' Pamela said. 'Give my best wishes to Edward. There – I must go. Where's the speech, Lucy? What have you done with it?'

'It's here, ma'am,' Lucy replied calmly, and, indicating the way with her open hand, she escorted Pamela across the room to where the women were waiting.

30

At the northern end of the Bakhoto valley, the road zigzagged upwards to a height of more than a thousand feet, emerging between two peaks at a vantage-point known as McIntyre's Saddle. From here, tourists driving to the Northern National Park stopped to survey the vast bluish savannah, and the thick dark jungle of the Ngozi Hills in the distance.

There was a dusty car park by the road, with half a dozen safari Jeeps, and a kiosk where a couple of young boys sold bottles of water, disposable cameras and nuts in twists of paper. Solomon parked the truck as far as possible from the little crowd, then opened the back to let Beatrice and Joseph out. They said goodbye to Stephen, and for half an hour the two of them were able to walk about in a dip of land below the car park, looking out across the northern plains, while Solomon made arrangements for Stephen to return to Kisuru in another lorry. After that the three drove on down the mountain road, entering Shala territory for the first time. And Solomon started singing a traditional Kishala ballad, thumping his hand rhythmically against the outside of the truck door.

Beatrice hummed Solomon's song, wrapping her arms around herself as the lorry bumped along the road. The last time she had stood on McIntyre's Saddle, staring across the sea-like vastness of the savannah, she had been a small girl holding her mother's hand. That first sight of the northern wilderness – the land of her mother's Shala ancestors – had flooded her young mind with mysterious feelings of pride and regret. It seemed to her that the whole of human history, right back to the remotest epochs, had been present in front of her, and a vast invisible crowd was watching her from the plain. Now, as she listened to Solomon's voice, those childhood memories seized her heart again. Despite the weight of fear and shame that had pressed down on her since she had regained consciousness, her blood was suffused with excitement. She reached out her hand towards Solomon, pressing it against the boxes that separated them.

By the time it was dark, they had crossed forty miles of savannah and the road surface had deteriorated so much that the lorry was grinding along a rutted track at less than ten miles an hour. Solomon stared out at the high walls of grass illuminated by the headlights, his drowsiness intensified by the whining of the engine. Then, suddenly, an antelope sprang out on to the red track just ahead of the bonnet, running along in panic down the road, before bouncing away into the grass. A little later, while Solomon's heart was still racing, the headlights picked out a female giraffe and her calf, standing stock still beside a baobab tree to the left of the road.

At about eleven o'clock, the truck reached the point at which the road crossed a dry riverbed, and after that the landscape became hilly again. Massive tree-trunks appeared out of the darkness, not isolated shrubs stripped of their leaves and bark, like the thorns on the savannah, but vast perpendicular sequoia and mahogany trees, standing apart from one another in the silver grass, their branches raised up in the darkness. In the distance, at the ridge of a low-lying hill, Solomon could see the light of a fire, and a couple of electric bulbs suspended across the track.

Beatrice had taken a tranquilliser, and was fast asleep. As long as it was light, Joseph sat next to her, looking out through his spyhole at the grassy wilderness. Then he replaced the whisky case, put a rug over his daughter, as the temperature began to fall, and tried to stretch out. But the continuous rolling and pitching of the lorry, the smell of exhaust and the roar of the engine made it impossible to sleep, and he was still awake when the truck came to a halt. Solomon tapped quietly three times on the partition, and almost at once Joseph heard men's voices outside. Then the engine stopped. Immediately the darkness was filled with the noise of cicadas, bird cries and the screeching of animals in the distance.

Solomon looked down from the cab. Behind a wooden barrier, two men in fatigues and T-shirts were pointing automatic rifles at him. Next to them on the side of the road there was a shed, with a rocking chair in front of it, where another soldier was watching from under a peaked cap as he smoked a cigarette. Further away, isolated in the darkness of the trees, he could see a small house, its wooden steps and veranda lit by a paraffin lamp.

One of the men approached the truck. 'Get down,' he said, still pointing his gun at Solomon. 'Show me your papers.'

He climbed out and handed the soldier his licence.

'Where are you going?'

'Upshala.' Solomon's eyes were fixed involuntarily on the end of the soldier's gun. He added, making himself look up at the man's yellow T-shirt and unbuttoned tunic: 'I have important goods for General Abako.'

'What goods?' He turned aside to spit on the ground. 'If you are carrying contraband, the major will impound your vehicle.'

'No, no. They are legal goods – I have a trading permit. Please see for yourself.'

The second man stepped forward from the barrier, and the soldier by the hut also stood up, threw down his cigarette and ambled towards the lorry. 'What's happening? Who is this person?'

'He says he's making a delivery to General Abako, Corporal,' the big man replied.

'To Abako?'

'That's right, sir,' Solomon said. 'I supply the general and his staff with many important goods.'

'And who are you?'

273

'Solomon Ouko. A businessman.'

The corporal raised his cap a little to scratch his forehead. 'Let me see your documents.'

'I was just going to show your men the cargo,' Solomon replied, indicating the back of the truck.

The corporal watched him fiercely. 'Where are your papers?'

'In the cab.'

But the other two men had already reached the back of the lorry, and were thumping the doors with their fists.

'Open it for them,' the corporal said. 'Then show me your identification.'

Solomon walked slowly along the side of the lorry, unlocked the door and pulled it open. The two soldiers had already lowered their guns. The big man in the yellow T-shirt shone a torch into the back, while the other – a teenager in baggy clothes – gazed at the boxes. For a few moments no one spoke, and Solomon heard the rhythm of *lingala* music coming from the little house beyond the checkpoint. Then the young soldier put his hand out towards a box of Johnnie Walker. 'Alcohol,' he said.

'Whisky and cigars,' Solomon replied. 'Scotch for the general. I'm sure he wouldn't mind if his brave soldiers in the field took something for themselves.'

Immediately the youth pulled a case from the stack, lowered it to the ground and started to tear it open.

'Leave that,' the corporal said. 'Fetch the major's dogs. Tell Private Mwenje to bring them. The dogs will save time,' he went on, watching Solomon cautiously. 'And now your papers, Mr Ouko. *Businessman*. Bring them to the office.'

The soldiers disappeared into the darkness beyond the road-block for a few moments, re-emerging with two Alsatians, which immediately started barking and growling around the truck.

'What's wrong with them?' the corporal said.

'They are unhappy tonight, sir. Perhaps there's a lion nearby – a hyena.'

'Then why are they barking at the truck?' the corporal

demanded. He turned to Solomon. 'What have you got in here? What is upsetting the dogs?'

'I don't know, Corporal. Perhaps they would like some whisky.'

'Show me,' he insisted. 'Take out the boxes.'

'Of course,' Solomon replied, remaining where he was by the barrier, and taking the cigarette carton from his pocket. 'However, if I have to spend too much time here, General Abako will want to know why his delivery has been delayed.' He pulled a roll of banknotes from the packet. 'His Excellency is expecting me to reach Upshala by this time tomorrow, and he is a man who always rewards good service.'

The sergeant stared at the money for a moment, then glanced over his shoulder towards the little house in the forest. 'Just show me what you are carrying,' he said hurriedly. 'Let me see for myself.'

'I have cases of whisky and cigars. They belong to the general – he has paid for them. The paperwork is here.'

'Nothing else?'

'Nothing.'

The young soldier was being dragged closer to the lorry by the two dogs, which were now barking at the undercarriage.

'There's no one in the truck?'

'No, Corporal. I had a man with me yesterday – he slept in the back of the van. There's no one there now. I expect the dogs can smell his bed.'

The corporal nodded. 'And the whisky?'

'Your man has already opened this box,' Solomon said. 'It's damaged. I cannot deliver it to the general like this. You take it, Corporal.'

'The major also likes whisky,' he replied, nodding to the man in the yellow T-shirt to take the box. 'And he smokes cigars.'

'I would be glad to let the major have a case of whisky for himself and a box of cigars,' Solomon said. 'One moment, Corporal.' He went over to the back of the lorry, and disappeared into the darkness, then returned with a wooden box.

'These are expensive cigars, high quality. I'm sure the general would understand.'

'Shall I take this to the major, sir?'

'Yes. If he is busy, do not disturb him. Put the whisky and cigars inside the house.'

'Now the paperwork, Corporal.' Solomon smacked his cheek to kill a mosquito as he walked back towards the cab. 'I have it all in here.' He stood on the footrest and reached inside. 'But, you understand, I really must continue my journey at once.' Turning, he held out his licences, along with the thick bundle of banknotes, raising his voice over the continuous whining of the dogs. 'Perhaps we could talk somewhere quiet.'

'Give me the papers,' the corporal replied. As he set off back to the hut with the papers, he called: 'Michuki, tie up the dogs, then take this box of whisky to my office.'

Solomon approached the hut, ushered inside by the corporal. As he did so, he saw a light going on in the house by the trees. A man's voice called: 'Corporal Kiviutu! Where are you? Report to me at once.'

The corporal stiffened.

'Perhaps we can conclude our business quickly,' Solomon suggested, with a smile. 'I don't want to trouble the major.'

But there was a look of intense doubt in the corporal's eyes, which were staring at the money in Solomon's left hand. 'I must show him these papers,' he said at last. 'Stay here.' And he hurried off down the path to the bungalow.

Solomon slipped the money back into the cigarette packet and stood at the railings. The young soldier who had brought the dogs was now standing on guard below the hut, gazing into the dark forest, then up towards Solomon.

'Where are you from?' Solomon asked. 'You're not from the north. You're not Shala.'

'The Shala are our enemies,' the boy said. 'I am Bakhoto.'

'Ah, from the south,' Solomon replied genially. 'Now, the south is beautiful – not like this terrible country. I also come from the south, from Kisuru. I hate the wilderness. I hate this forest – this dark, watery jungle. In the jungle you are never safe – something is attacking you all the time: insects, lions, snakes, leeches, spiders, bandits, or you fall into a pit.' And when the soldier nodded, peering into the pitch-black distance, Solomon added, 'I miss Kisuru very much. I hate to be away from home. When were you last with your family?'

The boy said nothing.

'Haven't you been on leave?'

'I have been here for six months. The major says I will go home after five years.'

'Five years,' Solomon repeated. 'And the major? Where is he from?'

'From the coast,' he said. 'He is a rich man – a big man.'

'I'm sure he is,' Solomon said, glancing at the half-illuminated stretch of track dissected by the barrier, and the constantly moving black wall of vegetation beyond.

'This is the major,' the boy said. 'He's coming now.' He stamped his right foot, coming to attention.

The corporal was walking briskly towards the checkpoint, followed by a chubby man in a clean uniform, with a pistol strapped to his side. He had wire-rimmed spectacles on his nose, and was flourishing Solomon's papers. 'Good evening, Mr Ouko,' he said, in English.

'Good evening, Major.'

'I see you are travelling to Upshala with important goods for our high command.'

'That is correct, Your Excellency.'

'Good, good. How interesting. So, this is your van.' And turning away, he shouted: 'Torches! Bring me some light here!'

The corporal produced a large torch from the hut, handing it to him.

'Let me see now.' He flashed it at the side of the lorry. 'Universal Exports. Is that your company, Mr Ouko?'

Solomon hesitated. For the first time his stomach contracted in fear. 'I am the proprietor.'

'You're a well-known man. At least, *I* have heard of you. I can't say that Corporal Kiviutu recognised your name but, you see, he doesn't read, do you, Corporal?'

'No, sir.'

'The fact is, we have been expecting you,' the major went on. 'All three of you.'

Solomon looked down at the dirt road and the gleaming toecaps of the major's boots.

'Well, your friends can't be very comfortable in there,' he went on, pointing at the side of the truck. 'I'm sure they'd prefer to sleep in my bungalow. It's not a bad place. They say it was built for an English doctor. He was killed by Patrick Ochola's men, but the plumbing is still working.' He nodded to the sergeant. 'Tell the men to open the back. Let's see what Mr Ouko is transporting.'

Joseph and Beatrice climbed out of the lorry and stood on the dirt track, while the man in the yellow T-shirt shone a torch into their faces. On the ground around them were a dozen boxes of spirits, cigars and medical supplies.

'Well, Mr Ouko,' the major was saying, 'it seems you are carrying unlicensed goods after all. Corporal, tell the men to reload the van, then drive it into the camp. I am going to interview Mr Ouko and his friends. Report to me when you're ready.' Turning to Solomon, Joseph and Beatrice, he pointed them towards the bungalow.

'I'm sure you wish I had not stopped you,' the major said, as they entered the little house, 'but you should be glad I did. You should all be shaking my hand and thanking me. The road is blocked between here and Upshala. There was a battle today

278

and the army has been clearing rebels from this part of the province. No supplies are getting through, not even army supplies.'

Beatrice looked around the living room, which was empty except for a few folding chairs and a camping table on which the major slapped down Solomon's papers.

'Shall I tell the cook to bring you something to eat? She made a goat stew today, Shala style.'

'That would be kind,' Joseph said, staring towards the major's round face.

The major raised his voice. 'Michuki! Go and fetch the cook. Tell her I have visitors. She must come with her daughters. They can serve us.' The major unstrapped his gun belt and laid it on the table. 'The general will be pleased you are safe,' he said, examining his three prisoners. 'You are Joseph Kamunda, I suppose.'

Joseph bowed his head.

'And this is your daughter, Beatrice.' He gazed at her approvingly.

'And may we know your name, Major?' Solomon asked.

'I am Jonathan Kiongwe.' He broke off from his scrutiny of Beatrice, reached for a bottle of Scotch and poured himself a glass, then handed the bottle to Solomon. 'Here. Why don't you drink some of your whisky?' And he added confidentially: 'We all drink out here. The men hate the jungle. They are terrified at night – always afraid. They think every noise is a lion coming, a leopard, an evil spirit, the ACP . . . If they didn't drink, I am sure they would go out of their minds.'

Private Michuki had come back to the house with three women in traditional Shala clothes, a mother and her teenage daughters. They took a step or two towards the major and, without saying a word, knelt on the floor in front of him. 'Dinner for my VIP prisoners,' he said, addressing them in Swahili. They got up and withdrew to another room.

'I commandeered this house when I was posted here,' the

major went on. 'I had to stop the men stripping it bare. Our soldiers are like ants. When they find a piece of property, they remove everything – not just the furniture and tools, the cooking pots, dishes, clothes, no, no. They tear out the stairs, the roof, the water pipes, the doors, the glass in the windows – everything. A man will spend an hour pulling a few nails from a wall . . . I promise you, they're very industrious. I have seen Corporal Kiviutu strip the copper wires from inside a telephone. When the army moves out, nothing is left behind, nothing at all.'

Solomon held up his glass and took a sip. 'The men are poor,' he said. 'They are not like their officers. If they have a new door or window-frame, that is something important in their village, but for a man like you, Major . . .' he paused, scrutinising the major's orderly table '. . . for a wealthy man, a Big Man, war brings greater rewards.'

'Today it has brought me a lorry full of whisky and cigars,' he replied. 'All that drink must be worth a lot of money.'

'The cargo is worth ten thousand dollars in Kisuru,' Solomon said.

'And what is the general paying you for it?'

'Twenty thousand.'

The major raised his eyebrows, his glass almost touching his lips.

'The price depends on supply and demand,' Solomon went on smoothly. 'In Upshala there is great demand, little supply. But out here, in the middle of this jungle, there is no demand at all, so the cargo is worth nothing – not even a thousand dollars. Who could pay for it? No one has any money. It will only be stolen by villagers.'

'That creates a dilemma, Mr Ouko.'

'Yes. If the owner wants to make a profit, he must first get access to the market.'

'And you can do this?'

'You are a soldier, sir,' Solomon said. 'I am a businessman. I know how to sell things.'

The two sisters had come back into the room, carrying bowls and a cooking pot, which they put on the wooden floor. Then, kneeling once more, the younger girl filled the bowls with stew, while the elder offered them first to Joseph, then to Solomon, and finally Beatrice.

'If I owned these goods,' the major said, 'just hypothetically, the goods and the lorry . . .'

Solomon took a spoonful of stew.

'. . . I would need an agent to sell them for me.'

'And if I were to act as your agent in this transaction,' Solomon replied, 'I would ask for a small cut, enough for my expenses, and a safe escort to Upshala.'

'How could I know that you would pay me the money?'

'The escort would come with us,' Solomon said. 'Your men could keep us under guard until the money is paid.'

'No, no. These men could never do that,' the major said dismissively. 'They are country boys, Mr Ouko, simpletons – *pumbaru*. None of my men understand the city.'

'Do you have a relative in Upshala, Major, someone you trust?'

But the major turned to face him. 'You are typical Shala,' he said. 'Shala are like Asians. They are always doing business, always looking for profits. They are nature's thieves.'

'I was brought up in Kisuru, Major. I believe that every tribe in Batanga has a gift for business. I have met naked Bontai herdsmen who have grown rich from tourism. In this country everything is business – politics, war, even rebellion.'

Joseph cleared his throat. 'Excuse me, Major.'

'Mr Kamunda?'

'You said that the road to Upshala is cut off, that the army is clearing the area. How can we get to Upshala from here?'

'Not on the highway. You will take the road to the west, through the Ngozi Hills. It's further, but the ACP are not operating there.'

'How long will it take?'

The major smiled. 'Why do you ask? Are you in a hurry?'

281

Joseph's eyes lingered on the man's fleshy face and bulging, ironic eyes, before dropping to the cooking pot on the floor, the two Shala girls squatting beside it. 'No,' he said quietly. 'There's no hurry.'

31

To the north of the major's post, the road continued for seven or eight miles through the hardwood forest. Beatrice sat in the back of an army Jeep, opposite Joseph and Solomon. Their wrists had been handcuffed behind their backs, and a young soldier, perched beside the driver, turned round every few minutes to point his gun at them, then looked back anxiously into the open country. Beatrice was in extreme pain. Every time the Jeep hit a pothole, the handcuffs dug into her wrists and the metal seat thumped against her bruised body, making her eyes water. But it was impossible to lift her weight off it for any length of time, and she concentrated on not crying out, staring up past the treetops towards the sky, her mouth shut tight.

'If he agreed to your terms,' Joseph was saying, 'why has he not sent the lorry with us?'

Solomon shifted his position. 'He said he wanted to be sure the road was open. He'll send the cargo later.'

'That could be true,' Joseph said. 'He'd rather lose us than the whisky.'

They were silent for a while, and Beatrice tried to straighten her legs. 'At least we're alive,' she said. 'The major might have killed us. I thought he would.'

'Apparently it's more profitable to sell us,' Joseph replied. 'I wonder what we're worth to him. Promotion? A new posting? Or is it just money?' He glanced up at the soldier in the passenger seat who was pointing his rifle into the elephant grass. 'Money, I expect.'

'You see up there?' Solomon said. 'Those hills? That's the Ngozi Highlands. They start there. Soon we'll be in the jungle.'

'We already are,' Beatrice said, looking up into the high treetops.

'No, no. This is forest – look at the trees. They're wide and tall, like city buildings. There's space here and big animals. The jungle is different. There's no space for anything. It's cramped – it squeezes the life out of you.'

'Your family lived in this country?' Joseph asked.

'I was born in the Northern Territory,' he replied. 'Not here, further east, in the farming country.'

'I never thought of you as a country man,' Joseph said. 'I would have said the city was in your blood.'

'I came to Kisuru when I was five – five or six, I don't remember.'

'Why did you leave home?' Beatrice asked.

'I ran away,' he said lightly. 'My father left us when we were small, and afterwards my mother started to live with another man. He was a farmer: he had goats and chickens, lots of cows. He was a typical Shala, very proud of his cattle. Then my mother and this man started to have children, but they had only daughters, and our stepfather began to hate my brother and me because we weren't his own sons. He said we were taking food for nothing. He stopped us going to school and made us look after the cattle. We had to keep them safe at night, watching out for lions. If any of the cattle were lost, he beat us. One time he beat me so hard with an *ugali* paddle I was unconscious.' He shrugged, sitting up a little to release the pressure on his hands. 'I thought I had died.'

'So you ran away,' Beatrice said.

'My brother died from a fever during the rainy season. After he was buried, I ran away to Upshala. Then I went to the railway yard at night and hid under the seat in a train going to Kisuru. The guards were always looking for children on the trains, but they didn't find me. During the journey there was a *mzungu* in my compartment – I can remember him exactly. He was a priest with thick spectacles, sitting by the window reading a black

284

book. He knew I was under his seat, but he didn't tell anyone. When the inspector started poking under the seat with his stick, the priest told him not to concern himself. He said he would take care of everything. Later he shared his lunch with me. And in Kisuru he took me to a refuge for street-children.' He gazed up into the treetops, trying to release the tension in his neck, then looked across the Jeep at Beatrice's face. 'I often think of that man,' he said. 'He changed my life. When I was a child, I used to think Jesus had sent him to look after me.'

'Why not?' she said gently, leaning towards him as far as she could and returning his gaze. 'Children understand things. They have generous hearts. That's why they're so easy to love.'

The track was veering to the right as it climbed. In the course of the last mile or two, the elephant grass had fallen away from the roadside. Beatrice watched it recede into the distance, confined to the lower ground, as they approached the edge of the jungle. Then, quite suddenly, the view to the south was shut out altogether as the track entered a tunnel of vegetation and the Jeep slowed, struggling over a road surface broken up by giant roots.

'Look at the soldiers,' Joseph said quietly. 'They're frightened.'

The young man in the passenger seat had put his rifle to his shoulder, ready to fire, and was repeating the same phrase under his breath as he peered into the undergrowth.

'What's he saying?' Beatrice whispered.

'He's saying, "Celestial Peace, Celestial Peace",' Solomon said.

'He ought to have more faith in the army,' Joseph remarked drily. 'Hasn't he read the papers?'

'Stop talking,' the driver hissed. He speeded up, keeping to the middle of the road where the ground was less broken.

'What's the matter?' Beatrice asked.

'It's nothing,' Solomon said. 'They're just nervous.' But as he was speaking, something in the vault of green above Beatrice caught his eye and he stared up.

'What is it?' Joseph asked.

'I don't know. I thought I saw someone looking at me—'

'Be silent,' the driver barked.

The road had been running along the top of a narrow ridge, rising continuously for the last fifty yards or so, and now all at once the Jeep emerged through the roof of the jungle into a limitless expanse of sunlight. They could see the rust-coloured track rising and falling along the line of the hilltops ahead, and all around it, as far as the horizon, the undisturbed darkness of the jungle. The driver slowed, and the boy with the gun spoke more rapidly, pointing at the trees ahead.

'What's happening?' Joseph asked.

'ACP,' the driver said. 'They have been here.'

An area of jungle had been cleared on one side of the road, and there were the marks of fires, animal bones, the carcass of a goat and, to the right, visible to Beatrice, a narrow foot-track leading down into the trees.

The young soldier was now arguing with the driver and the Jeep stopped. 'He says there are bodies hanging on the trees,' Solomon said.

'Where?'

'Ahead – next to the road.'

Joseph twisted his head to look past the soldiers. 'I can't see anything.'

The driver revved the engine and moved forward, and the young soldier fell silent, his eyes fixed on the trees in front of him. Then the driver said, 'Oh, Jesus!' The Jeep continued to roll forward, while the boy stared at the perimeter of the clearing.

Beatrice followed the direction of the driver's gaze towards the middle branches of a tall hardwood tree, standing on its own near the edge of the jungle. Five corpses were hanging from ropes tied to the same large bough, the bodies of a man, a woman and three young children. As the Jeep approached, she saw that the children's hands and feet had been cut off, and that the woman's body had been sliced open, so that her entrails hung down from her belly, almost reaching the ground. A wooden sign had been suspended around the neck of the man, written with large letters in Kishala and Swahili: 'Informer'.

'What have they done to him?' Beatrice demanded, staring at the man's featureless scaly black face. 'What is that?'

'They have skinned him,' Solomon said. 'They peeled his face off. That is what they do to spies. Now the ants are eating him.'

'What are they saying?' Joseph asked.

The young boy was railing at the driver, who continued to gaze at the mutilated bodies.

'He wants to go back,' Solomon said. 'The rebels who did this are still here – nearby. He can feel them watching us.'

The driver put up his hand for silence, then half lifted himself from his seat, his eyes searching the clearing with a kind of terrified determination. 'There's no one,' he said, sitting down. 'They've gone.' He started to drive on, but almost at once there was a crackling sound somewhere in the jungle to their right.

'Machine-guns,' Solomon said.

The boy started shouting again and the driver slammed on the brakes. There was another burst of automatic gunfire, followed by three single shots.

'Perhaps it's the army,' Joseph said.

They waited in silence. Then the boy was talking again, speaking rapidly, continuously, as if he hadn't time to unburden himself of everything he needed to say. The driver replied in a few words.

'They're going back,' Solomon said.

The driver made a three-point turn on the track, and the boy turned to the prisoners, pointing his gun at Solomon. 'Get out,' he said. 'Hurry up.'

'We can't,' Joseph said. 'The major ordered you to take us to Upshala. You must drive on or you will be court-martialled.'

'We cannot go to Upshala,' he said, pointing his rifle at Joseph. 'The road is closed.'

'You must take us with you.'

The driver had finished his turn, and he shouted at the boy,

287

who jumped out of the Jeep and went to lower the back. 'Get *down*! Get out or I will shoot you.'

'I can't move – you've handcuffed me.'

The boy glared at Joseph. 'Down,' he repeated, as Joseph wriggled off the bench and landed on the track. 'Out! Out!' he yelled to the others. 'You, too!'

The gunfire had stopped, but as Beatrice manoeuvred herself from the back of the Jeep to the ground, there was an explosion in the jungle. A plume of smoke rose from the bottom of the valley.

The driver shouted an order, and the boy tugged hard at Solomon's shoulder so that he fell to the ground.

'What about the keys?' Joseph said. 'You must unlock us.'

The driver stamped on the accelerator and the boy looked about in terror.

'The keys,' Solomon insisted, as he struggled to his feet. And when the boy seemed not to hear him, he said calmly: 'Listen to me, *kijana*, if you don't give us the keys, I will personally come back as a ghost and haunt you. I will visit you every night. I swear it.'

There was another exchange of gunshots in the valley, followed by a second detonation. The driver shouted again, put the vehicle in gear and started to drive away. 'I will curse you!' Solomon roared, as the boy ran after the Jeep. 'I swear to God, I will haunt you every night!'

The young man was sprinting along the track, yelling to the driver, who took his foot off the pedal just long enough to allow him to jump up and grab the rollover bar. Then, as the Jeep accelerated away, he turned round, took aim with his fist and tossed something shiny towards Solomon, then sank down between the benches.

'We must keep moving,' Solomon said, as he unlocked Beatrice's handcuffs. 'We have to get away from this battle.'

'Then what?' Joseph peered out into the jungle. 'We could

be a hundred miles from Upshala. You said you knew this route.'

'I've never used this road. I always go on the highway. All I know is, there are dead people in the trees, a battle is going on down there and Upshala is that way.' He pointed northwards.

Joseph nodded nervously. 'All right. Let's get out of this clearing. Bea?'

She had bent double and was vomiting on to the grass.

'Here, *mchumba*,' Solomon said, coming up to her. 'Come with me. It's going to be all right.' He took her hand.

They walked towards the family hanging from the teak tree, hurried past and disappeared into the deep vegetation. Without the Jeep, there was no engine noise to block the clicking and whistling of birds all around them, and the mysterious hissing of the jungle, as it panted and exhaled in the heat. At first Beatrice was conscious of these sounds pressing in on her, as if she was being smothered, but gradually the pressure seemed to lift. After a few hundred yards the road began to drop below the treetops, continuing downhill until it crossed a stream beneath a solid dome of branches. Joseph stopped short in the middle of the path, ten yards from the water, and held up his hand. 'Something's wrong,' he whispered. 'Listen.'

Beatrice closed her eyes, concentrating on the wall of sound. Her stomach and bloodstream were so charged with fear that she was lightheaded. Now, as her panic intensified, she felt strangely weightless and disembodied. 'I can't hear anything,' she said, almost inaudibly. 'Only the hissing.'

'That's right,' Solomon replied. 'No birds. No animals.'

Joseph's eyes were darting from tree to tree. 'What is it?' he whispered. 'What do we do?'

'Keep moving,' Solomon said. 'Beatrice, let me carry you.'

He lifted her in his arms, and started to cross the stream. But after a few steps, he stopped in the water, staring ahead. Beatrice followed his gaze. A young boy was standing on the opposite bank, his eyes hidden by the peak of a baseball cap. He was dressed in a pair of shorts and a T-shirt with the words *All-Star 22* written across it. His left arm was bandaged above the elbow, and he was holding an automatic rifle, which he was pointing towards them. Without any apparent movement, two other boys appeared from the shrubs beside the road, and a group of teenage girls rose up from the ground beyond the stream, their heads covered with wide, rubbery leaves. Each of the older boys was holding a gun, and the tallest child – a girl in camouflage trousers – was carrying a rocket-launcher on her shoulder. Then something splashed in the water behind them, a man's voice gave an order in Kishala, and the children took aim.

32

Ed and Mike Owens were sitting in wickerwork chairs near the bar of the George VI Hotel, Upshala. Ed had arrived late that afternoon, and had immediately been taken by Mike to visit the refugee camps nearest the town. Now, exhausted by the heat and humidity, he was gazing out through the tall windows on the other side of the room towards the high street, where a dozen white UN Land Cruisers were parked in the mud, and a Ngozi tribesman dressed in a long gown was herding a half-starved cow down the middle of the road.

'Nils has been here since last summer,' Mike said, nodding towards the fragile-looking man who had sat down opposite them. He had a bald, sunburned head, and was staring at the beers on the table through a pair of wire-framed spectacles. 'He came out with Emergency Unlimited.'

'Hey, all right, don't remind me,' Nils protested. 'I worked for those bastards. Nobody warned me.'

'What are you doing now?' Ed asked.

'I'm on your staff.' His lips expanded in a brief, ambiguous smile, and he glanced at another man who had come up beside him. 'I'm running the trauma unit at the hospital.'

'It's one of the best hospitals in East Africa,' the other man said, patting him on the shoulder. 'The more Nils drinks, the better he does – isn't that right, Nils?'

'This is Frank,' Nils said indifferently. 'Have a drink.'

Frank nodded to Ed and Mike, and called the waiter.

'Ed's taking over as regional director for the UNHCR,' Nils explained. 'He just got in from London.'

'Nice job.'

'Tell me about the hospital,' Ed said.

'We've got everything we need,' Nils replied, 'all the kit. The problem is, it's too good. The refugees are getting better medical care than anyone else in this shit-hole. People in the town don't understand why they get this treatment. We've got families in Upshala dying of malaria because they can't afford the drugs, but in the camps, drugs are at a discount – there's a glut of them and the supplies just keep coming. Some of the refugees are rich from trading drugs and food – Jesus, some of my doctors are making a fortune.'

Frank raised his glass towards the others. 'Here's to the aid business,' he said, with a grin. 'Photograph 'em, feed 'em, fuck 'em.'

'We're spending more and more on security,' Nils went on. 'The drugs disappear from the hospital so fast we don't even have time to enter them on the register. They get stolen off the trucks. Of course, the guards are a waste of money – they're the biggest thieves of all.'

'Anyway, you've got enough?' Ed put in, after a pause. 'I mean, the hospital's working well.'

'Sure it's working. We've got some good doctors, and the nurses are terrific. The convent school was burned down by the ACP last year and the nuns came to work in the hospital. We've got clean linen, clean floors, clean bandages every day, clean equipment. It's like Switzerland in there.'

'Excellent.'

'Is it?'

'I think he means it's a good idea to have a clean hospital,' Frank suggested with mock patience, as if he was talking to a child. 'Rather than, you know, operating in a sewer.'

'Well, it's fine, so long as you never think about what else is going on.'

'No, you can't do that,' Frank replied at once. 'It's impossible in any case. You'd go crazy. Believe me, I tried it once. I started writing a book about the development business, but had to give up. Nobody can figure out the consequences of all these Land Cruisers. Besides, who wants to know?'

'What happened to the book?' Ed asked.

'It's in a drawer. It was about Somalia mostly. I got offered a job when I was halfway through and I needed the money so I never finished.'

'You were in Somalia?'

Frank nodded towards Nils. 'That's where I met this guy. We were working in the refugee camps on the Ethiopian border – the Ogaden.'

'That was a fucking racket,' Nils interjected.

'In Somalia you could see the whole process work itself out from start to finish,' Frank said. 'It was like a case study: from perfectly normal, shitty little African country, to total basket-case in one decade. I got there at the beginning of it, in the eighties. Siyaad Barre's government wanted Ogadeen refugees in Somalia. The Ogadeen were allies of his clan – they boosted his support in the west of the country. So the army encouraged them to come in, and the government always exaggerated the numbers. They said there were at least a million and a half refugees, and the Western media bought into it. They even ramped up the numbers, for luck. Two million, more than two million – who's counting? The bigger the number, the better the story. When the UN actually did a census, they reckoned there were three hundred thousand refugees, four hundred tops, but nobody wanted to hear that. The UN figures were never quoted.'

'Tell them about the scams,' Nils said, picking up his beer and holding it up to the light.

'It was like Upshala,' Frank said, 'only a lot bigger. We had these refugee camps that were pretty well established – they were fifteen, twenty years old by the end. People had settled down there, got married, raised kids, made their fortunes. You had rich Ogadeen families who kept a place in the refugee camp just so they would go on getting free food and medicine, free schools. The women stayed in the camps, the men went back to Ethiopia to look after their flocks. The next generation bought a house in the town and went into business. Enough supplies were coming in to feed four times that number of refugees, so food was incredibly cheap. Merchants used to drive up from Mogadishu, buy food and drugs in the camps and truck them back to the city. Just like they do here. All the NGOs knew it was happening, but nobody had the guts to stop it.'

'You don't need to sound superior,' Nils said, holding the beer close enough to smell it. 'You didn't blow the whistle. Nor did I.'

'I was working for Africa Lifeline,' Frank went on. 'We were supposed to be helping the worst cases – starving children, chronic diseases. The starving kids was our big sell. All our brochures had pictures of children with flies on their faces. But we were in the wrong place. The children in the camps were healthy. We had photographers coming out all the time looking for half-dead children. They used to come up from Mog for the day, so they were always in a hurry. I drove them around the camps, and they were saying, "These kids are crap – they're too fat. We need skinny ones – big bellies, big eyes, thin little arms, ribby chests." Usually I ended up taking them to the hospital to photograph sick children. They weren't starving, but they looked kind of rough. It was the best we could do.'

'Meanwhile, the economy was getting fucked up,' Nils said, looking up from his beer, half of which he had drunk in a single draught. 'The farmers couldn't sell their crops because of the free food everywhere. Prices were down forty per cent. Peasant families were destitute because of the aid. They couldn't pay for their seed and were forced to sell up. And guess who was buying the land?'

'The merchants from Mogadishu,' Ed suggested.

Frank nodded. 'Merchants. Friends of Siyaad Barre. People with connections. So there was a kind of loop going on. The government created the refugee crisis to bring in supplies; they issued permits to their friends to trade in food and drugs; and those friends got to buy thousands of acres of farmland from bankrupt peasants. It suited Barre. The farmers didn't support him, but the merchants did. In the end, there were big estates all down the coast of Somalia owned by friends of Siyaad Barre. They were exporting bananas and lemons through Western corporations – cash crops. It was big business. But the backbone of the country – the smallholders and herdsmen – were totally fucked up.'

'So were the pharmacists,' Nils added. 'There was a good pharmacy sector in Somalia before the crisis, the old Italian system. But after the aid agencies had finished with the place, every chemist in the country was out of business. There were so many drugs being sold on the streets, why would anyone pay the proper price to a trained pharmacist? There was no point doctors writing prescriptions any more because people just went out and got whatever they liked. A lot of them died that way.' He finished his beer and immediately tried to catch the waiter's eye.

Frank had also emptied his glass, and was staring across the table at Mike and Ed, without appearing to see them. 'What I don't understand,' he said quietly, 'is the journalists covering these international fuck-ups. They know what's going on, but they never write about it. All they do is drive around looking for poverty porn and reprint the NGO press releases. Whatever happened to investigation? I mean, fuck it. There were hundreds of journalists in Somalia. They were everywhere.'

'They came to report the American invasion,' Mike said. 'That was the story, the cock-up military intervention.'

Nils had got another glass of beer, and looked about cautiously as he put it down on the table. 'Sometimes journalists come to a humanitarian crisis,' he remarked. 'I was in Ethiopia in 1984. I had a job with the World Food Programme. The UN booked our team into the Addis Ababa Hilton.' He wiped his lips with the back of his hand. 'Now, that's a cool hotel, really, with a great swimming pool – and the food, the restaurants . . . Everyone was staying there – journalists, NGO types, celebrities, famine tourists – the whole circus. Each morning my colleagues and I used to put on our safari suits, pick up a packed lunch from Reception and drive off to the airport. Then we would get into this little Cessna, hired by the WFP, and fly up to the relief camp at Korem. We were measuring the severity of the famine – the death-rate, numbers coming into the camp each week. My responsibility was to organise a triage. I spent months examining half-dead bodies, thousands of them, tens of thousands in the end. There were more bodies than you could count, squirming and groaning on the scrubland, trying to sit up, gesturing with their hands for food. They had walked for miles to get to the camp – the journey almost killed them. And every hour more people arrived. I had to decide which ones could be saved. In the end, I could make a decision in a few seconds. I could tell from the eyes, the gums, the stomach – the eyes most of all. I used to assess over a hundred patients a day, seven days a week. My record was a hundred and fifty-six in a single shift. That's one every two or three minutes for eight hours straight.' He paused, and his thin, sunburned lips almost disappeared in the neat line of his mouth. 'Then in the late afternoon we got back on our natty little plane and flew back to Addis, to the hotel, the bar, the television. Usually there was time for an hour or two by the pool – a nice swim, a shower, a steak for supper, chips, mayonnaise, beer, ice-cream . . .' He drained his glass. 'A lot of us put on weight in Ethiopia. I had to work out in the hotel gym. It was a kind of reaction, eating like that. You felt sick all the time – disgusted, emptied out – like you'd flown out of the ordinary world and landed in hell. Literally, in the inferno. When you got back, you needed to reassure yourself – you needed to fill yourself up.'

Nils put his glass down, and Frank surveyed the table. 'How about a round of whisky?' he said. 'We can't drink beer all night.' He signalled to the waiter again.

'Let's drink to development workers,' Nils said, 'the ones who realise they're causing more harm than good, but keep doing it anyway because they can't give up eighteen-year-old African pussy.'

'No, no, that's not you, man,' Frank said. 'Don't be hard on yourself. That girl you were with last night had to be twenty-five.' He chuckled, then tipped back his glass.

'Or how about a toast to the most hypocritical NGO?' Nils went on. 'The most shameless fundraising campaign. Let's raise our glasses to those bastards at Emergency Unlimited.'

Ed leaned forward, ready to get up. 'What about the soldier who makes the most money by stealing military supplies?' he said. 'Don't forget, Mike, we're seeing Abako at ten thirty.'

'Okay. I'll meet you in the hall at ten.'

'Good to meet you all,' Ed said. Nils was peering about the bar with an expression of genial disengagement. 'See you in the hospital, Nils.'

Nils nodded enthusiastically, but Frank intervened, with a stage whisper: 'There's no point telling him now. He never remembers anything that happens after dark.'

'Is he all right?'

'We'll get him to bed in a hour or two, if he hasn't picked up a girl. Don't worry about Nils. He'll be fine in the morning.'

Ed and Mike walked up the steps of General Wilson Abako's headquarters, in a bungalow overlooking an abandoned coffee plantation near the northern outskirts of Upshala. Two guards came to attention as they approached, their guns jostling the bougainvillaea, which hung down from the veranda roof. As they entered the sitting room, a thin officer with an elongated neck came forward to greet them. 'The general will be here in a few minutes,' he said in English. 'I am his aide-de-camp. Please sit down. Would you like something to drink?' Without waiting for a reply, he clapped his hands. 'Bring these gentlemen filtered water.'

'It's very good of the general to see us,' Ed said. 'I know he's extremely busy.'

'General Abako is always anxious to co-operate with the United Nations.'

'I hear there has been a battle to the north,' Mike remarked.

The officer's lips were still for a moment, pouting slightly. 'Nothing unusual. We are always keeping up the pressure on rebel forces. Our men are engaged in action almost every day somewhere in the war zone. You should not be influenced by rumours.'

'This time there were a lot of refugees,' Mike said. 'The town's full of them.'

'There are always refugees. They are a natural product of war. I'll tell the general you are here.'

Ed glanced at the watercolours of elephants and zebras on the opposite wall; then he looked out through the window at the end of the room, beyond a mahogany table, which framed a valley of overgrown coffee bushes, falling away to the north and terminating abruptly at the foot of the Ngozi Hills. 'We need to keep the army happy,' Ed said quietly, when the officer had gone. 'Try not to piss off the aide-de-camp.'

'They're packing up,' Mike whispered. 'There are no papers, no maps, nothing – you see? That guy is military intelligence. He's here to evacuate the general. I'd put money on it.'

'Then why's he meeting us?'

'Business,' Mike said. 'He still wants the supplies. Why are we meeting *him*?'

'You know why.'

'And if the army doesn't control the roads?'

'Well?' Ed folded his arms. 'Do you think that's true? Has the ACP taken them?'

'That's what everyone's saying. One thing's certain: these people won't tell you the truth.'

'All right. Keep quiet. He's coming.' Ed put his glass of water on the coffee-table and stood up. 'Good morning, General.'

'Yes, yes, good morning.' The general nodded at them, his hands buttoning his tunic over a white T-shirt and the heavy gold chain that hung round his neck.

'It's very good of you to see us,' Ed began.

'I agreed to see you, not *him*,' Abako replied. 'Captain, show this man outside. Give him something to drink while he waits.'

'If you don't mind, General, I asked Mr Owens to assist me. He's here as an adviser to the UNHCR. He has a good knowledge of the area.'

The general watched Mike for a moment as he straightened his uniform. Then he sat down behind his desk. 'So? What do you want?'

'We need the army's co-operation with the delivery of emergency supplies,' Ed said. 'At the moment fewer than half the trucks are getting through, and there are three camps that no one from the UNHCR has been able to visit for more than a month.'

'You must take up your complaint with Patrick Ochola,' the general said. 'Perhaps he can give you protection. My men are fighting a war, Mr Caine. They are not bodyguards for the white community. We are in the middle of an offensive, clearing the rebels from these hills.'

'I understand,' Ed said. 'But if the supplies are not getting to the refugees, the UN is effectively handing valuable material to the ACP. Nobody wants that, General – not the UNHCR, certainly not President Wachira. It would be better for everyone if you could give them safe passage to the camps.'

'I'll do my best,' he said. 'Is that all?'

'I would need to see the results for myself,' Ed said. 'My colleague and I will have to visit the camps.'

'That's impossible. There is a security issue. You speak of refugees, but we have reports of ACP guerrillas in these camps – many hundreds of rebels. There are arms, explosives, automatic weapons. We must keep the camps sealed off while we bring the situation under control.'

'Of course, General,' Ed said politely, getting to his feet. 'I will explain the situation to my superiors in Geneva. I'm sure they will agree with me that, under the circumstances, all emergency supplies must be cut off at once. Thank you for giving us so much of your valuable time.'

'I don't think that's a wise course, Mr Caine,' the general said, also getting up and going to stand in front of the fireplace, holding a fly-whisk across his shoulder. He surveyed Ed and Mike with a kind of sceptical resentment. 'Let me ask you something, Mr Caine.'

'General?'

'Do you know what is the biggest headache for an army in Africa?'

'Disease?' Ed suggested.

'Logistics. My staff spend more time keeping the men supplied than fighting the enemy. In Africa you have to plan for twice the quantity needed, three times. Roads are blocked, bridges washed away, the ACP ambushes our convoys. Sometimes whole lorries disappear. Warehouses are looted and towns destroyed. There are major highways that cannot be used for months at a time. Do you understand what that means?'

Ed waited in silence, and Mike folded his arms.

'The supplies that come through are very expensive. The food in the refugee camps,' the general pointed his finger at Ed, as if he was accusing him, 'that food – those little bowls of maize – cost as much as dinner in the Kisuru Hilton. Really. I'm not joking. My staff have made the calculations. And how do you think these supplies are paid for?'

'By the UN,' Ed said.

'No,' the general replied. 'The real price is paid by my men. They pay with their lives to keep these people supplied. Have you thought of that? If they receive some benefit from the supplies – if some of the material is mislaid on the road – is that unreasonable?'

'Do you want the UN to pay the army?'

300

'If the UN will continue to supply the camps, I am willing to discuss how to safeguard these deliveries, how to ensure that a good proportion reach the destination. Everything in this world has a price, Mr Caine. We need to find a way of maintaining supplies that is acceptable to you – to the UNHCR – and to those who risk their lives to keep the roads open. What do you say? I am only trying to be fair.'

33

Five soldier-children were walking ahead of Beatrice in single-file along the narrow footpath through the jungle. Her own guard – a girl of twelve or thirteen in a UNICEF T-shirt and combat boots, her thin bare legs spattered with mud – marched directly in front of her, clutching a rifle in both hands as she peered up at the trees. Ahead of her, two boys armed with machetes hacked away at the branches and vines that choked the narrow tunnel. From time to time the column reached an intersection of dark, indistinguishable paths. The young man at the head raised his hand, and everyone stopped. Then Beatrice watched intently as he crouched to examine the signs that marked the way – a flayed lizard nailed to a tree, a single large tooth on a stone, blue and yellow parrot's wings tied with string. He took his time, reading these omens, his forehead creased as if he was studying a book. Then, when he had made up his mind, he pointed in the direction of the path they should take, and they marched on.

They had been forbidden to turn round, so Beatrice had no way of knowing if her father and Solomon were still behind her. Rain had been falling heavily most of the day, but she was unbearably thirsty – her lips and tongue were throbbing, her mouth tasted foul – and all through her head there was a thumping sensation of heat and exhaustion, as if her brain was burning up. Her waterlogged sneakers continually rubbed the skin from her heels and the soles of her feet, and every step caused her pain, but the whole day as they marched along, she had used her remaining strength to concentrate on her guard and the young ACP lieutenant at the front of the line, obeying every order at once, convinced that if she stumbled off the path or tripped she would be shot. On three occasions when the column halted, the guard had raised her Kalashnikov, silently taking aim at Beatrice's heart. Each time, Beatrice had closed her eyes and tried to pray, certain that she was about to die, her whole body shaking violently. And by the evening, she had the impression her system was incapable of generating any more adrenaline, that she no longer had the capacity even to panic, but could only walk or stop walking on command.

Late in the afternoon, when the rain had stopped, the column paused beside a small stream. Five footpaths converged there, but when the leader moved on, he didn't take any of these tracks, but set off instead into the screen of burdock and bulrushes that covered the surface of the water. Then, for half a mile or more, moving upstream, the guards and their prisoners stumbled over rocks and waded through muddy pools, until blue sky began to appear through the trees to the right of the river. Beatrice found herself walking into an area of cleared ground, with a few thatched huts and a field of cassava, surrounded with the seething density of banana trees, shrubs of every kind, and hardwood trees half strangled with creepers.

'You can sleep here.' Beatrice's guard pointed her gun at the flattened grass between two huts, and she immediately dropped to the wet ground.

She had tripped on the riverbed and fallen into the mud, and now as she stretched out her legs she discovered a constellation of leeches attached to her jeans. She stared at them in silence, poking their black bodies with a finger.

'Hey, *hababu*,' Solomon said. He had arrived at the hut with his guard and was standing over her, blocking the sunlight. 'Be careful. Don't try to get them off. They leave their heads under your skin.' He said something in Kishala to his guard, who handed him a lighted cigarette. Then Solomon crouched beside her. 'This child is from my home district,' he explained quietly. 'I've promised to help him if he gets us food. You stay still. This won't hurt . . .' He pressed the end of the cigarette to one of the fat, slug-like bodies. 'There! He doesn't like that.'

Beatrice had leaned back against the wall of the hut, but immediately sat up again. 'There's something wriggling on my back.'

'Turn round,' he said. 'Pull up your shirt.'

'What is it?'

'Hmm. It's okay. It's only a bug. It's not going to bite or anything.'

A bright green millipede, eight inches long, was writhing about in the small of Beatrice's back. Solomon tried to brush it off with his hand. Then he rested the lit cigarette carefully on its head, causing the insect to curl up in a frenzy.

'What's happened?'

He flicked it into the grass. 'It's all right. It's gone. Let's kill these leeches.'

Beatrice turned slowly, but her lips were trembling and when she tried to say something, she began to cry. Solomon glanced anxiously at the guard, who was standing a few yards away smoking a cigarette. Then he sat on the ground, put his arms round Beatrice's shoulders, and held her tight.

'We're going to die,' she gasped. 'Look at us! We're going to die in this disgusting jungle. Why don't they just shoot us?'

'Ssh. Don't say that. You're going to be all right. I'll look after you.'

'But you shouldn't even *be* here,' she protested. She was shaking so violently now that her words were almost inaudible. 'Oh, God – God, it's my fault . . .'

He continued to hug her, resting his chin on top of her head, until she was calmer. Then, holding her head in his hands, he kissed her.

'Don't leave me, Solomon,' she whispered. 'Stay with me.'

'I'm here,' he said. 'I'm stubborn, remember? You won't get rid of me.' Looking across the clearing, he added: 'Here's your father.'

Joseph was limping towards the huts. 'Oh, Baba!' Beatrice said, sitting up and wiping her face with her hands. 'You've hurt yourself.'

'It's not serious. I sprained my ankle. If I had a stick, I could walk quite well.' He sat down slowly, with his back to the wall of the hut.

'We must get rid of the leeches,' Solomon said, sucking the burning stub and applying it to another of the shiny black bodies on Beatrice's jeans. 'It will be dark soon. We should check each other while we can.' Silently he signalled to the Shala guard for another cigarette.

'Don't worry about me,' Joseph replied. 'You two look after one another. What's the matter, Bea? You're shaking . . . Rest your head here. Lie on me – that's it. You need to sleep. We all do.' He added, glancing at Solomon: 'Have you any idea how much further they're taking us?'

'This boy tells me we'll be there tomorrow,' Solomon said. 'We're heading for an ACP base high in the hills.'

'Does he say why?' Joseph said. 'I mean, what use are we to them?'

Solomon concentrated on Beatrice's leeches. 'There!' he announced, surveying Beatrice's legs and ankles. 'That's the last. You'll bleed for a while. Try not to rub the wounds.'

Beatrice sat up from her father's lap. 'All right. Let me do yours,' she said. 'Give me that cigarette. You, too, Father. Roll up your trousers.'

'No, no. I'm all right.'

'Don't be impossible, Baba. Quick, before the cigarette goes out. These things will give you a fever.'

Joseph started to pull up his filthy suit trouser-legs.

'There – you see? You've got lots of them.'

'Look where they've put us.' Joseph gestured towards the open space in front of the huts. 'This is a Ngozi village. Other tribes bury their dead on the mountains or out in the jungle, but the Ngozi keep them at home, between their

305

houses. That's their custom, so their ancestors remain among them. You see that stone in the grass?' He waved at the great tufts of elephant grass on the edge of the village. 'That's the *masiro*, the burial stone. Our guards don't like it. They've gone to sleep by the river. I suppose they think we'll be too frightened to run away.'

'We don't need ghosts to guard us,' Beatrice said. 'Who could survive an hour in this jungle? All those paths leading nowhere . . . Okay, Father. That's it. Disgusting things. I wish we had a bandage or something.' She threw a dead leech into the grass. 'Now, Solomon, hold still.'

Joseph rested his head against the hut wall, closing his eyes. 'You know what I keep thinking about?' he said. 'A while ago I had a very strong desire to go to confession at the cathedral – a real hankering. It was the Feast of the Assumption, but we were busy in the ministry, and I never made it. Too late now. We'll never find a priest out here. The ACP kill them.'

'We're going to get out of this place,' Solomon replied.

'You will. Not me. I'm too slow.' He looked towards the burial stone. 'We have to face facts. I'm ready to die.'

'Don't say that, Father,' Beatrice protested. 'Please don't. You mustn't give up – not ever.'

'Anyway, you said you need to get to confession,' Solomon put in.

'Well, I missed my chance. I'll just have to face God as I am, sins and all. You must pray for me, Bea. Here comes your guard, Solomon.'

The young Shala boy hurried back and threw down three canteens of water. Then, glancing at the other soldiers spread out along the bank of the river, he pulled a plastic bag from under his T-shirt and dropped it on the grass. 'Hide that,' he said. 'Eat when it's dark.'

Solomon said something in Shala, and the boy strode away.

'"UNIMIX",' Beatrice read out, peering into the bag: '"Therapeutic High Energy Food" – it's for starving children.'

'Keep it hidden,' Joseph said. 'He must have taken a big risk to help us. We can eat it in the morning to give us strength.'

She shoved the bag behind her father's back, in the shadow of the wall, and sat down to unscrew the lid of her water bottle.

'Do you really think it matters?' Solomon asked, as he watched Beatrice drink.

'What?' Joseph replied.

'What you were saying about going to confession – seeing a priest before you die.'

'Oh, yes, it matters all right. When I was a boy at the Sacred Heart Academy, they drummed it into us. The Four Last Things – Death, Judgment, Heaven and Hell. The headmaster used to tell us in assembly, "In a hundred years, everyone in this room will be dead." People don't talk like that any more. Everyone likes to pretend it's easy to get to Heaven, that we can avoid all suffering in this world and the next. But only a fool could believe that. Nothing good was ever easy.' He paused. 'It'll be dark soon. We should take it in turns to stay awake.'

'You think they'll attack us in the night?' Solomon asked, looking towards the stream, where someone was firing a rifle into the air.

'Those children? Who knows what they'll do?'

'You rest,' Solomon said. 'I'll wake you in a few hours.'

'All right.' He leaned back and closed his eyes. 'Make sure you do.'

'You should lie down, too,' Solomon urged, taking Beatrice's hand. 'You need to sleep.'

She stretched out beside him, staring up into the sky, which was suddenly getting dark. 'Do you really think we'll get out of here?'

'Yes,' he said. 'Of course we will.'

'Where will we go?'

'Juba,' he said. 'It's not far. I've been there lots of times. And from Juba there are planes every week – to Europe, America, anywhere you like.'

307

'I'd like to go to London, please,' Joseph said, half smiling, without opening his eyes. 'If I'm going into exile, I'd rather be in England than anywhere else. We can live in a quiet street somewhere, Bea, or in the country, perhaps. Yes, in a cottage by the sea. That would be nice:

> *"An English home –*
> *. . . dewy pasture, dewy trees,*
> *Softer than sleep – all things in order stored,*
> *A haunt of ancient peace."'*

Solomon gazed down at Beatrice's face, listening to her breathing. Then, very gently, he kissed her forehead. 'You sleep, *hababu*,' he whispered. 'We'll keep you safe.'

But she opened her eyes, and looked at his large, handsome face, which was beginning to disappear in the shadows. 'I'm sorry,' she said. 'Look at us. This is my fault.'

'Ssh. Don't be silly. I chose to be here, remember.'

'And now you've lost everything – all your cargo.'

'My cargo?'

'Your whisky and cigars. You'd be in Upshala by now selling it, if you hadn't brought us with you.'

He smiled, brushing a fly from her face. 'You think I wanted to go to Upshala?'

'Didn't you?'

'No.' He lowered his voice. 'There was no business trip. Nobody's going to Upshala now – they haven't been getting through for weeks. The road's closed.'

'I don't understand.'

'It's simple.' He rested his hand on her shoulder. 'I've got my cargo here. And you're still alive.'

'Because of you,' she said. 'We're only alive because of you.'

'And what about me?' he said. 'Do you think I would be alive without you?'

Beatrice took his arm, feeling for his face in the darkness with her other hand, but he was already almost touching her, and suddenly she felt his lips exploring her face, kissing her forehead, the bridge of her nose, her open mouth. 'Hold me,' she whispered. 'Don't stop holding me.'

'I've wanted to hold you for a long time,' he said quietly, and squeezed her against himself.

'What's going to happen to us?' she asked, after a while.

'I don't know,' he said. 'But we're going to be together. Whatever happens, I'm staying with you.'

Ed was standing on the tarmac below the control tower at Upshala airport, dressed in a cotton jacket. Like everyone in the crowd, he had been squinting towards the west, where the aeroplane carrying Dr Salim Neguib, special envoy from the United Nations High Commission for Refugees, could be seen descending out of the sun towards the low, box-like houses of the suburbs. Ed turned away from the glare, taking off his dark glasses to rub his eyes and resettle his floppy safari hat on his head. Then, as the drone of the aeroplane intensified, he stared across the airport towards the high security fence that surrounded the UN warehouse, where a platoon of Pakistani soldiers in blue helmets had lined up to greet Dr Neguib. Ed's office manager, Eva, was standing beside him in the brilliant sunlight, and he folded his arms as he listened to her arguing with the pilot. The flight had been delayed in Cairo, and now that the plane was within sight of Upshala, Eva was ordering him to fly low over the runway, and circle the airport a few times before landing.

'We need a shot of the tail,' she said, raising her voice and blocking her other ear. 'Yes, yes. You have to show us the UNHCR logo. You can do that for me, no? . . . What's the point of coming if the plane flies out of the sun? . . . Listen to me, Alec; just go round again and land from the opposite direction – from the east . . . What's the matter with you? This isn't Heathrow. There's nothing to crash into, just a lot of sky.'

'For God's sake, Eva, let the poor man land,' Ed said.

'No, no!' She cupped the phone. 'I promised Salim we'd make

the TV news. He'll freak out if he gets no coverage.' And she yelled into the phone, 'The cameras aren't ready, Alec. Give them a few minutes. Do it – do it for me, sweetheart. Take your time.' She smiled, shaking her head. 'Uh-huh . . . God, you Englishmen, you're so foul-mouthed. Hey, you listen to me. I don't make any promises, right? You got to perform first . . . Okay.' She laughed. 'That's a deal. Yes, I know, I got it.' She switched off the phone. 'Salim's got a new PA,' she said, to Ed. 'She wants to see the menu for dinner tonight.'

'Do you have it?' Ed asked, raising his voice above the noise of the plane, which was passing over the airfield.

'It's at the office,' she shouted. 'She wants to know what kind of mineral water we have.' Ed stared at her, but she shrugged as she redialled. 'The special envoy likes still. Bubbles are bad for his stomach. Also, alkaline.'

'Eva . . .' he said reproachfully.

'Okay, okay. Too much information, right?'

'You sort it out. If you tell me any more, I might end up thumping someone – probably Salim Neguib.'

The plane was banking over the jungle to the east, and Eva called to the TV crew on the roof of the airport building, 'Are you getting this all right? U-N-H-C-R.'

'Tell the drivers I want to get out to the camps right away,' Ed said, as the plane came in, 'before we lose the light.'

'Dr Neguib may not want that.'

'Well, that's what he's getting. And I need to be alone with him in the middle car. Just you, me and him, right? Make sure everyone understands.'

Dr Neguib sat in the back of the Land Cruiser, checking his BlackBerry as he was driven away from the airport.

'I've updated my report, sir,' Ed began, holding the file for him, but Neguib shook his head, keeping his eyes on the phone, which he gripped in both hands. 'Of course, I can give you a summary, if you prefer. The situation's deteriorated in the last few months. We're going to see the two main camps today – I'm afraid that's all we've time for. I was hoping you might be able to extend your visit till tomorrow afternoon. With an early start, we could get up to the camps out in the Highlands and be back before dark. It's well worth the time.'

Neguib looked up from his screen. 'I'm afraid it's out of the question,' he said. 'I have to be back in New York on Wednesday. I'm hosting a seminar.' Tapping his BlackBerry, he continued: 'The people in my office were supposed to be making the arrangements. I do find it extraordinary that one has to do everything oneself. They haven't even booked the restaurant.'

Ed was still holding the file. After a few moments he opened it again. 'Well, Sir, the main problem with the operation has been the rate at which we're losing supplies. I've drawn a graph to demonstrate the impact of the ACP offensives since June. Here . . .' Neguib took the folder, squinting at it through his half-moon spectacles. 'Basically we're down to one road into Upshala, and even that's unreliable. In some months we're losing eighty per cent of our deliveries.'

Neguib turned the page back and forth a couple of times, looking at the graphics. 'Can't you make a deal with the ACP?'

'I've been working on it, but they're really in no mood to negotiate. They're getting everything they need as it is, and they're winning the war. What can we offer them? In a few weeks they'll be running the camps. The only thing we can do is cut off the supplies altogether.'

'We can't do that,' Neguib said. 'We need to run the programme as long as the donors are on board.'

'Well, sir, if the ACP take Upshala, our personnel will be flying out to Juba, and that will be the end of the programme.'

'You really think the rebels are doing that well? It's not what my people are telling me.'

'Of course the government denies it,' Ed said. 'And there's so little media coverage of the war outside the region that they can say what they want. The fact is, the army can't maintain deliveries. Upshala is isolated – it's an island in an ACP ocean. The Northern Provinces are under Ochola's control.'

'You've spoken to Wilson Abako?'

'Several times. I was hoping you might have a word with him yourself, Sir. He's been invited to the dinner tonight at the George. I persuaded the general to take a – well – a positive interest in emergency supplies. Basically, I bribed him to let our stuff through.'

'Yes?'

'The army's cut is forty per cent – that's what we agreed. It's enough to keep Abako in funds. In return, he's allowed UN personnel back into the camps, and promised to let the rest of the supplies through. Even so, we can't stop the army bullying the refugees. Whatever a family needs, they have to buy it from the military. Girls prostitute themselves for a bowl of *ugali* in the camps – for a little cooking oil.'

The convoy was moving slowly in and out of the potholes along Upshala high street, and as Neguib looked out of the window, he found himself admiring five young Ngozi women with bare breasts and gold rings around their necks. 'Are the people being fed in our camps?' he said. 'I mean, we don't want a full-scale famine on our hands.'

'No Sir, we don't. The food situation's all right for the moment – there's a stockpile from previous months. You'll see for yourself. The camps have a semi-permanent quality about them – with *dukas*, second-hand-clothes markets, even little restaurants. What worries me is that our relief operation is effectively supplying both sides in the conflict.' Neguib raised his eyebrows, turning back to Ed. 'I mean, if we stopped the supplies, the war would probably be over in a few months. Nobody has the money to continue without us.'

'Diversion of emergency supplies always creates a dilemma,' Neguib conceded. 'Actually, the high commissioner shares your concerns. It's one of the issues we're discussing in New York on Wednesday: emergency aid as a *casus belli*.'

'There's also the problem of aid demoralising the army,' Ed went on. 'Abako's men are deserting. It's a disastrous combination. Everyone knows the officers have been getting rich by selling supplies. It angers the men, boosting support for the ACP, and it virtually guarantees defeat in the field, neglect of the wounded, lack of basic care. No army could fight under those conditions. If the Wachira government falls, Sir, it could be argued that the UN aid programme bears a primary responsibility.'

'Yes, I see,' Neguib said, folding his arms as he turned to look out of the window. 'I do understand. It's certainly a compelling perspective.'

The car had turned off the high street and was lurching down an embankment to cross the shallow river that served as the town's principal sewer. On the other side of the stream, the track entered an encampment of huts covered with plastic sheeting, and a group of Ngozi children stuck out their hands as the convoy passed.

'This is the road to Camp One, Your Excellency. We'll be driving past General Abako's headquarters in a few minutes – in the coffee plantation over there. If you like, we can ring his staff and see if we can drop in on the way back to town.'

'Yes, yes, by all means.' Neguib sighed. 'Just as you wish.'

34

The Army of Celestial Peace had established its campaign head-quarters in an abandoned tea plantation on the cool upper slopes of the Ngozi Hills, less than fifty miles north-west of Upshala. Here and there in the undergrowth, as he struggled up the side of the valley, Joseph thought he could make out the vestiges of old telegraph poles, fence posts, the footbridge over a drainage channel; but everything had collapsed many years before, the timbers hollowed out by colonies of white ants or hacked down for firewood. Even the road itself had barely survived, running beside the river and almost overgrown with the hardwoods and giant shrubs that sprouted in the ditches, their lower branches cut away to clear a path for vehicles.

The column climbed all morning, pausing around noon at the crest of the hill, from which Joseph could see long parallel lines of tea bushes, now grown wild and sprouting to a height of twenty feet or more.

'We're almost there,' Solomon said quietly. 'Another hour, maybe. How's your foot?'

'Not so good,' Joseph said, touching it to the ground and wincing. 'I think it's swelling.'

'I asked if I could walk with you, let you lean on me, but the little man won't allow it.'

'I'll be all right.' Joseph began to lower himself to the ground. 'If they think I'm weak, they'll only shoot me.'

'Ssh, Baba!' Beatrice objected. Seeing the leader of the column set off again along a line of tea bushes, she added: 'Don't sit down. Give me your hand. We're going on.'

Joseph gave the appearance of an almost unnatural calm as

he straightened and walked on. For the last day and a half, especially since he had sprained his ankle, he had been preparing himself for death, expecting at any time to be pulled out of the column and executed by the side of the track. As he struggled through the jungle he had been muttering his rosary again and again, repeating at the end of every decade the act of contrition he had learned as a little boy: 'Oh, my God, I am heartily sorry for having offended thee . . .' until, by the time they reached the plantation, his mind had acquired a kind of fragile serenity.

At the brow of the next hill, he gazed down into the shallow valley of the plantation and the old estate gardens about half a mile away – an irregular diamond of flaming green, crossed by a series of colonial bungalows with thatched roofs and bounded by the river to the north. A group of drying-sheds and warehouses stood to one side, enclosing a yard full of anti-quated machinery, and at first Joseph could see no activity anywhere, but gradually, as he limped on through the tea bushes, he had the impression of subtle movement all around, as though some invisible force was agitating every branch at once. He fixed his eyes on the leaves of the bush directly ahead. There, half hidden in the shade, the fierce face of a young boy stared back at him; and a little higher, poking out from the leaves, the muzzle of his rifle caught the sunlight.

'So many soldiers here,' he said in a whisper. 'So many children.'

'Don't look,' Solomon murmured. 'Don't catch their eyes.'

Joseph limped on, his face to the ground.

From the cover of the tea bushes, the soldiers moved directly into the low buildings near the house and began to unload their equipment. Then they sat on piles of sacking to eat their rations. Joseph, Solomon and Beatrice were led out by the column leader, marched across the yard, past Land Cruisers parked in a shed, and into the main bungalow, where they were told to stand against the wall of a spacious whitewashed room. There was a large radio transmitter in the far corner, a laptop on a desk beside it, and a cassette player from which a man's voice was addressing a crowd in one of the Kishala dialects, his pitch rising in a series of rhetorical climaxes, each of which was rewarded with extravagant shouts from the audience.

Solomon looked out of the windows at the river, and the luminous green hills in the distance; then he turned to Beatrice. Her eyes were cast down to the floor, arms fidgeting, the whole of her body trembling. As he put out his hand towards her, a door slammed and a short, overweight man in a baggy suit marched into the room. He stood in front of them, scrutinising them with intensely suspicious eyes. 'Have you ever heard Patrick Ochola speaking to his people?' he asked in English. 'Have you seen him in the flesh?' He walked to the desk and stood with his back to the window, watching his prisoners, and listening intently to the rich bass voice that came from the cassette player. 'Our leader speaks like a prophet,' he said, as the crowd applauded. 'That's why the Makhoto block his radio transmissions – that's why they won't allow him to talk to journalists. If he had media coverage, he would win the hearts of all men, people everywhere, not just in Batanga.'

He turned down the volume and walked back towards them, nodding at Joseph. 'You are Joseph Kamunda. Your daughter is Beatrice. And this man is Solomon Ouko – a Shala.' He smiled guardedly, raising his finger at Joseph as if he had caught him out in a lie. 'I have been hearing all about you from the security forces – I listen to their conversations every day. The government believes you are dead. They claim they found your bodies hanging by the road, and they blame your death on the Army of Celestial Peace. And our forces might have killed you, seeing that you are Bakhoto. But they had orders to arrest you instead. After all, what would be the point of killing you when you are dead already? Therefore the Leader has given you a new life. He said to me, "Erastus, bring these dead people to me. Tell the children

316

not to harm them. I want to speak with them myself before they die for the last time.'"

'I am glad to meet you,' Joseph said cautiously. 'I have heard of you, of course. You are Patrick Ochola's principal adviser. Is that right?'

'No, not at all! The *kiongozi* does not require advice. He is guided directly by God.' He watched Joseph sceptically. 'But I am his spokesman. I explain the Leader's doctrine, his political strategy . . .' Starting to pace the room again, he added, 'I am the Leader's official biographer, also. I am writing a book about Patrick Ochola's life. When the Leader comes to power, my book will be read all over the world – it will be a bestseller.' He stopped where he was at the end of the room, gazing out towards the mountains.

'Would it be possible for my father to sit down, sir?' Beatrice asked. 'He's hurt his ankle.'

'Yes, yes, sit down.' Erastus waved his hand, without turning. 'You are not prisoners. You are guests of our Leader. His own doctor will attend to your ankle, Mr Kamunda, and you will dine with me tonight. I'm sure you are hungry.'

'Thank you, sir. We've travelled a long way,' Joseph said.

'The Leader will treat you however he likes,' Erastus went on, striding back towards them. 'Tonight he will feed and protect you. Perhaps tomorrow he will kill you. Whatever the Leader decides, it is always best. Maybe he will take this pretty young lady to Kisuru when he comes to power.' He stood in front of Beatrice, surveying her face. 'I must work now. Go and wash, if you want. Sleep for a few hours. This child will find you some clean clothes. She will show you to your rooms.'

He gave orders in Kishala to a girl of about seventeen, with brightly coloured beads plaited into her hair, who had come in and was waiting by the door with her eyes cast down respectfully. 'Later she will bring you back here,' Erastus told them. 'Tonight is a special occasion, a celebration. We received important news today, a message from the front, from the

Leader himself. Our forces are close to Upshala. They are in the suburbs.'

Joseph hesitated, helplessness and fear gripping his heart. 'What about the army?' he said.

'They are retreating, Mr Kamunda! Your soldiers are running away.'

'And the south?' Joseph asked. 'Kisuru?'

'Our special units are ready to rise up in the capital. The whole city is awaiting the Leader's orders.' Erastus looked him in the eye. 'Very soon I will go to Kisuru myself. We will start to govern. You look sad, but there is no reason. Everything is going well. Our people will be free at last, Mr Kamunda. Our future will be greater than our past.'

35

A few minutes after midnight, Ed was woken by the sound of mortar rounds detonating somewhere in the town. For a moment he lay on his back, staring up into the darkness, not sure what had disturbed him. Then a second explosion shook the room, lighting up the interior for an instant. Immediately he rolled off the bed and crawled as fast as he could to the window, where he sat in his boxer shorts, watching the tracer bullets and flares across the northern suburbs.

In the lull that followed, he became aware of a high-pitched piping sound coming from the bed, and it was a few moments before he realised that his phone was ringing.

'Hello? Mike? What the fuck's going on?'

'I've been trying to get hold of you. Are you all right?'

'I'm fine.'

'You watching the battle? You should get yourself downstairs. Go to the basement. Everyone's down there.'

'Where are you?'

'On the roof.'

There was another flash, followed by a rumbling detonation, and Ed ducked below the window frame. 'Is this the army?'

'No, it's the ACP. They're about two miles away. They're not moving yet, just saying hello – shelling the 'burbs. You see those fires along the river?'

He peered out again. 'Yes.'

'That's the market. It could hold them up all night. There's still quite a lot to loot down there.'

'What does it mean? Are they coming in or not?'

'I expect they're waiting to see what the army does.'

'And?'

'Abako's already flown out. He left hours ago. That's when I realised something was up. His men can't get away fast enough. Frank and I were watching them from the bar. They're not even bothering to loot the high street.'

Ed squatted with his back to the wall. 'So, what do we do? Have the rebels reached the airport?'

'I don't know. There's no answer from the blue helmets.'

'Jesus. So much for our evacuation plan.'

'I was thinking we should drive over and take a look,' Mike said.

'Can you get a car?'

'I'll find something. Meet me downstairs in half an hour – out the back, the service entrance.'

The moment he left his room Ed could hear the uproar in the hotel lobby. The yelling intensified as he hurried downstairs. The power supply had failed, and he had an impression of bodies writhing about chaotically in the darkness. At first it seemed impossible even to cross the lobby. He began to push his way between the jostling arms and shoulders, but was shoved back by a furious Batangan soldier, who pressed him against the wall until another mortar round exploded on the street outside and everyone dropped to the floor. In that instant the faces in the crowd were lit up – Batangan soldiers, hotel staff, white civilians, all prostrate and terrified. Then, in the middle of the lobby, Ed spotted an acquaintance of his, a German engineer, getting to his feet with a large suitcase. He was trying to reach the front door, followed immediately by his wife, who held their little boy in her arms.

'Hey, Marcus?' Ed called. 'What are you doing?'

'Leaving, of course.'

'By road?'

'How else? The airport's cut off.' He paused at the entrance. 'My driver tried. There's no way through.' Putting down his case, he added to his wife, 'Wait here, Hannah. I'll be back in five minutes,' then disappeared into the stream of soldiers and refugees that filled the high street.

Everyone was getting up again, but Ed managed to move along the wall towards the reception desk. The hotel office had been taken over by Batangan soldiers; he could see the manager standing in the doorway of his little room, arguing with a man in a black beret.

'We are requisitioning all vehicles,' one of the officers announced, shouting into the din. 'If anyone has a car – any kind of vehicle – they must hand it over. Anyone using a car without permission will be stopped on the road. They will be treated as rebels.'

Ed struggled on round the edge of the room, heading towards the corridor that led to the service entrance and the car-park steps. There were fewer people at the back of the hotel. Groups of foreigners and rich Batangans were trying to load their cars, arguing with the soldiers who were moving about in twos and threes, commandeering vehicles at gunpoint. In the midst of all the shouting, someone fired a shot and a woman screamed at the top of her voice. Then a Land Rover appeared out of the darkness and stopped in front of Ed. 'Hop in!' Mike shouted. 'Hurry up!'

'How did you get this thing?' Ed asked, as they accelerated on to the side road, turning away from the high street.

'I had some help.' Mike jerked his thumb towards the open back, where two teenage boys were leaning against the roll-bar, armed with Kalashnikovs and wearing UN flak jackets. 'I prom- ised them a hundred dollars each if we got to the airport and back.'

Ed's heart was pounding, and he tried to calm himself, breathing deeply. 'Marcus says the road's closed,' he went on at last. 'His driver couldn't get through.'

'I heard that, too.' Mike was driving along a narrow back- street, without lights, leaning forward as he peered into the darkness. 'But I've just spoken to Colonel Ali. His force was cut off for a while, but he counter-attacked. He says the airport's secure again, at least for the time being. His men have been collecting vehicles, too, bringing them back there. We should be able to evacuate your people.'

'Thank God.'

'As long as you can get a flight organised.'

'Eva's been talking to Juba. There's supposed to be a Russian cargo plane standing by. Jesus! Where are you going?'

'Short-cut,' Mike replied. The Land Rover had reached the end of the street, and all at once they could see nothing ahead of them except the black stream that marked the boundary of the town and a field of maize in the moonlight beyond. Mike accelerated through the muddy water and up the far bank. Then the Land Rover bounced across open country, maize stalks thumping the bumper. 'The army's set up a roadblock at the top of the highway,' he shouted. 'We'll have to bring people this way. Hold on. This is the main road – we're going to hit another ditch.' The Land Rover broke through a thin straw fence, lurched into a water-course, and emerged on to the empty highway. 'Okay, you can open your eyes now,' he said, as the car speeded up on the hard road, 'That's it. The airport's over here . . .'

The airport was guarded by a force of Pakistani infantry in the blue helmets of the United Nations, under the command of Colonel Ali, a middle-aged career officer. He approached Mike and Ed to shake their hands as soon as they got out of the Jeep. 'Well?' he asked at once. 'What's the situation in town?'

'Total panic,' Mike told him. 'Everyone thinks the airport's closed – which is a good thing or we'd have half the population of Upshala out here. As it is, they're heading south.'

'I've got twenty-five men at the warehouse north of the river,' the colonel said. 'I'd like to pull them out. We need them here and their position is dangerous. The rebels have almost surrounded them.'

'What's in the warehouse?' Ed asked.

'Medical supplies, mostly. Food, probably alcohol, too. My thinking is, if we withdraw, the ACP will waste time looting. It could hold them up for a few hours. The longer they stay north of the river, the better.'

'Yes, of course,' Mike said.

The colonel called: 'Captain, tell lieutenant Farsi to withdraw his men from the warehouse and report to me here.' Then he turned to Ed. 'So, Mr Caine, do we have an aeroplane or not?'

'There's a Russian transport plane at Juba, Colonel, an Antonov. It's supposed to land here at dawn.'

'All right. That gives us six hours to assemble your people.'

'And the rebels?'

'They're established in force to the north-east – up there, in the jungle. They could attack us at any time. If they do, if they fire on the runway, we'll have a serious problem.'

Ed looked towards the jungle. 'Even if they don't attack,' he said, 'even if we can get people out here in time, we still won't be able to evacuate them all. There isn't room on the plane.'

'We'll have to apply a triage,' Mike said. 'UN people first, Batangan VIPs, if we can get a second flight. The rest will have to fend for themselves.'

'You mean they'll die.'

'If we don't do our jobs, we may all die,' Mike replied. 'Let's take it in stages. Concentrate on the evacuation.'

The first UN evacuees reached the airport just before four in the morning – about forty expatriate professionals with pale, shell-shocked faces, crowded by Pakistani soldiers into requisitioned Land Cruisers and minibuses. By the time they reached the airport, several dozen Batangans had already arrived on foot and were now standing across the gates, blocking the road and demanding to be let in.

'I'd better talk to the colonel,' Mike said. 'Our people can't get in.'

'Why not drive around them?' Ed suggested.

His phone was ringing. 'Hello – Eva? Are you here? I can see three vehicles outside the airport . . . You're *not*? Why on earth? . . . Say that again. How many are missing? . . . Okay, I know about Marcus. He's gone south with his family.' He listened for a while, closing his eyes. 'That's a lot of people, Eva . . . Yes, I realise that. Hold on. I'll see what I can do. I'll ring you back in a minute.' He turned to Mike. 'Eva's asking about the Shala interpreters. She's got seven of them in her office, plus their families. Thirty people in all. They're terrified. They say the ACP will treat them as collaborators – they'll be cut to pieces.'

Mike took a deep breath, running a hand through his hair. 'There's nothing we can do,' he said. 'The plane's going to be overloaded as it is. They'll just have to go south.'

'But there's no transport.'

'Tell Eva they must get out of town – on foot, if necessary. Tell them to go to the junction with the Kisuru highway, and hide there.'

'They'll be killed, Mike. The ACP are bound to find them.'

'Just tell them to get to the highway,' Mike repeated. 'And tell Eva to come here at once or we'll go without her. Where is she, for God's sake?'

'At the hospital, looking for Nils.' Ed dialled Eva's number as Colonel Ali marched across the tarmac towards them.

'What's happened to our evacuees, sir?' Mike asked. 'I can't see the vehicles.'

'They're coming in now,' the colonel replied. 'I told them to head for the service road.' He pointed at the long fence that ran the length of the runway. 'That way they avoid the crowd.'

'Good,' Mike said, as Ed said goodbye to Eva. 'It's getting bigger. You see? Out there, at the edge of the trees.' Ed and the colonel gazed where Mike was pointing, across the grassland between the airport gates and the trees. 'Something's moving. It looks like the whole jungle marching forward.'

'Batangan refugees,' the colonel answered, putting his phone to his ear. 'Lots of them. Enough to overrun *this* little airstrip.'

The UN Land Cruisers and minibuses had been making their way along the open land in darkness, heading towards the cargo hangar. Then the vehicle at the head of the convoy switched on its lights. At once there was a roar of protest from the Batangan refugees outside the gates. 'Follow them!' someone shouted, and a group of men broke away from the crowd and started to run alongside the fence.

'That was the control tower,' Colonel Ali announced, closing his phone. 'The pilot's heard reports of mortar fire in Upshala. He wanted to turn back, but I managed to reassure him.'

'What did you say?'

'That we didn't have any mortar fire here at the airport, and if he's worried about the airspace over Upshala, he should come in from the north-east.'

'Do you think he will?'

'I expect so,' the colonel replied calmly, keeping his eyes on the throng at the main entrance. Hundreds of people were now chanting in support of the young men who were trying to climb over the fence. In one place, where three youths had reached the coils of razor-wire, the whole structure was swaying outwards and their legs were dangling over the crowd. 'Lieutenant, tell the men to fire a warning shot over the heads of those people,' the colonel called. 'Move them back on to the grass.' He added, to Mike and Ed: 'The trouble is, they understand our strategy perfectly well, and it's not in their interests to make things easy for us.'

'Our strategy?' Ed asked.

'The evacuation plan.' The colonel stroked his moustache. 'It's the usual procedure on these occasions. Withdraw all foreign journalists, UN personnel, internationals of all descriptions, before things turn nasty. After that, the crisis is over – for the Western media, at least. There's simply no one left to report it. The ACP can kill every man, woman and child in Upshala, if they want – they can chop them to pieces with their *pangas*, one by one. They might as well be committing their crimes on another planet, for all the outside world will hear about it—' He broke off and gazed up at the storm clouds, which had parted to reveal the pockmarked, stony face of the moon.

'What is it?' Ed asked.

'An engine. It sounds as though he's circling to the north. Are we ready for him, Mr Caine? Are all your personnel accounted for?'

'All except Eva, Nils and three Italian nurses.'

'How many people are out there?' Mike asked, looking at the crowd beyond the fence.

'Three or four hundred,' the colonel said.

'We've got vehicles for forty or fifty at the most. The rest will have to walk.'

'They'll die fighting over the cars, if the ACP don't get them first.'

There was an explosion somewhere in Upshala, then several more in quick succession, followed by a low rumble. 'I expect they're breaking into the banks,' Mike said. 'I'd better get going.'

'What do you mean?' Ed said. 'You're coming with us.'

'No.' Mike avoided his eyes. 'I'm heading back to town. I'm going to pick up the interpreters.'

'You can't be serious! Look at the crowd – they'll tear you apart.'

'I'll get through.'

'Even if you do, *then* what? Where will you go?'

'We'll drive to the coast, away from the fighting. We should be there in a few days.' He put out his hand to Ed. 'Don't worry about me. I'll be fine. I won't go till you've taken off.'

'Look, Mike, this is absurd—'

'Don't argue. You should be in the hangar, getting your people on to the plane.' He seized Ed's hand and shook it. 'Good luck. I'm going to talk to the crowd again – see if I can persuade some of these guys to organise a convoy with me.' Snatching up the megaphone that the colonel had left by the Jeep, he ran up towards the Pakistani soldiers guarding the main gate.

The two Jeeps containing Eva, Nils and the Italian nurses drove into the airport warehouse just as the silver fuselage of the Antonov appeared below the clouds to the north of the runway.

'Who's this?' Ed asked, stopping a few yards from Eva's Jeep and staring at a small Batangan girl, nine or ten years old, who had emerged from under a blanket.

'Her name's Mary,' Eva said. 'She's coming with us.'

'Eva, be reasonable . . .' Ed stared at her, then at Nils, who was crouching in the back of the Jeep, still in his green surgical gown, his hands and the sides of his face covered with blood. 'We can't bring unscheduled people on board. Everyone's had to make hard choices. We're all leaving people behind. It's impossible, anyway – what's going to happen to her in Juba?'

'What's going to happen to her here? Her mother died at the hospital. She must have climbed in when we were looking for Nils. I didn't see her until we were driving away. What was I supposed to do? Throw her on to the street?' She helped Mary out of the car. 'I think her hearing's been damaged,' she added. 'Either that or she's *loco*. Probably it's the shock.'

'Here we go,' a man's voice called. 'The plane's about to land.' Immediately the crowd in the hangar moved towards the open doors to look out at the runway. 'What a contraption – it must be Second World War vintage.'

'Jesus, he's coming in fast.'

'He probably doesn't want a rocket in his fuel tanks.'

'Listen, everyone,' Ed shouted, addressing them from the back of the Jeep. 'The plane can stay on the ground for just a few minutes. Only take on board what you can carry. Everything else has to be left behind. Don't delay the operation – don't put lives at risk. Be as quick as you can.'

The appearance of the plane, arriving out of the clouds into the dawn light, had an electrifying effect on the crowd outside the gates. Everyone rushed forward, pressing against the mesh and pleading with the Pakistani soldiers who remained on duty there. As the plane slowed down at the far end of the runway and started to taxi towards the hangar, twenty or thirty men leaped up against the gates, several climbing rapidly to the top. The metal frame sagged outwards under their weight. 'The posts will give way,' the colonel warned. 'Fire another shot.'

The sound of gunfire was followed by three distinct detonations somewhere between Upshala and the airport. Instead of drawing back, the crowd pushed up against the gates, which lurched forward. Dozens of men and women clambered up the mesh, now pitched at an angle that made it easier to climb. Within moments the entire fence broke free of its posts, and collapsed on to the tarmac.

'Keep firing,' the colonel called to the lieutenant. 'Don't let anyone approach the runway.' He turned to watch the evacuees as they ran from the hangar on to the ramp at the back of the Antonov. Then, as his men kept firing, the propeller engines, which had been audible the whole time, rose in pitch and the plane started to move down the runway towards him. 'Prepare to withdraw the men by sections,' the colonel shouted, taking his pistol from its holster. 'Wait for my order.'

As soon as the plane reached the end of the runway and started turning in preparation for takeoff, there was a furious roar from the Batangan refugees, and more than a hundred charged towards the soldiers. 'Wait for my order,' the colonel repeated, watching the plane complete its turn. 'Now! Fire and withdraw.' Then, standing calmly on his own, he waited as his men withdrew to the lowered ramp at the back of the plane, and disappeared inside. He looked around once more, then walked on to the ramp.

The moment the colonel was on board, the engine noise intensified and the plane lurched forward. There were shouts of protest as people lost their footing, and a pile of soldiers' kit bags tumbled across the gangway. 'Sit down, everyone,' a man called from the front of the plane. 'Hold on to the webbing.' Ed was standing next to Eva, who was squatting against the side of the plane, holding the little girl she had rescued. He tightened his grip on the rope net that hung from the side of the fuselage, but instead of sitting down, he peered through the open door, then shouted a warning to the colonel. A young woman in a yellow headdress had sprinted forward with her child in her arms, chasing the plane. As the ramp started to close, she drew level with the opening, thrusting the baby inside. The colonel took the little bundle and, lying down on the ramp, reached out to lower it on to the tarmac. Then he waited as the hold continued to close, and sealed itself tight.

'All present and correct,' he announced, standing up again as the plane accelerated in earnest. Ed watched the woman in yellow through the porthole. She had collapsed on the ground next to her child and was rocking back and forth, pounding her head with her fists, her mouth wide open as she cried. 'So many poor souls,' the colonel said. 'Look at them all. Even if we had a thousand men and six transports, what could we do for so many?'

Dozens of refugees were moving across the runway now, and by the time the plane rose into the air, Ed had lost sight of the woman and her child. He stepped back from the window and sank down next to Eva, his back to the fuselage. He glanced briefly at the little girl, then let his head drop back against the netting and closed his eyes.

36

Milton Abasi raised his head from the pillow, stretched his arm across the back of the woman who lay asleep beside him and grabbed his mobile phone from the floor. He glared briefly at the name on the display. 'Aunt Pamela?'

'Do you know what time it is?'

'Ten fifteen,' he said briskly, putting his index finger across the lips of his girlfriend, who had raised her head and was squinting at him. 'I'm not asleep. I've been at the office for hours.'

'At Makera?'

'No, Aunty. The club.'

'You mustn't go back to the Global Justice office.'

'Why?'

'Are you alone?'

'Yes.'

'Milton?'

'It's all right, Aunty. What's the matter?'

'I've just left a meeting at State House. The ACP has taken control of the slums. Makera's full of weapons. They're preparing for war—' A police siren wailed over her voice.

Milton swung his legs over the girl and sat up. 'What does that mean?'

'It means you've got work to do,' she said. 'Is there anything in Makera you need to get?'

'I don't know.'

'Well, *think*, Milton. Use your brain. Is there a safe? Documents? Money?'

'I emptied my desk – I haven't been there for weeks.'

'All right. I want you to do some jobs for me this morning. After that, get yourself home and start packing.'

'Where am I going?'

'You're coming with me to London.'

'Oh, Aunt Pamela, you've got to be joking!'

'Stop babbling. I want to see you at Deepak Zaidi's office in half an hour. You have some papers to sign. We're moving our investments out of the country. Milton?'

'Yes, Aunty, I understand.' He switched on the bathroom light and screwed up his eyes. 'What are you going to transfer?'

'Everything,' she said.

'The club, too?'

'*Everything.*'

'Wow.' He leaned over the basin.

'Yes, wow. Don't be late.'

'All right,' he said. 'But can't I leave tomorrow? There's stuff going on tonight.'

'Milton, don't make me lose my temper. I hate losing my temper in the morning. We're going this evening. Everything's arranged. Someone will pick you up at three o'clock and take you to the airport.'

'Yes, Aunty.'

'Now go and see Zaidi. I'll be waiting for you.'

Two bright yellow minibuses had come to a halt on Kwamchetsi Wachira Avenue. They stood in the annihilating heat next to a lorry full of soldiers. Stephen Odinga darted across the road, avoiding the army truck and skirting the back of the buses. The passengers were leaning out of the windows or clinging to the doors, and above their heads, small children sat on rolls of bedding tied to the roof-rack, their legs hooked over wooden chairs and cooking pots. Nobody spoke. They watched the soldiers in silence, following Stephen with their eyes as he leaped over the sewage in the gutter and ran towards Aberdare Fried Bananas.

'Why aren't you at work?' Martha asked, taking a banana fritter out of the bubbling oil with her tongs.

'Everyone's left,' he said. 'They've all gone – the receptionists, the salesmen, everyone. Machi told me to get out.'

Martha studied his eyes, instinctively putting out her arm to Ruth.

'The army's taking over,' he went on. 'They're stopping Shala boys and asking for ID. Lots of Shala have been killed. You mustn't stay here. You must take the children home. Where's Tom?'

'I don't know.'

He frowned angrily. 'Pack up. Take the kerosene and the cash.'

'I have to let the frying pan cool down,' she said, stuffing the cash into her pocket and turning off the stove. 'I can't carry it when it's hot.'

'Leave it.'

'Stephen! It's our only pan—'

'I'll bring it later. Get Ruth home now. And don't go into the Bakhoto districts, you understand? Keep to our own corridors. Hurry! I'll come and find you tonight. If things are bad, we'll go to the nuns.'

'Mrs Caine?'

'This is Sarah Caine.'

'My name's Damian Woodard, ma'am. I'm ringing from the British High Commission.'

'Oh, my God, what's happened? Is it Ed?'

'Your husband's safe, Mrs Caine. I wanted to confirm your arrangements for leaving, your flight this afternoon.'

'Yes, I've – er . . . I've been packing. Actually I went in to clear my desk at the office, but nobody was there except the caretaker. He said there were Shala boys with machetes on the street – boys he knew, his neighbours' sons. Everyone's afraid, aren't they?'

'It's very important that you and your son are ready to leave

332

at two thirty,' Damian said. 'A minibus will come for you then.'

'It seems strange,' she said. 'It's so peaceful here. That's what I told Ed. You can't imagine anything really terrible happening in Aberdare, can you?'

'There are riots downtown. Shops and hotels are being looted. It's only a matter of time before the violence reaches the suburbs.'

Sarah was silent, watching Archie as he ran up the lawn towards the house, chased by Ory.

'The government's going to declare a state of emergency,' Damian went on. 'After that, it'll be much harder to leave. Mrs Caine?'

'Yes, I understand,' she said. 'We'll be ready.'

Martha and Ruth sat in the corner of their shack, behind the open doorway, keeping their legs drawn up so that they were out of sight from the courtyard. For a long time they were silent, staring at the wooden slats of the wall opposite and listening to the gunfire and shouting a few blocks away. Then Ruth raised her head, looking at her sister in the half-light. She mouthed, 'I think someone's coming . . .'

Martha pressed her hand over her sister's lips. Immediately she heard footsteps in the muddy corridor and a man ran past the house in the sunlight. She drew Ruth's head tightly to her chest. They could hear the man moving about in the courtyard behind them, pushing open the door of the neighbours' house. Then he approached the Odingas' shack, casting a shadow across the floor as he squatted in the open doorway. Martha took hold of the machete that was lying beside her.

'Martha?' a voice whispered. 'Martha?'

She raised the blade, waiting for him to step forward.

'Hey, Ruth? Martha? Speak to me. It's me – Stephen. I've found Tom.'

Ruth let out a little cry, jumped up and stood in the light by the door.

'Where's Martha?'

'I'm here.' She stretched out her hand to touch him.

He barely glanced at her. Instead he laid his rifle on the ground, took Ruth's wrists and examined her face. Then he looked around the little room. 'What's happened? Where's the front door?'

'They took it before we got back. They stole our cooking oil, too, and the millet. There's nothing to eat.'

'It doesn't matter,' he said. 'We're going to the nuns.'

'They wrecked Mr Ngumi's bicycle shop also,' Martha said. 'He's gone – we haven't seen him.'

'Ngumi was a Bakhoto,' Stephen said.

'He was a good man, Stephen. He was always kind to us.'

'Follow me,' he said, picking up his gun. 'Ruth, take Martha's hand. Don't say a word.'

The traffic around the junction of Kwamchetsi Wachira Avenue and Kenneth Makotsi Road had stopped. Three army lorries were parked in the middle of the crossroads, under the signpost for the airport, and soldiers had spread out from there to interrogate drivers at gunpoint. Sarah sat in the British High Commission minibus, holding Archie on her lap, her heart thumping, her hands and feet cold in the air-conditioning, as she watched four men in uniform carry a prisoner across the pavement towards the Prosperity Butcher's Shop. They were lifting him by his arms and legs, and the man was screaming, flailing so violently that one of the soldiers lost his grip.

'What are they going to do to him?' she asked. 'He looks absolutely terrified.'

'Don't ask,' the woman sitting next to her replied, in a monotone.

'Apparently the army has developed a cunning new technique for interviewing Shala and Ngozi suspects.' The bald man next to the driver kept his eyes on the soldiers. 'They hold the prisoner down, and use a broken bottle to circumcise him.'

'Oh, for God's sake, Keith!'

'I'm only telling you what my housekeeper said.'

'But can't we do something?' Sarah exclaimed, pressing her hand against the window. 'We can't just sit and watch – it's horrible.'

'It's nothing new,' a man at the back said. 'The Bakhoto always used the security apparatus to terrorise their enemies. The only difference now is that they're losing the war and things are escalating.'

'For God's sake, why won't they let us through?' the woman next to Sarah demanded. 'Can't you go and talk to them, Keith? Can't you explain?'

'No need,' he said. 'Here comes one of them now. Not a happy bunny, by the look of him.' Lowering his window, he greeted the soldier politely in Swahili.

There had been intense fighting in the northern districts of Makera all through the night. Thousands of residents had fled downtown and the corridors around Stephen and Martha's house were blocked by evacuees, mostly mothers and young children. They were moving slowly, in silence, carrying rolls of bedding and cooking pots on their heads, while fresh platoons of ACP guerrillas moved in the other direction, loaded with assault rifles, grenade launchers and boxes of ammunition. Stephen led Martha and Ruth as quickly as he could out of the crowds and along a series of deserted alleyways just a few blocks from the frontline, trying to reach the Universal Exports building on Kwamchetsi Wachira Avenue where he had left Tom hiding.

He stopped a couple of blocks from the Global Justice site, took cover and signalled to the girls to do the same. Ruth crouched in the mud behind Martha, gazing at the blackened doors of the shacks, the bullet holes in the tin walls and the plastic dome of a hair-drier looted from a salon, which had been abandoned in the sewer.

'What's the matter, Stephen?' Martha said.

'ACP.' He pointed towards the next junction, where they could see an officer in jungle fatigues standing behind a half-demolished house, watching the area to the north through a pair of binoculars.

'We'll have to go back,' Martha whispered. 'It's not safe.'

But Stephen shook his head. 'No, I'll talk to him. We're Shala. He'll let us pass. Stay here.'

Martha's eyes widened in alarm, but she pressed her lips together, turning to take hold of Ruth, while Stephen walked towards the ACP commander. Before he reached the junction with the demolished buildings, an ACP soldier appeared from one of the shacks, pointed his gun at Stephen and called to the officer.

'Who are you?' the officer demanded, coming up to them. 'What are you doing here?'

'He was spying,' the soldier said. 'We must shoot him.'

'Well? Are you a spy?'

'No, sir, I'm a Shala,' Stephen replied, in Kishala. 'Stephen Odinga. I'm taking my sisters to safety.'

'Why are you bringing them this way? You want to be killed by Bakhoto?'

'We're going to the nuns, sir. It's safe there.'

The officer narrowed his eyes. 'You live in Makera?'

'Yes, sir.'

'Why aren't you fighting for your people?'

Stephen's face darkened. 'I was working, sir – I had a job.'

'So you let others fight for you – is that it? Are you a coward, city-boy?'

'No, sir.'

'Maybe you think you're too good for the ACP.' He stepped right up to Stephen. 'Look at me, Odinga.' Stephen raised his eyes from the ground and returned his stare. 'I will make a deal with you. Are you listening?'

'Yes, sir.'

'Take your sisters to the nuns. Then come back to Makera.'

Stephen's eyes moved sideways and the officer raised his voice. 'Every Shala youth is a warrior. Even slum-boys like you. Go that way, to the south. If you turn right, the Bakhoto will kill you.'

'What did that man say?' Martha asked as they approached Kwamchetsi Wachira Avenue. 'I thought he was going to arrest you.'

'He trusted me.' Stephen surveyed a line of army trucks parked along the avenue at the edge of the slums, and a great number of soldiers standing about. 'He could see I'm a Shala.'

'I hope you don't trust him,' Martha said.

'And why not? He's fighting for us.'

'He's fighting for the ACP.'

'And the army? Do you think they care if we're ACP or not? They see us and say, "They're Shala."'

'The ACP killed our father, Stephen. Have you forgotten that? They are murderers.'

For a moment he said nothing. Then he started counting the lorries, running out across the corridor to get a better view. 'We can't get out here,' he announced. 'You'll have to go back that way.' He pointed as he crouched beside the girls again. 'Go around the soldiers. You understand?'

Martha nodded. 'What are you going to do?'

'I'll come out later, when they've gone. If the soldiers see me, they'll kill us all. You go with Ruth. If anyone stops you, pretend to be Bakhoto. You can do that. You can pass for Bakhoto girls.'

'And Tom?'

Stephen's eyes moved away from her face. 'Perhaps they haven't found him,' he said. 'He may get out on his own. Go on. Get to the nuns.'

He watched Martha run off, followed by Ruth's tiny figure. At the crossroads they turned to glance back at him, and he waved them on. When they had disappeared into the next corridor, he got up and started to withdraw, keeping his eyes on the lorries, before turning and making his way back to the ACP position.

'Well?' the officer demanded, looking up from his map as Stephen approached.

'Stephen Odinga, sir. I have information.' He wiped his forehead with the back of his hand. 'The army is over there – on the avenue. They're going to attack.'

The commander lowered his map. 'How do you know?'

'I counted six lorries, more than forty men, sir.'

'You're telling the truth?'

'I swear it, sir,' he said in Kishala. He raised his voice so that the other men could hear: 'I swear it on my father's spirit.'

For a moment the officer watched him in silence. Then he said: 'All right, Odinga. You can do something for your people. Is that what you want?'

'Yes, sir.'

'Listen to me. I am Captain Omondi. You're an ACP soldier now, and I am your commanding officer. Understand?'

'Yes, sir.'

'You're going to take a message to the ACP command – you know where that is?'

'By the railway tracks.'

'All right. Hurry. Tell them what you've seen. Tell them Captain Omondi requires reinforcements with mortars and rocket launchers.'

'Yes, Captain.'

'Go, then – quickly. Come back at once with the answer.'

'God, what now?' the woman next to Sarah demanded. 'I can't believe it! They're clearing the traffic.'

The police sirens had been getting louder for several minutes, and the soldiers had broken off from inspecting the passports of the High Commission staff. They were squinting in the direction of the noise.

'That's an awful lot of blue lights,' Keith observed.

'It's Pamela Abasi,' the driver announced. 'That's her car.'

The police convoy had moved out of the queue of traffic heading east to the airport, and was now travelling at high speed on the wrong side of the road.

'That's the way to do it,' Keith said. 'Why didn't *we* think of that? One, two, three Jeeps, two Mercedes – and a Special Bureau armoured car. They can clear the road with a couple of shells, if they have to.'

Sarah looked towards the approaching cavalcade. The first big Mercedes, escorted by a Jeep and a motorbike outrider, glided past, followed by another Jeep and the second gleaming car.

'That's the lady,' the driver said admiringly. While he was still watching, one of the soldiers tapped on his window.

'Well, well! He's giving back the passports,' Keith said, with a kind of false calm, as the driver lowered the window. 'Quick, let me see them. Thanks, Joshua.' He checked them rapidly, one by one. 'Okay, that's it. They're all here. Looks like we're free to go.'

Sarah had taken a long breath as Keith counted the passports. Now she exhaled slowly and silently, clutching Archie.

'What's the betting Pamela Abasi will back in a decade or so?' the man in the back said, as they drove off. 'When Ochola's screwed up even more than usual, she'll probably fly home and run as the anti-corruption candidate. God knows, she could end up as president.'

37

'Do you hear that?' Solomon asked quietly. He was lying next to Joseph in the windowless room they shared. 'Are they celebrating? Do you think they've won the war?'

'Perhaps they're panicking,' Joseph replied. 'Clearing out.'

All around the farmhouse, there were bursts of automatic gunfire, and in the background a complex chant had started up, first a Kishala phrase, repeated in unison by the young men, then a high-pitched descant from the women in reply.

'What does it mean?' Joseph asked.

'I can't hear.'

'Shala music always sounds mournful to me. Even your wedding songs are sad.'

'They're getting closer,' Solomon said. 'Here are the drums.' They listened for a moment. 'That's it,' he announced. 'It's a celebration. The rhythm tells you – there, like *that*. It means they've had a victory.'

'God help Batanga,' Joseph said, then added in a whisper, 'Someone's coming.'

The singing was louder, as if the celebration had entered the house, and a man was calling for Erastus Mboya.

'I'm going to look out,' Solomon said. 'Perhaps the guard's gone.' He rolled away from Joseph and crawled in the direction of the door, feeling his way in the pitch dark, while the crowd outside shouted, 'Mboya, Mboya!' Someone close at hand fired an automatic weapon. Finding the door-handle, he lowered it slowly, opened the door and looked out.

'Well?' Joseph got up.

'There's nobody around,' Solomon said. 'Everyone's with Mboya in the big room.'

'Then you know what to do,' Joseph said quietly. 'Find Beatrice and get away.'

'We're all going,' he replied.

'We've been over that. We'll all die if I come. I'll slow you down. Go on! If she's alive, get her out of here, Solomon.' He held out his hand. 'You have my blessing.'

Solomon turned to him. 'You're giving me your blessing now because you think I can save her?'

'I don't know if you can,' Joseph said. 'Perhaps she's already dead. But you sacrificed everything for her, *kijana*. I give you my blessing because of that – because you love her.'

Solomon took his hand. 'Beatrice would never agree to go without you. There are cars here. We're going to drive out. You as well.'

'But there's a whole army outside. Those children will kill us.'

'Only if they catch us. And they're getting drunk – listen to them. Tonight nobody's in charge.'

Joseph peered out at the empty hallway from behind Solomon. To the left a short flight of stairs climbed to the living room, and at the other end, next to the kitchen, a back door led out into the yard that separated the house from the farm buildings. In between there were half a dozen doors, all closed, and the guard's chair, opposite Joseph and Solomon's room, which was now empty.

'You try this side,' Solomon said, indicating the right as he strode towards the sitting room. 'She's here somewhere – she must be.' Finding the first room locked, he tapped rapidly on the door. 'Beatrice! Bea! Open up!'

The chanting of Mboya's name had been getting more rapid and insistent, until the sound coalesced into a single roar. Then, as the gunfire resumed outside, Mboya's voice could be heard for the first time, addressing the crowd in Kishala.

'She's not here,' Joseph whispered. He had looked into the three rooms nearest the kitchen – a dormitory for the guards, a small office or storeroom, and a windowless room where the maids slept. 'She could be anywhere – out there on the farm, in the fields . . .'

'What's in those cupboards?' Solomon asked, pointing at the office next to Joseph. He disappeared into the little room to investigate, while Joseph, still keeping his eyes on the hallway, backed towards the kitchen door. As he reached the end of the corridor, he heard a short intake of breath from the kitchen, and something landed on the floor with a metallic clatter.

'Solomon?'

'I'm here.' He emerged from the office holding several sets of car keys. 'Toyotas,' he whispered. 'We're going to borrow a Land Cruiser from the ACP.'

There was another noise from the kitchen, and Joseph drew back. Solomon handed him the car keys, then crept up to the door and pushed it open. 'Who's there?' he whispered in Kishala. Hearing only rapid, shallow breathing, he put his head round the corner and peered inside. A small girl was crouching on the floor with her back to the wall, staring out at him with an expression of concentrated terror. Her T-shirt had been torn, so that one of her breasts was exposed, there was a bloody cut on her forehead, and she was holding an automatic pistol in her small hands, raising it towards Solomon.

He put his hands up, taking a step towards her. 'You don't want to shoot me, little sister,' he said in Kishala. 'I'm not going to hurt you.'

She glared at him, pointing the gun at his abdomen.

'I want to help you,' he went on quietly. 'I can take you away – you can go home now. The war's over.'

'I'll kill you,' she said.

'No. You won't kill me. I'm your friend.'

She shook her head. Solomon, keeping his hands up, knelt in front of her. 'My name's Solomon. What are you called?'

342

'Don't talk.' She straightened her arms as if she was about to shoot, but there was confusion in her eyes.

'It's all right,' he said. 'I'm like you, a prisoner. Tell me, what's your name?'

'Winnie,' she whispered very quietly.

'I'm looking for the woman prisoner, Winnie.' He put his hand out towards the gun. 'Beatrice. Do you know where they've put her? She's my friend. We're going to get married.' Almost imperceptibly, when she heard these words, the muscles in the girl's thin arms began to relax, and the muzzle of the gun dropped a few inches. 'You don't want to kill me,' he repeated. 'I won't let anyone hurt you.' In a sudden movement, before she could raise the pistol again, he snatched hold of it and, pointing the muzzle at the ceiling, prised it out of her fingers.

'Where have they put her?' he asked again, getting to his feet and checking the gun over.

'If I tell you, they'll kill me.'

'I'll look after you,' he said.

But she had folded her arms, and her eyes were fixed on the floor.

'Come on. They mustn't find us here. Tell me where they've put her.'

'She's in the farm,' Winnie muttered. 'The tea shed.'

'Show me.' He put out his hand towards her. 'Hey, Winnie, show me where she is.'

Erastus Mboya's booming voice had been obliterated by the chanting of the crowd. Someone started beating a drum, which was answered by several others, far away across the estate. At once the chorus rose an octave, the sound intensifying and broadening out until it seemed to fill the darkness around them. Solomon nodded to Winnie. 'Where is she?'

'At the end – there,' she whispered, pointing across the yard.

The tea-drying shed was one of the low, wide buildings that enclosed the yard. In the section nearest the farmhouse, exposed to view through an open doorway, there was a concrete area where the ACP commanders kept their cars, petrol supplies and spare tyres. In the middle were the makeshift barracks that Joseph, Solomon and Beatrice had walked through when they had first arrived at the camp. At the far end, adjacent to a shed containing the diesel generator, was the old estate office. 'There are always guards,' Winnie said. 'You can't go there.'

'We'll drive,' Solomon said. 'Come on.' He strode across the corner of the yard and into the garage. 'Try and find the key for this one,' he told Joseph, standing in front of a new-looking Land Cruiser with World Health Organisation markings on the bonnet. 'Don't set off the alarm.' To Winnie, he said, 'Bring me a knife.'

She looked at him in terror.

'I'm not going to hurt anyone. Just get a knife from over there – a machete, anything sharp.'

She ran to the side of the garage and the open door. Then she hesitated, glancing back at Solomon and Joseph before gazing towards the house, her arms folded over the torn T-shirt.

'Winnie,' Solomon called, from the back of the garage. 'Stay with us. We'll get you out of here.' She watched him for a moment, shaking her head. 'I promise you,' he said. 'They won't hurt you any more.' He lifted two five-gallon drums of petrol and started carrying them to the car.

Winnie peered outside. There was a prolonged roar from the crowd at the front of the house, and Erastus's voice could be heard once more, amplified now through a loudspeaker. 'History begins tonight,' he declared. 'You are witnessing the rebirth of Batanga. The Shala will be great again. And our enemies . . .' he paused, and the high-pitched wailing that had greeted each of his perorations gradually died away '. . . our enemies,' he went on, in a lower voice, which filled the whole farm, 'all our enemies will be destroyed.'

Winnie glanced back into the garage. Joseph had climbed into the Land Cruiser and was trying the ignition keys, while Solomon

344

loaded cans of petrol into the back. Then, as the cries of 'Ochola, Ochola,' started again, she peered out nervously into the dark yard, and ran out, charging diagonally across the open space towards the house.

'She'll tell Mboya,' Joseph said, watching her disappear. 'Go and find Beatrice. Take the car. I'm staying here.'

'What can you do?'

'I can delay them,' he said. 'I'll immobilise the other cars. Go and find Beatrice. Don't argue. Just get her out.'

'She won't go without you.'

'Persuade her.' He held the door for Solomon. 'Go on, *kijana*, I'm trusting you. Keep her safe.'

Solomon got into the driving seat and switched on the engine. 'We'll be waiting for you at the end of the barn,' he called, putting the car in gear. 'We won't go without you.' And he drove out into the yard.

Joseph snatched a screwdriver and a box of matches from a shelf behind the door. Then he unscrewed the cap of a petrol can and, struggling to lift it with both hands, started pouring petrol on to the concrete floor around the cars, muttering to himself again and again, 'God forgive me – God forgive me . . .' He was still listening for Erastus, who seemed to have broken off from his speech, while the crowd around the farmhouse continued to shout. Then as Joseph threw down the empty petrol can and took the matches from his pocket, Erastus roared into the loud-speaker, 'Find the prisoners! Bring them to me – do it now!'

'From the gates of Hell, deliver my soul,' Joseph whispered, standing at the door and holding out a lighted match. Then, turning his head away, he dropped it, and limped as fast as he could along the outside wall of the barn.

Pausing to look back from the far end of the building, he could see the fire bursting out of the garage door. A group of soldiers had already gathered in the yard, their faces smudged red in the firelight. He watched as they backed away when an explosion threw the flames towards them. Then he hurried round the corner of the barn.

The WHO Land Cruiser was parked outside the office with the driver's door open. 'Get into the car!' Solomon shouted. 'Come on. Hurry!'

'Beatrice?'

'I'm here, Father,' she said, stepping forward from the dark. She took Joseph's hand to lead him to the car.

'Get in the back!' Solomon said. 'Lie on the floor!' He moved with them to the car, pointing the gun in the direction of the yard as they climbed in. Then he jumped in, stamped his foot on the accelerator and drove off at great speed, just as something hit the car from behind with a deafening thump. 'What was that? Lie down! Lie down!' He leaned to one side, peering over the dashboard and keeping his foot on the pedal.

'They're firing at us!' Joseph shouted, holding Beatrice's head. 'They'll kill us before we can leave the plantation!'

The car hit a pothole as it accelerated, leaping into the air and coming down so hard that Joseph cracked his forehead against Beatrice's skull.

'Are you all right?' Solomon called.

'We're still alive.'

There was a burst of machine-gun fire somewhere behind them, and Solomon said nothing for a few moments. He was driving at high speed along the estate road, heading south between parallel lines of tea bushes. The burning barn was visible in his mirror, but he could see no sign of movement on the road, and the gunfire was fainter.

'This is the highway coming up,' he said, slowing and rolling down his window. 'There's nobody here.'

'Keep going, for God's sake,' Joseph said.

'Left or right?'

'North-east,' Joseph said. 'I mean, turn left – *left*!'

The car hit a deep rut, bouncing violently as it emerged on to the highway.

'All right,' Solomon said, as he straightened out. 'What now?'

'Now we keep going, as fast as we can. Just don't stop. We need to reach Sudan before the sun comes up.'

38

When dawn came, Stephen was lying on his stomach behind the wall of a burned-out barber's shop on the airport road, aiming his assault rifle at the Bakhoto soldiers he could see moving about in the golf club to the north. There was a continuous high-pitched whining in his ears, his head was throbbing, and his mouth was dry with hunger and exhaustion. But his brain was in a state of extreme alertness, and every part of his body – the hands gripping his rifle, his heart, his bloodstream – was charged with a drug-like feeling of exaltation.

Stephen's platoon had emerged from their cover in the middle of the night to advance in silence across the no man's land of collapsed corrugated shacks towards the enemy positions. They had covered twenty yards or so before anyone fired a shot. Stephen had stayed close to Captain Omondi, ready to run back to ACP headquarters with messages. But when the shooting had begun he had let go of his rifle and dropped to the ground, too frightened to open his eyes, while gunfire sounded all around him. Automatic rifles were strafing the wrecked buildings where his platoon had taken cover, and someone opened fire with a heavy machine-gun. One of the men lying nearest to Stephen was wounded at once and rolled about, screaming. But other ACP men kept firing into the army lines, and when Stephen opened his eyes again, he saw Captain Omondi standing over him, yelling and pointing towards the enemy.

He got to his feet and stumbled over the wreckage of tin sheets, but he was thrown into the air almost instantly by the force of a mortar shell detonating in front of him. After that he lay on his back for a long time, unable to hear anything, staring up at the tracer bullets and flares. He could see men moving past him in the darkness, heading towards the enemy, and he struggled to get up again. Gasping for air, he rolled over in the mud, managing to get on to all fours. His hand was pressing down on something warm and soft, and he peered down at it, perplexed, until he realised he was holding the severed leg of an ACP soldier, still encased in its boot and camouflage trousers.

For a moment as he held up his hands, entirely covered with blood, a sensation of panic and disgust filled his stomach. But instead of crying out, or trying to hide in the rubble, he stayed where he was, kneeling upright. Then, picking up his gun, he leaped to his feet and ran forward. All at once, his mind was clear and he understood what he had to do. He was no longer trying to save himself; he was no longer acting alone. He was a man, a Shala warrior, part of a great nation, and in his mind, the chaos of the battle had been transformed into the single, all-encompassing imperative of killing the Bakhoto. Other men were charging towards the enemy, and Stephen roared like them. He could see three government soldiers in front of him – young boys with round faces, staring up at him in the light of a flare – and as he ran, he fired his weapon into their chests, yelling at the top of his voice.

That first assault had been over in a couple of hours, and for the rest of the night it was impossible to know whether the army was surrendering or preparing to counter-attack. But now, in the first light, Stephen could see for himself that the enemy had abandoned its roadblocks on the avenue, and that the units in the golf club were also withdrawing.

Captain Omondi came up behind him, lying low and watching the road for a few minutes before he spoke. 'How many Bakhoto on those roadblocks, Odinga?'

'They have all gone, sir,' Stephen said.

'Are you sure?'

'Yes, Captain.'

'All right. Go out there and make a reconnaissance.'

349

'Sir?'

'Go and look – see what's going on.'

Stephen shuffled back from his firing position, and sat up against the wall.

'If the area's clear, signal to me. I'll bring the platoon to join you. Understand?'

'Yes, sir.' Stephen glanced at the soldiers in the golf club, then up and down the empty road.

'Go on,' Omondi repeated. And as Stephen turned towards the road, he shouted after him: 'By the way, Odinga, that's not Kenneth Makotsi Road any more.'

'No, sir?'

'No. It's Patrick Ochola Road.'

'And Kwamchetsi Wachira Avenue, sir? What is that called?'

'We'll call it Shala Avenue,' Omondi replied, thrusting out his chin. 'Yes. It's Shala Avenue now.'

From the roadblock on the junction of the airport road, Stephen's platoon could look down the deserted avenue, past dozens of looted shops and ruined stalls, towards the business district to the south. Bursts of gunfire continued throughout the morning, as the ACP drove the army out of the city, and there was almost no traffic. By noon people were starting to leave their homes and pick their way through the rubble on the streets, as they set about reclaiming their property. Then, over the course of an hour or so, a large crowd began to fill the avenue, moving up from the centre of Kisuru, and making its way towards the roadblock.

'You see these people, Odinga?' Captain Omondi said, studying the crowd through his binoculars. 'Do you know who they are?'

'No, sir.'

'They are Wachira supporters – they are Bakhoto. The Shala are not leaving the city. Why would they? We have won the war.'

Stephen watched the dust rise up as the crowd flowed along the avenue.

'Kisuru is full of Wachira's people,' the captain said. 'There are thousands of them in this city. Not just small people, Odinga, but Big Men – rich officials, businessmen, politicians. They will try to creep past us, hiding in the crowds. You must learn to read their faces. Can you tell a Bakhoto VIP by his appearance? The Bakhoto have wide, round faces – especially the rich. Their cheeks are fat and greedy.'

A minibus and a delivery van had reached the checkpoint. Omondi's men were ordering everyone out, making them line up on the road. 'These people must be searched,' the captain declared. 'But you have to look out for the VIPs, Odinga. You must be vigilant. Now, that man there.' He pointed into the mass of bodies. 'He is important. He is a big man. You can see from his attitude – his eyes.'

Stephen followed as Omondi strolled towards the man. 'Who are you?' he demanded in Swahili. 'Show me your papers.'

'My papers have been stolen, sir,' the man replied, in a deep voice that Stephen recognised at once. 'Our house has been destroyed – our possessions were looted. That is why I am taking the children to their aunt in McPeak.' Stephen stepped closer to scrutinise the familiar chubby face of Sergeant Mburu, with its wet, shiny lips. Mburu rambled on, keeping his eyes fixed on Captain Omondi: 'Their aunt lives in McPeak, Officer, but we are Shala. My family are all Shala.'

Stephen glared at him in silence, then looked down at the children – four girls and a boy, about the same age as Tom.

'What is your job?' Omondi demanded.

'I am a trader.'

'No. You are fat,' he replied. 'You are a parasite. Let me see your hands.'

'My hands?'

'Show me.' Mburu held them out. 'These are not trader's hands.' And he turned to Stephen. 'What's the matter, Odinga? Do you recognise this man?'

351

'No, sir.' He stepped back, folding his arms. 'I don't think so.'

'You see he has shaved,' Omondi observed. 'He is in a great hurry, but he has taken the time to shave. What does that tell you?'

'I don't know, Captain.'

'You must think. This is your job. He has changed his appearance. He has shaved off his moustache.'

Stephen glanced at the children again, still standing next to their father and staring up at the captain.

'Odinga,' Omondi insisted, watching him intently. 'You *do* know this man.'

Stephen nodded reluctantly, and at once Mburu put his hands out towards him. 'Oh, please, sir, don't harm me,' he said. 'You and I, we are only small people. We shouldn't be at war. I am not your enemy.'

'Well?' Omondi fixed Stephen in his gaze.

'He was a policeman, sir,' Stephen said. 'He used to patrol the avenue. His name is Mburu.'

'Deal with him,' Omondi said.

'And the children, sir?'

'Deal with them, too,' he replied.

'No, no, I beg you, sir,' Mburu broke in. 'Let the children go to their aunt. They are innocent, sir – they are good children. They have done nothing.'

Stephen glanced towards the Convent of the Sacred Heart. 'I will see to it, Captain,' he said.

But Omondi was still watching. 'Let me see for myself. I want to watch you doing your job. This is a Bakhoto policeman. Show me what you can do. Set an example to the other men.'

'Yes, sir.' Stephen glanced at the members of the platoon who were standing round. 'I will send him to St Jude's for interrogation.'

'No. You will shoot him right now – here on the road. I want you to do that. Execute him yourself.'

The children had started crying, and the eldest put her arms round the others.

'Make the children be quiet, also,' Omondi said. 'I don't want to hear them.'

Stephen glared at them, and as he did so, he caught sight of a red baseball cap moving through the crowd of ACP recruits outside the convent. His uncertainty intensified. 'Perhaps this man has useful information,' he said again. 'We should send him to St Jude's for questioning.'

'You know him – you can question him yourself,' Omondi replied. 'Shoot him in the leg, then see what he has to say.' But Stephen was still watching the red cap moving between the soldiers. Omondi followed his gaze. 'Well? And who's this?' he demanded. 'What is this boy doing here?'

'He's my brother, sir,' Stephen muttered. 'I will tell him to go.' And he shouted as Tom approached. 'Go away, you fool. Get back to the others.'

Tom stood where he was, holding out a plastic bag. 'Martha sent me,' he said. He glanced nervously towards the convent, then back to Stephen. 'She told me to bring you food.'

'Tell her never to send you here,' Stephen went on, his voice rising. 'Go on! Go away!'

Tom lowered the bag to the ground, staring at Stephen in silence.

'Take the food with you,' Stephen yelled, as Tom turned away. 'I don't want it!' An intense sensation of heat and pressure filled his head, and for a moment the whole street seemed to go dark. Then, running forward, he snatched the bag and threw it after Tom. 'Go! Get back to the others.'

'Now the prisoner,' Omondi roared, pointing at Mburu. 'Do it now!'

Tom had turned back, rubbing his head where the bag had hit him. Then he stood gazing at Sergeant Mburu, who had dropped on to his knees and was holding his hands out towards Stephen. 'Please listen to me,' Mburu was sobbing. 'Please, sir, let my children go. I am your neighbour. We are not enemies. We are both creatures of God . . .'

'Go, Tom! Go away!' Stephen yelled, ignoring everyone else, the blood pounding in his temples. 'Run!'

'What is the problem?' Omondi cried out. 'Shoot him, Odinga. We must have justice.'

Stephen aimed his rifle at Mburu's chest, and looked down at his face.

'What about my children?' he begged. 'You must let them go. What harm have they done?'

'Be quiet,' Stephen replied. 'You cannot give me an order.'

The soldiers behind him were now chanting together, 'Shoot the rat, shoot the rat! Shoot him, shoot him, *shoot* him!'

Stephen stepped forward, lowering his rifle. Tom's red baseball cap was still visible at the edge of the crowd, but Stephen concentrated on Mburu, pointing his gun at the man's shiny forehead, then his big shoulders, and the bulging front of his shirt. The soldiers' chanting was getting louder, but as Stephen raised his gun to his shoulder to take aim, the sound died away and, for a moment, the whole road seemed to be quiet. He took his hand off the trigger to wave the flies from his head, and Omondi crept up beside him. 'This is man's work,' he said quietly. 'You are bringing justice to this country. You are bringing freedom.' Then, quite suddenly, Mburu jumped to his feet and leaped towards Stephen, reaching for the rifle. Instantly, Stephen fired into his head.

'The children, too,' Omondi yelled. 'Go on, shoot them!' The children were kneeling on the road, the oldest girl holding her hands up as if she was praying to Stephen, while the others wailed and sobbed. But Stephen had already turned away from the policeman's exploded head, and the captain roared, addressing the other men: 'You see these little rats? Do you want them to become big rats? All right! You know what do to.' Glaring at one of his men, he said: 'You show me. You are a soldier. You can perform this simple task.'

Stephen gazed towards the convent on the other side of the road. Tom's red hat was still visible, bobbing from left to right as he ran through the crowd. 'This is justice,' Omondi was declaiming. 'This is what justice means!' As Tom disappeared into the convent gates, there was a burst of automatic fire.

Beatrice lay awake on the back seat, bouncing about in the dark as the Land Cruiser flew over the rough surface of the old highway, heading north. From time to time the car braked, rolling her forward, and Solomon switched on the headlights to assess the state of the track in front of him. Then he revved the engine, turned off the lights again and drove on in a low gear.

Joseph was sitting beside Solomon with the rifle across his knees, peering up through the windscreen at the moon, the silvery outline of the vegetation all around and the intricate mass of shadows below. They had been driving downhill for most of the night, but now, just before dawn, the road had entered a tunnel of vegetation on the side of a steep hill and started to climb once more. For a long time the darkness seemed to consume everything, until they emerged on to a ridge above the trees and the sky to their right began to turn red.

Solomon stopped the car.

'What are you doing?' Beatrice asked, from the back.

'We're trying to see where we are,' Solomon said.

Joseph was examining the road map he had found in the glove compartment, holding it up to the reading light. 'We need a landmark – a river, a range of hills, anything.'

'I'm going to drive into the bush,' Solomon said, 'into that gap. We must stay hidden till it's night again.'

'They could easily find us.' Beatrice leaned forward between the seats.

'They'll spot us if we stay on the road. We might run into an ACP patrol.'

'Either way it's a risk,' Joseph said, massaging his temples with his fingertips. 'If we only knew where we were, we could make a proper judgement.'

'What if they find us again?' Beatrice said. 'They'll hang us from the trees.'

'Well, we can't stay here.' Joseph gazed across the treetops at the enormous disc of the sun. 'Either we hide or we keep moving. There's no smoke in the hills. Perhaps the ACP have moved south.'

'What are those?' Solomon asked, leaning forward and peering up. 'Up there, those big birds.'

'I don't know. They look like eagles.'

'Yes, it's a fish eagle – a waterbird.' He drummed on the wheel. 'That means there's water over there.'

Joseph returned to the map. 'The only water between Upshala and the desert is the river – here. I've been assuming the tea plantation was this area. But perhaps it's further north – where the river bends round the hills. That could be it . . . How many miles have we done?'

'About forty.'

'Then I suppose we might have reached this tributary.' He pointed at a wide, sand-coloured line. 'It's marked as seasonal. If that's where we are, we're not far from the border.'

Solomon lowered the windows and they sat in silence as the sun rose, listening to the wilderness all around them. On the plantation there had been only a rough, rhythmic croaking of bullfrogs all through the night – the din had filled Solomon and Joseph's room – and in the daytime a kind of overheated silence, as if every living creature had fled the war. Here, in open country, it seemed to Joseph that Nature had woken from a dream. Vervet monkeys quarrelled back and forth across the hillside, and honeyguide birds chattered somewhere close at hand. Then a bright orange jacana broke cover below them, and zigzagged away along the skyline.

'What shall we do?' Solomon asked.

'Let's drive to the next ridge. Slowly. We don't want to frighten anyone.'

The pitted murram road rose to the left, away from the rising sun. Then, for several hundred yards, it climbed the embankment. Solomon stopped the car at the top, and everyone got out. The plain below them was watered by a wide, muddy river; and beyond that, almost at once, the jungle ended. From then on, all the way to the horizon, they could see nothing but scrubby, rust-coloured earth, pockmarked with vegetation and traversed by the highway.

'Where are we?' Beatrice said.

'Near the border,' Joseph replied, pointing with the map. 'Sudan starts somewhere out there.'

'Can you see anyone?' Solomon asked. 'Dust? Smoke?'

'Not a thing.'

'Yes,' Beatrice said. 'Something's moving in the desert. See? A cloud of dust.'

'It could be Sudanese guerrillas. This is a war zone, too.'

'No, it's antelope,' Solomon announced. 'Hundreds of kob. They're coming to the river.'

'Well, there's no point waiting here,' Joseph said. 'We could be in Juba by tonight if nobody spots us.' He walked back towards the car.

Solomon put out his hand to Beatrice, but her eyes were fixed on the far distance, where the desert was transformed into a pale pink vapour rising to the sky.

'What are we going to do in Juba?' she asked.

'Get to England.'

'How?'

'We'll find a way.' He put an arm around her, and she rested her head on his shoulder.

'I'm so tired,' she said, and when he moved in front of her, she asked, 'What are you doing?'

'I'm thinking. If I kiss you,' he said, 'something is certain to stop us. It always does. Ever since the party at the school, when the fire started.'

She smiled. 'We haven't even had dinner yet.'

'We'll have dinner in London.'

'Do you promise?'

'Yes, I do.'

She peered up at his face, pushing him gently away with both hands so that there were six inches between them. 'And after that? How will things be in London?'

'We'll be together.'

'Yes? And what about your freedom?'

'Freedom?'

'You know what I mean. A man like you – you could never be satisfied with one woman. It's not in your nature.'

'Nature changes,' he said. He took her hands, gripping them firmly. 'Do you want to be with me? I mean always with me.'

'Is that what *you* want?'

He nodded. 'I want to marry you.' He raised her hands, ready to kiss them. 'Will you marry me? *Will* you?'

She lowered her eyes, swallowing hard. 'Yes,' she whispered.

'You will? Really?'

'Yes, I will.'

He bent down to kiss her, holding her face between his hands, but as their lips touched, Joseph called from the car: 'Come on, children. Let's not wait about here all day.'

The border post consisted of a single wooden pole across the road, next to an empty hut. There was a calendar hanging inside the kiosk, above a magazine photograph of a woman with blonde hair and bare breasts. On the outside of the shack someone had painted a cartoon of a child with a Kalashnikov, crossed out in red, above the legend 'Armed conflict is bad for your health'. On the other side of the road, an old stone sign read, 'Juba 60 miles'.

'We could do it in a few hours if we're lucky,' Joseph said, staring north along the straight road as Solomon poured the last drum of petrol into the Land Cruiser. 'It depends on who we meet along the way – the Southern Sudan Liberation Movement, the Sudan Liberation Army, the Sudan People's Liberation Movement, the Sudanese Army – or our friends the ACP. They have bases up here – Khartoum's been supplying Ochola for years—'

'Father,' Beatrice broke in, 'can you please stop it?'

He raised his eyebrows. 'I'm only reviewing the situation.'

'Let's review it when we get to Juba.'

'No,' he said, putting an arm round her shoulders. 'I'll do better than that. I promise I won't talk about it till we get to England. Things are peaceful there. They haven't had a civil war for hundreds of years. Believe me, when we get to England, all these things here – the war and mayhem – will be hard to believe, hard to imagine. You'll see.'

'All right,' Solomon said, tossing aside the empty can. 'That's all our petrol. Let's go.' He climbed back into the car and started the engine.

Part Five

39

Sarah brought Mike a mug of tea, and put it on the little table beside him. He had laid his crutches on the floor and was lying down, resting his ankles over the arm of the sofa as he looked out at the terrace of Victorian houses and parked cars on the other side of the road.

'You know Ed wanted to resign when he got back to London?' Sarah said. 'He blamed himself for everything. He refused to go into the office. He just sat here, writing furious reports.'

'And they bought him off with a promotion. That's the UN for you.'

'Well, I think we deserve a few years in Switzerland,' she said. 'I mean, Ed does. At least he'll be taken seriously – his voice will be heard. We're going out this weekend to find a house. We've already enrolled Archie in the international school – it's really fabulous, such interesting parents.' She sat down opposite him. 'What's going to happen to Batanga, Mike? Do you think Patrick Ochola will hang on to power?'

'I don't see why not. He controls the security apparatus. Besides, most people in Kisuru are pleased Wachira's gone. It'll take Ochola a few years to erode the goodwill.'

'What about you?' she said. 'Are you going back?'

'In the new year, perhaps. I've got a few things to do in London first: meetings with DfID, physiotherapy, seminars, articles to write. There's a guy at the Home Office who wants to talk to me about Bakhoto refugees – the exodus has taken everyone by surprise . . . I like being in London every now and again,' he added. 'It's good for one's sense of perspective.'

'Here come Ed and Archie,' Sarah said, getting up and going into the hall to meet them.

'Hey, Mike.' Ed appeared at the door, pulling off his coat. 'How're things?'

'All right. You?'

'Okay. We're surviving. What did they say at DfID? Did you talk to Oona Simon?'

'No. They fobbed us off with Clive Bird, him and a couple of teenagers from the Africa section. I knew it'd be a waste of time.'

'They won't meet Joseph?'

'To tell the truth, I didn't even ask. They're so smug and patronising. What's the point of subjecting Joseph to all that sarcasm? Bird was saying, "Of course Wachira was corrupt – he's an African. Africa's always been corrupt – but at least Batanga was stable, blah, blah . . ." At one point, he started lecturing me: "You know, it doesn't do to disrespect the Big Man in Africa – it just *doesn't do*!"' He imitated Bird's hectoring voice. Then he added, in a different tone: 'Of course, they're quite pleased about the coup, really.'

'Why?'

'They can start handing out money again. Ochola's got a clean slate, no record of defaults. He's making the right noises about corruption. They can unload some of their cash on him – emergency post-conflict funds. There's a whole separate budget for that – it should be enough to keep the Shala gentry in whores and Mercedes for a decade or two.' He shifted his weight, sitting up a little on the sofa. 'Basically, Ochola can have what he wants. He'll be a billionaire in a few years. No wonder there are so many revolutions in Africa. What other profession pays that well?'

Ed ran his hands through his hair. 'What do we tell Joseph? He's expecting to meet Oona Simon.'

'There are still people we can introduce him to,' Mike said, 'people he ought to see. It just won't be so official . . . Oh, come on, Joseph knew the British were turning a blind eye. The region's too important.' He lifted his right foot painfully off the sofa and swung round. 'Still, it must be hard for him. So much for incorruptible old England.'

'True. He's pretty depressed. He saw Pamela Abasi on TV a few nights ago, taking up a new post in Geneva. I think that was the last straw. He rang me in a terrible state.'

'It can't have done much for you, either,' Mike said.

Ed shrugged. 'What can you do?'

'But doesn't it bother you? You'll be working with her soon. What are you going to say when you run into her at some Swiss cocktail party?'

'I'll say, "Hello, you smug bitch. I understand you have a hundred and fifty million dollars that belong to the Batangan people. Do you want to give it back?"'

'Yeah, yeah, that's great,' Mike said, leaning down to pick up his crutches. 'You do that – put it on YouTube. You'll be a hero. Permanently unemployed, but a hero.'

Someone was knocking at the front door. 'That should be Joseph,' Ed said, but after a moment, Mike heard Solomon and Beatrice's voices in the hall.

'Look at this place! You didn't tell me you lived in such a big house!'

'Hey, Solomon.' Mike manoeuvred himself to his feet. 'How's things?'

'Good. They're good.' He came up to shake Mike's hand.

'Well, I should be congratulating you,' Mike went on, as Beatrice came up to kiss him. 'You're a lucky man. When are you getting married?'

'Soon,' he said. 'As soon as we can.'

Mike swayed a little on his crutches. 'So – what else? Have you heard from Kisuru? You weren't looted?'

'No, no. Machi hung out signs saying we're a Shala organisation. We're doing business with Ochola now. Luxury imports. We're getting a merchant's licence.'

'And you, Bea? I expect you're working already.'

'Actually, I'm thinking about going on with my studies,' she said. 'I met a Batangan girl who's doing law at the LSE. She was saying I ought to transfer my degree. She's going to help me with the application.'

'Well, that's great,' Mike said. 'Why not? You can make a new start.'

'Here's Joseph, now,' Ed put in, glancing out of the window. 'I'll let him in, love. Do you want to get the champagne?'

Mike was shocked by Joseph's appearance. His shoulders were frail, his neck seemed much too thin for his shirt, and there was an exhausted, disengaged look in his eyes. But he came into the room with his head erect, nodding calmly to everyone.

'Hello, Father!' Beatrice stepped up to kiss him.

'Hello, my darling.' He embraced her, then said to Sarah and Ed: 'I'm sorry I'm late. I took the wrong turning at Shepherd's Bush. Nobody could give me directions – until I was rescued by a taxi driver.'

'I'm glad people are helpful,' Sarah said.

'Oh, yes, on the whole – most friendly and helpful. And my flat is very comfortable. It's next to the flyover, but it's a good place. Everyone in the block seems to be a recent arrival like me – Somalis, Iraqis, Venezuelans, Libyans . . .'

'It's thrilling,' Sarah said. 'When I was growing up, England was so stuffy and provincial. We needed some new blood. And, really, we *are* a nation of immigrants, aren't we? It's what we've always been.'

'Do you think so? Oddly enough, that's what the lady at Westminster Council told me when I was applying for my flat. I didn't like to disabuse her, of course, but it seems to me Britain has mostly been a country of *emi*grants. That's certainly how it appeared to us Africans.'

'So, what about the new government in Batanga?' Ed said. 'Nobody in the FO predicted it and, of course, now they're all saying it was inevitable, that it's the turn of the Shala to have a taste of power.'

'Well, that's true, isn't it?' Sarah said, holding out a glass of champagne for Joseph. 'I mean, the Shala were denied their rights.'

'True enough. And now the Bakhoto will be denied theirs, along with the rest of the tribes and the Asians.' Joseph looked down at his glass. 'I suppose that's political progress, Batanga-style. The tribe wins again, with all its stupid grievances and paranoia, the pettiness, bad blood. In fifty years, nobody in power has ever once explained what it means to be a Batangan, to be the citizen of a nation that encompasses all the tribes, recognises the rights of all. There's no public culture, no shared history, nothing to hold us together. And now the ACP.'

He stared into the middle distance, and nobody spoke for a moment until Beatrice took his arm. 'Come on, Father. We're celebrating tonight, remember? We should count our blessings.'

'Yes, of course. You're right. I'm sorry.' He raised his voice, fixing his eyes on Solomon and Beatrice: 'Well, I'm sure you all know what I'm going to say. I have an official announcement to make about Beatrice and Solomon. They're going to be married. They – er, that is, Solomon – came to see me last week and asked my permission. Of course I'm delighted. I have given them my blessing – not that they need it in this country. Honestly, I had no hesitation. They love each other. I know that.' He held up his glass. 'Here's to Beatrice and Solomon. May they enjoy many happy, fruitful years together.'

'Well, Joseph,' Mike said, after supper, dropping down on to the sofa beside him. 'What about you? How are you finding London?'

Joseph shook his head. 'Beatrice is quite right,' he said. 'We should count our blessings. We're lucky to be alive.'

'But?'

'Well, it is a little strange to be unemployed for the first time in my life, to be out of the loop all of a sudden. I keep expecting the phone to ring or someone to call by.' He glanced about the room, focusing for a moment on Beatrice's face. 'I expect I'll find something to do. You said you'd talk to your contacts at DfID and the Foreign Office – Oona Simon?'

'Yes, I did. That's right.' Mike looked down at his swollen foot. 'In fact I – well, I had a word with Clive Bird yesterday. He knows all about you, of course.'

'Do you think there's a role for me? Martin Sykes always used to say I should work for the Africa desk – we joked about it.'

Mike took a long breath, glancing rapidly at Joseph. 'Bird's team has been badly caught out. They're trying to catch up with the Ochola government. After all, they ignored him for so long and now, overnight, the ACP are in charge and the Foreign Office is clueless. They don't have a single friend in the regime.'

Joseph nodded.

'The fact is, they're embarrassed. They don't want to admit how wrong they were. They assumed the Bakhoto would hold on to power for another thirty years.'

'Well, I can't tell them much about the ACP,' Joseph said, 'but the region more broadly – I have a comprehensive, long-term overview. It would be good to get working soon, while my contacts are up to date. One can go stale pretty fast.'

Mike hesitated. 'They'd be crazy not to involve you in some way, Joseph, but you know my view . . . I'm just not sure they have the good sense.'

'Still, you gave them my contact details?' he asked. 'They know where to find me?'

'Yes, absolutely. Of course. They all asked after you.'

40

Joseph buttoned his raincoat as he came up the stairs of the tube station and hurried outside, under the partial shelter of the flyover. He was carrying a plastic bag and a small, collapsible umbrella. When he reached the Harrow Road the wind instantly blew the frame inside out, so he stood in the rain trying to push it back into shape. Then he stuffed it into a bin and marched on past a row of Moroccan cafés and kebab bars. At the Williams betting shop he crossed the road and strode on past the sports centre towards the front door of his building.

There was a smell of fried garlic in the stairwell, and as he passed the first landing he could hear a man and a woman arguing in a Nilotic dialect that reminded him of Ngozi. On the next level, a baby was screaming over the sound of a TV quiz show. When he reached his own flat on the fourth floor, and was searching his pockets for the key, he could hear the muffled barking of a dog somewhere on the next storey.

Joseph checked the answer-machine for messages, and poured himself a glass of whisky from a half-bottle by the sink. Then he took a small chicken pie from his plastic bag, put it in the oven and sat down at the table. The kitchen window overlooked the elevated section of the Westway, which was no more than fifteen yards away. But it was hard to see the road in the darkness, or the concrete pillars that supported it. For twenty minutes or more, he gazed out at the headlights rushing past in both directions until he had the dizzying impression that the traffic was flying unsupported through the air.

Joseph ate quickly and washed up, then poured himself another drink. He went into the sitting room, picked up a copy of *Jeeves and the Feudal Spirit* from the table and sat down on the sofa, beneath a picture of the Sacred Heart. The dog had stopped barking on the top floor, and the whole block was quiet, except for the applause of the TV show somewhere below him. But he didn't start reading straight away. Instead, he leafed though the photographs on the table beside him: an old picture of his wife on the wide veranda of their house in Kisuru and, beside it, a photo he had taken of Beatrice and Solomon, standing together in St James's Park. For a long time he stared at the faces of his wife and daughter, until finally, turning away slowly, as if he was afraid to lose sight of them, he took a mouthful of whisky, put his spectacles on and opened the book.

41

By around six in the evening, a northerly breeze had started to agitate the dust and litter along the marketplace on Shala Avenue. Martha stepped back from the kerosene flame, holding her frying pan at arm's length. Carefully she picked out four deep-fried bananas with her tongs, and arranged them on the newspaper. Then, putting everything down, she stood for a moment in the hot shade of the kiosk and took a drink from her water bottle, waving away the flies. All around her, traders were crying out and crowds of shoppers moved between the stalls. A group of policemen were drinking beer nearby, below a sign that read, *Half the World Groceries – Under New Management*. Further away, on the other side of the street, dozens of schoolchildren in white and grey were walking away from the convent. Martha squinted into the low sun, trying to spot Tom and Ruth in the crowd, but instead her eyes came to rest on the dark blue uniforms of a Special Bureau patrol. She put down her water.

'Aberdare Fried Bananas,' she cried defiantly, using her tongs to drive the flies from the customers' food. 'Best value in Kisuru. Only ten shillings.'

'Your prices have gone up,' a woman said, lifting her long skirt as she stepped over the gutter to approach.

'Yes, ma'am. These days, I have to pay the wholesaler double.'

'Ah!' The woman sighed. 'How are we supposed to live? Everything is expensive.' But she was looking at the fried bananas on the paper. 'I'll take one for the journey home – just one.'

The Special Bureau soldiers had moved out into the middle of the road, holding up the traffic as they demanded identity papers from the driver of a minibus taxi. As her customer strolled away, Martha caught sight of Stephen, in an officer's tunic with epaulettes, tapping his baton on the side of the minibus as the driver answered his questions. Then he nodded, said something to his sergeant, and the patrol moved on across the road, meandering towards Martha's stall.

'We'll have something to eat here,' Stephen announced, surveying the market. 'Sergeant, tell the men to buy themselves some food.'

'What are you doing?' Martha demanded, in a low voice. 'I told you not to come.'

Stephen folded his arms, his swagger stick pressed to his side and his face fixed in a frown as he looked away from his sister's eyes. 'You are not my commanding officer,' he said quietly. 'You cannot tell the Special Bureau what to do.'

'Five bananas, ma'am,' the sergeant said. 'Here is the money.'

Martha took the cash in silence, and dropped a couple of bananas into the bright yellow oil.

'Where are Tom and Ruth?' Stephen asked.

'They'll be here soon.'

'Are they working hard?'

She glared at him. 'You know Tom. He doesn't think about his future. He sees soldiers on the street and he wants to be a soldier.'

'I'll talk to him,' he said. 'I'll tell him to work.'

'But he sees your life,' she retorted. 'What is he going to think? Your example is important to him.'

'I'll explain,' he said. 'He'll listen to me.'

'They're coming,' she said, glancing up from the frying pan and nodding towards the crowd that was crossing the street near the junction. 'Please, Stephen, go away. I don't want Tom to see you.'

'Don't say that,' he said. 'Look, I brought you money.'

'I don't need it.'

'Don't be stupid. It will pay for the school fees.' He unbuttoned his tunic pocket and took out a roll of cash. 'Give it to the nuns. It's enough for the whole year.' He held it out to her.

She put down her tongs and wiped her face with a cloth. 'I can't take it.'

'Then I'll give it to them myself. You think they won't accept money from a soldier?'

Tom and Ruth had stopped a few yards away, and were watching them in silence. 'They're here.' She took the roll of notes and slipped it into her belt. 'Talk to Tom, guide him.' The moment Stephen turned round, Tom broke away from Ruth and ran towards him.

'Hey, *kaka mdogo*,' Stephen said, putting his hand on his brother's head. 'Tell me you're behaving yourself.'

Tom stared at his black beret without a word.

'You working hard? Listening to the teachers?'

He nodded, his eyes fixed on the automatic pistol in Stephen's holster.

'The most important thing,' Stephen said, 'is to work hard at school. If you don't work hard, you'll never have a good life.'

'Can I see your gun?' Tom asked, putting out his hand. 'Can I hold it?'

Stephen crouched and unbuttoned the holster. 'Are you listening?' he said. 'If you don't work, you'll never get a good job. Nobody can join the Special Bureau if they don't work hard at school.' He handed him the gun.

'It's so heavy!' Tom weighed it in both hands, before trying the handle and putting his finger on the trigger. 'Is it loaded?'

'Yes.'

He took aim at the dust. 'I bet you killed a lot of Bakhoto traitors with this.'

Stephen watched Tom's excited face. 'You remember what I told you,' he said quietly. 'You work hard. Promise me?'

Tom nodded.

'Ruth,' Martha called. 'Take Tom to Mrs Buwumbo's salon. Sit quietly and do your homework. Don't get in her way. I'll come and test you when I close up.'

'Wait a minute,' Stephen said, taking the gun from Tom and

putting it back in his holster. 'Come here, Ruth.' He put out his hand towards her, and she looked at him with her head on one side. Then he drew her towards him, holding her tight. 'I miss you, little sister,' he said. 'You don't miss me, but I miss you.'

'We remember you every day,' Ruth said. 'We pray for you in your dangerous work.'

'It's not so dangerous,' he replied. 'The war's over.' He relaxed his grip. 'You helping Martha?' She nodded. 'You need to look after Tom, too. Don't let him waste his time daydreaming. Understand?'

'Yes,' she said, backing away.

'I'll see you soon.' Stephen got to his feet, brushing the dust from his trousers. To Martha, he said: 'They look well. You can see they're happy – they have peace of mind, thanks to you. It reminds me of being a child. When I was a child, my mind was at peace – do you remember?'

'Yes.'

'Now I always have a lot of problems – many troubles and responsibilities.'

She was struck by the pain in his eyes. 'Whatever you have done,' she said, 'whatever is troubling you, Stephen, you must never lose hope. You know we love you. The children miss you. You can still change your life.'

He looked at her for a second, but his eyes were no longer focused and he stepped away. 'Tell me if you need more money,' he said, straightening his cap. 'Ask for anything. Anything at all. I will get it for you.' Turning from the kiosk, he walked off between the stalls, heading back to his men.

Acknowledgements

Writers of fiction don't normally acknowledge their research sources. But *Ten Weeks in Africa* is the product of a great deal of labour by people other than me, and I want to recognise my debt to them, while accepting full responsibility for any errors or confusion my fictional use of their material may have engendered.

The elements of my story came from many sources, but certain particularly powerful and vivid books provided the inspiration for some of my characters and the broad shape of the plot, notably Michaela Wrong's *It's Our Turn to Eat*, Aidan Hartley's *The Zanzibar Chest*, and Michael Maren's *The Road to Hell*. I also gleaned countless details and insights from the work of Robert Calderisi, Paul Collier, Mike Davis, William Easterly, Jonathan Foreman, Matthew Green, Martin Meredith, Dambiso Moyo and Linda Polman, among others; from interviews conducted by the photographer Steve Bloom with Nairobi shopkeepers in *Trading Places*; from the biographies of Dar es Saalam street-children collected by Kasia Parham for *Dogodogo*; and from the testimony in the *Voices of the Poor* series edited by Deepa Narayan and her colleagues.

All of these writers, unlike me, are experts in their respective fields, and many have lived and worked in Africa for decades. Lacking this background, I was extremely fortunate to be able to show drafts of my novel to a number of readers with experience in East Africa, or in the world of international development, each of whom made the generous sacrifice of time required to proofread a book-length manuscript, and offered invaluable corrections and advice. Some of them have asked not to be named, due to the official nature of their work. I am deeply grateful to my anonymous readers, as I am to those whom I can acknowledge in print: Beth Capper, Jonathan Foreman, Justine Hardy, Robin Heber-Percy and Maggie Murphy.

Ten Weeks in Africa owes its existence to the support and guidance of my agent, Clare Alexander, who encouraged me to pursue this story from its conception. I was also extremely fortunate in my editor at Sceptre, Drummond Moir, whose sympathetic and astute readings strengthened the book in countless ways; and in Hazel Orme, who copy edited the text with great skill and enthusiasm.

Finally, and leaving the best till last, it is impossible to conceive of the book's development without the constant collaboration of my wife, Caroline. She helped and advised me throughout the process of research, plotting, writing, and above all editing – a role which obliged her to read almost every draft of the book. *Ten Weeks in Africa* is dedicated to her, with all my love and appreciation.